The Gaze of Zeus

Terry Kroenung

Molpadia Aulis Expedition #1

Rare Moon Press

To my fellow autistics
both diagnosed and not;
stim away, you heroes

and

To Janet
Who's tolerated my 'uniqueness' for 25 years;
it ain't gonna get better, honeybunch

Contents

Contents

A note on Molly's peculiarities

Molly's autistic idiosyncrasies and tics may seem over the top, but I assure you they aren't. And how do I know this?

Because I'm autistic and I do all of them. In fact, I'm doing a couple as I type this.

Yes, I exaggerated some of them for literary effect, but none are fictional. They are mostly a form of stimming, which is shorthand for self-stimulation: repetitive motions that serve to calm us down. Some, like the shoulder twitching to settle clothing and sensitivity to light and sound, come from our need for sameness, predictability, and having to subdue the storms of sensation we live with.

The synesthesia **is** fictional, as I don't have that, though autistics are more likely to than the general population. Combined auditory and olfactory color synesthesia (chromesthesia) does exist, though it is one of the rarer forms.

Traumatically-induced synesthesia, as opposed to being born with it, is quite rare but not unheard of. The brain is a strange and wonderful thing and has a high capacity for adapting itself to injury.

So what's real and what's not?

Other than Steampunk, not a lot of historical science-fiction gets written. Why, you ask? Because it's a lot more work.

Sure, you don't have the headache of worldbuilding, but worldbuilding is fun. You can make up whatever you want. With science-fiction set in a rigid past, you have to research everything until your eyes bleed, on top of wrangling the science end. But for this autistic author, research is the fun part of writing, so there's that (as proof: I was given the World Book encyclopedia for Christmas when I was 9).

Anyway, a great deal of reality lurks here. Ahmed Hassanein, Djuna Barnes, and Harry Grindell Matthews were real people, as were Eugene Bullard, Bricktop, Constantin Brancusi, Man Ray, Kiki de Montparnasse, Cole Porter, and Hadley Richardson. The British Empire exhibition was as described, as was the Paris Olympics. All geographical descriptions are as accurate as I could make them.

The restorative masks after the Great War were absolutely real, though I have no evidence of a woman getting one. They were a godsend to soldiers with the most gruesome facial wounds imaginable (a consequence of popping one's head ever the edge of one's trench).

Incredibly, the 'death ray' actually existed (!) and there's even film of it in operation, where Matthews ignites gunpowder at a distance. It wasn't a city-destroyer, though.

To help with unfamiliar things and places, an extensive (SO extensive) glossary is included at the end.

The Gaze of Zeus

Also by Terry Kroenung
www.terrykroenung.com

<u>Novels</u>
Brimstone and Lily
Jasper's Foul Tongue
Jasper's Magick Corset
Paragon of the Eccentric
Rapiers & Rogues

<u>Drama</u>
The Three Musketeers
Coolness and Courage
Blood and Beauty
Gentle Rain

<u>Nonfiction</u>
HeartSnark

<u>Anthologies</u> (contributor)
Customs, Castles, and Kings, v. 2
Broken Links, Mended Lives
False Faces
Found

<u>Awards</u>
Colorado Gold Literary Award
Paragon of the Eccentric (winner)
Brimstone and Lily (finalist)

Independent Publishers Book Award
Brimstone and Lily (Bronze Medal)

Next Generation Indie Book Award
HeartSnark (finalist)

Colorado Short Story Contest
"The Day the Earth Couldn't Stand Still"
(winner)

Prologue / Libyan desert, 1923

"Effendi! The demons are coming!"

Ahmed could hardly hear his man's words over the roar of the sandstorm, but the terrified tone cut through the dreadful noise well enough. So did the sound of the enemy engines. At least the Fascist aeroplanes were grounded by the screaming sands. Their motorcycles and armored cars were trouble aplenty to his poor camels as it was. He prayed that they and the brave men who rode them had escaped. Bad enough that he and young Farouk were trapped. To lose the entire expedition to these Italian bandits would be a tragedy.

At least Farouk had found this shelter. Well, blundered head-first into it, anyway, falling through the hole in the sand with a yelp. Ahmed had been more than happy to accept Allah's gift and dive in after him, Il Duce's bullets nipping at his expensive boots. All he had been able to take with him had been a single paraffin lantern, twenty meters of line that he used for lowering buckets into wells (not much use against bullets), and his Webley. He broke it open and checked it for seemingly the tenth time. Still only the three rounds left. Packed on the camels were several thousand, but they might as well have been at the bottom of the Red Sea for all the good they did him now.

Something tells me that the Egyptian Olympic team will need a replacement epee fencer next year.

Despite the gravity of his situation Ahmed Hassanein Bey laughed, struck by such a trivial and absurd concern. Granted, a good sword would do him a world of good right now, as the pistol was about to become a particularly unattractive paperweight. But he had graver concerns than the Paris Olympiad. If he perished in this cavern, then the world would remain ignorant of the outrages Mussolini's troops were committing against the poor Senussi tribesmen. Murdered with poison gas, as if it were the Great War, except that the Libyan freedom fighters had no masks to protect them. Their keffiyehs had proved poor substitutes. Scores of them lay in their defensive positions around the oasis, lungs blistered and burst. That would most likely be the fate awaiting him and young Farouk. No sense in storming such a tiny entrance when a single canister of death would serve. So Ahmed's options were few. Unless...

"We shall draw the fangs of the demons," he told his comrade, who shook like a desert mouse pinned by a falcon. He thrust the lantern at the teenaged boy. Give a man a job and he will concentrate on that instead of his terror. "We are an exploring expedition, yes? So, explore." Ahmed pointed to the black maw of the cavern behind them, far away from the feeble light of the entrance or the lamp. "Find us a way out. Or, at the very least, better cover so that we may sell our lives more dearly." With that he ended Farouk's hesitation with a slap on the shoulder that told him that for now they were equals.

Farouk nodded, leaving his Enfield rifle with his sheik in case the Blackshirts poked their Roman noses into the crypt. The lantern became a drunken firefly as it diminished into the further reaches of the cave. By feel Hassanein examined the magazine. Six rounds, and one in the chamber. *Bless you, lad. Perhaps we'll be lucky, and I can bleed them enough that they'll grow tired of the sting in the storm and leave us be. Surely, they would prefer chianti and cannoli to chasing us about.* He stroked his black moustache, wishing that he had not lost his canteen in the mad scramble for safety. They would not last long without water, even if the Italians gave up the chase.

2

As if in answer to his hope, he detected an animal-like scrabbling sound near the entrance. Since he knew that it was blacker than Jahannam to anyone peering in, Ahmed moved boldly to the hole in the roof, only an arm's reach up. Barely shoulder-width, not much light came from that direction, either. Even with the sandstorm there should have been more than that. So clearly something was blocking it. Reversing the rifle, he gauged the location of his target and rapped upward with the speed of a striking snake. A wet crunching sound rewarded him, followed by a limp form in gray.

And a grenade.

He dove like a champion swimmer, landing in sand and burrowing with the enthusiasm born of imminent doom. After ten seconds of that, however, it became clear that his fate was not of the explosive variety. Twisting his head, he saw in the weak light from above that the bomb had not been armed. A relieved sigh filled the cave, louder than the storm. Ahmed scrambled to his feet, kicked the groaning Fascist back to sleep, and snatched up the grenade. It looked like a large egg covered in alligator hide. A nasty surprise for his friends should they grow bolder.

A search of the luckless Italian produced the longed-for canteen, a knife, matches, and an electric hand torch. Nothing but the latest and best for Benito's boys. He had no luxury to linger and hunt for more. Chattering Italian voices reached him from outside. Firing a single round out of the cave entrance to encourage Latin caution, he retreated back into the cavern's bowels in search of Farouk, making sure to announce his presence in Arabic so that the nervous aide would not attack him.

The storm's growl faded to eerie silence after he had gone only fifty paces. Fear of the Blackshirts lessened as well, replaced by the primeval terror of the dark and subterranean. That murk greedily devoured his torch's yellow beam. Ahmed had been in tombs and catacombs before, most recently with that odd writer woman in Paris with the unusual, clipped manner of speaking and the even stranger name. Molpadia. Named after an Amazon by her eccentric archeologist father.

3

As tall as an Amazon, that was certain. Rattled off facts like a human *Encyclopedia Britannica.* Never looked him in the eyes. Rigid face. They had explored the underbelly of the so-called City of Light together, after he had given a lecture with Rosita Forbes about their first Libyan expedition. Bones and skulls for kilometers. Six million skeletons, they said. But that had been a known quantity. This filled him with more dread, not being able to see or predict what awaited him.

At the same time, he had fantasies of Aladdin, of finding a magic lamp and calling forth a djinn that would grant him wishes. It would certainly get them out of what seemed to be a fatal predicament. He doubted that the Italian grenade would accomplish the same thing, though if it came down to it he would rub it hard before flinging it at his murderers. Perhaps they would do him the courtesy, before bayoneting him, of explaining precisely why they had burst over the horizon, shooting first and asking no questions. What sin had his tiny band of geographers committed? They had not violated any restricted military boundary that he was aware of. Nothing but dunes and dark rocks in all directions. No installations, no encampments, no secret facilities. What were they protecting? Or did they believe he possessed something of strategic value?

Ahmed laughed. At one time, perhaps, in Cairo when he had been an aide to General Maxwell, that might have been true. He had been privy to a myriad of secrets then. But no longer. The war was five years gone. Whatever intelligence or plans he had once possessed were now less valuable than galoshes on a camel. Too bad. Having something of value to trade for their lives would be a wonderful circumstance. Not that the Fascists seemed to be in a trading mood. They looked to be more interested in searching unresisting corpses than in negotiating.

His booted shin collided with a boulder. He slowed. The cave had grown narrower, the ceiling lower, the floor more cluttered. Now he had to crouch, keeping the beam aimed at his feet. Where was Farouk? Hopefully, he had not tumbled into some dreadful pit. Though that might be preferable to whatever horrors the Blackshirts might be planning. Their

4

viciousness would likely rise with their frustration.

It was while stepping over a rock and inspecting the cave roof that he fell into that dreadful pit.

That was his first thought as he pitched forward. It turned out to be a soft sandy ramp, steep but free of solid objects that would fracture skulls or break spines. Hassanein took no chances, however. He twisted around as he gained speed to slide feet-first. Digging in his boot heels, he jammed the butt of the Enfield into the sand until he slowed and stopped. The torch sailed past him, but he managed to snatch it before it vanished down the slope. Its light did not reveal where the end of the descent might be, but the angle looked to be lessening. Possibly an ancient watercourse, left by the currents that had created the cavern. Since he was far beyond effective range of his pursuers, he ventured to find his ally.

"Farouk! Where are you?" No reply. "It's only me, Sheik Hassanein! The others are still outside!"

Still nothing, though he fancied that he heard movement farther down. Zigzagging to control his speed, he skied toward the noise, using the Enfield as a primitive pole. The sound grew louder but somehow did not much resemble the clamor a handsome young Egyptian might make. When the ground flattened out he found himself in a wide chamber, some thirty meters across and with a ceiling twice as high as before. Hassanein noticed that his torch had somehow grown stronger, illuminating a greater area. His puzzlement at that impossibility faded when he saw that the walls contained a naturally phosphorescent mineral activated by his electric device. This created a glow similar to stained glass windows on a cloudy day, but it was far better than the torch's limited range. It showed two things of great interest.

Farouk, standing on a rude stone platform that had clearly been carved by the hand of man.

And a stream of shining black water at its base. That was what the sound had been.

Tongue thick from thirst, as he had been husbanding the canteen's contents until he found his friend, Ahmed flung himself at the noisy black water. But just before he could

5

plunge his face into that blessed freshet he was repelled as if by a stone wall...by Farouk's passionate cry.

"Effendi, no!" The young man held up a hand like a magician flinging invisible power. That and his terrified tone produced the desired effect. Ahmed skidded to a stop, frowning. Boots barely a meter from the small river, he directed the torch beam into it and gasped.

Scorpions. Untold thousands of them, racing through a shallow trench.

Yelping, he scrambled away from them. They did not pursue him but maintained their frantic pace, all racing in one direction as if called by something. More kept coming from a cleft in the wall. He would not have believed that there were that many of the wicked things in all of Libya. Where were they all going?

"I actually waded into them in the dark," said Farouk with a shiver. "Thank Allah for this ledge." He knelt on the platform, made of carved stones of great antiquity. Letters and pictures had been etched into them. Behind him sat a smaller structure that might have been an altar. All of it seemed to have been thrown up by men in a hurry to leave.

Ahmed gauged the distance across the swarming venomous mass. It looked to be about three meters. With his long legs that was possible to jump. The chest-high platform edge made it more difficult. He held up the rifle. "Here!" Farouk caught it with ease. When his sheik offered to toss the grenade, however, the lad gulped.

"Is that strictly necessary?"

"It is if you wish to get out of this. Those Fascists are certainly coming."

Fatalism crept into Farouk's eyes. "Ah, well. Being blown to bits would be quicker and less awful than...that." He eyed the unslacking stream of scorpions.

With eyes half-closed and a grimace on his face he held out his cupped hands. When the little bomb landed harmlessly in them, he still waited a long moment for the inevitable disaster.

"You're still in one piece," Ahmed informed him. "Now set the thing down and grab me if I misjudge this." He backed up

6

a few paces, grinding his boots into the soft sand for better purchase. Recalling his days on the Oxford athletic fields, though fencing had been his forte, he sprinted toward the platform for a long jump that would permit no second attempts.

It was a near-run thing in the end. His front toe overstepped and squashed several of the little monsters, causing him to slip and not gain the push-off he had hoped. Stretching his full length with a yell, his fingers just managed to snare the platform lip. But as he hauled his weight up, accumulated dust and sand made his hands slide back. Only Farouk's last-second clamping of one wrist saved him from tumbling down into an awful fate amongst the stinging creatures below. Even then it took some doing for the slender boy to haul up his heavier master. At last, however, they both lay panting on the platform, backs against the altar.

"Well done," Ahmed told his comrade. "Safe as houses."

A dull boom echoed far back up the slope, from the other end of the cavern.

Farouk sighed. "Our house has burglars, Effendi."

"Il Duce's dogs grew tired of waiting. They must have blown a breach. They are no doubt pouring down here like those scorpions."

"What shall we do?"

Ahmed stretched and stood. "Find a way out. If there is none, then we shall sell our lives so dearly that they shall tell stories of us at Blackshirt reunions a century hence."

A bleak look curdled Farouk's face. "I prefer the first one."

That earned him a laugh and a clap on the shoulder. "As do I. But if it is our kismet, we shall not complain." He listened, but heard no more sounds yet over the hissing of the scorpions. "Have you explored beyond this point?"

"No. Too dark, until your torch excited the walls."

The glowing rocks still provided light, more than should have been possible from his little electric toy. "Indeed. I wish I knew the science that would explain this. But that must wait for another expedition, eh?"

He turned to inspect the altar, if such it was. The same sort

7

of carvings and letters as graced the façade of the platform were found there. Ahmed recognized them with a bemused snort. "Attic Greek! What the devil would they be doing this far into the desert?" His brain searched that corner of his mind that still warehoused old school lessons. Those neglected classics courses came in handy now. "I think I can piece this out. Someone took a great long while to carve so many words. Guard our backs with that rifle. Have no hesitation to shoot the first man who appears. For he shall do the same to you."

As Farouk lay prone on the platform, trusting his master's judgement, Hassanein ran his finger along the letters, which told the story of the objects resting on the altar. These were a shattered stone the size of a football, filled with odd metal and crystal bits he could not identify, and an ancient unfired clay bust of great beauty...and greater strangeness. He read aloud both for Farouk's benefit and to assure himself that what he said made a sort of sense, as odd as it was.

We followed the dying star across the sands for six days. It shot over the oasis like a bolt from Apollo's bow, with the sound of many lions. Our curiosity overruled our sense of safety. By the time we found the great pit we had lost a man to the sun and another to an adder. There was much grumbling and a near-mutiny nearly forced us to turn back. The crater smoked like the volcano of Sicily. Mastering our fear, we crept to the lip to spy our quarry. Not a star, but a broken stone, pitted with heat. White gems gleamed within it, but it was too fiery to approach for another day. Saying a prayer to Hephaestus, we pried out two of the gems with spear tips. The rest would not come free of the dead star.

Shrill voices rapid and angry Italian could be heard echoing from far up the cavern passages. Farouk added his own anxious tone. "Effendi! Time grows short!"

"Be firm of purpose," Ahmed instructed him, reading more quickly. He had to know what great secret had led men so many millennia ago to place the altar here. It might be their salvation.

As the sun was sinking, I held a torch up to one of them to inspect it more closely. It held a blue fire in its core. But I let the flame get too close. When it touched the gem Zeus' lightning blazed from the opposite side. My hand was singed and I dropped the gem. Less lucky was the poor slave tending his camel in the path of the bolt. He shrieked and melted like wax in a flame. We all prayed to the gods to spare us the same fate. Our priest declared that we had offended the lords of Olympus by tampering with their star. It was decreed that we erect an altar to them and their gift, as a tribute and a warning. With water running low we had little time, but we did our best. While we cut and stacked stones our priest, no mean sculptor, crafted an image of a new god that had just come to him in a dream. Then we placed the deadly gems in it for eyes and set it in a place of honor beside the fallen star.

Let no man disturb them, for this is a thing beyond our ken. Its power is reserved for the Olympians. To mortals it can only be an uncontrollable curse.

Ahmed looked up at that god's image, sculpted in pinkish clay that was now hard as stone thanks to thousands of years of dry desert heat. Beautiful and weird at once, it showed the fierce features of a supremely handsome youth. But the stunning lad had pointed ears, ram's horns, and dozens of shark's teeth in his pretty mouth. His bulging eyes were the glittering white gems from the meteor, with vertical cat's pupils painted onto them.

That came to their priest in a dream? An opium dream, most likely.

A bullet split slivers of rock from just above his head. He ducked behind the altar, Webley ready. "How is it with you?" he called out to Farouk.

The Enfield boomed, causing a shriek and much commotion at the top of the slope. "Still firm of purpose!" the youth laughed. "Though that papist might be a little less so."

That earned him a blizzard of bullets from the enemy. "Enough foolish crowing. Get back here under cover."

Farouk fired again and slid back until he crouched beside Ahmed. His muzzle smoke streamed back behind them. Hassanein squinted at it, then glanced back toward the cave's dark rear. He sniffed fresh air.

9

There's another entrance! And the Blackshirts don't know it. We may survive this yet.

In the next few moments he had cause to doubt that thought. The battle grew as hot as the desert above, with the Fascists using their numbers and training to pin the explorers behind the altar while maneuvering down the slope. Soon they occupied all of the ground at the bottom, well-hidden behind boulders. Ahmed and Farouk were down to a pair of bullets each. When they held their fire, no easy targets being in sight, the Italians did the same.

The reason became clear when a tall officer, almost skeletally thin, strolled down the sandy slope as if there were no possibility of being shot. He wore the standard black shirt and jodhpurs with tall boots, his head crowned with the same low black felt fez favored by Il Duce, the right side covered by a thick tassel. But instead of the usual fasces device, it had a death's head with a dagger between its teeth, the whole surrounded by what looked to be electrons, as if it were a new and dangerous element. Incredibly, despite the heat, he also wore a long black leather coat with huge pale lapels. It seemed to give him no discomfort.

What really made Ahmed's eyes widen, though, was his glass left hand.

It rested on his jeweled sword hilt, another absurdity in the circumstances. A cigarette in an onyx holder smoldered between its dark green, brass-jointed fingers. He lifted the tobacco to his thin bloodless lips and slipped it between crooked teeth that were made all the more disturbing by white receded gums. It was a mouth Ahmed had last seen on a bleached skull in the Negev Desert. In fact, all of him seemed to have been recently resurrected from a morgue. No color enlivened his face. The skin was yellowish and stretched over the facial bones like a drum. Even though the cavern was dim, his eyes were hidden behind dark motorcycle goggles, which Hassanein considered a blessing. If they were as disturbing as the rest of the man, they would not bear examination.

"Ahmed Mohamed Makhlouf Hassanein al-Bulaki," he said in a dry papery croak that might have come from an animated mummy. The accent was Umbrian, but overlaid with something else. Eastern European, possibly. His voice had been damaged, probably by the same agency that had taken his left hand. Scars were just visible at the edge of the coat's collar. Those hidden eyes might have also suffered. "An aristocrat of Egypt. Fine lineage. Educated at all the best schools. Honored by the effete English for service in the war. An MBE, yes? Scholar, diplomat, adventurer. Handsome as a motion picture actor. Lovely moustache, by the way. I envy it. And I hear you have taken up the aeroplane. That must make your country nervous and proud at the same time. Nasty machines." He waved his false member. "My last flight in one was... unfortunate."

"You have the advantage of me, sir," Ahmed called out, keeping an eye on his flanks in case the man's monologue was a ruse to hold his attention while the soldiers moved in.

The fellow's laugh resembled a serpent choking on a child. "Advantage! Yes, that is true. In all ways, it would appear." His boot heels snapped together, the pointless spurs clicking. "Colonel Pasquale Terremoto. My parents had a macabre sense of humor."

It struck Ahmed that the colonel's first name referred to Easter and his surname meant 'earthquake' and 'terror.' *Let us hope that it's Farouk and I who can orchestrate a resurrection.*

"And is this your idea of a joke?" he asked, using his pistol barrel to indicate the platoon of Blackshirts. He reached a hand up to grasp the base of the bizarre clay bust atop the altar. To his relief it moved. "Attacking a harmless explorer's expedition?"

"Oh, no. My taste in mirth runs in...other directions." The twist he gave to the phrase chilled Hassanein's blood. "And as for you being harmless, that is not strictly true, though I will grant that you have no such intention. You are, as the Americans say, in the wrong place at the wrong time. Unfortunate for you, but there it is."

The bust turned until it faced the rear of the altar. Ahmed prayed that the Italians could not see the maneuver in such low

11

light. "You want this artifact, yes? That is what all of this is about."

"You are welcome to the artifact, as you call it. I just need its ---" Terremoto consulted an aged parchment that a small round man in civilian clothes and spectacles handed to him. "Its eyes. Apparently the crystals are of some scientific and military value. We are on a sort of scavenger hunt, you see."

"Scavenger. Like vultures. Or maggots."

The most disturbing smile imaginable split the colonel's horrid face. "Oh, shush. You'll turn my head."

That was precisely what Ahmed had now done with the bust. He used the knife he had taken from the fallen Blackshirt to begin prying one of the white gems from its face. "Right now I'd like to turn it until it breaks. But I suppose that's a poor negotiating ploy."

"Assuming that we are negotiating at all is the real mistake. As you said, I have the advantage of you."

"True. But how many men are you willing to lose getting these baubles?"

Terremoto shrugged. "Why, all of them, of course."

It gratified Ahmed to see several of the troops react poorly to such a cavalier dismissal of their lives.

His opposite number continued. "We all swore an oath when we joined the Squadristi. *Dulce et decorum est*, yes?"

The first gem was almost free. "But you would prefer that the *pro patri mori* be applied to only us, though."

Terremoto blew a smoke ring. "That would involve rather less paperwork for me, yes."

With a sigh Hassanein caught the first eye and set it atop the altar. It was faceted, not natural. Someone had worked it. "Here's an idea. We give you the damned eyes and you go back to Rome a hero. Even less paperwork."

"Would that that were possible. But you see..." The awful colonel shrugged. "Witnesses."

He frowned at his cigarette, which had gone out.

The Egyptian fished out the matchbox and lit one, keeping the flame out of sight. To Farouk he whispered, "Cover your eyes. If this works, run for the rear."

"And if it doesn't?" the youth asked, still looking down the Enfield's barrel.

"Then shoot that demon in one of his goggled eyes."

Terremoto had discarded his dead cigarette and replaced it with a fresh one. He held it out for the civilian with the parchment to light. Ahmed held the burning match up directly behind the crystal, lining it up with the men and praying that the altar's inscription was not a mere metaphor.

"Colonel, let me help you with that."

The briefest touch of the flame to the gem created a stupefying blue-white light. Ahmed kept his head down, not looking directly at it so that he would not be blinded. True to the words of the anonymous Greek, a bolt of energy flared out of the crystal. Not precisely Zeus' lightning, it was a straight beam that resembled a welding torch. Startled, Ahmed dropped the match, which ended the bolt's existence. He risked a look at his target. Against his hopes, his aim had not been true. It had passed behind Terremoto and struck the edge of the passage, liquefying the rock and making it run like hot butter. All around chattering panicked Italian filled the air. One man tried to run back up the slope but his colonel, the only man unfazed by the beam and the only man wearing protective lenses, coolly shot him down with a Luger. Then he ducked out of sight behind an immense outcropping just as Farouk sent a .303 round his way.

"Well, I should thank you for proving that the good Doctor Rospo's parchment is no fraud," he said with a sour chuckle.

Ahmed's mouth was still hanging open in awe at what he had just done. No wonder the Fascists wanted the gems. They would be the source of unrivalled military might if used to power a weapon. And if somehow Mussolini's scientists managed to mass-produce them...

He seized the bust, wrapped it in his keffiyeh, and thrust it into Farouk's arms. "Get this out of here. They can't have it or the world will burn." To ram home his point he lit another match and sent a second blaze of doom at his foes. Again it struck no one, but it did cut a small stalactite from the ceiling and drop it between two soldiers. Between that and

Terremoto's execution of one of their comrades, their morale was rapidly declining. None of his orders to advance was being obeyed with any alacrity. With the time that bought him, Ahmed scrawled upon the back page of one of his expedition notes. He stuffed it into Farouk's clothing, along with the torch. "If you escape these devils, get the head and that eye to this person. If they are about to catch you, bury it deep in sand and lead them away from it. Can you do that?"

"With my last breath and last drop of blood, Effendi," Farouk swore, handing him the rifle.

Ahmed kissed him on both cheeks. "Allah be with you. Run when I start shooting."

"You are staying here?"

"I must destroy this other eye, and the Fascists with it. Now go!" He felled the bravest of the Blackshirts with a rifle shot.

Without hesitation the lad ducked his head and dashed off into the gloom behind them. A final bullet encouraged more caution in the Italians, though their well-concealed colonel's pistol kept them from retreating. He propped the empty weapon atop the altar as if it still posed a threat. That drew a bee-swarm of bullets, but he had already ducked behind the stone bulk. Soon Terremoto's men would decide that Ahmed was less danger to them than their own commander and charge. When they did, he hoped to dispatch them all at once. Because he had the proverbial ace up his sleeve.

The grenade.

His penultimate match sent another gem-boosted bolt at the Italians. That made them squeal, but it also drew nearly constant fire. Ahmed's only hope was to draw them into the open. Already he could hear orders being given for suppressive fire and enfilade. He would not last long. If he ran after Farouk, they might both escape the cavern but would be at the mercy of a platoon of pursuing Blackshirts with vehicles. No, he had to even the odds and make them think that their prey was not worth the cost. If that meant that his family would only be left with a sad memory, so be it. Allah's will be done.

He hauled down the crystal-filled stone from atop the altar, nearly dropping it onto his foot. Its weight was far greater than its dimensions had led him to believe. One end was burst open, most likely from the initial impact. White lights glittered inside it. Placing that side around the gem, he set it all atop the grenade. A firm knot tied his bit of line to the pin. After testing to ensure that the stone was heavy enough to secure the grenade against a hard tug, he wriggled the pin halfway out. There was a tense moment when one of the Blackshirts grew bold and rushed him, but the Webley's final round winged him. The luckless fellow tumbled into the trench of scorpions, shrieking. It was a sign of Terremoto's leadership that no one risked fire to drag the man out.

Ahmed unwound the cord and prepared to pay it out to its full length. To buy himself more time he lit the last match and feigned preparing another energy blast. When the Fascists yelped and ducked, he bounded off the rear of the platform while they were not looking, the line unwinding behind him. He pulled the slack out of it and crouched behind the stoutest boulder at hand. That provided him with a slim view of the altar. It took a full three minutes, but eventually Mussolini's minions grasped that their quarry had bolted. The whoosh of a flamethrower told him that they were clearing out the scorpions to effect a crossing. Then thirty men with pistols and rifles bounded onto the platform, heads silhouetted against the phosphorescent walls. As they paused to hunt for him behind the altar, he muttered a prayer, lowered his own head, and jerked the line as hard as he could.

The resulting light was brighter than staring into a carbon-arc stage lamp. Ahmed thanked every god with a name that the force of the blast went away from him, for it brought down the very rock ceiling of the cavern there. Augmented by those extra-terrestrial crystals, the grenade's explosion destroyed everything in its path. An immense rush of sand and dust came his way, choking him. Satisfied that even if all the white gems had not been destroyed they would never be found under tons of debris, Hassanein crept after Farouk.

But the lad had already escaped through a cleft in the rock that was all but invisible. Only the air rushing in from the dying sandstorm betrayed its presence. Ahmed waited an hour for the wind to completely diminish, then risked poking his head out. No Farouk. No sign of any of his other men or their camels either, not that he had held out much hope of that. Just a glorious Saharan sunset. Recalling that the oasis lay north, he put the purple-red glow to his left and trudged toward it. Two hundred meters on he found what had been the other entrance to the cave.

All of it had collapsed into a great shallow crater, now filled with sand. He saw no sign of life in it. But a hundred meters beyond he found remnants of the hasty Blackshirt position that had been set up when they had trapped him. A motorcycle with sidecar sat there. From the tracks he saw that there had been another, but it had recently left, also going north. Its tracks had no blown sand in them. Two sets of footprints came up to it from the south. From the pit.

Someone had survived.

Whoever it was had casually abandoned all of the troops. No search had been attempted. If Hassanein had been prone to wagering, like his fellow English students at Oxford, he would have made a certain bet on which two men were most likely to have saved their own skins. That Terremoto had all the signs of being a callous survivor.

Ignoring that possibility, and hoping that their paths would never cross again, he examined the transport that would either save him or doom him. When he found the fuel tank full and two canteens equally so, he sent thanks to heaven. He sank onto the seat, head on the handlebars, absorbing all that he had just endured. Impossibilities abounded but after all, there are more things in heaven and earth, Horatio...

Replenished by water and a brief rest, Ahmed Hassanein kicked the cycle into life and headed to the oasis to find his men. Then they would take stock and all head south again. This expedition was not yet completed. And if Farouk was not with them, they would mourn him, honor him, and breathe a sigh of relief that the last of Satan's eyes had not fallen into Fascist hands. Or even worse, Stalin's.

He decided not to mention this day in his report to the National Geographic Society.

1 / *Paris, June 28, 1924*
Latin Quarter, 5th Arrondissement

Her face was bothering her again, so Molly removed the wretched thing and hung it on its peg.

Avoiding the gleaming brass urn that half-mad Major Lawrence had awarded her in Mesopotamia – too much like the mirrors she had banned from her home – she clenched her fists the mandated five times, touched the tip of all five coat hooks, and returned to the kitchen, making sure to step on only the white tiles in the hall. Not for the first time she told herself to get a long carpet so she would not be obliged to make that awkward dance. At least the kitchen had three-foot square flagstones, all the same pale gray color. That only required stepping on tiptoe occasionally so the bottom of her foot would not touch a seam between two stones. Doing that made her squirm as if she had stepped on a moist slug. Then she would have to wipe her feet three times to make the feeling go away.

The morning light was far too bright, despite it being barely past dawn, so she yanked the second layer of curtains across the window above the sink. Calm settled upon her distressed mind, as if a screaming baby had quieted. Though most of the world dreamed of basking in the glorious sun of Paris, Molly could barely tolerate it, or any other intense light. She bathed with the aid of a single candle and wore smoked glasses most of the time when out of her single-bedroom flat. After adjusting a dirty cup that was out of alignment with the others on the counter and catching an inadvertent glimpse of her shattered features in its cobalt blue surface, she settled into her chair at the pristine table to see what the *Herald* had to offer.

It took a few moments, as the sections were not even and she had to spend no little effort straightening the paper's edges. By then the tea kettle whistled, which sounded like a banshee from the pits of hell. She threw herself at the stove to slide the pot onto a cold burner and thus quell the storm in her ears. Muttering a Sufi chant she had learned in the Transjordan, she let her anxiety settle itself while preparing the chai. Once the tension eased, she let out a long breath and returned to her Sunday paper.

Though everyone told her that she should improve her French, which was charitably termed a work-in-progress due to the Midwestern American accent and creative use of verbs, Molly preferred to read the English-language *Herald* to a local journal, at least first thing in the morning. The irony of otherwise being a master of 11 other languages (kept sharp with an hour of daily practice) was not lost on her. She did peruse the Parisian papers after that, armed with the fresh knowledge of events, to get the French take on those issues. It would be a poor journalist who would dismiss the opinions of the people she lived amongst. Those views would be predictable for some of the stories. The Olympic Games, of course, only a week away. National pride was running like a Caucasian stream at high snowmelt. This would be the country's first opportunity to put on a grand show since the Armistice had ended the Great War, not quite six years before. Naturally, the Germans had been pointedly not invited.

Her single eye scanned the pages. Other headlines inspired professional interest, mirth, or bemusement. French and Belgian troops still occupied the Rhineland, to encourage Germany to pay its colossal war debt. The American banker Dawes was finalizing a plan to satisfy all sides. Italy had elected Mussolini's clownish but dangerous Fascists to a huge majority two weeks earlier and there was much hand wringing about the implications of that, particularly since the result had been obtained through thuggish intimidation. On a more hopeful front, Germany's own clown, Hitler, had just been thrown into prison for his attempted coup the autumn before. In Moscow, the expected power struggle following Lenin's passing in January had many analysts predicting an early demise of the Soviet Union. Molly had her doubts. That absurdly-named Stalin had already been installed by his mentor Lenin, and not even Bukharin or Trotsky seemed up to the challenge of surviving him, let alone supplanting him.

Of less state import, the great Italian actress Duse had passed away. Whether it had been from the shame of her country's recent electoral shenanigans was open to debate. Some fool in England had managed to convince the British authorities that he had invented a death ray and they were permitting him to demonstrate it. Hopefully if it, by some miracle, did actually function as advertised he would aim it away from the new British Empire Exposition that had opened on Wednesday. Her London writing and exploring friends had invited her to attend it with them and she would rather not have the site turned into a smoking crater before then. But to judge by the inventor's photograph, he was unlikely to be more than a clever confidence man. Buster Keaton had just released *Sherlock, Jr.* back home. Apparently, the wild stunts were beyond even his typical level of insanity and he had literally broken his neck with one of them.

"That would never happen here," Molly mused aloud, lifting a bit of buttered baguette to her reconstructed mouth. It had taken her a trying year to retrain her ravaged throat to speak again. It was much huskier, almost mannish now, in keeping with the tall, muscled frame she had always had. "The French prefer their films to be historical and significant."

The sound or, more likely, the butter, caught the notice of a ragged bundle on a rug near the door. It snuffed and animated itself onto four dwarfish legs. Mostly white, only twelve inches tall at the shoulder, with a gray-brown patch imitating a saddle on its back and long, furry, drooping ears of the same color, the low-slung dog shook itself with the sort of languorous vigor expected of a French hound. His length and wavy curls made him seem like a Lhasa Apso that had been tortured on the rack by cruel Inquisitors. Hector was eternally shedding and canine snow floated in a bit of sunbeam that evaded the doubled curtains. Before the morsel could disappear into his mistress' mouth he had ensconced his shaggy self at her feet, dripping chin resting on her knee, soaking into the green silk of her robe. His gaze, difficult to make out through all the facial tangles, was placid yet demanding, like one of Louis XIV's tax collectors.

Molly put words into his mouth in precisely the manner that so annoyed her when others did it with their animals. "If you give me that yummy treat then no bipeds need die here today." She did it in a comical music hall French accent, another thing that would have made her roll her eye when done by anyone else.

Hector accepted the bit of bread she gave him with an almost tender grace. His liquid brown eyes gave her 'the look,' angling for more, but she shook her head and pointed to the chair on the other side of the table. With a derisive but adorable snort that puffed out his fuzzy lips, he slunk there as if on his way to the guillotine. When he hopped onto the seat, sat erect, and put one paw onto the table, resembling a boulevardier warring with ennui, Molly laughed and relented. She tossed him another bit, which he snapped out of the air with casual ease.

"See, this is why I have no need of a lover," she told him in the curious tone that unnerved people. Flat, emotionless, lacking music, words uttered too quickly. "All you men act just the same in the morning." Lover...as if that could ever be an option now. Her hand rose to scratch an imaginary itch on her equally-imaginary nose. Half a dozen years it had been gone, blasted away by the Boche grenade that had stolen the rest of her face, and still it taunted her. She froze halfway up, then set down her bread to flick the fingers of both hands for half a minute, staring at a stain on the floral wallpaper. When the trance ended she felt better, though she could never say why.

Though the itch was a phantom, the ache in her left shoulder was not. Jason and Hecuba had been particularly unforgiving the night before. Her parries had been weak and both of her la canne chausson masters had reinforced that error with punishing strikes. From the first she had insisted that they pay no regard to her missing left eye, that they freely attack the blind side so she could learn to adapt. They had taken her at her word with the typical Gallic enthusiasm in such matters, a sort of friendly cruelty that meant that one belonged to the chosen circle. To Molly's credit she had returned the favor with American gusto Saturday night, snapping out accurate low kicks in retribution. That had earned her a swirling salute from Jason, who had only accepted her as a pupil because his salon was empty due to the cemeteries being so full. His reluctance at training a woman, a grievously injured one at that, in savate and jiu-jitsu had not been entirely mercenary, however. He had told Molly that he had seen at once, in that fierce remaining eye, her desperate need to be independent, to be capable again. Even if she never had need to employ his techniques outside of the salon, the training alone would go far in replacing some of what she had lost in the war. And that had been much more than the fist-sized absence of flesh and bone that her mask covered.

She winced, rested the sore left arm on the table, and picked up her tea with the right hand. The spiced chai soothed many ills, as it had ever since she had been introduced to it as a teenager on a dig in Tibet in 1908. That had been the trip where she had discovered a great many things. Her love of the ancient East. A natural writing talent that paired well with dogged inquisitiveness and later made for a successful career as a field reporter. The confusing attraction to both those in trousers and in skirts that had sent her fleeing back home.

Not that she had ever told her father of that, of course. Despite his towering achievements Nathaniel Aulis was unready to handle sexual confusion in a fourteen year-old. She had concocted a story about bandits and sand fleas and how her tender self was just not quite ready for the hardships of archeology. At nearly six feet and over one hundred sixty pounds, her tenderness had been an open question, but he had accepted the fiction as gospel, or pretended to, and returned her to Chicago.

There she had flung herself into the joys of the Field Museum in Jackson Park again, using the parental prestige to gain access to any part of the collection she wished. Inadvertently she had contrived to give herself the equivalent of an Ivy League education in natural history and geography by the time her father retired from field work four years later. Hardly had he put his feet up than his daughter had kissed him on the cheek and bounded off with Hiram Bingham on his second expedition to Machu Picchu.

Molly sighed, shook out the last few drops of chai, and addressed her dog again. "Too much introspection, Hec'. Going all Marcel Proust with this teacup. That way madness lies."

Hector whoofed and bounded from the chair to dance before his mistress. He knew that when her Spartan breakfast was done he always got his walk. Molly rubbed his scruffy chin and stood, ignoring the twinge in her skull. That was such a constant, as was the ringing in what remained of her left ear, that it scarcely deserved notice anymore. After aligning the dirty cup with the other dishes in need of washing, making sure that they were in two perfect rows, she went to her bedroom to change.

Molly threw on a well-worn rust-colored cashmere cardigan – it was still cool in the early morning in late June -- over her favorite old pink silk blouse, then stepped into an equally broken-in brown tweed skirt. She could not abide most new clothes and generally bought from high-end second-hand shops. It took great wear to properly soften fabrics so that her over-sensitive skin could accept their touch. Even then she constantly shook her shoulders and arms to make garments settle properly. More than once someone had inquired if she suffered from St. Vitus' dance.

If only that were the case. It'd be easier to manage than whatever this is.

With her beloved cavalry boots laced up to the knee (following three frustrating minutes for Hector as she kept redoing the laces to get the pressure even on both legs), Molly felt ready to face the Paris streets. They were veterans of the desert war and had come through demonstrably more unscathed than she had. Getting them on required the usual inflexible ritual: right stocking first, then the left, then the left boot and the right. Not only did they remind her of better days, as she had worn them on all of her expeditions before the carnage of 1914, but they had low heels. Her height attracted enough attention without augmenting it with impractical fashion accessories. A charcoal gray picture hat with a wide drooping brim and navy blue sash was her one concession to la mode of 1924. If she had had her way she would dress in trousers at all times, as she had in the field, but she had grown tired of the looks that habit earned her here and generally submitted to popular taste when unavoidable. When interviewing people or dealing with editors and the like it was a small sacrifice to not draw undue judgement. Her lack of eye contact was already a hindrance.

She returned to her door via the usual tile-dance. With the tips of the coat hooks gently tapped again, she tugged on tight kid gloves and snapped Hector's lead onto his collar. After uncoiling it from around her knees when the over-enthused dog circled her like a cyclone, she snagged a scarf and an ash stick from the hat rack beside the door and ventured out, making sure to hold the leash with her unbruised arm. Some liniment was in order when she returned, and aspirin as well, one of the few German inventions she could bring herself to use.

Hector dragged her down the five flights of narrow stairs and onto the Rue Le Goff as if in pursuit of the mother of all squirrels. For such a short funny-looking animal he was amazingly strong. She winced at the sun, too bright as always despite it being barely seven in the morning, and pulled her hat lower onto her brow. Even though her street was tiny, narrow, and mostly in shadow due to the tall, elegant limestone buildings, the sun seemed to always find her. Turning onto the Rue Soufflot and putting her back to the east to reduce the pain, Molly urged Hector toward the nearby Luxembourg Gardens, making sure not to step on any pavement cracks.

The gardens' regimented geometric arrangement always calmed her. Initially she had moved near it because her mask-maker's shop was just to the west. Now she was glad she had. All the trees and flowers were in full bloom, the color chasing away the memory of winter. Summer's warmth always gratified her. As long as she could remember she had preferred heat to cold. Wandering the deserts of Egypt and Asia had never bothered her. Now, with the cruel damage she had suffered, cold was even more of an enemy, piercing the savaged tissues like Hun bayonets.

Her curse asserted itself as she strolled down the walk. The other curse, apart from the scourge that drove her compulsions. That one had been born of trauma and shell-shock, augmenting a minor tendency toward rituals that she had always had. But the talent, for want of a better word, for noticing things that most people did not and for extrapolating them into inferences, that was innate. Her 'Sherlock Holmes eye,' some had termed it, to her irritation. Archeology had developed it, certainly, as had interviewing and journalism. As long as she could recall, though, it had been there. Someone would enter her room and begin to tell her some news and she would wave a hand and beat them to it, informed by their manner, some smudge on a sleeve, a facial tic. Then she would go on to ask them about their aunt with a heart condition or their dyspeptic cat. If she had earned a nickel every time someone had jokingly (or not, in the Orient) called her a witch, she would be living in a maison on the Champs-Élysées. But despite her observational skill, interpreting people's emotions was still difficult for her.

Only three pedestrians passed her, all too intent on their own journeys to pay her any attention. That suited Molly fine. It saved her having to pretend to interact. Her tight Mona Lisa smile, all that she could ever manage despite much practice, tended to annoy people. They thought her rude. The first passerby looked to be a war widow with money troubles and a useless son. After her came a defrocked young priest with a sad affinity for choir boys. Last was a newly-affianced young woman who had been honeymooning without benefit of clergy, but not with her intended.

Shaking her head at the little miseries she was reluctantly informed of, she kept her eyes on the treacherous paving lines and hurried to the park. She let Hector snuffle in the grass and shrubbery, searching for canine treasures. Her own sense of smell was inexplicably sharp, despite the absence of her nose. The doctors had explained that the real organs of scent were high up in the skull, actual protuberances of the brain. Those she had not lost. And something about the shock of her wartime ordeal had reshaped the way she experienced odors.

Molly smelled in colors.

She heard sounds in varying hues, as well, a result of the same devastation. Occasionally it all overwhelmed her and she would have to seek refuge in a silent dark room until the chromatic storm subsided. Generally, though, it merely gave her warm and beauteous sensations, like an opium dream without the side effects. When she had first experienced the sensations, in the hospital near Amiens, she had shrieked and curled into a quivering ball, fearing madness. But a patient doctor had explained it all to her and brought in others with the same condition to assure her that it was not insanity but a blessing. Molly was not prepared to go that far, but she had adjusted over the years and learned to accept and manage the 'gift.'

Sitting on one of the new green chairs the city had just spread about Paris for its citizens, she squinted at the circle of statuary around the central green space in front of the Baroque palace. All twenty of the pieces were of famous women, a fact which always amazed and gratified her. As she admired the nearest, that of Clémence Isaure, she sniffed the wet grass and saw the white statue bathed in a golden bronze glow. Her altered sense of scent did not usually match colors with the look of the thing she smelled. Goldfinches in the tree behind her twittered, causing the statue to take on silvery sparkles as well. The thought of gold, silver, and bronze made her think of Clémence's supposed founding of the Academy of the Floral Games, that ancient poetry prize celebrating its seven hundredth anniversary. Naturally, she was also reminded of that other venerable competition, even older, that Paris was about to host. There would be literary medals awarded there, too, she had read, and also in painting and sculpture. It all made Molly sigh with the satisfaction of fine things coming together.

At this hour, the gardens had few visitors, chiefly the usual dog walkers and shy lovers slinking home after a tryst. It was Paris, after all. The latter was hardly something Molly could claim familiarity with, at least not since her wounding. No one was beating a path to the door of a woman who looked like the picture of Dorian Gray. But animals were drawn to her like iron filings to a lodestone. As if to prove the point, a gorgeous brindled greyhound broke free of its owner's grip and loped up to her. When it began to lick her hand she cooed to it and stroked its muzzle. That provoked the usual jealous reaction in Hector, who poked his own brushy white snout in between her hand and the interloper. Just as she managed to separate them and give them one set of fingers each, the round middle-aged lady who had lost the sleek hound waddled over with apologies. She was dressed in pre-war fashion, no doubt what she had worn in her youth, with a hat even larger than Molly's.

Abandoned by her husband for a younger and prettier woman. The dog was his. Living in reduced circumstances. Prefers red wine to white, and rather too much of it.

"I beg your pardon, madame," she said, reaching for her dog's collar. "Actaeon has lost all his manners and ---"

She stifled a gasp and pulled the greyhound close to her, frozen. Molly's hand stopped petting Hector as she realized that the woman was staring at her in horror, mouth agape. As their eyes met that expression mingled with sorrow and pity, the emotions Molly loathed the most. For an instant she frowned, wondering why the stranger was so distraught. Then it struck her why the sun seemed so bright today.

She had left her mask at home.

Her head dropped down in a defensive reflex, the brim of her hat mercifully hiding the repulsive black cavity. Muttering a string of 'I am so sorry for you's,' the older woman tugged her greyhound back across the lawn. That anguished series of words hung in the air as a black and green mist with monstrous little winged fiends cavorting in it. Molly felt sorry for her, too. She knew well how stomach-churning a sight she was, particularly the first time. The left and center of her face resembled a wet clay bust punched by Gene Tunney, then scooped out with bear claws.

Tugging the scarf up to cover as much of it as possible, shaking her unfashionably-long dark hair down to hide the empty eye socket and missing ear, she made a reluctant Hector turn for home far earlier than was his wont. But he made lemonade from the lemons and happily sniffed everything and everyone on the return trip. Too many people decided to stop and adore him, trying to lure Molly into the conversation that she could not abide even on a normal day. Twisting her body away from the bad side, with her left hand fiddling with the hat, she would mutter inanities she had heard others say and proceed onward as soon as politely possible. Her journey seemed to take years. Every passerby appeared to stare at the freak. Truth be told, though, few of them even noticed her, save to marvel at her height. Most eyes went to the adorable cavorting hound. That had been one of her reasons for adopting him in the first place.

So distraught was she that when her foot accidentally stepped on a pavement seam, she kept on going without performing the usual cleansing ritual. Nor did she count the steps between doorways or do any of the other secret tasks that kept her from dissolving into a puddle of emotion. She saved all that for the moment the door shut behind her and she had released Hector's lead. As he dragged it toward his water bowl she dropped the stick and rubbed her palms together so quickly that they blurred. If she maintained that pace they might burst into flames. Then she tossed her hat onto the rack and softly banged the back of her head against the door while twiddling her fingers. At the same time her knee tendons flexed in time with the head rapping while she clicked her teeth. Her eye traced the outlines of windows, furniture, and rugs as if she would draw them. For nearly five minutes she remained there, waiting for the mental storm to dissipate. By the time it faded and the banging ceased, Hector sat before her, head cocked, wondering where his post-perambulation biscuit might be.

Molly fetched his treat from the pantry. The scarf came off and returned to its place on the hat rack. She picked up the cane and did the same for it. With a huge sigh she wiped a tear from her eye and stomped into the hall, not neglecting the tiles and hooks. On the wall hung her face, the one she insisted on showing the world. Painstakingly designed and constructed by Anna Coleman Ladd in her Red Cross Paris studio, the mask was made of incredibly thin copper, painted in realistic flesh tones, with rubber and leather contours. It attached to round smoked spectacles that held the latex left ear and covered an ever-staring false brown eye. When necessary Molly could remove the glasses and attach the appliance with almost-invisible wires. A separate pair with clear lenses could also be used when it was too dark to justify the others. Touching it with gentle fingertips, almost like a lover, she freed it from the peg and set it onto her empty face, connecting the wire behind her head and beneath her hair, grown out for that purpose. No trendy bob for her.

From when she had permitted mirrors in the house, she knew that the effect was remarkable. Those who had known her before 1918 said so. Not perfectly natural, of course. That would be impossible. But Mrs. Ladd had exerted her considerable artistic talents even more on her behalf than on the countless others with similar damage. Molly supposed that was because she was a woman victim. The only woman victim, so far as she knew. Was that true? Surely there had been at least a few others, unlucky to be standing where a stray shell had landed near a hospital where they had been tending the wounded. At any rate, the artist had spent much time and many trial versions before presenting Molly with the finished face. Plaster casts, photographs of her strong-planed but unremarkable features from every angle, experiments with a vast variety of materials, paints, and cosmetics. And with clever employment of makeup and hat veils the edges were practically invisible. In the end even T.E. Lawrence had gasped in astonishment, pronounced it a triumph, and embraced her. As he had spent a year with her in close quarters in the Arab desert, that was good enough for Molly.

It itched, it pinched, it often felt like a marble façade despite weighing only eight ounces. But behind it Molly felt as safe as if it were a steel blockhouse. She wondered if the Greek tragic actors had felt the same way about theirs.

Thus secure, she tracked down Hector and removed his leash. The bits of rubber in the mask smelled orange, but that sparkling vision soon faded. She spied the mail from the previous day. It had come after she had left for her training session with Jason and Hecuba, and she had been too beaten up to worry about it when she had returned. Now she sorted through it while returning to the kitchen for more tea. But halfway through the stack she gasped and fell into her chair, tea forgotten, an open letter in Arabic hanging from her fingers.

It was from a dead man.

2 / Rue Le Goff

Barely a man, though. Just out of boyhood and more beardless than Molly if memory served. Farouk Al-Khasera had been the protégé of that irritatingly handsome Egyptian fellow, that suave moustached Hassanein who had attached himself to her like a barnacle when she had gone into the catacombs to be alone. She had considered having a go at seducing him while down there, banking on the murk to be her face's ally, but in the end her nerve had failed. 'I am grooming Farouk for great things' he had told her, his voice presenting as pastel blues.

Yes, if you consider becoming a pile of bleached bones in the desert a great thing.

She had read of Ahmed Hassanein's fabled expedition in Libya, his trek across its desert from north to south. While the official account would appear in the *National Geographic* magazine in the fall, her close contacts in the worlds of archeology and geography had afforded her access to many of the particulars. Near the Sudanese border he had discovered significant ancient rock art and a pair of lost oases at Jebel Uweinat and Jebel Arkenu. But her sources also hinted at dark events that would likely not appear in Hassanein's forthcoming book. Interviews with other expedition members spoke of much death and suffering, even occult happenings (she put that down to Arab excitability and the tendency to embellish a good story for Westerners who wanted their money's worth). What was certain, however, was that poor

Farouk Al-Khasera had vanished into the desert with some sort of priceless artifact. Neither he nor the object had ever been seen again.

Yet here he was.

Handwritten, the letter showed all the signs of haste. Smudged ink, misspellings, odd abbreviations. Above all, it was brief, two sentences only. The first reminded her of who he was and how they had met, while the other pleaded with her to meet him at the Panthéon at noon that day or else many millions might die.

Millions? Really? Her toes began clenching in a fast rhythm.

At first she feared that her Arabic had failed her. But a careful re-reading assured her that 'millions' was correct. Well, the word was, anyhow. She rather doubted that the true meaning could be, though. Youthful hyperbole, no doubt, intended to get a reaction from her.

Perusing the note, written on the blue form of the Tubes Pneumatique, the underground air-powered message system, she noted that it had had been posted the day before from a downtown telegraph office and dropped off by courier. That meant that Farouk was in some danger, or believed himself to be. Otherwise why not simply knock on her door or wait for her? Was he being pursued and feared leading them to her? Had he escaped from someone and was reduced to lurking in the shadows until he could find an ally? And why write in Arabic when he spoke passable French. She had found him personable and charming in that language. A sort of code, to prevent casual eyes from reading it?

That would mean that his captors aren't Arabic speakers, then. Not that it much narrows the field. Paris isn't full of them.

A tentative sniff at it made her mind reel with clashing colors. All manner of reds, golds, and greens exploded behind her eye. Spices. Turmeric, cumin, fennel, coriander. The thing reeked of curry. Farouk had written in or near some sort of Indian cookery. Paris was awash in refugees from the British raj. Ever since the revolutionary hub in London at India House had been broken before the war, France had been the center of their activities. Madame Cama, in particular, was visible and vocal. Molly had attended one of her talks on the equality of women and come away impressed. There was no shortage of homes and restaurants where Farouk might have hidden... or been held. That would necessitate inquiry into the political leanings of the owners of every establishment in Paris, a daunting prospect. She would have to investigate that if Farouk missed his appointment at the Panthéon.

A calming caramel shade filled her vision as her index and middle fingers thrummed the edge of the kitchen table, as fast as a hummingbird's wings. In counterpoint to it her head bobbed a fraction of an inch, at perhaps half the speed. Absent a table she often drummed her thighs or a chair arm. It was her default thinking position, a sort of waking trance that resembled the Eastern meditation she had learned, and still practiced, in Tibet. Aware of her surroundings (and that people were generally staring at her in discomfort), Molly could organize her thoughts best this way. She gazed into a corner, where the wallpaper pattern made, to her eye at least, an image of the Buddha. It actually was a pair of cartoonish iris blossoms.

After perhaps half a minute the trance was broken when an interloper drenched her lap in a gallon of cold mucilage.

Molly gasped and jerked. Hector almost seemed to smirk as he shared his dripping muzzle with her, just refreshed at his water bowl. His shaggy coat was good for two things, absorption and shedding. Strangers, seeing her clothes covered in hair, assumed she had a white cat.

"You, sir, are a trial," she informed him. He hopped into her lap as if shot from a mortar. "And a kangaroo court, at that."

After smooching his nose and hugging him, she nudged him back onto the floor. She had always preferred animals to humans. If she met someone walking a dog, she would speak to the dog first, avoiding eye contact and conversation with the owner until forced to. And the feeling was mutual. Creatures of all types flocked to her like she was St. Francis of Assisi. At times that was adorable, as when the swallows had nested in her windowsill. In other circumstances, as when two cobras had cuddled up to her in her sleep on a dig in Egypt, it had been rather less so. On balance, however, it had proved more blessing than curse.

Right then it leaned toward curse, as she examined the ruination of the skirt she had only just put on. It looked like the remains of a particularly prolonged birth. "I hope you're happy with yourself," she told Hector, who turned circles and whoofed. She turned to go change, then decided that since she would have to adopt new garments later for her rendezvous with Farouk, she might as well wait. A potentially hazardous meeting would require an ensemble more suited to self-defense (or fleeing) if it came to that.

Since she was already drenched, Molly washed dishes, always a perilous task. Part of her curious brain wiring was that she did not always have the same fine motor control she had had before the war. Then she could manipulate tiny tools to expose artifacts in soil or rock, painstakingly liberating them like a surgeon. Now her fingers tended to grip either too tightly or the reverse. Her house keys would drop to the ground of their own accord. Glass would shatter in her grip. This last was an obvious household hazard come washing time. The problem was not so frequent that she had need of a servant. But on occasion she would need to hie herself to a shop to replace crockery. Wine glasses, in particular, gave their lives for her. Alcohol's relaxing effect, so welcome in times of pain or stress, often worsened her already tenuous coordination.

Oddly, though, her condition never seemed to affect her savate work. Perhaps the large muscles involved were more immune. Or possibly the focused exertion itself provided a therapeutic effect, which had been the point of undertaking the discipline in the first place. Ballet class had certainly not been in the cards. It struck her, however, that many of the movements had a dancelike feel, especially as taught by her strict masters. Hecuba had eagerly adopted some of the swirling Eastern maneuvers that Molly had learned in London from the suffragettes before the war. After watching a five-foot girl of seventeen take down and subdue a mountain of a bobby, she had insisted that her political friends teach her the rudiments. That had resulted in two punishing weeks of delightful abuse, but her muscles had learned permanent lessons there.

Of course, the assignations afterwards had often been more delightful.

Molly shook those images out of her head, charming as they were. That sort of touching was dead and gone for now, unless she paid for it.

This time all her dishes survived the washing. After drying them and restoring them to their proper places on the shelves (arranged by color and style, handles to the right, edges perfectly aligned) she swept the floor. Intermittently she would imagine an attack and respond, broom in hand. *Coup de pied bas. Direct bras avant. Fouetté.* Anyone spying on her would have thought her mad. But since her neighbors had already come to that conclusion, she felt no concern for their opinion.

Sweeping done, she dusted with a towel that she had used to dry her skirt, alternating between adjusting an errant knick-knack and defending herself with the cloth against imaginary foes. Found weapons were a special favorite of Jason's. Frequently he would dump a load of household objects into a corner of the salon and invite students to explore ways to use them. Umbrellas, magazines, lamps, clothesline, hats, rubbish bins. She had grown quite resourceful with them. When a new student had suggested that she merely remove her mask and make an attacker faint, she had thrashed him with a tightly-rolled magazine (the ends as solid as fire logs) until he poured claret from several head wounds. It had taken the combined efforts of both masters and another student to get her to stop.

Another drawback to this confounded new brain. The fearsome rages.

They only lasted perhaps ninety seconds, but they were horrific. Most often they only involved property damage, but in rare instances where she felt threatened they could turn on people. Strangers, always. Her doctor thought they were a type of seizure brought on by shell shock and aggravated by her wounding. Molly had much experience with soldiers who had suffered more than the mind could stand. She had seen many of them at the mask studio. Poor souls who twitched, or jumped out of their skins if a book was dropped on the floor, or who went on long crying jags for no reason. Quite a few grew violent over the slightest of frustrations, as she did. Though she could respond with cool detachment to a Parisian road accident -- organizing witnesses into treatment teams and saving the lives of all involved -- bumping her head on a bookshelf turned her into a rampaging Hun. Death and suffering re-sculpted the psyche. In fact, it was her belief that there was no such thing as a war veteran who did not suffer from some form of that. How could they not?

After an imaginary battle where she subdued two thugs with a throw rug and a soup ladle, Molly finished cleaning and straightening the flat. After two cups of water and more aspirin, thirst and head pains being companion weaknesses for her, she removed her mask again, shrugged her shoulders three times to get her blouse in the proper place, and sat down to get some writing done. Procrastination was her bête noir and she had to force herself into her little office on a strict schedule. She feared little after so eventful a young life, but a blank page could cause palpitations. And a poorly-written page was almost as bad. That was what she faced now. The article about Mesopotamia, newly-christened Iraq by the idiot British, was a mess. Vague, disjointed, confusing. Her editor at *Collier's* would use it to light his cigars if she turned it in like this. It was a comparison between pre-war and post-war Baghdad, based on her memories of the former and her interviews with friends and current residents for the latter. An in-person take on the current situation would have been preferred, but the magazine had refused to pay for her to go (*as if I could bring myself to do it in the first place, with all the terrible memories*) and money was tighter than usual.

Molly refused to touch the generous checks her family kept sending her. They still labored under the false hope that they could buy their way into her good graces after the shabby treatment they had meted out. When the war had started, they had expected her to leave the Middle East, not join Lawrence as a spy and sniper. Somehow fighting for a people's freedom reflected poorly on the family. She was supposed to have returned to Chicago to knit stockings for the troops and campaign for war bond drives. It had been bad enough that her father had vanished on that ill-advised Persian expedition in 1915, abandoning his retirement in search of some silly magical artifact Alexander had supposedly used to defeat his enemies. His eldest daughter going native and getting herself three-quarters killed had given her mother and aunts apoplexy. And the disfigurement had nearly unhinged them. Only her wild brother Titus had retained the saving grace of a macabre sense of humor. He had called her behavior "cutting off your nose to spite your face." So relieved by that had she been that she had hugged him, a thing she normally avoided at all costs.

So they sent long letters blaming Molly for her predicament, as if living in the City of Light were some sort of affliction when compared to Illinois. Her mother managed to give the impression that her daughter's maiming had been a crueler blow to the family matriarch than to the actual sufferer. None of them had ever visited after the first trip to her hospital room in late 1918, when she had been evacuated from Syria to Cairo and then to France. Their expressions reminded her of what witnesses to leprosy must have looked like in Biblical times. 'What have we done that God should smite us so?' Granted, she had been in a whopping great morphine fog and might have recalled events poorly, but subsequent encounters, including her one visit home two years later, seemed to confirm that impression. That event had been marked by awkward conversations, much averting of the eyes, and a relentless faux cheerfulness that had made Molly want to tear out her remaining eye and stumble off to Colonus.

Her refusal to accept their money, an incredible $30,000 worth so far, nearly half the salary of the President of the United States, meant that Molly had to earn her own living, which was all she had ever wanted. So she had spiked the checks onto her desk with a Turkish bayonet as a monument to her dignity. She had no patience for women who behaved like fragile blossoms that needed tending. Neither did she think much of those who fell back on a man's protection or support.

Lawrence and his Arabs had tried that when they had first employed her as a guide and informant, her knowledge of the desert and the Turks often proving greater than that of the locals. The coddling and patronizing had ceased when she thrashed a man who attempted tribal liberties with her and then rescued that same man when he had fallen down an old well in the midst of a battle. There were few things men appreciated more than a comrade who could outshoot and out-drink them, she had discovered. If she could also out-think them, well, that was initially embarrassing to the male pride but if it saved lives and brought victories, who were they to second-guess Allah?

All of this ran through Molly's mind, costing her fifteen minutes of writing time before she shook her head clear and began pacing the room. This was not getting the damned article done. After many trips across the office, seven in each direction, teeth clicking every time a foot landed, she growled and cranked the gramophone. Once Bach's *Goldberg Variations* began filling the June air with their honeyed silver notes, the tension melted from her shoulders and spine. Sitting again at her bruised Underwood, which had suffered nearly as much battle damage as she had, Molly quit thinking and let the words flow.

They came almost as if sent to her in a trance, as if she fell into some mystical state and creative phantasms possessed her fingers. It always amazed and surprised her to read what they had typed, particularly if she let the pages sit for a few days. She rarely recognized herself in the phrases. The person who could invent such poetic compositions seemed leagues apart from the damaged husk behind the mask, so spare of words in conversation. Often, she could barely croak out a polite hello when speaking one-on-one, though giving a speech to hundreds never fazed her. Nor did playing a role onstage. Amateur theatricals had always been a passion for her. The flat tones she normally had would vanish when focused on being someone else. But then, makeup and an assumed persona were merely variants of the mask, weren't they? Only when revealing her true self did she seize up like an unlubricated engine. That had always been the case. Her wounding had worsened it but had not created it.

She felt certain that some of her skill with words stemmed from her linguistic talent, the facility with which she acquired tongues, particularly those of verse-loving Orientals. Speaking

Arabic practically demanded a poetic sensibility in the speaker. More than once she had watched a semi-literate camel herder hold an audience of equally uneducated nomads spellbound with musical words that he invented on the spot. Rhythmic starbursts of sound, generally about things that a Westerner might assume were foreign to such hard men: tenderness, the laughter of children, sunlight glistening in water. Lawrence had reveled in it and had taught her to appreciate the capabilities of the language, so rich in simplicity and complexity at once. Eventually she had gained more than a little competency in verse herself, to the extent that her fellow soldiers not only ceased to snicker at her when she tried, but would actually commission words from her to commemorate a victory or a lost comrade.

But it did drain her, snaring the proper words with mental grappling hooks and hauling them onto the page. After an hour or two of battering away at the keyboard she felt as exhausted as if she had run several kilometers. Stretching, she reminded herself that she had an assignment to cover the upcoming Olympiad. At least someone else would have to do the running there. La canne was to be a demonstration sport and her masters would be part of that. An easy article to write. She had yet to decide on an approach toward other sports. The professional athletics writers would handle their bailiwicks more competently than she could. Her angle would have to be cultural. There was no hurry, the games ran all summer.

After a nap in her heavily sun-proofed bedroom, Hector snoring at her feet, Molly wrenched herself awake, not entirely sure of the time or even of the day. Eventually she convinced herself that it was not dawn and got her bare feet onto the plush Yemeni rug. Yawning, she noted that her dog had already abandoned the bed. Perhaps he had to go out. As she had no desire to deal with a soiled carpet, she padded into the sitting room to find him. Sure enough, he was at the door. But instead of gazing wistfully at it, he was growling as if a cat were taunting him on the other side.

"What is it?" she asked him, leash in hand. She watched him for a few moments, noting the odd behavior. Alerted, she exchanged the lead for a heavy stick and seized Hector's collar.

Her ear pressed against the door. Slight metallic vibrations turned her vision red and silver.

Someone was picking her lock.

Making sure that its tip would not catch on the jamb if she had to slash down, Molly raised the cane, heart pounding. She had never used her new savate skills on an actual unwilling opponent. Even in the war she had rarely fought hand-to-hand. But she trusted in Jason's training and Hecuba's confidence in her. With a quick snap she unlocked the door and threw it open.

Her stick came down on empty air.

Hector's rapid barking sounded like a Lewis gun, filling her head with orange pinwheels. She held him back while taking a step into the dim hall. A black fedora vanished down the stairs. The dog nearly dislocated her arm with his desire to pursue, but she feared losing him if she let him go. Once his nose locked onto a scent he tended to keep going forever, oblivious to all else. Molly hauled him back. As she was closing the door she saw that one of the lockpicking tools had fallen to the floor. A kick sent it spinning inside. Once the door had slammed shut and locked again, she released Hector and dashed to the kitchen window to get a glimpse of the intruder as he emerged onto the street.

That same black hat popped into view on the sidewalk, bounding from the doorway. As soon as the man arrived there he stopped, collected himself, made sure not to attract any more attention. He had the presence of mind not to look up at Molly's window, which disappointed her. Though the brim hid his features, it did not hide the one salient detail of the man's garments.

His priest's collar.

Of average height and build, he looked like any Catholic priest. Black suit, white collar, cross. His tight black driving gloves were different, and not needed for warmth by this time of day. And the small leather doctor's bag caught the eye, as well. Molly rather doubted that he was a Papal physician making a house call to ease her suffering.

She also rather doubted that it was entirely coincidental that Farouk's pleading letter and this house-breaker had arrived within hours of one another.

The curious stranger continued west, the same way she and Hector had gone on their walk. It struck her that he might have been lurking in the park, waiting to ambush her if she had gone to a more secluded spot. Or perhaps he had been about to break into her flat while she was out, but the absent mask sending her home early had prevented him. *Lovely thought.*

Shivering a bit, she returned to the door to pick up the dropped burglar's tool. It turned out to be a bone-handled stiletto with an exquisitely narrow and wavy blade. Molly knew something about picking modern locks, thanks to spending so much time around soldiers and bandits. The unusual design of the knife's blade meant that it could serve as a sort of rake pick, moving the lock's pins while a torsion wrench held them in place. Not ideal, not as good as a purpose-built rake. This said that her visitor was not a professional. He was desperate, too, if he was attempting such a bold operation in a public hallway in broad daylight.

She smiled as it struck her that her mask lay on the office desk beside her typewriter. That amateur would likely have wet himself if he had remained to face her. A screaming half-faced woman with a bludgeon, snarling dog in hand. Well, no one had to know how truly lacking in viciousness Hector truly was. He might slobber at a miscreant's feet and make him slip and fall. That would be the extent of his attack capabilities, unless Molly were directly threatened.

As if reading her mind, he snuffled her chin. She hugged him and went to fetch a biscuit. "You're a fine watchdog, you are," she told him. "Kudos."

He accepted his crunchy tribute and her accolade as no more than his due. Molly sat at the kitchen table to examine the dagger more closely, even daring to part the curtains to let in more light. Brief digging into her old kit bag produced a magnifying glass, so useful when working with intricate artifacts. She scrutinized the knife as best she could, longing for her lost binocular vision. But the examination bore fruit without it.

The dagger's blade was damascened and about eight inches long. It had no sharp edge. *Hmm. A presentation weapon, then, or an ornament. Strange that he would have left it on my doorstep. I must have spooked him half to death. But a priest would hardly wear it openly. Not that he's likely to be a real priest anyhow. If he is, then they've grown feistier in this new century.* Shaped in an S-curve, the silver guard had been molded into a fairly realistic adder, fangs bared. It was the handle, though, that most caught her eye.

For it was made of a petrified human finger.

Anyone else might have dropped the thing in disgust. But it was hardly Molly's first encounter with body parts. She had held all manner of fossilized, mummified, and even fresh organs in her thirty years. Tombs, digs, graves, and the battlefields of the Great War, not to mention mirrors, had inured her to such things. So she pushed on with her scrutiny without a hitch, though her teeth did start clicking.

The finger was from a large person, probably male from the girth. No way to tell if it had been taken from a cadaver or had been unwillingly donated in life. If the latter, that said something about its owner that hardly bore contemplating. *Some creepy secret society? Does a finger bear some special significance? Politics or religion, no doubt. Possibly both, which always makes for a particularly nasty combination.* She decided that the aid of a doctor or specialist might be needed. Though an archeologist with much experience disinterring the formerly living, she was no anatomist.

Something stung her mind as she considered the bone. Fingers were called phalanges. Phalanx bones, because they were arranged in a rank like ancient Greek hoplites. Could that be the reference here? *Obscure enough for a secretive political group. Spanish, perhaps? Falange means phalanx in that language. Italian, too, come to think of it.* She snorted with the comical yet sensible nature of that train of thought.

The silver pommel was a clenched fist. That would seem to reinforce the political and symbolic nature of the weapon. A badge of honor and recognition, most likely. On a whim she twisted it, unscrewing it from the threaded tang. Sliding the hollow finger bone off as well, her remaining eyebrow shot up as a tiny bit of rolled parchment fell out of it, about two inches square. She hoped against hope that it was not actual human skin. That would hardly be a surprise, the way things were looking. Inked onto the parchment was a single word: *Ardire,*

Ah. Then this is an Italian toy, not a Spanish one. Ardire ...'to dare.'

She applied the magnifier to the parchment. The ink was not on the surface, but embedded into it. A tattoo. So this *was* real skin. Whether or not it belonged to the finger's contributor was an open question, though. What did that word, combined with everything else, suggest to her?

Italian stormtroopers in the war had been called Arditi, a variant of *Ardire* . As she recalled they had been tough and effective, gliding into enemy trenches, knives in hand, to pave the way for the infantry. Elite troops, no doubt high in morale and full of themselves. But they had not used this sort of blade. Perhaps it was a special award of some kind.

That word, *arditi*, gnawed at her. She had heard it more recently. In the news someplace. Mussolini? No, before him. That writer who got up a band of misfits and took Fiume as a Versailles Treaty protest. The name came to her quickly. Molly's mind was staggeringly good at retaining obscure facts, though she had a difficult time remembering the names of people she had just met. D'Annunzio, that Decadent writer. Gabriele D'Annunzio. His followers called him the Poet, sometimes even the Prophet. He had been in the Arditi, as she recalled. Ginned up a group of veterans in black shirts and fezzes to occupy part of the Dalmatian coast because they thought Italy ill-served by the treaty terms. *Probably inspired Il Duce. Thanks a lot, Gabriele.*

So her lock had been picked by some Italian freedom fighter posing as a priest? One so green that he had fled at the first sign of discovery, leaving behind his precious icon, probably bestowed at his initiation ceremony? His superiors would be doubly-annoyed by that. Something told her that their sense of humor regarding his losing their sacred object as a clue at a crime scene would not be great. Dragging the Seine might produce a garroted priest by the next morning. She would have to inquire further, ask some friends at the Sûreté or Foreign Affairs. They might have more particulars about the group's aims. Poincaré, especially, liked to keep up on troublesome overseas groups.

As she was putting the knife back together, preparing to hide it in a drawer for further inquiry, a silly thought struck her. One should employ all of one's senses. So she held the finger up to her mangled face and sniffed. Though they were much fainter, the same colors that had struck her when smelling Farouk's letter showed up again. Deep red, rich gold, jungle green. In the same swirling pattern, too. That was how she knew that it was identical. Smells that were merely similar would might have the same hues, but the motions would be different.

Just to be certain, she separated the parchment from the hilt and tried it. Muted cloudy gray this time, like a fog. With hints of mustard yellow. So the handle smelled of the user, but the tiny note held its own scent, a bit of the creator. Beyond all expectation, one thing was now clear. The burglar and Farouk had both been in the same curried atmosphere, and recently.

Molly reassembled the dagger and popped it into her handbag, a heavy steel-beaded affair with a shoulder strap. No sense in leaving it for that housebreaker to find if he came back hunting it, as he certainly must. She reminded herself to change the lock, to get the most secure available. And to jam a chair's back beneath the knob when she retired for the night. Having downed a quick lunch, half of it claimed by Hector as taxes, she changed into a perfectly respectable and even fashionable drop-waisted blue dress *(good thing flat bosoms are in, I'm all the rage naturally)* with a high enough hem to permit free movement. Then she clenched her jaw and pulled on the fashion accessory that she hated most, stockings. After slipping on comfortable flat-heeled shoes, she donned her mask, augmenting it with cosmetics to increase the realism, using the only mirror in the house, in her compact. Then she plopped a different big-brimmed hat, a yellow one with a veil, onto her head and made for the Panthéon, curved black walking stick in hand.

3 / *Place de la Sorbonne*

He paced to and fro on the Place de la Sorbonne, the wretched clerical collar biting into his neck. How the devil had he worn one for so long without choking? Foolish belief, he supposed. A man will tolerate all manner of tortures to be part of what he considers a great idea. The half-healed brand inside his forearm was certainly proof of that. A livid red fist that he would carry to his grave.

Which might await him much sooner than he had thought if he did not get the dagger back.

A mother and small daughter passed him, smiling and nodding. No doubt they had just left Mass and were basking in their own belief, certain that all that mumbled Latin made them special, made them the Select. Would that it were so. He had once thought the same, till they had pilloried and ejected him for loving the wrong person. Correction: for getting *caught* loving the wrong person, too publicly for them to avoid the issue. Ejected from the only real family he had ever had, for an offense so common in the Church that it was the subject of jokes and snickers.

Not that his present brotherhood were much better on that score, though at least they cared little for whose skin he touched, so long as he did not draw attention to them and their activities. Their idea of defrocking involved removing said skin. He rather doubted that their reaction to his losing the *Ardire* dagger would be more magnanimous.

Curse that Aulis woman! Only the one eye and she had still spotted him when he had passed her near the Luxembourg Gardens. The penetrating look that monstrous face had given him...as if she had reached into his soul and read everything there in two seconds. His mentor had warned him about that, of course, but it had sounded too much like magic to be credited. Now he wondered. He had watched her habits for a week, routines so ingrained that they were almost set in granite. She had never deviated. So when she had taken that absurd-looking dog of hers for its morning walk, he had been sure of thirty-two minutes to search her flat for the Gaze of Zeus. Even spying him as he headed for her building had not caused her to turn around. She had kept on to the gardens. Something had brought her back, though, just as he was about to climb her stairs. Getting out of sight around the alley had been a miracle.

His tender nature had been his downfall. They had given him poison to take care of the dog, but he had not had the heart to use it. When he had snaked the flexible little periscope beneath her door and seen her head toward her bedroom, yawning, he had seized his second chance. Going back empty-handed would have been disastrous, and not just for him. Poor Rene, they had made clear to him, would also suffer if he failed. After losing his church for the young man, he dared not lose him, as well. So he had waited a decent interval, until dog and master seemed fast asleep, to try again. But nerves had moistened his amateur hands, slowed the process, caused mistakes. One clumsy jab too many and the beast had come to investigate, then his mistress. There had never been a chance to bribe the animal with the meat he had brought.

What to do now? He finally decided to calm his nerves with a glass of wine and think things through. Sitting outside the brasserie, he admired the Baroque dome of the Chapelle St. Ursule. Now that was how architecture should look. None of your steel and glass. Modernism and Futurism left him cold. *Give me statues and stained glass and ornament. I want a building with passion.* Cardinal Richelieu had built that church. Another man who did not tolerate failure in his minions. What would he say about the clock in the façade being a quarter of an hour slow? Probably burn a few Protestants and call it a day. Too bad that times had changed. Even after the recent international bloodbath you could not get away with that sort of thing now. It all had to be done in the dark, quietly. His auto-da-fe would have to be a private throat-cutting, if it came to that.

Not with his dagger, though.

That thing would never serve for such a task. A bauble, not a weapon. Merely a showpiece. He had better retrieve it or his mentor would show the others his head. One hand slipped into his jacket pocket. Yes, the garrote wire was still there. Better for his purpose. Stab someone and they might cry out, bleed all over you, even fight back. But the wire…

While sitting there in the shadow of St. Ursule, he relived his initiation. Sliding up against the naked flesh in the crypt, the blindfold never permitting the sacrificial lamb to see him coming. Looping the wire over the lad's head before he could guess his fate. The sweat erasing the friction as his own bare skin made contact from behind. Jerking like lovers at the moment of release, which in his case had been completely accurate, despite the hooded witnesses. When the dead head had lolled, he had sighed and collapsed beside the corpse. His mentor had immediately sliced off the skin from over the silent heart. *Ardire* had already been inked there, ready for that moment. Like St. Teresa in ecstasy he had lain, panting, scarcely noticing when the branding iron had seared his arm. Only the deluge of icy water had brought him to his senses again.

It had been like being born and giving birth at the same time.

When the gloved hand came down on his shoulder his heart leapt nearly as high as the dome. A dry barking laugh told him that it was not a police arrest, but his mentor. His midwife, present at his rebirth. The woman who had branded him. At least, she claimed she was a woman. With the husky voice, strong sinews, bold facial planes, and short black hair he had been forced to accept that on faith. Beautiful either way, though. Her dusky skin, a lovely café au lait, hinted at some African or Middle Eastern blood. Catalessi's fingers tightened upon him like a raptor seizing a mouse.

"Careful, Soffocare," she chuckled, one finger teasing along his jaw line. "Anyone might get the idea that you bear a guilty conscience."

He forced a smile, attempting nonchalance. "What could a simple parish priest have to be guilty about?"

"Let's ask your former incarnation about that, shall we?"

She ordered a coffee and leaned back in her chair. The midnight blue cape she wore caught the slightest of breezes and danced in the air like a condor. Beneath it she wore a red silk blouse and a man's wool waistcoat, with a long gray matching skirt. Shiny boots with wicked, pointed toes peeped out from beneath the hem. Soffocare thought she looked like an avant-garde opera impresario, rather than the icy assassin he knew her to be.

"Poor Soffocare, so out of his depth on his first assignment." He gasped and jerked at that. "Oh, relax. We all leave much to be desired at first. What virgin is ever worth a damn?"

That forced him to recall his own deflowering, at the hands of a drunken uncle. He shuddered.

"That bad, was it? Ah, well, let us roll up the bloodstained sheets and press on. I gather that you are not hoisting that glass in celebration of your transcendent triumph in obtaining the Gaze of Zeus?"

Soffocare's silence might as well have been a shrieked confession.

"Ah. Too much to hope for, I suppose. Outwitting a one-eyed faceless scribbler and her clownish cur." She held up one elegant hand, clad in gorgeous gray lambskin. One of the benefits of belonging to an Italian secret society was the quality leatherwear. "No excuses, please. They make my head cramp. And that would be pleasant for neither of us. I saw her notice you near the gardens. And saw you panic. You give her too much credit, you know. She can't read minds, it only seems like it sometimes."

She accepted her coffee from the waiter with a mannered nod. "Never push. If a plan goes sideways, dance in the same direction. And why the deuce did you pick her lock, man? All you had to do was knock."

That launched Soffocare's eyebrows up. "Knock? She would

see me."

"And...? You're dressed as a harmless cleric. That would have disarmed her long enough for you to overpower her."

"But the dog ---"

"Hardly the hound of the Baskervilles, is it? A garrote works on any throat, you know."

As her protégé's head hung in shame, Catalessi responded to a mild buzzing in her waistcoat pocket. She plucked out a gunmetal box the size of a cigarette case, with an elegant feminine nude painted on it. Across a tiny screen a line letters paraded to the left. With a nod she returned it to its pocket.

"Your luck has returned. According to this new toy of Rospo's, she's left the apartment. Eabroni picked that lock with rather more facility than you showed. The foolish dog let itself be locked in her lavatory. He says that there is no sign of the Gaze or of Farouk's letter. So evidently, he has not given it to her yet. It was unfortunate that we lost him in the Gare du Nord. A clever little Arab, to escape the Hindus and then us. Obviously, he has the god's head well-hidden." She sighed and lit a Sobranie. Pungent smoke surrounded her attractive androgynous face, making her even more intimidating. "Seguire has followed her to the Panthéon. So that ruse has worked. She expects to find Farouk there. If he shows, then we will simply let him lead her and us to the prize. Unless he is fool enough to bring it with him."

"In which case...?"

"Then you will have two orgasms with your little wire this time."

While she smoked the gold-tipped Black Russian, she tapped out a message on her tiny device, giving their two comrades instructions. Soffocare finished the wine, visions of his last communion service itching in his mind. He had nearly dropped the chalice, so nervous had he been. The monsignor had brusquely commanded his presence and it could only have been for one reason. They had been discovered. What a fool he had been to have risked all on an open assignation. When he had entered the monsignor's office, hand trembling on the latch, he felt like Dante entering into ---

"Bloody hell!" he shrieked, choking off the sound as the

other patrons turned to stare. He clutched his agonized hand, tears welling in shocked eyes. Catalessi was still twisting the burning end of the cigarette in his flesh.

"Oh, don't act so surprised," she told him with a warm smile, as if she were offering him a chocolate. "Consequences, dear boy. Lessons learned. And it's nothing compared to the last burn I gave you."

With a wink she lifted the steaming wound to her mouth and licked it with a surprisingly soft pink tongue. "Now, listen carefully. This is what we will do."

4 / Olympic Village

"Allez!"

The room, reeking of leather and sweat, boomed with the stamping of feet, the squeak of shoes on the piste, and the heady ring of steel. A dozen pairs of fencers maneuvered for advantage. Soon a few victorious yells echoed in the hall, punctuating the grunts and gasps of those exchanges that continued without a touch. Coaches barked instructions and reminders. Head up. Watch your footwork. You call that a riposte? Sabers smacked onto masks with alarming thumps. Foil tips moved like silvery hornets. Heavy epée guards clashed with solid clunks when the fencers lunged at the same time.

Ahmed Hassanein's sparring partner tried a flèche, but as usual he telegraphed the move. All he earned for his trouble was a bruising jab to his sternum as Ahmed picked up the incoming epée blade and held it aside with his bell. Muhammad saluted, chagrined, and backed up to his line again. The next time it was Ahmed's turn to remonstrate with himself, as he left his knee too far forward and his opponent gladly took advantage of the error.

Silly mistakes like that kept occurring. Finally, his coach told him to quit wasting Muhammad's time and to go take a break. "Come back when you're ready to focus on the bloody Olympics, eh?"

Ahmed stripped off his mask and toweled the sweat that blinded him. An assistant handed him a mug of water with honey, lemon, and salt added. As he guzzled it, he lay his shamed weapon in its canvas bag and shoved open the door. Outside he could find sunshine, better air, and perhaps some balance. The first two struck him instantly, but the last was still lacking. Until he could find an explanation for that strange phone call, he would want for mental equilibrium.

Before him lay the Olympic Village. That was what they called it. A new feature of the Games this time, putting the athletes together for camaraderie. And because it was cheap and convenient, it had to be said. Plus, the frisky young competitors would be easier to control in a city renowned for romance. Ugly little cabins, like a summer camp for teenagers. To be fair, that was just what the Olympics were.

Beside that was the stadium, a monster holding 45,000, he had heard. Too bad it was so far away from the sights of Paris. They were in Colombes, a good fifteen kilometers northwest of the city center. In fact, most of the venues of these Games seemed to be scattered hither and yon, either from poor planning, money woes, or a desire for inclusion. Local politics, no doubt, played a large role, as usual. His previous experience, fencing in the 1920 Games in Antwerp, had shown him that. It was worse here, though. After all, the French had literally invented bureaucracy.

It was not all bad. He understood that the fencing competition would be held at the Vélodrome d'Hiver, near the Eiffel Tower. That would be splendid. Even from this distance that glorious monument soared above all else. The other two men on his Egyptian team had never been there. A song from the war came to mind. "How you gonna keep 'em down on the farm, after they've seen Paree?" But that was immediately shoved aside by another, more pressing thought, as impossible as it seemed to be.

Farouk was alive.

The voice on the phone had been barely a whisper, the message cut off midway, but it had certainly sounded like the poor lost boy. "Effendi, it is me...Farouk. For now, I live. But they are coming for me. The *Ardire*. I have the head and the Gaze. They are safely hidden. But you must meet me at noon today at Voltaire's ---"

That had been all. The telephone clattered as if it had been dropped. Shouts and running feet could be heard. After a few moments someone else had picked it up. Whoever it was had said nothing, had merely listened to Ahmed's anguished appeals for Farouk to find him at the Village, then hung up. Clearly the poor boy was being pursued. How had he survived the desert all of those months? Where had he been since? Why had he not gotten word to Ahmed before this?

Naturally Hassanein's mind leaped to the Blackshirts and that repellent Terremoto. Had he also escaped the cavern and the Sahara by some miracle? Then Allah must have been busy that day. Or was some other group involved? An artifact of such power as the otherworldly crystal eye possessed would naturally attract unscrupulous men. It was unlikely that even fear of the glass-handed colonel would prevent gossip about something so extraordinary. Word must have gotten out. In that case, he would be in as much danger as Farouk. Care would have to be taken.

But what did Voltaire have to do with it? The philosopher had been dead for nearly a century and a half. Nothing occurred to Ahmed, so he shook his head and returned to the hall. After more fruitless drills and sparring, and more berating from his coach, he gave up and returned to his cabin. While bathing and dressing it struck him that he needed assistance, as he was by no means an authority on Paris. And the perfect person's name came to mind. Someone who not only was a resident and knew the streets, but was an expert in archeology. If she could aid him in finding the place where Farouk would be at noon, she might also be invaluable once they had the article in hand again. Satisfied that he had stumbled onto the best course of action, he donned his best white linen suit, accented it with his favorite walking stick, and set out for the Rue Le Goff.

As he was departing one of the other fencers stopped him with a message. A small man in a big car had been asking for him. Frowning, Ahmed asked to be shown this car. From an unobtrusive window he spied the vehicle. He knew something about autos and immediately saw that this one was special. It was a shining new Isotta Fraschini Landaulet, painted a rich purple, with two sets of seats in the rear, blinding heaps of chrome accents, and beautifully-spoked, white-walled tires. Built for luxury and speed. Hardly the best choice if one wished to be unobtrusive. The driver of this marvel wore nondescript dark chauffer's clothing. His hat brim hid his face.

Ahmed toyed with the notion of marching boldly up to him but abandoned that in favor of caution. Instead, he had the fellow who had alerted him go there. While he was gushing to the driver about the wondrous qualities of Italian engineering and design, spouting out statistics about cylinders, torque, and the like, Ahmed crept up by a roundabout route to its rear. Making certain that the mysterious driver's attention was fully diverted, he thumbed the catch on his cane and slid out its hidden treasure of Sheffield steel. A moment later both splendid rear tires had perished to the sword's point. Any pursuit would now be problematic.

He gave his friend a wave and hailed a taxi. The other fencer had already agreed that if pressed by the stranger he would say that Ahmed had gone sightseeing in Montmartre. Perhaps the entire thing was utterly innocent, but such an inquiry coming dead on the heels of Farouk's panicked call was unlikely to be a happy coincidence. In hindsight he wished that he had not blurted out his location to the unknown listener on the phone. Something dark was spreading its wings about him.

On the long ride toward the center of the city he had leisure to admire its beauty again. Yes, Cairo and Damascus had his heart and could claim their own aesthetic marvels, but Paris had been lovingly designed for the eye. Its proportions, scale, balance, symmetry, and ornament belied the blood that had run its streets. The Revolution, Napoleon, another revolution or two, the conflict with Prussia, the Commune, and then the Great War. No wonder the exhausted French embraced cafes, art, and fine living. Just ahead of him the Eiffel Tower, originally intended to be temporary but now as permanent as the Île de la Cité, pointed a latticed finger at God. In the distance Notre Dame did the same, rather more directly. Somewhat between them he could make out the domes of the Panthéon and Sorbonne, near where Ms. Aulis lived. Graceful bridges across the Seine hardly seemed strong enough to bear traffic. Pretty mansard roofs everywhere one looked, with lush parks and woods providing the well-watered greenery that all Arabs appreciated.

What he did not appreciate, or even notice, was the nondescript little green Renault following him, its driver dividing his time between watching the road and reading words on a small gunmetal box...code sent from a little café near the Sorbonne.

Paying his driver in front of Molly's building in the 5th arrondissement, he stared up at the elegant five-story limestone pile, so representative of the neighborhood. Most of the structures around it were the same. The little street was scarcely longer than a football pitch. Here it was quiet, but at the corner an army of autos and buses made quite the rumble. He gave way at the entrance for a burly priest who rushed past him without a word. Then he consulted the directory, discovered that Molly lived on the top floor, and began trudging up the stairs with a sigh. After fencing all morning his thighs registered many a complaint about that, but eventually they delivered him to her door.

It was open.

Not quite closed would be a more accurate description. Someone had locked it upon leaving, but it had not latched due to a corner of the small Turkish rug inside the door being bunched up against the jamb. Ahmed frowned. From what he knew of Molly Aulis, based even on that single meeting, she was utterly incapable of doing such a thing. Her dependence on order and ritual to get through life forbade it. He squinted and peeped into the flat through the half-inch crack. An instant later he burst through the entrance, sword loosened and ready.

Someone had, in the parlance of the Americans, 'tossed' the place. Drawers had been emptied, their contents strewn willy-nilly. Cupboards hung open, their shelves in disarray. Furniture had been moved away from the walls so that secret compartments might be found. The large carpet in the sitting room had been rolled up in case there might be a secret door under it. Some bits of Oriental statuary had been smashed in case they might have contained the object being searched for. A Croix de Guerre from the French government, awarded to

Ms. Aulis, astonishingly enough, lay on a shelf next to her British Distinguished Service Order. Papers and envelopes littered the floor like giant snowflakes. From what he could tell the flat had been charmingly appointed before being ransacked, decorated in green and gold fabrics and art pieces from all over the world. Even the slanting garret ceiling had been painted with a delightful Arabian scene.

The bedroom and office had received no gentler treatment. Apparently, the interloper had been hunting for both documents and something smaller and more tangible, more easily concealed. He had moved the typewriter but not removed Molly's current work. A glance at it showed Ahmed that she was writing an article about Mesopotamia. Her style was crisp, structured, just as one would expect from her. But it also blazed with dry wit and sparkling humor that was not the sort of thing that sprang to mind having met her. Perhaps she had not been at her best that evening. The catacombs of Paris were hardly conducive to jocularity.

A thump reminded him that he stood in a crime scene. Was the perpetrator still here? Or had he returned? Ahmed poked his head out of the office. The front door had not moved. To protect his flank he eased over to it, pulled back the rug, and locked it. More banging. Someone was most definitely in the apartment. From the sitting room he could see all of the flat. Nothing came to view. That only left one uninspected spot.

The lavatory.

His sword slid free of the cane body, sniffing the air like a hound. He held it gently in his right hand, all his epee training settling there. In the other hand he gripped the cane like a baton, ready to respond with either. Still more noises came from behind the narrow door next to the bedroom. The home invader seemed to be too intent on his task to pay attention to potential danger. With two fingers of his left hand Ahmed unlatched the door, sword arm pulled back for a quick thrust if needed.

His foe burst from the lavatory with the ferocity of a striking adder, sending him sprawling onto his back against the rolled carpet before he could respond with either blade or cane. Hassanein found himself pinned by his enemy, utterly helpless. All he could do was squeeze his eyes shut and await his fate, which came with horrifying swiftness.

A warm tongue bathed his face, accompanied by relieved whining.

Hector had been trapped in the tiny room for nearly an hour, listening to someone who had not been his Molly tear the place apart. That stranger had shoved him into his prison mere seconds after entering, clearly prepared for the dog. Now he thirsted for revenge. But this human was not the bad man, he smelled nothing like him. So Hector fell back to his default position, which was 'lick biped until love or treats were given.'

Ahmed had been reared with the traditional Muslim distaste for dogs, particularly being licked by them. But he had also loyally served the British during the Great War and had learned to appreciate his allies' love for the beasts. Eventually he had even acquired one, a charming greyhound named Trixie, to aid him in tracking spies in Cairo. So he was of two minds at the moment as to the proper response to his dire situation. As the dog was doubtless Molly's, respect won out over murder.

He reached up to both rub the animal's scruffy white whiskered face and gently push it aside as he rolled out from under. Adorably silly-looking, the dog was short-legged, long-bodied, and fuzzy, as if a blend of terrier and giant dachshund. The clownish thing kept jumping up at Ahmed even when he stood. His joy at being released from immurement was obvious. It took several minutes to calm him down, requiring water, petting, and biscuits found in the pantry. Then the distraught dog proceeded to search the entire flat for his mistress, capable nose huffing and snorting. Eventually Hector assured himself that Molly was gone and plopped himself in front of Ahmed, head cocked, as if seeking an explanation.

"Sorry, old boy," the Egyptian told him with a shrug, scabbarding his swordstick, "I don't know where she is." He gazed around the demolished apartment once more. "I wish I did."

He considered calling in the police, but decided that it would only delay him. Missing his appointment with Farouk would be disastrous, presuming he could determine where that would take place. It would take some care on his part in leaving the flat. If a neighbor had heard any commotion then the place might be under watch. Ahmed's description would go to the nearest gendarme and he might be detained. That he could not permit.

Leaving Hector with food, water, and assurances that his beloved Molly would return, Hassanein opened the door a few millimeters to survey the hall. Only one other tenant occupied this attic floor and that door was closed. He waited a full minute for it to open. When it did not he tiptoed out, walking down the side of the stairs to reduce the likelihood of betraying squeaks. After reaching the street without incident, Ahmed adopted a casual air and strolled east along the Rue Soufflot, away from the crowded Boulevard St. Michel area. As he walked he kept an eye out for anyone suspicious while considering his next move.

No one ambushed him. He was not dragged into a waiting car with curtained windows. Bullets did not snap past his ear. By the time he reached the Rue Saint-Jacques he had relaxed enough to admire the lovely architecture and the growing crowds of Sunday families out after church, if not in lieu of it. But his whirling mind had still reached no conclusion as to where he was likely to find poor Farouk. With only thirty minutes until noon he began to despair. And then his prayers were answered, by a house of death.

Strictly speaking, the Panthéon celebrated life, that of France's greatest men, but it was technically a mausoleum. The bones of dozens of the nation's most notable lay there. Originally Revolutionary martyrs, but since those days it had become a repository for others who had served the state, including authors such as Victor Hugo. With no other inspiration striking him and Farouk's deadline approaching, Ahmed shrugged and approached the massive structure. Hugo's novels had once enthralled him, so perhaps a visit to his crypt would not be amiss. It also struck him as apposite that Rodin's *The Thinker* had until recently resided there. Perhaps that was a good omen.

As intended by its designers, the building was a grand machine for overwhelming the visitor. Its magnificent dome, actually three of them layered inside one other, had been an inspiration for America's capitol and Ahmed could see why. When combined with the stupendous portico, so obviously modeled on the original Panthéon in Rome, and crowded with immense Corinthian columns, the effect was to make the observer whole-heartedly believe that only men of worth could possibly be interred there. It reminded him of the imposing masses of stone that his own countrymen had left from their ancient glory days, the northern side of the Edfu Temple of Horus in particular. The sight almost pushed Farouk's plight from his mind.

As he climbed the steps to the entrance he looked up at the broad pediment, where the motto 'To the great men, the grateful homeland' had been carved in grand gold letters. So intent was he at marveling at the three-meter high portal that he nearly collided with a pair of somber priests lingering at the door. He apologized to the holy men, whose dour faces immediately incandesced with pleasure upon seeing him. For a moment Ahmed thought that they must have met before, but he dismissed that as impossible. They did not speak to him, but did hold open the door for him to enter, following at his heels.

Five steps into the building it was their turn to bump into him, as the Egyptian stopped dead to wonder at the Panthéon's interior, which somehow surpassed its magnificent outside. His first thought was of the Blue Mosque in Istanbul, for both places staggered the eye with their perfectly proportioned columns, vaulting, and domes. Here the ornate Eastern tile work was not in evidence, but exquisite sculpture and vast murals took its place. Everywhere Ahmed looked was decorated like a wedding cake, in artfully worked marble. It was the glory that was Greece and grandeur that was Rome writ large, so large as to be terrifying. He was somewhat disappointed that the French had not hired choirs to sing oratorios for the visitors.

"Breathtaking, eh, monsieur?" commented one of the priests. His accent was not purely Gallic. Hassanein decided that the fellow must have been born far in the south of the country, possibly even in Switzerland, for he detected a hint of an Italian melody.

"Truly," Ahmed agreed, in all sincerity. Here the French had done nothing by halves.

The priests nodded and moved off. He favored them a brief glance, thinking that they must have come to the priesthood later in life, after much hard living. Both had the look of men who had seen battle and pain. That was hardly surprising, as those who had not were now few and far between. Perhaps the Great War had set them upon a more peaceful path. No one could blame them for wanting to save souls instead of taking them.

After gaping upwards like a goldfish for a few moments longer, the oculus of the dome fairly demanding it, he took a deep breath and ambled along the perimeter of the Baroque nave, admiring the epic art. Huge and realistic, the paintings were academic in style as might be expected for such a site. They were chiefly religious scenes from French history, such as the burning of Jeanne d'Arc. In contrast were the Revolutionary touches, such as the sculpture commemorating the National Convention. Given the militant irreligiosity of Marat, Robespierre, and their ilk, it made for a jarring tone.

Few visitors were present, perhaps two dozen, as it was a church morning. In so cavernous a space they did little to fill it. So, when the two priests slunk off into a corner near the entrance to one of the crypts, Ahmed noticed. They had acquired a furtive aspect, glancing about as if fearful of discovery. His spy sense from the war immediately tingled his brain. Heat flushed up his spine and his senses heightened. With nothing else to do, Farouk's meeting clearly a lost cause, he assumed a nonchalant air and meandered in the same direction. He watched them disappear around a corner and accelerated to catch up. As he rounded it, he ran into an old man. When he realized who it was colored lights of epiphany exploded in his head.

Voltaire. His statue, at any rate.

5 / Panthéon

Molly could tell that other visitors to the Panthéon were staring at her, but she did not care. Standing in a corner near the monument to Diderot and gently banging the back of her head against the stone wall helped calm her. It was not as if she was likely to harm herself. Her thick felt cloche provided ample shock absorption. She needed it after the echoes of voices and footsteps, which flooded her vision with a garish kaleidoscope of azures, whites, and ochres. And the hellscape of a floor pattern had been even worse. All the other patrons must have thought she was practicing flamenco dance moves as she desperately tried to step on white tiles instead of colored and negative space instead of lines. The floor was much too busy for her walking or her vision. By the time she reached the safety of the corner her heart was pounding with alarming speed.

While the ritual continued, she considered several things to distract her mind from the overstimulation. Would Farouk come as promised in the letter? Had he already been recaptured? Or worse? And why so many nude statues in a tribute to Diderot?

She had arrived thirty minutes early so as not to miss Farouk and so she could survey the enormous place for possible trouble. Though the Egyptian youth had doubtless selected it for its very public nature, there were too many places to set up an ambush. Niches, crypts, statues, columns. If someone plotting mischief had preceded her there, they could be lurking in any number of spots, particularly if disguised.

Was the entire thing just a trap? She had once used a similar ruse in Damascus to snare a Turkish agent. Let him escape and followed him to his handler. It would help if she knew who the enemy actually was. No one she could see in the vast mausoleum looked particularly sneaky.

Mothers, kids, an old couple, priests, more than one veteran sans limbs.

Priests. Damn.

Especially sturdy, those two. They looked to have seen more action than would likely be

found in a Paris church. Their hard eyes were not the product of taking too many sordid confessions. And after her late experience with a so-called man of the cloth, Molly was not disposed to give them the benefit of the doubt. She scanned the nave once more, saw no sign of Farouk yet, and followed the suspicious pair toward the stairs to the crypt below, behind the enormous new sculpture of the National Convention. It did not escape her that there might be only one exit, so she did not rush into it. But it was nearly noon and she had to get there.

Sure enough, there was old Voltaire first thing, standing on his pedestal in the vestibule, quill pen in one hand and book in the other. Not that she had expected him to have walked away since she had last visited, three years earlier. The French had decided to make him stare at Rousseau's monument for all eternity. That seemed unnecessarily cruel (and typically French), as they loathed one another.

Well behind him in the crypt proper lay the red marble sarcophagus itself, repository of the old reprobate's bones. A shiny gray orb lay atop it, like some sort of prehistoric egg or a leftover cannonball, resting upon a carved laurel wreath. Beyond it a large fan window in the wall let in some light, though the area was still quite dim, which concerned her. With her smoked lens it was often difficult to see indoors. But she could see well enough to note the strange decorations on the tomb. Molly wondered what Voltaire might have to say about the angels. Maybe that heavy orb was there to keep him from bursting out of his grave in protest.

The priests kept walking, seemingly intent on viewing other

memorials further along. Molly hung back, barely noting the walrus-moustached and coverall-clad workman who polished Voltaire's pedestal as she adjusted her mask a bit. It itched, but no more than usual. She returned to the crypt entrance to see if Farouk had arrived yet, passing a young mother (her observatory skill said that she was a war widow with a pension) with two small daughters (one was a love child born while the deceased husband had been in the trenches) in adorable straw hats, and a swarthy elegant man in white (Middle Eastern, patrician, served in the British Army, somehow familiar). All of them stopped to admire the statue, the mama explaining who Voltaire had been and why the nation had saw fit to make him the Panthéon's second occupant, after Mirabeau. Some of her recitation might have angered the man even more than the angels did, for the lady showed little appetite for his more irreligious views.

There was still no sign of Farouk. The little family proceeded along the passage. After a few moments, the man in white did the same. Molly noticed that he turned back twice to look at her. She worried that she now had three potential adversaries to keep tabs on. When he shrugged and moved on, she relaxed somewhat and kept looking for Farouk. Rather than spotting him, however, she saw two officious-looking gentlemen heading her way. One carried a pair of brass stanchions connected by a bit of red velvet rope.

"Pardon, mademoiselle," the taller one said, tipping his homburg (some prison time, favored pomegranates). Molly thought the appellation was a bit much, as she was thirty years old, but the light *was* low. With the mask, cosmetics, and veil most people took her for younger anyway.

"Oui, monsieur?" Politeness never came easily or naturally to her, but she had seen enough people engage in it that she could briefly adopt their mannerisms, particularly in a pressing case such as this. "Is there a problem?"

"Only a minor one." As he spoke his colleague (heavy drinker, divorced, owned a cat) was blocking off the entrance by spreading the stanchions to create a barrier. "A scheduled inspection of the great Voltaire here. It will require perhaps fifteen minutes. If you would not mind?" He waved one hand to indicate that he would prefer that she leave the area for that time. As he did so Molly saw something that told her all that she needed to know about him.

Forcing a smile through her veil, Molly nodded and did as he bid her. The official muttered a "Merci" and headed off to catch the others in the crypt to inform them, as well. No other visitors were nearby, having already been informed of the temporary closing. His short round partner produced a small magnifying glass and proceeded to squint through it at Voltaire's rump in a clumsy way that did not inspire confidence that he knew what he was doing. She stopped a few paces away to pretend to examine a mural, angling herself so that she could observe that corridor despite its being on her blind left side. Mother France's functionaries seemed to have the same sharp edges as the suspect priests. Something was clearly about to happen that the good bourgeois citizens around her would be horrified to observe.

The little workman had moved from the statue to the far side of Voltaire's sarcophagus, beneath the window, wiping it with a cloth to make the marble gleam. A large clock chimed noon, its low bongs creating vibrating white circles for her. That made the fellow with the magnifier straighten up and stare toward the entrance. His hand twisted the head of the glass and removed it, leaving a nasty secret stiletto in its place. When he did so the cleaner lifted his cap to Molly, removed his shaggy moustache, and winked.

It was Farouk.

Cursing under her breath, she mentally kicked herself. *How did I not notice that? Lawrence would've cut my rations for overlooking such a simple disguise.* By the time she had completed the silent upbraiding, he had slapped the lip covering and cap back in place. He moved around the stone monument and headed toward her, not noticing the weapon in the other man's hand. Molly advanced to meet him halfway after making sure that no one else was coming from the main nave of the Panthéon. All she saw was a hunched-over former soldier on crutches, one trouser leg empty, perhaps ten paces behind her. Farther down the crypt the taller official was returning, with the two priests and the man in white trailing.

Is he the ringleader?

"Pardon, monsieur," she said to the inspector, distracting him so that Farouk could pass between her and the corner. "Do you perhaps see my little lace handkerchief anywhere? I believe I dropped it."

His face twitched and he gave her a brusque head shake without even pretending to look for it. "No. Nothing here."

Farouk had nearly made it to her. Only three steps more. But the inspector's partner had increased his pace, reaching inside his coat. "Are you certain?" She adopted the precious little-girl-lost tone her mother used so effectively to manipulate men, much as it made Molly cringe. "It was a gift from my poor beloved Gaston, lost at Verdun. It's all I have of him." But inside she felt nauseous and anxious, heart pounding.

Despite himself the man dropped his eyes to the floor. As he brought them back up Molly punched him in the throat with the curved steel handle of her stick.

Quick and savage, the blow collapsed him against Voltaire's image, gurgling, unable to sound an alarm or alert other patrons. Molly spanked the stiletto from his weakened fingers, kicking it against the sarcophagus. "Run!" she hissed to Farouk, who had stopped dead, eyes agog at her attack. "Find a gendarme!"

She shoved the incapacitated inspector into the path of his onrushing partner who, rather than catch him, mercilessly shouldered him aside to crash into a wall and then the floor. A blood lust that she had seen in the eyes of desert assassins flared up in his. Molly began to back up to rush off with Farouk. Then she saw a tingle of triumph at the corner of one lip. Forewarned, her one eye darted up into the brim of her hat. And her cane snapped up before her face like a military rifle salute.

Just in time to block the garrote wire that had looped over her head.

The one-legged veteran had turned out to be part of the gang pursuing Farouk. He had abandoned his disguise, unstrapping his leg with some sort of clever quick-release mechanism. Anyone watching would have credited Saint Genevieve, for whom the Panthéon had originally been built, with a miracle. But now they were all in the crypt corridor, out of sight. So the attacker had been none too worried about observation. His crutches slapped onto the marble floor, making Molly see a silver wave. However, that did not cause her to miss his advance from her blind side, for she had long ago sewn a mirror to the underside of her hat brim.

She felt his momentary shock at the failure of his ambush. That half-second slackening was all she needed. Rounding her shoulders and shoving her hips back, just as Jason had taught her to, she stretched him out so that he came up on his toes. The cane hooked the wire, stripping it from one of his hands. Before he could react, she thrust a shin behind his lead foot, stood up with a strong shrug, and tripped him to crash onto his back with a *whoof!* He left a hint of camellia scent behind him as a memento of the encounter, its faint earthy honeysuckle tingling her brain with pinkish-yellow.

None of it had saved Farouk, though. His pause to stare at this fighting lady archeologist in a skirt had cost him his opportunity to escape. In fact, Molly saw that he had actually retreated toward Voltaire's sarcophagus again. *What's he doing back there?* The lead official had sent one of the priests around to bear-hug him from the rear, after shoving the man in white toward the central rotunda and telling him to get out. Now the young Egyptian struggled in his grip while the other false man of the cloth closed on Molly, wicked blade in hand. She knew how deadly knives were, worse than guns at close quarters. You could stab someone four times in a single second. His cruel grin spoke volumes about what would happen when he reached her. This would not be his first murder, likely even not his tenth.

Molly's savate masters and her experience in the war had taught her not to surrender the initiative. Reacting was nearly always more dangerous than acting. Too many options to consider. Before the thug could quite reach her, and before her fear made her vomit on the sacred floor, she flicked the end of her stick at his blocky face. When he rocked his head back and batted at the stick with his free hand, she bent low and snapped out a stylish shoe at his knee. That locked his onrushing leg, stopping him in his tracks with a growl of pain. Orange flashed in her vision. But he still raised his knife to throw it. Molly swung her handbag by its strap, smashing his brutish mug with dozens of sharp metal beads. She spun away, putting the tall white statue between them, and went to help Farouk.

The lad's cap and crepe hair moustache had already come off in the struggle to free himself from the grip of the faux priest. Try as he might, though, no amount of wriggling was getting him loose. He gave up too many kilos to the other man, despite the almost effeminate beauty in that one's face. At least the bastard seemed eager not to kill him. *He can't lead them to the Gaze if he's dead.* Molly approached them with her stick held like a rifle with bayonet, mindful that she was one against many, something Jason and Hecuba had always warned her to flee from. But Farouk's well-being was in her hands and, like in *Macbeth*, returning were as tedious as to go o'er.

"Release him," she commanded, checking her hat mirror as her teeth clicked. The one with the garrote had regained his feet. Now she saw to her surprise that it was a dark-skinned woman as tall as she was, with a mannish beauty that might have attracted her in different circumstances. "The police are coming."

"I think not," said the first official, the one who had waved her out and thus unwittingly displayed his clenched fist brand to her. She detected a hint of unneeded vowel at the end of the last word. Italian? "The nearest gendarmes are dealing with a timely auto crash on the next corner. Convenient for us. Not, alas, for you." He cocked his head, peered at her. "You are no ordinary woman, madame, that I will grant you. As a mark of respect, I allow you an opportunity to depart, despite your interference. My colleague with the crushed windpipe might not agree, but still..."

Molly shook her head, making certain to keep turning to prevent another ambush. Two were down, but that still left the miraculous cripple and this pair. Plus, the man in white. Where had he got to? She adopted the character of a dashing film hero, a swashbuckling Douglas Fairbanks type. "Impossible. You have my friend. He would consider it a breach of courtesy were I to abandon him." She shrugged. "Arabs. What can you do?" She carefully slid her rear foot up against her front heel as she spoke.

"Cut his throat. That I can do."

"You've shown a marked reluctance to do so already. I'm guessing that you need something that he has hidden? You let him escape so that he might lead you to it, but instead he came here to me. Awkward."

Now the other man shrugged, foolishly creeping toward her. He had closed the distance when he should have moved back. "That was a known risk. But it has paid off for us because the little imp predictably called his master and brought him here. Perhaps he knows where the Gaze is." His voice raised a bit, though still low enough not to attract attention beyond the corridor. "A trade, Hassanein? The lad for the Eye? And pray don't insult my intelligence by feigning ignorance. I know it is you, though my idiot associate here failed to recognize you despite my instructions to him."

The slim, elegant man in the bespoke white linen suit eased into view from around the nave corner. He might have escaped but had chosen to remain. And now Molly knew why. She recognized him as the charming fellow explorer who had insisted on visiting the catacombs with her the previous autumn. With a hint of a smile on his handsome mouth he stopped a few paces to Molly's right, giving her a nod to show that he remembered her, also. Weight on both feet, right foot slightly forward, he assumed a contrapposto attitude, letting the straight stick hang lightly from his fingers.

"The lady Aulis and I are of one mind here. My friend comes with us. I fear that negotiations are at an impasse, as we diplomats say." He gave a hard look at the woman Molly had knocked down, who had been furtively moving toward them. When she stopped, he went on. "Besides, I have no idea where your deadly toy is. I thought it was lost in the desert. Hoped and prayed that it was. I had not known that the young man was even alive before today."

"Then I bid you au revoir. We shall have to return home and continue to encourage him in other ways. The human body has much potential in that arena, yes? So many nerve cells, just waiting to be...stimulated." Hassanein jerked and the man held up a wavy bladed dagger with a bone handle, the twin of that in Molly's handbag. "Ah, ah, ah! I advise you to embrace discretion, not valor. You are overmatched here."

The one Molly had kicked appeared, limping but still clutching his knife. From the sour glare he gave her he was itching to wet it. Behind him the tall striking woman in man's clothes blocked their easy escape into the rotunda. She held her garrote in both hands again, flexing and releasing the wire. Something in her manner told Molly that she, rather than the overconfident official, was in charge. *That one bears watching. Careful with her.*

The pretty one controlling Farouk moved first, propelling the young man around Voltaire's statue by a hand on the youth's collar. He was barely older than Farouk. To Molly he looked to be the weak link in the chain of brutes, but it was probably too late to exploit that now. Later, perhaps, when she had managed to get out of the current mess. *When. One thing about surviving the Great War the way I did, you worry less about any other trouble that comes your way. One simply assumes that you'll sail through it.*

When she smiled at that the lead official asked, "You find humor in your predicament?"

She scratched her brow as if it itched, attracting his attention while her right foot snaked slightly ahead of her front. The stick remained in its bayonet's attitude, even with one hand holding it. "No, I find humor in your predicament."

The limping man moved next, jerking his head as if to hurry his boss along before their escape could be impinged by curious throngs or police. But Molly had pinned that gentleman in place with the need to have the last word. "How so?"

"This is a Punch and Judy show and you haven't noticed."

He frowned, the tip of his odd knife dropping a bit. With that encouragement Molly flung her cloche directly into his face. In reflex he flinched, eyes closed. She launched her long legs in an explosive lunge, both hands back on the stick. Its narrow tip caught him just below the sternum, just as she had rehearsed, driving the breath from him, and sending his knife clattering to the floor. While he still gurgled, she hooked his neck with her cane and spun him into Voltaire's marble effigy. That worthy proved stronger than evil even in death and the arrogant criminal sank to the ground, blood seeping from a scalp wound.

Time seemed to slow down for Molly. She could tell that many voices were crying out, for her vision was cluttered with sound-colors. Charcoal gray clouds to her left, amplified by the false ear, told her that the villain she had kneecapped was moving on her. Whipping her head that way to bring him into view of her eye, since the hat mirror was gone, she felt a hot rush of alarm at how close he had come despite the bad knee. His knife already lanced out at her and she was in no position to block or avoid it. All her muscles tensed to absorb the blow.

But that deadly fang never pierced her. Instead, the arm holding it jerked and went limp. From the top of the shoulder, near the bull neck, grew what looked to be a narrow bird's beak. It sniffed about in all directions, making the fellow yelp, then vanished back inside his coat. As he clapped a palm onto the spot, face twisted in pain, Ahmed Hassanein felled him with the sword cane's empty housing. Molly nodded in relief and thanks, which earned her a quick salute with the blade.

The handsome priest still held onto Farouk, but his eyes were wide with shock and confusion. It seemed that he had been promised an easy snatch of a helpless young man. He had not been prepared for resistance. His gaze shifted to the eerie woman. As Molly had suspected, she turned out to be the ringleader. She coolly scanned the scene, assessing her casualties. Three wounded, at least two so badly that they were lost to her. If she had any hope of escape to fight another day, she had to cut her losses.

"Kill the whelp," she commanded in a warm chocolate voice. "Fortune has favored the well-dressed this day."

Now Molly saw that Farouk was not being held only by his collar. His captor had a wire garrote looped loosely about his neck as an added encourager. After hesitating, the pretty one seized it in both hands and prepared to yank it taut. Ahmed and Molly both flung themselves at him, knowing that they were too far away to intervene.

Fortunately, their aid was not needed. An instant before the wire could bite into Farouk's throat, his would-be killer yowled and shook his right hand as if hornet-stung. That was close to the truth. In Farouk's fist Molly saw a glint of steel, now tipped with crimson. He had scooped up the stiletto of the first man Molly had struck.

So that was why you went back into the crypt instead of running. Clever boy.

No doubt cursing himself for not having kept his prize in the bear hug that had immobilized his arms, the chagrined priest shoved Farouk at the onrushing pair of rescuers and fled into the rotunda, a handkerchief disguising his wound. Molly let him go, after noticing that the terrifying woman had already vanished. She collected the wobbly Farouk, whose legs began to buckle from who knew how much running and hiding. Turning him over to Ahmed, she ushered them up the stairs to join the general population of the Panthéon visitors.

Just in time, too, for a cluster of little girls in their church finery, accompanied by a nun, were inbound to investigate the Voltaire crypt, rope barrier or no. They paused to pay their respects to the false priest, who played his part well enough, uttering a few Catholic pleasantries before disappearing into the growing crowd.

While that was happening, Molly dashed back to sweep up fallen weapons and search the two defeated enemies. Hassanein caught on at once and stalled the group further with a few questions about the building, acting the confused foreign tourist. She plopped her hat back onto her head, straightening the mask and smoked lenses, while rummaging through pockets. Other than noting that both men had the clenched fist brand inside their forearms, she found little of use other than a strange little metal box with a glass window and some buttons. That went into her handbag next to the *Ardire* dagger. At home she could examine it thoroughly.

Dragging both unconscious men into the corner behind the sarcophagus, out of casual sight, she arranged them into a scene of attempted robbery and violence, leaving a wallet and cash spread across the floor. Then she straightened her dress and adopted a ridiculously vacant persona. She sauntered up to Ahmed and said in a cheery tone, "There you are, darling!

Always wandering off. What would you ever do without me? Shall we go?

6 / Bhagwa's Restaurant

Five acrid smoke rings hung in the air of the restaurant's crowded back room, almost in a parody of the Olympic symbol. Considering the meeting's sinister purpose that would have been appropriate.

"Citius, Altius, Fortius," Colonel Terremoto pronounced in an artificially low pitch. He even threw in a false echo for bravado, sounding like a pompous stage announcer. His papery rasp from the war wound to the throat made it all the more disturbing. "That should be our motto, too. 'Faster, Higher, Stronger.' The man's ubiquitous cigarette, this time scented with clove, burned in its onyx holder, the remarkable glass hand supporting it. That member's fingers, like the rest of it, were dark translucent green. Though they had no independent movement on their own, they could be manually manipulated and posed.

"Faster, higher, stronger...than what?" asked the dusky man across the table from him, a black-turbaned and black-bearded young fellow in white chef's togs with the burning eyes of the freedom fighter.

"Not what. Whom." The Italian removed his bowler hat, which looked wildly incongruous on him, and hung it on the back of Dr. Rospo's chair. He was in Harris tweed mufti, his Blackshirt uniform hardly being the thing for a man in disguise. The questioning Indian raised one eyebrow when the colonel's head came into view. Harsh electric light from the bare bulb above glared off the shining platinum plate that served as a goodly portion of his skull. It resembled a metallic yarmulke, only off-center to the left.

"English anti-aircraft artillery," he explained, tapping it with his ersatz hand. "A word to the wise. Raising one's arm to ward off a barrage is...ineffective." His long nose pointed to the placid scientist to his right, whose own nose was buried in a papyrus of great antiquity. "Luckily, the good doctor here was able to engineer some clever improvements."

Gurdwara Bhagwa nodded. "One more tally onto the ledger of Pernicious Albion, then."

"Indeed." Terremoto tapped ash into a tray and took another draw on the cigarette. "Though I believe that the correct phrase is 'Perfidious Albion.' Yours, however, has a certain pungent cachet that I must admire."

That brought out a slight smile from the dour Indian. "My small contribution to our joint enterprise."

"But not the last or least, certainly?"

"By no means. Do we not possess hundreds of millions of reasons, and as many soldiers, for the cause?" With a tight smile he added cryptically, "And my old gods, now incarnate." The sturdy Bhagwa sipped his tea. "You were saying...stronger than whom?"

"Why, Albion, of course. Is that not why we are here? And the Gaullic fools who presently host us, all unknowing. In fact, all three words of Coubertin's phrase apply to our scheme. We shall be faster than their intelligence services, higher than their air defenses, and stronger than any force they can send against us. Already we have proven the first to be true. They are utterly at sea as to our aims."

"One hopes so. I was the unwilling recipient of British attention at Amritsar five years ago. A thousand peaceable citizens shot to pieces by their guns." The Indian's expression took on a tragic faraway aspect as he relived the massacre of 1919. In Jallianwala Bagh Garden fifteen thousand had gathered to protest the arrest of two of their leaders. Brigadier Dyer had brought fifty Gurkhas, blocked off the exits, and made them fire for a solid ten minutes. "I fought for the white bastards in their war, nearly died for them. Many of us did."

He held up one arm, yanked up the white cotton sleeve. In the muscled forearm were two round wounds, nearly overlapping. A finger pointed to the lowest. "That I had at Neuve Chapelle, bleeding for the thankless British to save the ungrateful fucking Frogs." The finger moved half an inch. "And that was my pension payment at Amritsar, waving at the Gurkhas to stop, vainly hoping that they might listen to a fellow soldier." His hand waved, punctuated by a disgusted sigh. "At least you were an actual declared enemy."

"True enough," Terremoto agreed, blowing more smoke rings. The smell of the rich tobacco fought with the aroma of curry from the nearby kitchen. "You have been cruelly used, all of you. If only your great mutiny had succeeded, India would now have its own place at the assembly of nations." He stubbed out the cigarette, dropped its remnant into the ashtray. "An ancient people, a proud people. And a civilized people, despite what your occupiers believe. There we are alike. Fallen empires, thirsting for redemption." The Italian gestured toward the man to his left, a bland middle-aged fellow, square of jaw and mild of eye. "Today I offer you that very thing, in the person of this esteemed gentleman."

The person in question tugged on his wool vest to smooth it over his stomach, nodding to Bhagwa. In the liquid R's of a Gloucestershire accent he said, "Harry Grindell Matthews, at your service, sir."

"He means that literally. Our friend here has just met with disappointment and disparagement in his own country. Scoffed at him, they did, despite his successful demonstration of a most remarkable invention."

Half-smiling, Bhagwa played along with the dramatic build-up. "And that invention would be...?"

For the first time Rospo spoke, struggling a bit with the French that they all used as a *lingua franca*. Now that he was on solid scientific ground, he felt confident in addressing his superiors. "A death ray." He paused to let Bhagwa master the belly laugh that almost escaped him. "Well, not strictly speaking, though it could be indirectly lethal in various ways. It generates waves similar to radio waves, but in much shorter wavelengths. With sufficient power it can interrupt and shut down the magneto of an engine, stopping it. In fact, our learned associate has already demonstrated that in England. Turned a motorcycle into a paperweight. Just imagine applying that to enemy aircraft." He pantomimed a plane falling from the sky, slapping his palm onto the table. "Or seizing the engines of the vaunted Royal Navy."

Terremoto grinned, an especially disturbing sight. "It can ignite gunpowder at a distance, he says. Apparently, this has been shown to journalists, so we need not take his word for it. A more robust version might blind enemy troops, or boil their blood."

Matthews grunted, pointing to his left eye. "Nearly no vision here, thanks to the machine." His hands balled into fists. "No vision at the War Office, either. Claimed I was a fraud, concocting tricks to fool them into throwing money at me."

Bhagwa shrugged. "It seems that you gave demonstrations. These were not regarded as satisfactory?"

"No. They wanted me to immediately surrender my plans, explain precisely how it worked, before parting with a farthing. I wasn't born yesterday. They wanted to set their own boffins onto it, steal my invention."

The colonel's palms turned up. "Perfidious Albion, yes?"

"Most perfidious," the Indian muttered. "But it sounds as if there is only one of these gadgets and that it is mostly experimental still?"

"Funding will change that," insisted Matthews. "I can't conjure devices out of thin air."

"Il Duce's Divisione Scienze Marziali will happily aid you there," Terremoto assured him. "My understanding is that sufficient power has been your principal stumbling block?"

"It has. I can use a generator, but for war use the thing would have to be the size of a locomotive. Hardly practical if it's not mobile."

"What if I said that we can supply you with a source of nearly unlimited energy, and that it would be not much larger than the tip of your thumb?"

The scientist grunted and tugged at his red bow tie. "I might, politely, suggest that you had partaken too freely of the product of the poppy."

Terremoto opened his awful mouth and outright guffawed at that. "Splendid! An egghead with wit! We shall get along famously." He turned to Rospo. "Communicate with our team and see what's keeping them. They should have returned with our prize by now."

As the round specialist nodded, rose, walked a few steps apart, and began fiddling with a small metal box, Terremoto continued. "I forswore the poppy after I was discharged from the army hospital. Better pain than a befogged mind. So, no, I do not speak of pipe dreams. I have seen this thing in operation with my own suspicious eyes. A marvel, a terrifying marvel. It boosts any energy put into it ten thousand-fold. A lit match touched to it brought down stone walls." His eyes met those of Matthews and saw the expected doubt there. "Naturally, you think me mad. But I barely survived the event. Dr. Rospo and I were the only ones to get out of that cavern. I lost many good men there."

"If this thing truly exists ---"

"The Gaze of Zeus exists," Rospo insisted, returning. "Soon it shall be in our hands again."

"Again?" Bhagwa asked. "You let something that valuable be taken from you?"

"When lightning bolts fly and rocks and sand are burying you, objectives change," said Terremoto with a shrug. "Just as we were about to lay our hands on the artifact, an idiot explorer blundered down a hole and literally tripped over it. But we have him where we want him and today ---"

"Er...perhaps not," Rospo suggested, indicating the communicator. "Catalessi hints at a, um, difficulty."

Terremoto's eyes narrowed. "Do tell."

"She says the Aulis woman and Hassanein are at the Panthéon, interfering."

"Details?"

"None. The message was cut off. When I just now sent an inquiry, it was received, but no corroboration code came back."

"Then perhaps someone else is reading our mail now. Irksome. But we may be able to turn that to our advantage later. Send a man over there to discover what mishap may have befallen our people."

A low feminine voice addressed him from the kitchen door. "Unnecessary. We have arrived, tails between our worthless legs."

All eyes turned to her. Catalessi walked gingerly, as if she ached in many places. Still dressed as a man, which was indeed her preferred attire, the tall raven-haired woman waved her surviving accomplices in after her. Eabroni, the bull-necked killer who had taken Ahmed's sword in his shoulder, limped in with his arm in a sling and a grimace on his unhandsome face. Pretty Soffocare had lost some of his allure due to the pout on his own features. A bloody handkerchief around one hand testified to his engagement with Farouk's stolen stiletto. The crew looked like they had just run with the bulls at Pamplona.

"Somehow I am not sanguine about the success of today's mission," sighed Terremoto. "Did you run into a mass of gendarmes?"

"No, Seguire and Seduttore performed well with the faked auto accident. That drew away all the police. Those two are watching Rue Le Goff again."

"Then what fearsome force has reduced Mussolini's finest to such a state? Bears?"

The new arrivals all exchanged glances. No one seemed eager to speak. Eventually Eabroni spat, "Aulis."

"The scribbler? The bone digger? You were all overcome by a one-eyed woman in a skirt?"

Catalessi advanced on him, striking the table with a fist. "No, we were overcome by your overconfidence! Your poor intelligence work. Someone has trained her in savate, among other things. She gave quite the demonstration. One man crippled, if not dead, and another out cold. And she is damned clever, too sharp to be any mere magazine writer. Not only did she beat us there, we failed to fool her with our disguises. Too cool by half. I'll wager she did more in the war than type supply requisitions."

Terremoto nodded as he took it all in. While he digested her words, he unscrewed the index finger on his glass hand. It went into a coat pocket, to be replaced by another that looked identical. As he twisted that one onto the hand, he looked past her to the others. "Eabroni, do you concur with her statement?

Is this what happened?"

The squat thug approached the table, leaning on it as Catalessi was. "Yes, sir. That bitch took us apart. Her and the Egyptian. Fair stuck me like a bug in a collection, he did."

The colonel made a humph sound and extended his artificial hand to lay it atop Eabroni's. "An appropriate figure of speech." His wrist twitched and some mechanism hissed. Where the new finger touched Eabroni's skin a dimple appeared. With a yelp the henchman yanked his hand away with a frown.

"What did you ---?"

With a sigh and the disappointed look a parent might give a shoplifting child, Terremoto explained, "Consequences. While it would be lovely to think that we are all motivated by love, by altruism, by a simple desire to do the right thing, it is a sad truth that the misbehaving puppy may require a sharp rap on the nose with a rolled-up newspaper. This applies to collectives as well as to individuals." He waggled his left hand. "So here we have the newspaper." Eabroni clutched his own hand, face taut and pale. "And there is your nose. Consider it rapped."

"It burns!" the stung man hissed.

"As well it might. Fear not, it shall go quite numb in a moment. *Conus geographus*. A cone snail found in the Red Sea. Dr. Rospo informs me that it is the most venomous animal on earth. Hundreds of different poisons in its sting. Over a thousand times more deadly than cyanide, if you can imagine it. No antidote. More's the pity for you, eh? Fascinating creature. Lovely shell. Collectors adore them. Shoots a tiny harpoon into its victim. The good doctor was kind enough to create a rather special dose for me to use. Quite large enough on its own, but it has been augmented with blue-ringed octopus venom and a soupcon of pufferfish. In one of our tests we dispatched a Nile hippopotamus with it. Quite thrilling to watch."

In the time it took for Terremoto's little speech, Eabroni had collapsed against a rear wall of the room. His comrades scattered, none of them meeting his eyes. The entire stung arm had turned blue and that cyanosis was creeping into his jaw. When the victim tried to speak only gibberish came out, as he could not form words with a paralyzed tongue and lips. He clutched at his stomach, then bent over to spew an enormous quantity of vomit, splashing the concrete floor. With enormous will he struggled to pull his knife from inside his coat and lunge at Terremoto. But after only a single step he collapsed, torso spasming as he struggled to breathe. Half a minute later he lay still, air bubbling out of his dark lips, sightless eyes open.

Terremoto cocked his head to observe the dead man's face. "Bad puppy! Bad!"

All around him were expressions of horror, disgust, and terror. Interestingly, Bhagwa seemed merely annoyed. "I would appreciate some warning next time. A messy death during the lunch hour rush is hardly a good advertisement for my restaurant."

"You act as if I disciplined him in your main dining room. Get a hose and a mop and all will be well."

Catalessi mastered herself, refusing to be cowed by the display. She called for two employees to remove the body, which task they performed as if it were a daily chore. Perhaps it was. "Is this supposed to frighten us into obedience? Into being better soldiers for your enterprise?"

"Why? Did it not work? I can always kill someone else if you weren't paying attention." Terremoto replaced the deadly finger with the original inert one. "We play for high stakes. Remember that. One does not bring down an empire with stern words. I have seen how the English treat those who oppose them. The Irish in 1916, for instance. The Zulus. Hell, they burned the Americans' capital city to the ground. And yes, Mr. Bhagwa, I do not forget the suffering throngs of your country. Your revived gods have much to avenge."

Matthews blurted out, "And the Boers. I was there twenty-odd years ago. One of the soldiers, sad to say. A hundred thousand civilians shut up into concentration camps by Kitchener. A quarter of them died, mostly little children. And for that they made him a bloody Viscount."

"True. Excellent choice of adjective, by the way." Terremoto lit another Sobranie, using a cigarette lighter built into his middle glass finger. "We are between two hungry behemoths, the British lion and the Roman wolf. Neither is particularly forgiving. But we have already gone over the top against England and there is no retreat now. Consider me the file closer who marches behind the last rank on the advance and ensures that no one loses his nerve, because though the enemy *might* strike you down, I *certainly* shall."

Catalessi shrugged. "So we have gone over the top. In which direction? To what end? I have heard a great deal of sloganeering and charming ritual from *Ardire*, seen many pretty costumes, but what are we hoping to accomplish? I have no love for Limeys or Frogs, you know that. Think they own the world. Britain's fabled empire is just a giant trading concern, conquering ever more people to stuff the Bank of London's coffers. France is no better. They both got half my family killed in their Great War, with their incompetence and arrogance. How is your Il Duce an improvement, though? And what, specifically, is our mission now?"

"As to your first question, that will have to wait for a time of more leisure, when we can have a spirited geopolitical discussion like we were back in university. As to the second, and more pertinent one: well, our goal is simplicity itself." Again, Terremoto puffed out five smoke rings until he had another Olympic image. Then he ignited his middle finger and punched it through them. "We are going to test Mr. Matthews' death-ray on the crowd at the Olympic stadium."

7 / Rue Le Goff

Breezing out of the Panthéon in the guise of a cheerful couple, Molly and Ahmed watched Farouk go in the opposite direction. Hassanein had already whispered to him to meet them at the Café Sirocco on the Rue Soufflot. Traveling as a pack seemed unwise in light of the knowledge that there had been others in the gang besides the ones inside the mausoleum. Farouk nodded, replaced his stage moustache, assumed the posture and gait of a man of fifty, and shuffled off on a roundabout route to the café. His two comrades were bound for Molly's flat, as she was concerned for Hector. Ahmed had not yet dared inform her about the condition of her home. As it was, she was showing all the signs of battle fatigue. Her arm wrapped in his felt cold. It trembled. Though the day was not overly warm, perspiration ran down her neck. She took rapid shallow breaths and complained of a headache. So strong in the fight, she now had to be supported or her wobbly legs might have given way.

He maneuvered her into a narrow side street and sat her on a bench. When he inquired as to whether she was all right, she did not answer. Her teeth clicked in a machine-gun rhythm and she began gently rocking. Fingers of both hands thrummed on her thighs. If he had not known better he would have thought her in some sort of epileptic fit. Deciding that whatever she was doing should run its course, he let her be and scanned the neighborhood for signs of pursuit. There were none. In fact, the street – little more than an alley -- was completely deserted. Relieved, he crossed his legs and waited.

After perhaps three minutes he detected a lessening of vibrations in the bench. He turned his head to look at Molly in polite inquiry, but otherwise did nothing. In another minute she clenched her fists and stopped rocking. Soon after that she spoke, though it was so low that he had to ask her to repeat it.

"You have a fine bedside manner, doctor."

"That is giving me too much credit. I really had no idea what to do, so I chose to let the patient treat herself."

"Would that all of my physicians had shown such wisdom." She took a pair of deep breaths. "I am... unusual."

"I had noticed that you are no run-of-the-mill woman, yes."

"Mama, there goes the madwoman, I hear children whisper when I pass." Molly fiddled with her face beneath the veil. "She fidgets, she twitches, she won't step on sidewalk cracks. If one arm itches, she has to scratch the other one, too, just to even things out. Touches every lamppost with the tip of one finger. If she forgets she goes back to the one she missed. Can't stand bright colors, especially red. Wakes up crying, afraid that the Turks are infiltrating the tents again. Has no trouble speaking to a crowd of two thousand in a theatre but can't look a single person in the eye across a table. Can handle a fatal traffic accident yet flies into a towering rage when her toast burns. Seeks out dangers that others would flee from, just to occupy her mind. Aeroplanes, skiing, deep sea diving, frenzied romances with the wrong sort of people. Several at once if she's really in a mood. Men, women, both, it doesn't matter. Anything for a sensation."

This was hardly what Hassanein, proper Muslim gentleman, had expected to be dragged into on the quiet Parisian bench. But he had seen this sort of urge to spill secrets before in shell shock cases. But had this single brawl caused it, or was it brought on by something more?

"Miss Aulis, if I may presume, you betray signs that are normally seen in war veterans."

"Very observant of you. That is precisely what I am, despite my frock. I was with Lawrence in the Arabian desert."

Ahmed eyes widened. "In what capacity?"

Now her toes were tapping in a complicated rhythm. "I was trapped in the Transjordan when the Arab Revolt against the Ottomans broke out in '16. Working on a dig near Kerak Castle, my nose in the sand, paying no attention to the whirlwind around me. The Turks assumed we were spies for the British and interned us. When they...abused...my friend so badly that she died, I decided to turn their suspicion into a prophecy. Escaped before they could show me the same attentions they had paid to poor Diana. I took a camel into the desert, got lost, and should have ended up a desiccated skeleton. By fool's luck, or fate, an Arab patrol led by Lawrence plucked my babbling self out of the sand. When I discovered what he was about – killing Turks – I offered him every legitimate service I could provide. To his credit he took me seriously. Naturally, some of his men did not and I had to teach them the difference between an ally and a whore. There were rather fewer testicles in our party on the return trip."

"You fought in the war, then?" Ahmed asked, genuinely surprised. "As a soldier?" Not that he hadn't seen some Arab women fight, but that was generally only *in extremis*.

"Not as front-line infantry a la the Western Front if that's what you're thinking. We were raiders, in the best desert tradition. I was a scout, a spy, a cultural liaison with the natives, a guide when we sojourned in lands I knew from my work. A sniper, too, as it turned out I had the patience and the eye for it." She laughed, though it came out more bitter than happy. "Still have that eye, though the other one has gone the way of all flesh."

Ahmed frowned. "I'm sorry. You say you were wounded?"

"Comprehensively. As near to death as one could be. Thus, the mask, the unblinking eye, the glasses. And the veil." She blew out a tiny laugh. "Got my DSO the hard way."

"A terrible thing. But you seem to have come through it well."

"Really? That laundry list of difficulties I gave you is largely the lingering effect. I admit that I was hardly well-adjusted before, but it all became worse by orders of magnitude when I left half of my skull on a hill outside Damascus." Molly shrugged. "Who's to say whether it was the getting wounded that caused it or the tally of Turkish souls on my register?"

"If so, you have much company in that regard."

"True. I've seen a great many of them, in the hospitals with me or in the waiting room at the mask studio. Pathetic lads, wracked with guilt for what they saw, what they did, or merely for having come home from it when millions didn't. As one of them on all three counts, I sympathize."

She leaned over as she sat, almost as if to vomit, but remained there, head bobbing, until Hassanein began to fidget. When she spoke again, he had to strain to hear her. "Sniping is bad enough, killing some poor unsuspecting sod from half a mile away. But hand-to-hand, feeling bone and cartilage crunch..."

Ahmed felt like reaching out, touching her shoulder to reassure her, but recognized that it would be a mistake. Instead, without moving toward her, he said, "They left you no choice, did they? You were attacked."

"Was I? They gave me a way out, all but shoved me out of that corridor. I went back in of my own accord."

"And Farouk is still alive and free because of that."

"Perhaps." Her hands waggled, a blur. "Four years of training. Savate, la canne, even jujitsu. The only woman at the salle, besides one of my instructors. So proud of myself. Independent, self-reliant, strong. No man will ever do to me what the Turks did to poor Diana, I told myself. Purely for self-defense. Never thought I would actually use it, of course. What were the odds? And the first time I get into a fight, I lose my mind. 'I find humor in your predicament.' 'This is a Punch and Judy show.' That's not just self-defense, that's being entertained by violence. What sort of person does that?"

"If we are to be judged by every casual word we say during a life-or-death struggle, who shall evade censure?"

Molly sighed, sat up, stretched. A wry smile wriggled at her mouth. "Your placid wisdom is positively annoying."

He raised his palms to the sky. "What can I say? Diplomat."

She finally gave him the same sort of examination she gave everyone else, pulling details of his life from gesture, manner, dress, voice. "A staff officer in the war if I had to guess. Not the

84

Western Front. My neck of the woods, as if there were any woods there. Cairo, I expect, working for the British. Allenby or, more likely, Maxwell. Raised in the East in a certain amount of privilege. You carry yourself like a blueblood who has no need to demonstrate his lineage. The accent has a whiff of jujitsu, though, so you were British educated. Manners of a courtier. Expert fencer, judging by your asymmetrical development and the lightness of your feet, not to mention that neat skewering of the fellow who nearly gutted me. I already know of your predilection for exploring. A neat piece work that, in Libya. *National Geographic* is publishing your account?"

He nodded. "Later this year, I understand. As you can no doubt imagine, I left out a few details."

"More than a few. It seems, though, that the irksome gentlemen at the Panthéon knew all about them."

"Alas, yes. From one of the two other survivors of the incident that I omitted. They have an ancient parchment guiding them. He seems determined to not only acquire the object you salvaged, but to gain a measure of revenge as well."

"That will likely be his undoing. I saw quite a bit of vendetta gone wrong in the desert. It sours the judgement."

"That it does. But it can also make a man a formidable adversary, in the short term."

"Then let us work to outlast him into the long term." Molly stood, stick tapping a beat on the pavement. "Come. Let us see if they are still watching my flat. I have to feed my dog and listen to your explanation of why people are so hell-bent on dispatching us."

As he also got to his feet Ahmed gave her a pained look. "Ah, yes. Your home. About that..."

The rest of the way there Molly grew increasingly agitated while he outlined what he had found in her apartment, though his description of his encounter with Hector made her cackle. She leaped over every crack and seam, tapped every lamppost, counted windows in buildings out loud. Often she would repeat particular words or phrases if their sounds calmed her. Her shoulders were constantly in motion, as if she were trying to shoo pesky flies from them. Once or twice she commented on the color of a noise, which gave Ahmed pause.

Rounding the corner to the Rue Le Goff, they slowed to take measure of the situation. Few autos were parked. Molly immediately seized upon one as the most likely, a small green snub-nosed Renault Torpedo with the top up. Its driver was engrossed in peering at a palm-sized metal box like the one in her handbag and only noticed the tall woman stomping toward the car, stick at the ready, when Molly was nearly in striking distance. With much rude language the driver dropped the device and slammed the gears. As the engine was already running, the auto lurched from the curb and before Molly could inflict her wrath upon it.

"That should keep them away for a while," she muttered, crossing the street to her building, "at least until they can change cars."

"Not very subtle about their surveillance," noted Ahmed as he rushed to catch up. At all times Molly walked with vigor and purpose.

"They've displayed an extraordinary amount of arrogance throughout this whole affair. I expect they will soon adjust their methods. In fact..."

She stopped inside her vestibule and gazed out at the street again. Her lips moved but made no sound, as if she were speaking to herself. After a long moment she slapped the door jamb and whispered to him, "There. See him? Pretending to paint that railing?"

Ahmed looked where she indicated, at the nondescript workman dabbing tiny swabs of black onto the wrought iron decoration along a set of steps. If he was a real painter then the client should have demanded a refund. Half the time he kept glancing at Molly's building. Once he reached into his supply box to consult yet another object resembling the one she had taken from the fallen official in the Panthéon.

"Less obvious than the one with the car, at least."

"Yes," Molly agreed, "because we were intended to spot the auto. Then we would think we were unwatched and maybe give something away. That's more cleverness than I would have credited them with."

"Do we chase him off, as well? Or ignore him?"

"The latter, I think. For now. Come on, Hector will be

frantic."

She led the way up the formidable series of stairs, touching every newel post with her right hand. Ahmed kept his cane ready, one inch of steel showing for a quicker draw At every landing they slowed to look ahead and prepare to be ambushed. But all was clear. They reached the top without incident, though Hassanein felt winded despite being an Olympic athlete. He noticed that Molly's breathing had not grown any more labored.

At her flat they inspected the door and its surroundings for signs of tampering. None were evident. Ahmed explained that he had draped a fine linen thread from inside his coat pocket over the door handle when he had left. It was still in place.

"Why, aren't we the sly one?" she teased. "General Maxwell had you doing more than look at maps when you were on his staff, eh?"

He chuckled. "Once or twice." His sword slid all the way out, point aimed at the door. "Ready?"

"Don't trust that thread? Or don't trust my dog?"

"The valiant Hector has already proven my equal once this day."

She snorted and opened the door. Toenails clattered on tile before falling silent on the carpet. Hector whined in glee and launched himself up into her arms. Molly tossed her cane onto a chair just in time to catch the shaggy bundle of excitement. His pink tongue slathered her face and neck, avoiding the masked portions.

"Oh, yes, you beautiful boy! Did you miss me? You had to defend your house against the nasty burglar, yes, you did." She kept up the baby talk while smooching and hugging him. It was a side of Molly that Ahmed would not have expected.

"What sort of dog is he? I haven't seen one like him before. A bit comical. Is he a mixed breed?"

She set Hector down and moved to the pantry door to scoop up a handful of biscuits. "Sacrilege! He's no mutt." A treat flew through the air and was expertly caught in Hector's furry jaws. "You're a blueblood, aren't you? Yes, you are." Another biscuit disappeared in mid-flight. "He's a proud specimen of the Petit Basset Griffon Vendéen. An old and noble breed."

"Not a terrier then? With the beard and moustache and that coat ---"

"Terrier? No! He's a proper scent hound. One sniff and he'll tell you what you had for breakfast last week. Yes, the coat does look like I gave him a wash and let it dry without brushing him, but it's supposed to look like that."

"How does he see through all of that fur on his face?"

Molly shrugged. "Don't know, but he has yet to crash into a wall, so he must manage somehow." She tossed three more biscuits so quickly that Ahmed felt certain at least two would fall to the floor. Yet the white and gray blur snagged each like an adorable cobra striking.

"Impressive."

"Yes, he's quick. I ---oh!"

Now she noticed the state of her home.

Immediately Molly began quivering as she looked around at the devastation. Though Hassanein had tried to prepare her, apparently his words had not done justice to the carnage. Given her need for order, ritual, and structure it no doubt seemed much worse to her than to him. Head bobbing, hands drumming on the table like an engine at high speed, she took it all in. Her teeth clicked until Ahmed feared for their integrity. After a minute of that she stood, fingers scraping at the insides of her palms over and over. She stepped toward one corner of the room, shook her head, went at another, stopped, moaned. With a growl her fists went up on either side of her head, shaking in the air. That quiver spread to all of the rest of her, as if she contained a small earthquake. Like a bird of prey she pounced on what looked to be an authentic canopic jar from an Egyptian tomb. It had been opened and searched, the lip getting chipped in the process. When she spotted that damage something exploded inside the woman. Grunting, she flung it at the wall. As it burst into clay shards she did the same to anything else she could lay her distraught hands on. Her belongings, whether intact or not, all became missiles. At the same time she kicked at everything in her path. For thirty seconds some tremendous demon possessed Molly Aulis, causing Hassanein to take shelter behind a decorative screen until the fit passed.

At last the sound and fury subsided. On her knees in the middle of her floor, Molly sank forward until her head rested on her arms, heaving deep racking breaths. For another long minute she remained there, each inhalation growing shallower than the last, until she was quiet. When she finally lifted her head up, hat and veil long gone, Ahmed saw that her face held a lost, confused look. It was a wonder to him that despite the mask and dark spectacles she could still project considerable expression. This one reminded him of a holy man returned from a trance-communion with his gods.

"I felt it coming on," she said, low and hoarse, "but couldn't stop it. I rarely can."

"You worried me," he told her, coming out from behind the screen. He hurried to the sink to fetch her a glass of water.

"I imagine so. It makes me feel the same." Still on her knees, she looked around. "It's worse for poor Hector. He's probably under my bed now."

Ahmed handed her the glass and wound his way through the war zone she had created. Sure enough, a bearded snout poked out from under her duvet. "The good soldier is in his trench, hiding from the bombardment."

Molly struggled to her feet, moving like a boxer who had had the worst of it in a long bout. "I'll coax him out in a minute. Have to wait for the muscles to unkink. These things are essentially brief seizures. It takes me a bit before I can function again." She shuffled to her kitchen table and sat with a wince. "I'm surprised that you aren't under there with Hector."

"I considered it, but feared I might take shrapnel on the way."

"Wise man." Hassanein stooped to begin cleaning up the mess, but she barked at him. "No!" When he started and ducked his head as if a club were aimed at it, she raised her palms and lowered her voice. "That won't help. Well-meaning as you are, you'd make it worse. I know where everything has to go, to the micron. If it doesn't end up that way, I'd just go off again."

"All right, then." He approached the kitchen, not getting too near to her. "Can I do anything?"

"You should probably go, harsh as that sounds. The police

will no doubt come snooping about before long. Someone was bound to have noticed us. I'm fairly well-known in this district. No sense in getting a proper Egyptian gentleman and Olympian tangled in this."

"Well, I can hardly leave you alone to ---"

Again she held up a hand. "Please. 'Alone' is what I do. It's my preferred mode of existence. There I'm at my best. People short-circuit my brain. So don't let that concern you." She sipped her water. "Besides, this isn't over. Barely begun, even. Better that you have freedom of action if I am detained. And you'll be safer in that Olympic village. Go back and prepare for your bouts."

Molly searched through her handbag and produced a business card. "Here. My telephone number at this address. Also at the Club de Archeologie in Montparnasse. I'm often there, pretending that I have social skills. If I have to cross the channel there is a number and address for my flat there."

Ahmed took it, frowning as he read. "1 Kensington Gore? I say, isn't that the ---?"

"The Royal Geographical Society, yes. I have a small lodging there. Through my mother I have dual citizenship. The British government owed me a favor because of a service I did for them. Didn't I mention my DSO?" She touched her mask. "And perhaps a bit of guilt may have entered into it. At any rate, that was the reward I claimed."

"It must have been quite a service."

Molly shrugged. "Let's just say that someone still sits on purple cushions because I was in the right place at the right time."

Chuckling, Ahmed handed her his card in return. It had been made especially for his upcoming time in Paris. "Just when I think your capacity to surprise has exhausted itself. Here is mine. The second telephone number is the Egyptian embassy. They will always know how to reach me, even if the fencing coaches do not."

The implication was not lost on Molly. "Ah, so this is something of a working holiday for Hassanein Bey."

"Particularly now. I should go there immediately and consult about this day's events."

"Be careful on the way. Shall I arrange a distraction for our friend across the street?"

"No, please, you should stay here and recover. I can manage him. Besides, I expect that he has orders to remain where he is." The Egyptian gazed about the apartment. "And you have much work to do."

"True enough. Until I restore order I shall be positively twitchy. You know that blessed
feeling of relief you get when a baby stops crying? That's how I feel when I straighten an out-of-place knickknack."

"Then I shall leave you to it." He made for the door, collecting his hat and stick. "It has been an unfettered joy to make your acquaintance again, Miss Aulis. You have restored my Farouk to me and dealt his captors a body blow. I hope that we may continue to punish them."

"I look forward to it. And I will keep you informed of anything I learn about this affair."

"And I shall do the same. You will be all right?"

"Oh, yes. I'm used to this by now. More's the pity."

Hector slunk back into the sitting room, head down, tail between his short legs. Molly made apologetic cooing noises and clapped her hands for him to come to her. As she was apologizing to the distraught hound Ahmed opened the door just enough to survey the hall. Satisfied that no ambush awaited, he stepped halfway through it, then turned back.

"Oh, before I forget. A remarkable auto has been following me."

Molly kept on adoring Hector, but spared him a glance. "More remarkable than a green Renault?"

"Quite. It's a rich purple."

She froze. "Purple? Large car? A rich man's car? Italian luxury and all that?"

"Why, yes. You know it?"

"Unfortunately so. Don't fret about it. It has nothing to do with today's business."

"You're certain? I punctured its tires so I could escape."

She hooted at that. "Really? Then you are my new hero!"

Hassanein spent the whole trip back to the village wondering what she had meant by that.

8 / Sûreté

Sanglier's moustache amounted to little more than an eyebrow-pencil smear across his lip, but he seemed enamored with it, so Molly refrained from ridicule. She may have had poor abilities at social interaction, but she knew that antagonizing the man whose aid he needed was poor tactics. Still, she kept staring at it, since her gaze naturally avoided direct eye contact. Thankfully, her dark glasses kept that fairly discreet. When she did look elsewhere it was to admire the fine view over his shoulder out of the wide window, where Sainte-Chapelle's ornate Gothic spire poked up over the more modern roofs like a particularly painful yet lovely harpoon.

Rather than wait for the Sûreté to find her, which would entail a great deal of work on its part and mean that they would be in a less-than-receptive mood when they arrived at her door, she had gone to them. After restoring order to her flat and taking a desperately-needed decompression nap in her darkened bedroom, she had mounted her beloved bicycle, a professional men's racing model that required her to wear her preferred split skirt, and ridden over to the Prefecture of Police headquarters on the Île de la Cité. Evading her watcher with the paintbrush had been simple. It was unlikely that he would try to break into her flat again, as the first search had proved fruitless. If he did, Molly had left him a nasty little surprise with an oiled floor, a wire trigger, and an old bit of fishing net she had scavenged while visiting Le Havre. To add to his potential distress, the net contained several dozen wicked fishhooks. Hector was locked in her bedroom, worrying a beef bone.

Affecting an attitude of civic concern and a desire to help, she had breezed into the Prefecture and asked for Sanglier, since she was familiar with him after a few other encounters, mostly when she was looking for details for a particular piece she was writing. They had a sort of bond forged by the war, for the detective had been a formidable raider of German trenches, an activity not for the faint of heart. His brass-knuckled trench knife, still stained with Boche blood, lay on a corner of his desk, mounted on a commemorative plaque by his admiring troops. Other deadly mementos of the war filled his office, for he was a noted collector, particularly of unusual weaponry. Unlike Molly, though, he bore his wounds, physical and psychological, much more lightly.

"Mlle. Aulis! What a delight!" he boomed, offering her a chair. With a snap of his thick fingers, he commanded that tea be brought to her. Not tall, but as sturdy as the Arc de Triomphe, he filled his fine suit near to bursting, none of it fat. His neck seemed too thick for his celluloid collar. He had not let himself go when the need to fight Huns had passed. Instead, he had simply transferred his love of infiltration and combat back to his police duties. Molly did not envy any criminal on the receiving end of his attentions. Once or twice, she had experienced that very thing when he had visited her savate salle. It had occurred to her at the time that he fought like his namesake, the wild boar. The bruises he had left her could attest to that.

I wonder what a mattress romp with him would be like? No, thank you. He'd leave me looking like a Picasso painting.

"Fine weather for the Games, eh?" he asked as they waited for the refreshments to arrive.

Molly's natural talent for small talk would not have filled a demitasse spoon. Her brain, even before the injury, had never had patience for that sort of thing. People would natter on about the weather, their children, sports, politics, gardening, servants, or how awful the trams were. When they expected her to follow suit, her throat would close up. So did her mind, only able to focus on something that actually interested her, in which case her devotion to it was fierce, her grip as unyielding as Milo of Croton's. She adopted a new interest every year or so, dropping the old favorite as if it carried plague, though the acquired knowledge or skill always remained. Thus had flute playing, bridge, juggling, flying aeroplanes, and the like, pursued with intense passion while they lasted, all come and gone. Besides her unending love of archeology and the East, only writing, savate, and amateur theatricals remained. The one paid her bills, the second kept her safe and sane, and the last seemed to be a sort of excellent psychological therapy. Somehow pretending to be an imaginary person permitted her to interact with people in a way the real Molpadia Aulis could not.

"Yes, I suppose so," she replied curtly, a bit irritated. Sanglier knew her conversational limitations perfectly well. Then, realizing that she needed to spread honey to catch this fly, she took on a new persona, making sure to keep it subtle enough that the detective would not notice and grow suspicious. For besides his evident physical attributes, he was no fool.

Her frame softened, became more feminine, her posture moved forward in the chair. She thought of herself as a girl named Chloe, educated but personable, reared with many brothers and used to interacting with men. Chloe knew how to talk to them, how to get what she wanted by stroking their sense of manly self-importance. Molly cocked her head to one side and smiled, a genuine warm one rather than the tight pained grimace her true self used.

"Cool and dry for the Opening Ceremony would be nice," she offered, taking care not to affect an accent different from her own. "We are supposed to be sunny France, after all. Jut the proper amount of wind at le Havre for the sailing. I gather that the rugby and football boys never mind a bit of mud, though."

"Yes, but their spectators might object, especially at the astronomical ticket prices."

Sanglier laughed and filled his briar pipe, banded with

engraved silver and gold. Molly laughed with him, more delicately, though inwardly she was in despair at the horrid stench he was about to inflict on her. She expected to leave the meeting with Vulcan's hammer pounding at her skull, a pain that would take another hour in her dark room to quell.

"I understand that le canne is to be a demonstration sport this time," he said, bowl fuming like Vesuvius and smelling nearly as bad. His broad hands smoothed his center-parted black hair down, already made as slick as a skullcap by pomade. "Is your salle involved?"

Molly saw black demonic shapes at the edges of her vision, perfectly matched to the aroma of the strong tobacco Sanglier favored. It was the same dreadful stuff issued to French troops during the war. Her temples immediately began to twinge. But her smile remained, as if part of her mask. "Two of our senior students will spar, yes. That will be the extent of the demonstration. One stole the other's girl, he claims, so we may have to alert the hospital staffs."

After more laughter, gamely forced on Molly's part, the policeman sat back and spread his hands. "To what do I owe the honor of this visit? I'm only too happy to help after the assistance you gave us with that nasty omnibus accident. Saved a couple of lives, I have no doubt."

Molly-as–Chloe waved that off. "Oh, any citizen would have been just as glad to pitch in."

"Perhaps. But most citizens couldn't have set up a battlefield triage station, applied a tourniquet, stopped a child from choking in her own blood, and, oh, yes, I haven't forgotten this one, pulled a grandmother from a burning auto."

"Well, when you put it that way, it does sound like I was awfully busy. I'm just happy that we lost no passengers."

"As am I. I'm also reminded that you alerted us to a Soviet agent planted in the Hotel Brienne. Quite a feather in my cap with the War Ministry, that was, though I do wonder that you insisted I take the credit. Which is why I am eager to assist you today."

Molly had stumbled over that choice bit of intelligence accidentally while investigating a completely unrelated story about the Armenian massacres of 1915. It had not escaped her that using it to make friends in the police would stand her in good stead someday. "That truly was just luck on my part. Though I am an expatriate, France is my home and I wish to see her safe. And as for the credit, well, where spies and Communists are concerned, the less they know of my involvement, the better. I don't enjoy looking over my shoulder. With only the one eye, it's so inconvenient."

He seemed not to know whether that was a witticism or not. She tittered a little to give him a clue. After returning a confused smile, he fell silent, puffing on his pipe until his desk resembled the lair of a dragon, inviting her to continue.

She let some of her assumed character dissipate now that she had hooked him. It had turned out not to have been as necessary as she had feared, but it was good practice anyway. And she could only maintain that sort of thing for a brief time. "You had an unpleasant situation at the Panthéon today. Just after noon."

"Heard about that, did you? Some sort of brawl. No one got a good look at it, the place had just opened and it all took place down one of the crypts. Looks like a robbery gone wrong, but after studying it for a while, it started to smell funny."

Nearly as bad as your wretched pipe.

"Two men down, near the Voltaire statue. Armed with knives. One had a crushed windpipe."

Sanglier's straight-stemmed briar descended to the edge of the desk. His gaze went narrow and hard, like a sniper taking a bead. She knew that look well, having made it herself dozens of times. "You are remarkably, and I should say suspiciously, well-informed."

"I come by my facts honestly. I am the one who damaged both gentlemen." When his eyebrows bounced up in surprise, she added, "They had it coming."

He mastered his astonishment. "I imagine so. It turns out that both were imposters with colorful criminal histories. Armed robbery, assault, forgery. One had just returned from the French Guiana penal colony."

Now it was her turn to be surprised. "That's possible?"

"In truth, not really. A few prisoners might eventually be eligible for release, but in practice they and nearly all others perish of disease or, it must be admitted, brutality."

"Was this gentleman the exception to the rule?"

"He was not. In truth, he was declared dead by their doctors a year ago." He smiled and let her absorb that. "We have discovered that some of our staff over there have been suborned. Corruption is rampant, of course, conditions being what they are. Some unsavory group had corrupted our people to falsify death certificates and smuggle a few prisoners out. All the toughest ones, the crème de la scum, if you will. Curiously, all were Italians. We imagine that some big operation requires their particular set of skills and absent moral scruples."

"Any clues as to who might be doing this?"

"None. Though I fully expect that a certain American lady is about to hand me some."

As she opened her handbag, Molly asked him, "Has the word *Ardire* ever come up in this?"

"Not until today. Branded on their arms, along with a clenched fist. Tougher to take than a simple tattoo. Few men are sanguine when facing a glowing red iron. I expect that it helped separate the wheat from the chaff at their recruiting center." His pipe smoked with a fury. "Damned secret societies. Everybody wants to have their own special little club."

"The word is Italian, curiously enough. It means 'to dare.'" She set the disturbing finger-bone dagger on his blotter for him to inspect. "I found the word on a parchment hidden inside the handle of this delightful artifact."

He squinted at it with a detective's eye. "More decorative than functional. A ceremonial toy. Given when the group adopts you. Probably a prize for taking that brand without flinching."

Sanglier picked up a pen and a notepad. It was time to get to work. "Tell me how you came by it. And how you bested these hard cases while wearing a skirt."

Completely abandoning her Chloe persona, Molly gave him all of it in her usual flat and fast speaking voice, staring at a spot near his left ear while tapping her foot like a metronome. The only details she kept to herself were Farouk's name and Ahmed's claim as to the capabilities of the mysterious crystal.

Until she had more proof of the latter it seemed wise to err on the side of disbelief. Besides, if it turned out to be true, better that any infiltrators in the Sûreté not be alerted. And the clever communication device also remained private knowledge. She knew well that French bureaucracy, though Byzantine, was also porous. Seemingly half of Europe's spies lived in Paris. That was chiefly due to France's central role in the continent's affairs, but the attractions of the City of Light played no small role. Give a choice of espionage there or in some flea-bitten African hamlet, it was an easy choice to make.

Sanglier listened with a bird of prey's intensity, wisely eschewing any interruptions as he took notes. He knew that breaking into Molly's narrative would be neither useful to him nor easy on her. And any questions he might have would likely be answered by her careful storytelling. After all, she was a professional journalist, albeit a prickly one. When she completed her tale, he remained silent for a long minute, ticking off points on his pad while chewing on his pipe stem. To Molly's great relief the choking cloud had dissipated as he had let the tobacco go out while listening.

He tapped out the ash from the briar's bowl while also tapping the paper in front of him. "So this is some sort of political jewel robbery?"

"So it would seem," she agreed, not wishing to send his sleuth's nose in too straight a direction yet. "I gather that the bauble has some sort of scientific value, though why Mussolini prizes it so highly as to make very public assaults is still a mystery."

"The Fascists do have a new team dedicated to technological espionage. This Colonel Terremoto's name has come up before in such affairs. They believe that science will win the next war."

Molly nodded. *Or avenge the last one.* "I saw enough poison gas and the like to believe that while they may be correct, they will also make the next war all the worse...if that's possible."

Sanglier's eyes went dark as he relived similar horrific memories. "Oh, it's all too possible. Four years in those trenches taught me to never underestimate modern man's capacity to conjure up new and exciting ways to inflict cruelty on his neighbors."

After another tense pause, he slapped the desk and grinned. "Well, that's a charming idea, eh? So glad that you came here to drag me down that sunny path. But at least I have the image of you thrashing those thugs in a frock and cloche to take my mind off it. Clearly your savate tutors know their business. Perhaps I should bring you in to give a course of instruction to some of the clods under my command."

Molly was well aware that this was mere charm, as he had more than once demonstrated his skill in that arena. But she played along, in the interest of remaining in his good graces. The Sûreté had resources that she could not hope to match. She wanted to ensure access to future information. So she forced what passed for a smile with her.

"Oh, I wouldn't want to damage any of the Republic's finest."

Naturally, that made him guffaw. "By God, I believe that you just might! I could film it. Sell tickets."

"We could book it as a double-feature with a Chaplin comedy."

For another few moments, things went on in that light vein. Once it had run its course Sanglier grew more serious. "As capable as you are, these gentlemen, and at least one lady, are no laughing matter. They have no compunction about abusing their own citizens and they will certainly have even less scruples about the welfare of an inconvenient foreigner who bloodied their noses. Mussolini is easy to laugh at, but he has proven himself savage enough if pressed. You made these people look silly. They will remember it. Please take care of yourself."

"Have no fear, I will watch my back. My front is being watched already, by a particularly clumsy spy. But your point is taken." She straightened in her chair. "And while I am gamely defending myself, what will you be doing?"

"Interrogating those unlucky to have encountered you in the Panthéon. No doubt they have many charming secrets that they will be more than willing to share. The one will have trouble speaking through his tracheotomy. If they prove recalcitrant, I shall mention your name."

"Try to leave their fingernails intact. Italian men can be so vain."

"Fingernails? What sort of brute do you take me for?"

"Ah, I forget myself. You are a French brute. You will resort to withholding their crème brulee. They will tearfully spill every secret they have."

Molly squirmed in her seat, eager to leave. She had reached her limit of social interaction, witty banter, and pipe smoke. It would take the rest of the afternoon to recover. "If you discover anything that I need to know to protect myself, please pass it along. As you doubtless know, I shall continue to pursue this, despite your reflexive intent to warn me off. They wrecked my flat. Fingered my belongings. Don't worry, I won't publish any of it."

He laughed and stood, reading her silent signals. "I don't know why I bother to converse with you, since you manage to cover both sides at once."

Standing as well, Molly collected her handbag and shrugged. "I believe in economy in all things." She looked him over, taking in the tiny details that no one else ever saw, synthesizing them into a story. "And tell your mistress that her cat is in need of veterinary treatment."

As he sputtered at her seemingly magical observation, Molly winked and strolled out of the Prefecture. She mounted her bicycle and raced off, enjoying the breeze on what little of her face could feel it. The whole way to the Café Sirocco she pretended not to notice the deep purple luxury auto that followed her at what its driver must have thought was a discreet distance.

9 / Salon Formidable

"Daaaarliiing!!!"

The turbaned matron swooped across the garish carpet, her golden chiffon wrap catching the air to waft in her wake like the tail of a particularly effete comet. Maroon harem pants gave her the silhouette of a seductive vase. She ducked under low-hanging satin drapery, arms stretched wide, a jade cigarette holder in one hand. Artemisia Formidable engulfed the new arrival to her Montparnasse salon, a plain but pleasant lady holding an infant. Ignoring the fussy baby, who seemed to resent being trapped between competing bosoms, the fashion designer kissed the young mother on both cheeks and then gave her a chastising glare.

"You are in bad odor with me, cherie! Vanishing from Paris without so much as a by-your-leave. Six months gone and for all I knew you had been kidnapped by bandits! We all felt your loss at my fall show." Artemisia's fleshy face could not hold her feigned outrage, however. The frown collapsed into a grin as she pinched the child's cheek. "But now I see that you were doing your own great creative thing, the only endeavor that trumps haute couture. Who is this delightful little gentleman, eh?"

The mother mirrored Artemisia's smile. "This is Bumby."

An imperious French eyebrow crept up. "Bumby?" Madame Formidable's voice held equal measures of surprise and disappointment at such a gauche choice.

Sensing this, the other woman hurried to explain. "Well, that's only my pet name for him, because he's so like a plump little teddy bear. His birth certificate says John Hadley Nicanor Hemingway." The resulting pause seemed to indicate that more explanation was in order. "Hadley, after me, of course. Nicanor, after some bullfighter that Ernest worships." She rolled he eyes.

Artemisia had not reached her vaunted status through a lack of tact. She clapped her hands and proclaimed, "Genius! The one for beauty and poise, the other for boldness and courage."

The rest of the women in the room, chiefly models but also some regular customers who knew Hadley, surrounded mother and child. Much cooing and giggling ensued. Only one remained aloof, lurking in a corner near the changing rooms. Her mouth wore a sour expression that seemed to be its default one. It served her well on the runway, its acerbic insouciance matching her exotic allure. Here and now, though, it was as out of place as an abattoir in a nursery school. Artemisia told her so.

"My Antiope seems less than enthralled. You could at least make a show of enthusiasm for glorious motherhood. After all, France can use all of the new men it can get."

The tall model wrinkled her nose. "They aren't French, they're American, yes?"

"A trifle. They are here by choice. As are you."

That made the young woman laugh. "True. I have made my bed and shall willingly lie in it."

"So mysterious! And so grumpy. Why do I keep you on, I wonder?"

"Because every time I wear your clothes the matronly cows drown you in francs?"

"Ah, yes, that's it. I knew there was a reason." Artemisia nodded to the door behind them. "Off you go, then. I'm in need of more rain. And remember, the photographer is coming today."

While her employer returned to gland-handing clients, Antiope slunk away as if her joints were made of silk. Even in quasi-male attire, a white shirt and woolen waistcoat paired with a simple gray skirt, she held the eye. Ever since the age of twelve men and women had stared at her. Sometimes it was because they wondered which sex or race she might be, but most of the time it was simple admiration. Her abnormal height first snared the eye, of course, but then one noticed the strong features, the huge dark eyes, sleek short black hair, the tawny skin with its buttery sheen and texture. When she smiled, which was as infrequent as rain in her native Algeria, she could outshine the sun and bend a man's will as if it were copper wire.

Not that she generally cared what any man wanted.

She disrobed and hunted through the garments on the rack for those assigned to her. Thankfully, they were what passed for normal clothes in Madame Formidable's atelier. Though it kept her employed, she was tired of always being dressed as the exotic foreign temptress. As if any of the lumpy housewives whom Artemisia catered to would be caught dead in that sort of thing. It seized the attention, though, brought customers to the door, and that was the point. But it also drew panting men to her like flies to shit, which was not only infuriating but a waste of everyone's time. Unfortunately, when she tried to explain her Sapphic disinterest most men believed it to be a mere ploy and tried all the harder.

And that, after the rape, she could not abide.

It was not as if being taken by force as a teenager had turned her against men. She had always known that her tendencies ran in the other direction. That sordid event -- at the hands of a relative, no less – had merely confirmed her desire to never be a victim of a man's grasp again. After running away from her home in Oran, if home was even the proper word for such a chaotic mess, she had ended up in Marseilles, living with a cousin. Marie had introduced her to some unsavory waterfront types who had taught her how to defend herself in exchange for her smuggling the odd package north. Her rapid mastery of knife, garrote, stick, fist, and foot had impressed her hardened teachers, who soon found more dangerous work for her as a spy in the local police prefecture. Twice she had had to dispatch gendarmes who had seen through her innocent guise. Another time she had castrated a too-bold idiot from another gang who thought he had found an easy mark. After that the lowlifes, at least, had steered clear of her.

And every soul she freed stained her own. Hardened her, chilled her. After a year she had become known as the Marble Viper.

Some called her the Amazon, of course, as all with no imagination tended to do when gazing up at her. Though it annoyed her, it had its uses, too, as the warrior tradition of those mythic women added its patina to her. Eventually she gave up and embraced it, naming herself Antiope and adopting an intimidating persona that tended to fight her battles for her.

Nude, a tower of light brown beauty, she held a jeweled satin bandeau by one narrow strap with a sneer of disgust. Not being particularly busty, she never wore such things. As it happened, her shape was all the current rage. But Artemisia must have had something in mind to include it with her outfit, so she sighed and struggled into it. Cream-colored silken cami-knickers went on over that, then the dress. A heavily-beaded silver chevron tabard affair, sleeveless and weighing the proverbial ton, it hung straight from her broad shoulders to her calves. With the matching headband of silver and pearls and a gleaming rhinestone flower and small white feather, accented with a long double strand of pearls hanging from her neck, even Antiope's jaded sensibility recognized that she was a vision.

If the boys back in Marseilles could see this, they'd wet themselves laughing.

To add to the imagined mirth of her former friends, Antiope sat at the make-up table to gild the lily. She amused herself while painting her face by taking stock of the various items on the table and around the room that could be used with homicidal intent. Eyebrow pencil: stab the face or throat. Powder: blind the victim before attacking. Hand mirror: shatter, use the shards to slash. Strand of pearls: strangulation, of course. Just as she was giving serious consideration to using all of them on Artemisia, the rest of the girls flooded into the room, chattering in half a dozen accents about babies, men, clothes, films, and a dozen other pointless topics.

"Ooh!" shrieked one, a slim blonde Austrian, peeling herself out of her frock. "Isn't that little Bumby just the most adorable thing on two legs? I could just squeeze the stuffing out of him."

"I'd rather squeeze something out of his adorable papa," countered the Spanish beauty beside her. "Have you seen him? He's dishy."

"That doesn't count for much, Lucita. You think anything in trousers is dishy." She pulled a gown from its hanger. "Even Antiope here."

The Latin girl winked. "Have you seen her backside in pants? Enough to make a man-loving gal re-evaluate her life choices."

Antiope stood, looming over every one of them. She slid the hem of her skirt up to expose what looked like two meters of smooth thigh above her stockings. "But this is easier for you to get your hands into."

The whole room went "Woo!" and the resulting laughter made the mirrors vibrate. After that settled down a pleasingly plump French girl named Cosette clucked in appreciation.

"Mon Dieu! Bring in a photographer and even this one pretties herself up. You look like a million francs today."

That pleased Antiope, much as it also annoyed her to admit it. She made a pretense of preening for them in a clearly ironic way, trying to maintain her pose as one of them. But that twisted a spot in her back that had taken the brunt of the fall onto the Panthéon's unyielding marble floor. While she silently cursed the interfering American who had been the cause, they all took notice when she winced, clucking in concern.

"It's nothing," she protested with a wave of one hand. "I slipped getting out of the bath and crunched my arse into my vanity table. Nothing that a little aspirin won't fix."

The Austrian model paused while donning a green skirt to waggle a silver flask. "I can do better than that."

"Ah," sang Cosette, "Herr Doktor Schnapps is in the house!"

Antiope had much to do that evening in her alter-ego and couldn't afford to be in an eighty-proof haze. "Thank you, Brigitte, but I'm clumsy enough on the catwalk in heels as it is. That would send me flying into the poor customers."

They responded to that with varying expressions of disbelief. The Antiope they knew was many things – prickly, arrogant, aloof – but clumsy was not one of them. Their declarations were interrupted by Madame Formidable, who burst among them like a stern kindergarten teacher.

"What is all of this chit-chat? Too much fooling about, ladies. Mr. Ray is here and he has better things to do than wait for a lot of silly girls. Hurry up and get dressed, please. He already has his camera set up."

Lucita peeped through the curtain at the main room of the salon and squealed. "Eeee! He's brought Kiki with him!"

The rest of them, except for Antiope, rushed to the curtain to see for themselves, dropping clothes and accessories all over the room. But Artemisia had anticipated this and blocked them with her fashionable bulk. Hands on hips, she barred the way like Horatius at the bridge. The half-clad models stopped, those in the rear crashing into the ones up front. It all resembled one of those American comedy films, the ones with the foolish policemen.

"Back, harridans!" she boomed. "When all of you are properly ready, then you may go out en masse to see Mlle. Kiki. Until then, you are under house arrest here."

Mumbling their juvenile discontent, the pack of models returned to their assigned places to continue dressing. After a few moments Cosette, brows furrowed in confusion, sidled up to Antiope. "What is a harridan?"

"An unpleasant woman. Bossy, irritating. A shrew."

The French girl snickered and dropped her voice to a whisper. "But surely that applies more to her than to us."

"Perhaps she was being facetious."

Cosette shrugged and fussed with her outfit, a daring little number that left little to the imagination. Artemisia believed in enhancing a model's natural assets. Brigitte, adjusting an earring, moved over to Antiope. "At least you didn't mention other synonyms, like termagant or virago. The poor lass's brain might have over-heated. Then which of us would have to wear that handkerchief of a dress?"

"Not me. Haven't you heard, I'm a virago." When Brigitte returned a puzzled expression, she explained. "The primary meaning of the word is a woman who adopts masculine manners, clothing, or behavior."

"Ah! Like Jeanne d'Arc?"

"As one example, yes. Or Antiope the Amazon. Only later did it become an insult."

"Well...you're a very nice virago, anyway." Brigitte looked her up and down. "And in that ensemble, who would ever guess?"

Finally, the models were all tidied-up, made-up, and dressed-up. Artemisia arranged them single-file in the order in which she felt most appropriate for the effect she wished to create in the observers. Antiope found herself at the end of the line, so apparently she was the 'big finish.' This was a scheduled photographic session for the new catalog and to advertise in newspapers and magazines. Madame Formidable had opened it to her favored customers, both to make sales and to provide an enthusiastic crowd as a backdrop for the models. So most of the fashions were tame as couture went, more wearable by the average woman than some of the more shocking looks used to create conversation and excitement. Fairly ordinary dresses, coats, and hats, with the Formidable twist that made them worth the price. No Antiope in a leopard skin this time, brandishing a short sword and shield.

A good thing, too. If she'd done that to me again, I might have cleaved her from the nave to chops, no matter what orders Terremoto gave me to keep a low profile here.

Applause and appreciative noises greeted the women as they paraded out onto the narrow, elevated platform to be viewed. The usual natural lighting from the wall of glass in front and the skylight above had been augmented by the photographer's own electric bulbs, which threw atmospheric shadows in odd places. That gentleman, a fierce-eyed young man in a tasteful dark suit and striped tie, called himself Man Ray. It was just the sort of name one would expect for an associate of the fringe artists and philosophers who called themselves Dada. Friends with the just-as-challenging Cubists, they were fond of quirky attention-getting spectacles such as stage productions called *Symphonic Vaseline* or *Cannibal Manifesto*, which generally were chaotic lunacies, the larger purpose difficult to discern. Supposedly they were revolting against traditional art and literature, which were a product of the decadent culture that had caused the Great War.

To Antiope they were confusing and gave her a headache.

However, Man Ray was not present this day to make any artistic statements beyond photographing pretty women in attractive garments. Quite aside from his startling avant-garde images, the American was known to be a wonder with a camera in a more conventional capacity. His portraits were poems in black and white. And his fashion work could turn the simplest of looks to a siren's aria that lured many a bourgeois housewife to demand that she be permitted to purchase the item. The irony of a Dadaist doing such work was not lost on him. He seemed to have a twinkle in his eye as he 'exploited the oppressor' by taking its filthy lucre. But, after all, renegade art paid very few bills.

To elegant yet chic piano music, each model strutted out alone for her moment in the couture sun, twirling and posing. Cosette winked, Brigitte pouted, Lucita simpered. The others sold the wares in whatever way best suited their particular charms. Antiope glided out last, her face set in a proud mask of what she imagined Diana might have looked like on the hunt: focused, imperious, resistless. A woman with no time for silly men and even less interest in appeasing them with a 'come hither' expression. She radiated hauteur to the point of distaste for this entire absurd exercise of selling clothes. A predator, daring anyone to approach within bow-shot.

And the crowd loved her for it.

All the assembled ladies leaned forward in their chairs. The few male escorts lifted their heads as if scenting danger but drawn to it, nonetheless. Even the gentlemen whose tastes ran to their own kind licked their lips and nodded. It never ceased to amaze Antiope how her utter contempt could be so alluring. Perhaps people took it as a challenge. All she knew was that no matter how hard she tried to project her disgust at the game that paid her bills, the more those she abhorred flocked to her. Her manicured hands reflexively clenched into talons with the dream of strangling some of them.

With a patrician shrug of her lovely brown shoulder, the translucent chiffon lace wrap slid down one arm. Snaring it with absent-minded ease, she trailed it behind her like the male dancer's cape in a paso doble. Artemisia had hung upon her just as she had left the dressing room. Every eye followed her, making Antiope feel like a cobra trancing its victim before striking. Free hand on hip, she reached the end of the catwalk, all but sneered at the patrons, then made a languid turn.

As she did so she had time to notice several prominent attendees, from Mrs. Hemingway and her writer acquaintance Fitzgerald and his wife, to Coco Chanel and her great friend Misia Sert. The latter pair, tastefully dressed and coiffed, must have been imbibing cocaine before coming to the salon. Their eyes were bright with its effects. Coco was no doubt evaluating her competition, as her own collection had debuted on May 5, as it always did. Behind them sat Bricktop, an American nightclub owner and entertainer whose red hair and freckles clashed with her half-African parentage. Antiope had enjoyed a casual fling with her one night, but the singer had returned to the arms of a man and that was that. Anyway, in her current situation Antiope could ill-afford intimate attachments.

Bricktop must have pulled some strings, because no less a light than Cole Porter played the piano. The white-suited American grinned at the trio of pretty boys who hung around him. He had once hired her to entertain at his legendary bacchanals, leading to her becoming popular enough to have just opened her own club. This seemed like an odd venue for him, but Porter was known to seek fun in unconventional ways.

Man Ray's flashbulbs made her see purple and gold for a moment. He had caught her just at the perfect moment, that split-second of stillness in her turn before she stepped off again. Applause and cheers followed her, reinforcing her self-image as the conquering matador. As she drew even with him before exiting, Antiope noticed that Kiki de Montparnasse had, indeed, made an appearance. She stood beside the photographer, her current lover. Well, one of them, anyhow, knowing her predilections.

Antiope could not recall the girl's true name. Naturally, no one was really named Kiki de Montparnasse. It was something simple and plain, that she did know. Kiki was the self-appointed Queen of Montparnasse, in effect Queen of the Bohemians in Paris, and somehow all of the other artists, writers, musicians, and their assorted fellow travelers had accepted that. It was quite an achievement for someone barely twenty-two. No doubt having been a celebrated artist's model, with all that morally suggested, had helped. She livened parties, sang, painted, knew everyone who mattered, lifted others up to the status of mattering, and generally brought light, if little heat, wherever she went. No one would call her beautiful, and she was already fleshy for her height. As time went on she would turn positively stout. Her sleek black helmet of short hair, with pointed spit curls swooping up to her pale cheeks, was all the rage now.

Peeking out from the dressing room, Antiope was amazed at the other man with Kiki and Ray. Graying and craggy, with a beard worthy of Moses on Sinai, the sculptor Constantin Brancusi was known to be a friend of the avant-garde photographer and his circle, but she would not have thought him interested in fashion. As she watched him sip red wine and beam at everything in a skirt, Antiope understood that fashion per se was not his objective today.

"Quite the swanky assemblage," noted Cosette as she lit a cigarette. "Some notorious characters."

"Not a lot of them with any money, though," observed Brigitte. "They're here to look, not buy."

Lucita giggled. "I don't know. I hear Mr. Porter throws huge parties that require lots of ladies' garments. And he has gobs of money."

"The ones with money aren't the ones you've heard of," said Antiope. "The wives of the rich are our clientele. The rest of them are here to make a good show for Madame."

Artemisia waved to her models to come out again en masse. Grumbling, Cosette stamped out her untouched smoke and led the way with a sunny grin plastered onto her cute face. Like obedient ducklings the rest followed, to renewed applause and babbled adoration. For the next few minutes patrons and models mingled, making chit-chat and ogling the Hemingway baby. For Antiope it was on a par with thumbscrews and chewing ground glass, but she put on a brave front for a while. One small part of her mind she dedicated to that while the larger part dwelt on reviewing the unfortunate events at the Panthéon and at Bhagwa's restaurant. Learning from her mistakes had kept her alive so far and it was a habit she intended to maintain.

Her thoughts were interrupted just as she came up with two ways she might have taken down Aulis and several more for dealing with the repulsive Terremoto. Though the latter was her current employer, bitter experience had taught her that all such arrangements were fleeting and that an exit should always be in hand.

"I'm sorry...what?"

Man Ray gave her a tight smile and repeated his request. "I'd like to shoot you."

Her response was to raise an elegant eyebrow. "Do I get a cigarette and a blindfold?"

Kiki giggled as if the remark were worthy of Oscar Wilde. "Aren't you adorable!" She wound her arm through the taller woman's and pressed up against her, not noticing how Antiope stiffened in automatic reaction. Much shorter, the green feather in her turban didn't reach Antiope's chin. "Do say yes! Manny's a whiz with a lens. All the best people pose for him. James Joyce, Picasso, even that Mrs. Hemingway's husband, Bumby's papa, though calling him one of the best people might be a bit premature. Gertrude likes him, though. I think her Alice is less in love with his oh-so-manly manner. Hard to take in large doses, she says." She uttered all of this without drawing a breath, as if it were a single breezy word. As vapid as she seemed, it was hard for Antiope to ignore her. Fairy lights seemed to glisten from her. Kiki's charisma was undeniable.

"The photos you just took weren't good?" Antiope asked Ray.

He fiddled with the knot of his tie with one hand and waved dismissively with the other. "Okay for quick fashion shots, I suppose." His French was halting, uncertain, with a distinct nasal Brooklyn note. "As a mere record of an event, they'll do." A passionate gleam lit his eyes. "But they're hardly art. For that I need time, the right light, preparation. And a great subject."

"Manny has an eye for what makes a great picture," Kiki assured her. "Did you see the one he just did of me?" She rummaged in her bag and pulled out a photo on good cardstock. It was Kiki from the rear, nude except for the same jeweled turban she now wore. Her arms were pulled in front, invisible to the camera. Now she was just a torso and head. It was an imitation of the great painter Ingres' masterwork *Le Bain Turc*, a reversal of the pose of the foreground figure. Only Ray had superimposed the f-holes of a violin onto Kiki's back. He had turned her into a harem girl, doubly an instrument for pleasure, a literal plaything.

"Striking," Antiope conceded. "Will you make me into an accordion?"

"Nothing so crude," Ray said. "More a study of, er, entwined limbs and dancing light."

With an impatient sigh Kiki explained. "He wants us to do it while he takes pictures."

"Ah."

Now Man Ray's lover was the one with the ecstatic light of inspiration in her face. "It'll be swell! All that frisky nakedness and slippery goings-on. That's my kind of art." She winked up at Antiope, not releasing her grip on her arm.

Ray hastened to correct Kiki's enthusiastic declaration. "You're overstating the case, honey. And scaring away our model." He shrugged at Antiope. "I need two contrasting figures for this. Light and dark. Tall and short. Frisky and aloof. How far you take it is up to you." But his unspoken heat left no doubt that he would be more than amenable to something more than a risqué photo session.

Antiope had no interest in participatory photography with Man Ray. Kiki looked as if she might be worth at least one naked hour. If nothing else, it would enhance her credibility with the Montparnasse community, as Terremoto desired. And the more notoriety the better, in both her lines of work.

"I could be convinced," she told them. "Have you a card?"

Ray instantly produced his business card, which had a disturbing image of a woman crying tears of glass. Accepting it, Antiope said that she would contact them soon. She turned away, hoping to get back to the dressing room and into her own clothes, when she was ambushed by Brancusi, who had been lurking a few meters away until his friends had concluded their business. He appeared before her, blocking the way to the door. Still holding the wine glass, nearly empty now, he lifted both hands up to her face.

"I see an African goddess," he informed her with a raspy Eastern European voice.

This sort of thing was irritatingly familiar to her. "So do I, every time I pluck my eyebrows in the mirror."

"You misunderstand me, atrăgător," he hurried to say, falling back on his native Romanian. "I mean no seduction, unlike my somewhat wild friends there. I wish to sculpt your face as an African mask. You have seen these? Marvelous! Such primitive power."

Brancusi was speaking her language now. That held more appeal for her that a romp with the morose American and his wiggly puppy Kiki. "I have. In museums. You have made them before?"

"Regrettably no, yet your face has inspired me to try. But all of my work is inspired by their aesthetic."

Antiope was familiar enough with Brancusi's art to admit that his style would transfer well to an African motif. Clean lines, suggestion instead of representation. Lovely curves doing the work of a hundred more complex manipulations. From what she had seen, his declaration that he had never made such a mask was somewhat hollow, even disingenuous. But perhaps he was being literal, believing that he had not really made an actual African tribal piece, only modern interpretations.

"I have no trouble believing that. I have admired your work for some time."

"It brings me joy to hear it, coming from such a cultured lady." His eye twinkled as he lifted his glass to her. "Your good taste is evident."

She chuckled and took it from him, sipping and returning it. Her mouth sang with the excellent Bordeaux. Clearly, he had achieved more success than most of the artists she knew. "As is yours."

"Then we are agreed? We shall commemorate our aesthetic joys at my studio?"

"I think that very likely, Monsieur Brancusi. May I call on you there?"

She accepted his card and a kiss on her hand. But before she could reach the safety of the dressing room, she found her passage obstructed for a third time in as many minutes. This time it was a stranger, a lumpy and dowdy woman in a frumpy woolen dress a decade out of style. Her dark hair was cut short, but in a mannish way rather than in the current fashion.

If this is another artist wanting to immortalize me or shag me or both, I shall garrote her here and now and hang the consequences.

"They all swarm you like honeybees to a blossom," she said in a throaty voice with no hint of seduction. It was all business, curt and sharp.

"I'm used to it," Antiope sighed with a shrug. "And this blossom comes with thorns."

"I can see that." The woman squinted at the model's hands. "And strangling vines, too, eh?"

"I beg your pardon?"

"Is that not what others say to you, with their last breath?"

Before Antiope's flushed mix of alarm and outrage could resolve itself into action, the stout stranger had vanished into the crowd. After searching for her and failing, Antiope finally gained the relative calm of the dressing room again. Only Brigitte was there, undressed to her knickers, the rest having remained to accept the plaudits and propositions of the patrons.

"Did you see that woman who was talking to me just now?" Antiope asked her.

"What, the one dressed like a homeless schoolteacher?"

"Yes, her. Came on to me all mysterious. Didn't make much sense. Do you know her?"

"I know of her. Adrienne Monnier. She has a bookshop in the Rue l'Odéon. *The House of the Friends of Books.* Knows anybody and everybody who writes and a great many who don't. Has friends in the Sûreté, so don't cross her."

Antiope frowned as she hung up Madame Formidable's gown. "Didn't speak or act like a bookseller. I thought she was coming on to me, but the words didn't match that."

"She's queer, but not your type. Likes her women brainy and attainable. Her beloved Sylvia has the bookshop across the street, the English-language one that gives writers a place to sleep. She published that shocking novel a couple of years ago, the one by the Irish fellow, the one with the absurd spectacles. Joyce. The book had a Greekish name. *Achilles*? No, *Ulysses*. That was it. So modern that you couldn't understand half of it. Full of dirty stuff, which would be the only thing that'd make me pick it up. I hear that the Americans burned it. No wonder so many of them move here."

"You're saying I'm not brainy or attainable?" said Antiope in mock-indignation.

Brigitte snorted. "You have different brains, the kind a street cat has. And you seem so unattainable that most people never get it into their heads to try. Tell me I'm wrong."

Since the Austrian girl's analysis was spot-on, Antiope could hardly contradict her. Instead, she gave her a tight smile and finished changing into sharp wool trousers, white blouse, green jacket, and black trilby. After wrapping a white Lanvin scarf around her slim neck and refreshing her camellia perfume, she managed to sneak out of the rear door before Madame Formidable could veto her leaving. Once out of the alley and back onto the Rue Stanislas, she headed south across the Boulevard Montparnasse, making for the cemetery.

Though tempted to detour over to the Aulis woman's flat and settle accounts, Terremoto had forbidden it. *Ardire* could ill-afford distractions during the critical phase they had entered. Instead, she had been directed to accept the romantic attentions of a well-dressed gentleman who foolishly thought that his identity as an agent of British Intelligence was still a secret. He had become a difficulty that needed her specific sort of attention, so she had asked him to meet her at Baudelaire's monument for a steamy rendezvous. But Antiope had a plan to gratify both her desires, francs and death. His mort would be a bit more than petit.

As she approached the site, she tugged the expensive scarf from her throat and tightened it between the hands that Adrienne Monnier had so admired. In her pocket was Dr. Rospo's communicator. Though she was not permitted to dispatch Aulis, she knew someone who could. By now they would be in place. And her obtaining the Gaze would buy Terremoto's total forgiveness.

10 / Café Sirocco

Just after dusk the Rue Soufflot was doubly awash in amber light from the newly set sun and the tall streetlamps. The Panthéon's resplendent dome loomed over one end of the block like an imperious maiden aunt. At the other the fountain's floral spray caught the light and made jewels hang in the air. A few autos and omnibuses passed, but most of the traffic was pedestrians, either tourists or lovers. Molly sat just inside the Café Sirocco, one of her favorite haunts and beloved of other professional explorers and travelers. It occupied an enviable corner site, its rich green awning decorated in delicate golden arabesques. Intricate scrolls and florals intertwined, leaving room for the name of the café in large swirling letters. Nearly all seats were taken, both inside and out, but she had called Abreek to reserve her favorite spot in the window, as far away from other patrons as the floor plan would allow. He was well aware of her limitations and necessities, having fought Turks with her in the desert. Several times Abreek had been her spotter on sniping missions. She hoped that those skills would prove unnecessary this night, but it was comforting to know that he was there if *Ardire* kicked up a row. Just in case, she had made a couple of other calls to ensure adequate support this time.

So far, she had not spotted either Hassanein or Farouk. They were not late, as she had made a point of arriving very early in order to reconnoiter. Another scan of the room, decorated in tasteful Arab style, or at least a commercial Gallic version of it, accented with various explorers' souvenirs and tools, showed that they had not snuck past her. Nor had any of the Italian agents she had already encountered that day. Naturally, it was of concern that they undoubtedly had more assets yet unrevealed, but there was little that she could do about that except remain wary. Already she had alerted Abreek to keep his sharp ears out for anyone speaking in Italian or with that accent. Truly well-trained operatives would, of course, not be so easy to detect. Lawrence's words to her during the war held true: *We do what we can to prepare. The rest is prompt reaction.*

Her teeth clicked in a machine gun rhythm while her toes clenched in counterpoint to it. After catching herself thrumming the table to the point of rattling the crockery, she had moved her fidgeting hands to her thighs where they would make no noise on her light wool skirt. Already she had arranged and rearranged the cutlery, flower vase, salt and pepper shakers, menu, and everything else within reach into perfectly straight lines. Anything to take her mind from the cacophony of conversations and clinking glassware all around her. It made jagged red shapes cavort at the edge of her vision. To anyone else it would have been normal cafe noise, somewhat subdued even. But to her it was like scrap metal tumbling down an iron staircase. *Too many people here tonight, and too animated in their conversations.* The more she focused on something else, though, the more tolerable it was.

Yet the situation was still better than back at her apartment. There she had spent another two hours trying to restore order after the dreadful wrecking by the searcher. The first pass before visiting Sanglier had merely collected the breakage and sanded off the rough edges. After that had come trying to replace every object back into the precise spot it had been before, to the millimeter. Otherwise, she would never get any sleep there again. At first, she had hoped that bare patches in the dust would aid her, but she had been so scrupulous in her cleaning that there was no dust present. Her habit of bringing back innumerable tiny souvenirs from her years of travel had made it all so much more complicated that she had burst out in a small tantrum again and had had to lie down with a wet cloth over her eyes, stroking Hector until the fury abated.

Eventually she had made enough progress that her pulse ceased to hammer whenever she surveyed the place. So she had put on her mask, walked the dog, made sure that her building was no longer being watched (*perhaps the Blackshirts have moved on to bigger game*), grabbed a stick from the stand beside her door, and strolled on over to the café by a confused route designed to detect a shadow. None had appeared then or since.

Now she began to relax and enjoy her mint tea. The only darkness was a slight lingering headache from the afternoon's rage, aggravated by the new lens she had put into the mask. Clear and thick, it had been carefully-crafted by her optician to enhance her limited vision at night, when it was at its worst. Though it worked well, peering through it strained her eye more than the everyday lens would.

To take her mind off the sound, she risked closing her eye for a few moments to take in the café's wonderful aromas. Ever since her maiming that had been the sense that she could rely on to calm her, so long as the ambient scents were not too strong. Soon the disturbing crimson lines of sound were subdued by warm, soft, bubbly forms of umber and sepia, shot through with gold-bronze. Molly could feel the muscles in her neck and shoulders uncoil as if tended by a talented Turkish masseur.

Memories of succumbing to the attentions of one of those talented gentlemen in 1918 came rushing back. On undercover assignment, she had followed her quarry into one of the more broad-minded and thus less respectable bathhouses. Playing her part had required her to strip down and submit to the establishment's attentions. The masseur she drew had not disappointed. He could have been the model for the main figure in Praxiteles' statue of *Hermes and the Infant Dionysus*, and proved amenable to much more than a simple rubdown. After months fighting in the desert, Molly had not been in the mood to resist.

Until he had tried to smother her with a wet towel while making the proverbial beast with two backs.

The knots immediately returned as she relived that panicked forty seconds. If the assassin had not slipped on the wet tiles, enabling her to reverse their positions and drown him in the pool, she would not be sitting in a fine Parisian café enjoying the spicy ambience.

The first, and only, person I ever killed with my bare hands.

Her stomach lurched at that, as if snakes slithered there. She clenched her hands until the nails made her palms beg for mercy, those same hands that had held the poor nameless Turk's head in warm perfumed water until his beautiful limbs had ceased thrashing. Nude, slick with sweat, steam, and passion, she had lain atop him, panting, feeling his pounding heart fade out. It had been a cruel parody of their breathless coupling.

And it had also been the last time that Molly had made any sort of love with her face intact.

A hand touched her shoulder, making her gasp and start. Her fingers snatched up a knife from the table as she came back to the real world.

"Easy now, sadeeka," purred a low honeyed voice. The accent spoke of oases and caravans and crowded markets in Eastern climes. "It would be a great inconvenience to have to launder my own blood from that fine linen tablecloth."

Molly blinked and looked up at the speaker through her veil. Abreek's broad brown face, full of life and laughter, matched his equally-expansive belly. Life had been good to him since the war. Then he had been half the bulk he was now, all lean leathery courage. He grinned through an enormous walrus moustache and a bird's-nest of a graying beard.

"Ah. Sorry," Molly said, peeling her fingers from the knife. As she continued speaking, she took care to adjust it on the table so that it was perfectly aligned with everything else. "Having one of my moments."

"Still taking holidays in your mind, eh? I can think of better places to go than the past, cherie. They say that the future is nice. Lovely weather, good food, not as many massacres. You should try it sometime."

She smiled despite herself. "It might make a nice change, at that. Can you attend to my future then? The good food part sounds nice."

"I'll send the new waiter over to mesmerize you with our evening specialties."

That made her scowl a bit. Change was not her forte. "What happened to Armand?"

"Can you believe it? He inherited a farm in Provence. Lucky bastard."

"Well, in that case I can forgive his callous abandonment of me." As she removed her hat and set it on the far side of the table, she spied Hassanein in the doorway, searching for her. Waving him over, she added, "Here's one who has stayed true."

Ahmed moved through the press of customers without seeming to look where he was going, effortless and elegant. His double-breasted blue serge suit fit him like a good fencing glove, its subtle pinstripe enhancing his slender form. He carried the same stick that he had employed to such great effect in the Panthéon, a pale gray homburg in the other hand. Heads turned to admire him, some people obviously recognizing him and nudging their friends to look. Hassanein seemed oblivious to it.

To Molly's great relief, introducing him to Abreek proved unnecessary. They immediately embraced, kissing one another on the cheeks with the warmth of old friends and not mere acquaintances. She held her palms up for an explanation.

"This fine fellow got me out of Istanbul when the war ended," said Abreek. "Used his diplomatic connections to pull me from a Turkish firing squad and onto a splendid aeroplane piloted by his glorious self. I owe him everything."

Ahmed waved away the praise. "He might be overstating the firing squad a bit. But we did smuggle his then much less bulky self onto a Felixstowe flying boat, along with the other unwanted items in our intelligence station there."

Abreek guffawed at that, then sobered as he looked down at Molly. "You never knew about it. That was after your...er..."

Molly growled, frustrated as always when someone tiptoed around her injury. "After I left most of my vaunted goddess-like beauty in the desert sand. Yes." When that made a gaping well of silence in the jocularity, she clapped her hands and went on. "Lots of gaps, I suppose, what with a year in the hospital and all. Good to fill in this one. Have a seat. Abreek's new waiter is champing at the bit to lure us toward something appallingly expensive."

With that the café owner excused himself to attend to the dozens of other guests. Ahmed slid into the chair beside Molly, laying his hat, stick, and gloves on a third chair. She noticed that he had maneuvered himself so to not leave his back to the room. It also did not escape her that he nodded greetings to at least four other tables.

"You've been here before?" she asked, perusing a menu that she already had memorized from many previous visits.

"Never, to my shame. Business has always kept me elsewhere since the war. But as this seems to be the favorite haunt of our sort of person, I do recognize a few faces." He indicted a lean weathered man with a spectacular moustache who was animatedly conversing with an elderly Negro in spectacles and fez. "Percy Fawcett. Soon headed back to Brazil again, I hear, to the Matto Grosso. Probably in town to raise funds and recruit personnel."

It irritated Molly that she had missed the legendary explorer of South America. True, she was working with one eye in a dim room through a veil, but she was still piqued. "Dangerous country, that. Irritable natives and fauna. But he's always come through before."

"Who is he speaking with? I can't place the man."

Now Molly had the advantage. "That's Ndugu Jasiri. You've probably never had the pleasure of meeting him. Long retired. He was one of Stanley's guides in 1871, on the expedition to find Dr. Livingstone. Lucky to have survived it. Burton said that Stanley shot his Africans as if they were monkeys."

"By the Prophet's beard! A living fossil."

"Don't let him hear you say that. He'll whack you with his stick. It's made from the penis of a white rhinoceros that made the mistake of charging him."

"How old is he? He must be ---"

"Somewhere around eighty-eight, if I recall. If he offers to play whist with you, beg off, unless you have more than one shirt."

"Promise you will introduce me."

"Of course, but not now. We're here to meet Farouk, remember?"

As if a signal gun had gone off, they both fell silent and looked the room over carefully to see if the young man had arrived. Though not spotting him, they did note at least three other renowned explorers of Africa, the Antarctic, and western China, as well as a few smooth ladies (and a couple of sturdy lads) she wouldn't have minded exploring herself. She also saw that a cuddlesome couple in the far corner near the kitchen door was actually her insurance policy. Ahmed and Molly checked the tables outside, also to no avail. Molly eyed the clock and sighed.

"I hope he hasn't fallen foul of our Italian friends."

Hassanein shook his head and returned to his menu. "Unlikely. After escaping them twice, he'll employ all of his considerable cleverness in avoiding them now."

"Well, I suppose if he can get out of the Sahara on foot, Paris should be light work."

"Yes. I'm dying to hear how he managed that."

A soft calm voice accented by sand and hardship explained, "Wild camels, effendi."

They both looked up at their waiter, dressed as were call of the others, in a dark green formal jacket, spotless tuxedo shirt, and black bow tie. His gleaming white apron reached nearly to his shoes. On his head he wore a brimless black kufi, embroidered in gold. Between cap and tie he sported a trim black beard and prominent moustache. The appliance was almost realistic in the café's low light.

Molly couldn't resist quoting *Hamlet* at him. "Why, thy face is valanced since I saw thee last. Comest thou to beard me in Denmark?"

Poor Farouk was out of his element there. "Er, mesh fahma," he said with a helpless shrug and an imploring look to Hassanein.

Ahmed patted the lad's arm and assured him in Arabic, "Don't worry. You weren't meant to understand. Miss Molly is having you on. Quoting Shakespeare again."

She gave him as apologetic a half-smile as she was capable of. Also in Arabic she told him, "A reflex. Sorry. I can reference ibn Arabi if you prefer. *"Whichever way Love's camels turn..."*

"Speaking of camels," said Ahmed, "someday you must tell us just how you took charge of wild ones and got out of Libya. And where you have been all these months. Your family mourned for weeks when I informed them that you were dead."

Glancing about, Farouk indicated that they should remain in Arabic, at least for important matters. Clearly, he did not trust that his good fortune in escaping his captors would hold. He opened the order pad and licked his pencil, going through the motions of playing garçon. "I had to hide long enough for all to think me food for vultures. Better that they go on believing it, effendi. At least until this affair is truly ended." His voice raised and he spoke in French. "May I acquaint madame and monsieur with our special offerings for the day?"

"Please do," said Molly, leaping into her role. She imagined herself a bourgeois housewife out on her anniversary dinner with her exotic diplomat husband. "This is our first time here."

Farouk went through the motions of outlining the café's offerings while they made a show of scanning their menus. They ordered meze to start, then vegetarian mujaddara for Molly and baba ghanoush for Ahmed, with kanafeh and lavender tea for dessert. After writing it all down and expressing vocal admiration of their taste, Farouk pointedly asked if Ahmed would consider adding a small serving of oysters to the order.

After trading glances with Molly, Hassanein nodded. "That sounds delightful."

While they waited for the meze appetizer, the couple made public small talk in French and spoke of meaningful matters in subdued Arabic. While doubtless someone in *Ardire* knew the latter language, based on Ahmed's encountering them in Libya, it was still a safer bet than the more-popular French. Each continued to watch for unpleasant returnees from the Panthéon or any strangers who seemed a bit too interested in them. Hassanein discussed the Olympics for the benefit of anyone listening and Molly did the same with Roy Chapman Andrews' recent expedition into the Gobi Desert. Dinosaur eggs proved more interesting to those eavesdropping, so she discoursed at some length about the amazing discoveries by the American. Since she knew the man personally, a family friend, she had details not widely published.

The meze arrived, warm and wonderful, redolent of the spices that made up its assortment of tastes. Molly's scent-colors kaleidoscoped from the fattoush's onion, garlic, purselane, and sumac. Likewise, the glories of the dolma and labneh made her want to sing Aleek's praises to the assembled multitude. It all took her back to a happier, pre-war and pre-wounded time where she would live with the locals and dig to her heart's content. Her social deficiencies were smothered by the hues that the food created and she babbled happily about those placid days until the main courses arrived.

When the entrees were placed before them Hassanein took over the conversation, sensing that Molly would soon return to form and fall silent. She gladly let the smooth Egyptian talk of his venture into the Libyan desert, outlining adventures that would soon appear in his National Geographic article. So captivating was he that soon the grating sound of forks and knives had all but stopped as most of those within earshot paused to listen. By the time the plates were cleared and dessert deposited in their place, Ahmed had finished his discourse to the applause of all.

The kanafeh, like all else served then at Café Sirocco, did not disappoint. Abreek made his with smooth semolina dough, creamy Nablisi cheese, sugar syrup, and rose water. Molly abandoned all thought of Fascist assassins and international intrigue as she submitted to the pastry's will. When they had nearly finished devouring it and were about to sag into their seats with the tea, Farouk arrived with one more small plate.

"Monsieur did order an oyster. The house offers its apologies for neglecting to bring it with your entrée."

He set the single bivalve before his master, leaning in close. In Arabic he added, "Abreek says he will protect me. I shall live above the café. If you need me, ask for me here. I have the terrifying head. Salaam alaykum, effendi, Miss Molly."

With a bow he vanished into the kitchen. Ahmed coolly addressed the oyster, inserting the special knife between the two halves. When he did so he paused, frowned, then recovered. Molly sat up, senses tingling. She could see that not only had the oyster already been opened, there was no actual meat inside. Instead, there was a tiny leather pouch. Its contents looked to be about the size of a glass eye, which amused Molly in an odd way.

Hassanein moved his chair subtly so that no one else in the room could see what was on the plate. Molly moved her cloche with a casual toss, placing it between the oyster and the plate glass window. Now it was invisible to all but them. With his skilled fingers Ahmed fully opened the oyster to expose the pouch, then tugged apart its mouth. He upended the contents into his palm, angling it to catch the light from the candle near Molly's arm.

Even with a single eye in a dark room, Molly could see that the otherworldly gem was a marvel. At first blush it seemed to be an enormous semi-worked diamond, but the eerie fire moving inside it disproved that. To Molly it seemed as if something alive moved inside the stone, in irregular patterns, not the perfect brilliant lines of a proper diamond. It did not have the fire one saw inside an earthly gemstone. Instead, this odd thing almost appeared to be a glittering vessel housing some sort of imp.

She shook her head and pronounced that to be absurd. It was merely a fancy rock from a meteor that someone had painted a black eye upon. Weird, that went without saying, but certainly explainable by science, given time for analysis. Leaning forward to get a better look, squinting her eye, she bunched up the tablecloth before her, not noticing that this propelled the candle directly toward the crystal.

Hassanein's trained reflexes saved the day. He snatched the deadly item from the flame's edge just as it was near enough to destroy the building. With a gasp Molly sat back, seeing the alarm and panic in his eyes. Until that moment she had not really believed his claims of the danger the gem posed. But anything that could so blanch the complexion of a bold Egyptian explorer deserved to be taken seriously.

"So it's true, then?" she asked in Arabic as he dropped the deadly bauble into its pouch again and stowed it inside his suit coat.

"All too true, alas," he confirmed, tossing off his tea and taking a deep breath. "The Fascists cannot possess this."

"Fascists? No one should have it. Throw it into the sea."

"A splendid suggestion. I was thinking that very ---"

Without being touched by either of them, the dessert forks rattled on their dirty little plates.

Molly cocked her head, stared. A few seconds later it happened again.

"Do you think Abreek has a poltergeist? Should we alert him to the need for an exorcism?"

"It's not his café that needs a priest," Ahmed said. "It's your handbag."

Sure enough, the rattling occurred for a third time. Now they could both see that it came from her purse, lying on the table beside her hat. Before anyone else took notice, she slid it into her lap and peered inside. A weak bluish light met her gaze.

"It looks ghostly enough, but it's actually fairly pedestrian, at least so far as this affair goes."

She plucked out the little electrical communicator she had taken from the injured man at the Panthéon. Its tiny screen glowed with letters in Italian. "Someone's talking to us."

"Not likely to us, but they don't need to know that. Can you read it?"

Molly gave him a sour face, as if he had insulted her intelligence. She practiced all her eleven languages for an hour each day. He smiled and raised his palms in apologetic surrender. "What do our violent Roman friends have to say to one another at this time of night?"

"It would seem that there's a meeting of evil henchmen at the Cimetière du Montparnasse in thirty minutes." She curled a finger at the lovers near the kitchen. They nodded and rose. "Shall we, as the new slang goes, crash it?"

11 / *Cimetiere du Montparnasse*

The new lens was less help than Molly had hoped in the murk of Montparnasse Cemetery. Apparently, the managers had not thought it necessary to install streetlamps for its residents. But she had suspected as much and, as her flat had been on the way, she had stopped off there to equip herself for the excursion. Leaving Ahmed to calm Hector, who had gone sorely unattended that day and was bouncing and slobbering like some sort of damp kangaroo, she dug into her old kit bag and found two working flashlights, American Winchesters with rounded copper ends intended to resemble bullets, but they reminded Molly more of 'every woman's special friend.' She traded the fashionable veiled cloche for a newsboy cap, as she had just doctored the thing and it might come in handy. Her dress she replaced with dark trousers, a long-sleeved khaki British army shirt, and her boots. When Hector proved to be too excited to leave home, she leashed him and took him along, stout ash stick in hand. After all, his nose could be of use.

They cut across the Luxembourg Gardens to save time, though they were forced to fend off a few begging drunks and one rather insistent robber who had laughed at Hector's teeth but not Hassanein's naked steel. Once the hapless thief ran off, they made better time, despite Molly touching every lamppost, cutting south and east via the Rue Vavin, down the Boulevard Raspail to Rue Huyghens and directly to the main cemetery entrance on the Boulevard Edgar Quinet.

Which, of course, was locked.

Molly scowled and glared at the immense posts that formed the gate. Its doors looked to be five meters high and offered no purchase for climbing. The two smaller iron doors, one in the wall on either side, looked to be just as secure. Had she interpreted the message incorrectly? Or had *Ardire* entered early and simply remained after closing time? But then how did they plan to leave once their business was concluded? And what was their purpose here anyway? Grave robbery? Did the cemetery hold some artifact that was needed to complement the alien gem?

She gave up contemplating motives and focused on getting into the place, teeth clicking. Hassanein went to the left in search of access, so she moved right, Hector's snout leading the way. Though there was enough ivy to make climbing the wall possible, she dared not attempt that on the main street, in case a gendarme took a dim view of it. Besides, having Hector complicated that sort of thing. After finding nothing of use, she backtracked to the gate, hoping that Ahmed had had better luck.

It was open.

Strictly speaking, the right-hand postern gate was cracked perhaps half a palm's width. She would have bet her remaining eye that it had been firmly shut not three minutes earlier. Hector poked his snout into the gap, whining. Something had caught his attention. Whether it was an Italian Fascist or merely a squirrel she had no way of knowing without investigating.

Well, that's why we came here.

Back against the opening, Molly leaned into it, forcing the heavy iron door open a bit farther. She waited until there were no passersby, then shoved her way in, hoping no assassin waited. When her throat remained uncut, she exhaled and snapped on her torch. No one leaped at her. In fact, only the dead were visible. Since the light made her a target, she switched it off, hoping that someone else was moving about with their own light. Seeing none, she put the wall to her blind side to preclude an ambush and allowed the dog to lead her back toward the direction that Hassanein had gone, in case he found a way in from there. And she wanted to find a landmark so she could get her bearings with the map she had stuffed into her glove.

It took quite a long time. This was no village churchyard. The place took up nearly fifty acres. From a previous visit with tourists Molly knew that some two hundred thousand people were buried in the Cimetiere du Montparnasse. It had been there a long time. In fact, 1924 was its centennial. Generals, statesmen, artists, writers, bankers, and all manner of ordinary Parisians lay there. And it seemed to be some sort of requirement that they all had to vie to out-do one another in ostentation and cleverness. Weeping angels on pillars, immense crosses, large sculptures worthy of the Louvre (some nude, which was disconcerting), and so many mausoleums that the grounds looked like a vast unlit city of stone. Molly jumped in alarm running into a statue of a reclining dog that looked remarkably like Hector. All the structures were butted up against one another, as space was at a premium. It was scarcely possible to walk anywhere but on the paved avenues.

Finally, she found an intersection that was on her little map. Risking the torch again, she found that she and Hector were at the northwest corner of the *grand cimetiere*, the large rectangular portion. Just across the Rue Emile Richard was the angular *petit cimetiere*. She had no need to explore that, as the *Ardire* message had indicated that they would gather at Baudelaire's monument, which was in the larger section. After sweeping the wall and the path with her lamp, she switched it off and moved south on the Avenue de l'Est. It would be a long time before she reached her goal, as Baudelaire lay on the other side of the cemetery. Molly hoped that she found Ahmed before then, having no taste to encounter a whole violent gang by herself.

Teeth clicking, she felt along with her stick like the blind woman she essentially was this night, trusting Hector to lead her true. Many hours had been spent training him to do that very thing, as she had chosen to take a realistic view of her vision. If something untoward happened and she lost the use of the eye, she would have to rely on him. Thus she did so now, having little choice. The torch's beam would be a help, but it would also steal her feeble night vision. And the quarter moon's light was little help.

After another fifteen minutes of picking her way through more disturbing, eerie tombs that made her feel as if Virgil should be guiding her and not Hector, Molly came to her next landmark, the lane that led to the large roundabout that lay slightly south and west of the center. There she turned right, tapping along with her low-slung guide dog. Now she noticed that Paris' nickname, City of Light, was accurate. The innumerable streetlamps and shop displays, plus automobile headlamps, made seeing significantly easier now that her eye was recovered from using the torch to read. More detail came into focus, the details of the tombs and monuments were sharper. She decided to rely on her memory of the map and reserve the flashlight for an emergency.

A pale monster appeared before her. Like Don Quixote's giant, it was actually a windmill, the most prominent structure in the cemetery. Monks had built it in the 1600's. Its vanes had been removed long ago, but the structure remained. Around ten meters tall at the point of the black slate roof, the mill was a cylinder of white stone, amounting to a motherly monument to all the countless thousands buried around it. Four lanes intersected there, connected by a circular one. A larger ring ran around that. Molly knew that from the mill all she had to do was walk north to the second intersection, turn left, and march to the wall. That was where Baudelaire lay.

Hector snuffed, froze, stared at the remnant of the mill. They were no longer alone.

Molly knelt, listening. Nothing. But if the hound's nose said someone was near, that was proof enough. She followed his example, lifted her mask's bottom edge up a bit, and sniffed. Reds, greens, and golds lit up her brain, as if Paris had decided to celebrate the cemetery's centennial with silent fireworks. And it was not just any random collection of those colors and patterns. Her synesthesia had experienced this one before, that very morning.

The complex curry of the restaurant where Farouk had written his note to her.

She tugged Hector back to her and crept rearward until she

lay in the shadow of a small tree. After wrapping his leash loosely to the thin trunk she moved out to her right, hoping that he would not bark or pull free until called, but not terribly concerned if he did. That would at least be likely to get a response from whoever was lurking in or near the tower. Knowing just where they were and what their intentions might be would help.

Well, the second one is easy. They don't have any benign reasons for being here at night.

Just like when she had maneuvered into a tough sniping position during the war, Molly crawled with glacial slowness from one covered and concealed position to another, cradling her stick as she had her rifle. This time the terrain was more advantageous, as there was hardly a square meter of open space. The graves were nearly all well above ground, providing solid stone bulwarks against observation and attack. Unless she strayed into the middle of a lane she was likely safe, unlike the open desert of her youth where it had so much more difficult.

Of course, this time I only have a bloody cane. If I'm up against a gun...

Another sniff gave her the same colors and patterns as before, but fainter. That told her that her adversary had stayed put and was on the other side of the windmill, facing Hector. It did not tell her, though, whether he was in the structure, hanging out of one of the small windows, or hunkered down at the base. She hoped for the latter, as it would grant her an opportunity to get at him. Since his spiced aroma was so strong, even out in the open and at a distance, it seemed most reasonable that he was not hiding inside the building.

Molly stood up, hidden by a sizable mausoleum with a prostrate angel atop it. From there she had a clear run across turf to the mill. Smelling told her that her prey had not moved and was still near the front, near the single door. The mass of stone was between her and him. She could approach unobserved.

Presuming he was alone.

That gave her pause. If the aromatic one had a partner who did not live or work in an Indian restaurant, how was she to know? The myriad hiding places that had aided her would do the same for him. No sense strolling into an ambush by assuming that Curry Man worked alone. A moment's fumbling brought a small clay flowerpot to hand, left by an attentive mourner to the mausoleum. After hefting it to gauge her throw, she lobbed it ahead of her, just where a hidden assailant at the mill's rear could do her the worst damage.

No response.

That was encouraging unless the potential foe had more discipline than the average soldier or criminal. Even more interesting, the man in front did not react, either. Was he asleep? He would not be the first guard on an outpost to succumb to that temptation. She set her stick in a good defensive position, flicking it behind her at random in case someone came at her there, and advanced on the old windmill. But she made certain to avoid the paved path, as any pre-arranged defenses would most likely be placed there.

Reaching the rear of the mill without incident, she kept her stick before her for rapid deployment, feet set for quick use as weapons if need be. Pausing to listen and smell, she confirmed that the person guarding this patch of cemetery lay just around the bend of the column. She took a deep breath, focused on the dangerous task instead of her many rituals, and dashed forward to engage him.

No one was there.

Frowning, she rushed around the entire structure, confirming that she was alone at its base. When she came back to the front she tried to open the door. Firmly locked. A look at the window showed that it was closed and no one leaned out of it with a weapon. Another circumnavigation confirmed the same for the other windows. Yet she could still smell the curry. Where the deuce was he?

If Hector had not started woofing that question might have been her epitaph. The dog's deep warning howls made her turn toward her blind side, just in time to spot a wisp of shadow from what little moon there was. With no time to bring up the stick in defense, all Molly could do was duck. Sparks exploded from the wall just above her head. She rolled across the grass until she was well clear of the building, then popped up in an en guarde position, stick high, point down. Her left hand was before her to deflect a weak-side assault. When no attack came, she looked up to find her enemy.

He stood on the wall, perpendicular to it, as if the law of gravity did not apply to him.

Molly shook her head at the impossible sight. After a moment she realized that he hung from a thin line that was attached to a harness. The other end led to a grappling hook that bit into the stone sill of a window just beneath the black slate roof. She had not spotted him before because he wore white, including pale face paint, to blend into the wall in the evening's poor light.

Well prepared. This is no guard, but an assassin. We were lured here. And those are some wicked pointy things he's using.

That was the extent of her ruminations, for the man on the tower let out more line, ran down the wall, and hit the ground running, flipping the grapple free as he landed. He unhooked it from his waist harness and let it lay as he reached her. Heart pounding, which filled her ears with booming sound that became orange waves at the edge of her sight, Molly feinted a retreat, selling it with a mostly false bleat of terror. The Indian, shorter than her but much huskier of build, chuckled and rushed at her with even more speed. Overconfident, he failed to recognize her lowered stick for the invitation it was. His left hand slashed at her face, while the right pulled back for a follow-up strike after she was distracted.

But his prey did not follow the plan. As the hand swept toward her, Molly switched her stick to her left, grasping it in the center. Right hand up to block the attack, she stepped directly into him, careful to hook the deadly katara in the fellow's right fist. That immobilized the dreadful push-dagger. She pivoted like a Spanish torero executing a verónica, just as her masters had taught her, using the attacker's own momentum to fling him past her. He stumbled and fell backward onto the grass. Given that opening, Molly pounced, stick raised to club his head.

Only the assassin did not stay down. Much nimbler than he appeared at first, he rolled backward and up onto his feet, spinning to face her. Molly checked her rush, not wishing to make his mistake. Back on guard, she settled into a crouch and tried a few circling feints, testing his reactions, trying to lull him into an error. He did the same. The only sound was hard breathing and the rustle of feet in wet grass. Despite her competence so far, Molly was beginning to tremble with fear and anxiety.

"The police are coming," she lied, trying a ruse. "You'd best scarper."

He laughed, short and cruel. "Let them come. We'll kill them, too. The old gods have returned for vengeance. Demons will feast on their hearts." His accent revealed him to be a high caste from around Lucknow.

With that he charged her again, careful to control his impetus this time and not let her pull the same trick. Expecting that, Molly calculated his reach and slid backward just as he pawed at her with his left hand again. A sharp rap on the knuckles discouraged him. Hissing, he withdrew it. Now she could see that he wore a bagh nakh, a tiger claw, on his palm. Nasty little curved knives projected down from the base of his fingers. That had thrown the sparks from the wall.

"Clever little white bitch," he snarled.

"Name-calling?" she chided. "And here I thought we were getting on."

Molly's bravado was forced. She was near to fainting with the distress of her second combat of the day. *Six years without this sort of thing and suddenly today happens.* Her teeth clicked and elbow tendons flexed, falling back on the rituals already. *Not good. Concentrate or die, like Lawrence always told you.* As she countered his attempt to flank her on her blind side (did he know of her infirmity there?), she wondered why he employed antique weapons. Purely for silence? Or did the choice mean something?

The 'white bitch' was instructive. Racial motives at play, it seems. Old weapons suggest that he and his fellows have a political interest in the ancient ways. Probably want the English out, like most Indians. The violence isn't Ghandi's way, though, so they disagree with his tactics. Former adherents who grew impatient? And he's from Lucknow. The

Mutiny of nearly seventy years ago was centered there. Nasty siege. Massacres. Simmering resentment and secret societies ever since? I've heard of less likely rationales.

Her adversary grew impatient with more than the Mahatma. He advanced again, with a growl this time, relying on feints and clever combinations to drive her back. Molly was appalled at how quickly an enraged fighter could move, nothing at all like her sparring sessions. More than once she blocked with the stick and delivered a punishing kick, but the Indian simply accepted the damage with a grunt and kept forcing her rearward until her back smacked against the curved windmill wall. She even broke his wrist with a savage strike, immobilizing the claw, but that did not completely deter him. The dagger jutting from his fist slapped the cane out of her hand, then snapped back for the killing thrust. Pinned to the stone by his weight, unable to knee his groin because he wisely set himself side-on, she only had one card left to play.

The flashlight's beam bored into his black eyes.

He yelped, shutting his eyes, and withholding the stab for half a second. Pausing to gloat had given her time to grab the light. By the time he thought to resume the thrust she had shattered his nose with its phallic end. Bellowing in pain and rage, he slashed in all directions with the katara. Molly had ducked beneath his arm and run past him, however. Frantically she hunted for her stick, pawing the grass in desperation. The assassin sensed where she was, turned, thundered down upon her. Still, she could not lay her fingers on her cane. At the last moment, though, they found the next best thing. She seized it and yanked hard.

The Indian's fallen climbing rope went taut when the vicious grappling hook bit into his arse. Completely surprised, he shrieked and fumbled at his backside with a broken limb and the other encumbered by the katara. By the time it occurred to him to cut the line, Molly had made that impossible by pouncing upon him and trussing him up like a calf at a rodeo. A heel stomp relieved him of his dagger. After frenzied struggling proved to him that he was immobilized, he began chanting in Hindi. Molly recognized it as a death prayer to Vishnu.

"Now my breath and spirit goes to the Immortal, and this body ends in ashes. Om. O Mind! Remember. Remember the deeds. Remember the actions."

While he kept repeating that, low and fast, Molly tried to interrogate him, keeping a watch out for any of his comrades who might have been alerted by the fight. A whistle brought Hector, trailing his leash. He could watch her back. Now she was shivering as if on an Artic expedition, her usual reaction to any sort of unpleasantness, from meeting a stranger to attempted murder. Her fingers snapped in a silently calming ritual while she caught her breath and asked him questions.

"Why did you attack me?" No reply, only the chanting. "Who sent you? Who do you work for?" Still nothing. The prisoner's words came faster now, more intense in tone. "What have I done to merit murder?" She switched to his own language. "Are you allied with the Italians, with *Ardire*? Did they promise to help you drive the British out?" That threw him for a moment, though it was unclear whether it was the mention of the Fascist group or hearing her speak Hindi with his own accent. He paused, cocked his head at her. "Do you think that murder will earn you merit, free your jiva from samsara? I think not. Your avidya is massive. This is not good karma."

Hearing his intended victim blithely discussing his reincarnation threw the man. Looking around as if some aid might come, he seemed about to respond. Then he sagged, head down, and began his chant again. Molly grumbled and stepped away from him, considering. Then she swore and reached for his right wrist. Too late. The brass talon on his index finger had already clawed through the thin white garment covering the thigh. It dug in three or four times, obviously administering something that she wanted no part of. Jerking her hand back in case he decided that he wanted some company in his afterlife, Molly grabbed Hector's lead and pulled him to a safe distance.

It did not take long. Though she could not have known it, the poison was the same that had Terremoto had employed to dispatch the unfortunate Eabroni in the very restaurant where the assassin had worked as a cook. She watched with distaste as the disturbing symptoms took hold: paralysis, retching, convulsions, stillness. No matter what he had done, such a hard death unsettled her. Once she was assured that he was well and truly gone, Molly eased up to him and removed the talon with painful care. She placed it point-down in a patch of soil at the base of the windmill, marking it with the man's katara point so that she could find it later for analysis.

Searching the twitching body made her skin crawl, but it was not as if she had never done that sort of thing before. In the war there had been plenty of dead Turks and Germans to be inspected for intelligence, many killed by her own Enfield. Too often they had lain in the desert sun long enough to make this search a sprig of daisies in comparison. Swallowing her distaste, Molly turned out his pockets and unwound the turban. Besides a recently-made chest tattoo of some sort of mythical monster, the dead murderer had few possessions. She imagined that his line of work discouraged carrying formal identification or small change. All she found was a leather packet containing a chilling photo of her walking Hector in the Luxembourg Gardens and a scrap of paper with 'CR4224' inked on it.

Perhaps he has a cache of other items nearby. Things that would've interfered with his movement.

After taking a few moments to calm herself with rocking and head bobbing, she made a hasty search by having Hector snort at the wallet and go hunting for twenty meters in all directions, but the dog found nothing. *Either he's a lone wolf or his masters are elsewhere in the cemetery on some other mission.* Pocketing the photo, which alarmed her more for having Hector as a potential target than because he had been stalking her, and the numbered paper, she headed off down the lane that led toward Charles Baudelaire's grave, alert for any other nasty surprises.

And she was not to be disappointed. Halfway along the path a statue of some long-deceased general, sword drawn and pointing to heaven, came to life like the finale of *Don Giovanni* and leapt at her.

12 / Cimetiere du Montparnasse

Only years of experience as a necessarily silent and disciplined sniper kept her from squealing.

Molly leapt back into defense, stick high, holding Hector well to the side while silently upbraiding him for not smelling the second ambusher of the night. She became even more miffed at him when the hound let out a welcoming whine and leapt up at the assailant for a chin rub.

"An evening constitutional in a necropolis with one's pet," said Ahmed Hassanein. "This we do not do in Egypt."

She sighed, mostly in disgust with herself, and relaxed. "You pose on gravestones instead? Is competitive gargoyle-impersonating a popular past-time?"

Sheathing his sword back into its cane, he chuckled. "Only when pressing necessity requires it." His head nodded in the direction she planned to travel. "Four other nocturnal mourners, apparent fans of *Le Fleurs de Mal*. They just passed this spot. I was up there trying to see you. Had to act quickly."

"We should both act quickly, in case they plan more mayhem." Molly gave him a hurried account of her battle at the windmill. The bit about the old gods and demons returning stumped them both.

"I agree, that was no ad hoc assault. Someone expended time and planning to get you. That's good."

She flexed aching muscles. "From whose perspective?"

"Yours. Mine. If you weren't getting in their way, they wouldn't have bothered. That may lead to more mistakes on their part. Cool professionals don't indulge in revenge."

"If it was revenge. Maybe we're close to breaking up their little plot, whatever it is."

"That letter/number you found. A code? A telephone number?"

"Could be. Let's ponder that later. Time to join the cotillion."

They continued to the intersection that led to the outer wall where Baudelaire's monument lay, taking care to walk on separate sides of the path, keeping out of the center and moving from one stone structure to the next. The wisdom of that procedure soon became apparent. After perhaps five minutes they turned left onto the final stretch of lane. Two minutes after that a whooshing sound made them duck behind cover. Metal clanged as something flew through the air, ricocheting off of a bronze horse's muzzle with a small explosion of sparks. It wobbled to a stop in the path, a body length from Molly.

"What is it?" asked Ahmed in a hoarse whisper, squinting ahead for the thrower.

"Indian chakram. Like a quoits ring from hell. A flying razor. Nasty thing. Look sharp, they usually carry several."

"Refresh my memory. Did we anger the subcontinent recently?"

"Not that I know of. It seems that the mahatma's pacifistic ways haven't been adopted by all of his countrymen."

"Is Mussolini allied with some Indian faction now?"

"Possibly. Stranger things have happened. I've given up trying to predict what this group is up to."

She yelled out an insult in Hindi, then dove for the fallen weapon. Its twin rang against the top of the stone grave she had just been hiding behind. Snatching up the first one, she rolled across the lane until she was tucked between a small mausoleum and a bronze figure of a Napoleonic officer.

"All well?" inquired her partner.

"Just peachy." She hefted the hollow ring, a circular bit of yellow metal ten inches across, very thin. "This thing could shave a bear. Glad I wore these gloves."

"Shall we return it, then?"

"Yes, let's. You get his attention, I'll flank him."

Based on the flight angle of the two hurled chakrams, their owner lay some twenty meters in front of them, just off the path on Molly's side. Using every bit of stealth at her command, she let Hector pull her through narrow gaps in the field of pale stone, taking care not to let the brass scrape against anything and give her away. That was Ahmed's job. He had drawn his sword again and was advancing parallel to her, popping up every few paces to tap the sword on a statue or drag his foot heavily. Twice a wicked chakram whistled at him. The second one would have bit into his flesh if his swordman's instincts had not parried it with his own blade. Molly used the noise of that encounter to risk a rush and get almost even with the attacker. Focused on his near-success against Hassanein, the dark-clad Hindu was unaware that his silhouette was spectacularly visible against the white marble wall of his covering structure. Remaining patient, she let him loose another at Ahmed, who cleverly feigned a hit by crying out. His attention now firmly fixed on his triumph, he never saw his own blade hissing through the night air from the right.

It bit into the shoulder of his throwing arm, a very lucky hit as Molly had no practice with such a thing; however, she had observed their employment on a trip to Rajasthan and knew the most effective technique. He yelped in surprise and pain, arm hanging useless. Several chakrams slid down it and clanged onto the ground. Making the mistake of bending down to recover them with his other hand, he yowled again as forty pounds of toothed basset seized his fingers and began shaking them with a growl. Unable to tell what was eating him, the fellow must have thought it was a punishing demon sent by his angry gods. His high-pitched pleadings for aid to at least half a dozen of them faded as he ran up the lane at a pace worthy of the best sprinters in the upcoming Games.

Molly crouched, giving Hector the adoration he deserved for a job well done. Gravel crunching behind her made her start, but it was Ahmed, sword point up, chuckling.

"I daresay that our element of surprise is now somewhat diminished," he said.

"If it ever existed," she shrugged. "Two ambushes already? This is a gauntlet, not an infiltration."

"Then we shall likely need our trump cards. Are they in place?"

"They should be by now. Let's go find out."

No one disturbed them the rest of the way to Baudelaire's tomb, which lay against the western wall of the cemetery. He had been buried there, against his express wishes, with his family. In a few minutes Molly and Ahmed reached it, weapons and reflexes primed, ready for any sort of trouble.

No one was there.

They conducted a hasty puzzled search for thirty meters in every direction, but they were alone. There was no sign of anyone save the dead.

"So the whole thing was just a ruse to let their assassins have a crack at us?" Hassanein wondered.

"They went to an awful lot of trouble," Molly pouted. "And they were very specific in their message about meeting at Baudelaire's grave. Their thugs were placed nowhere near it. Why entice us to this spot and not leave another vicious surprise?"

"What did the message say?"

"I just told you."

"No, precisely."

Molly paused, closed her eye, envisioned the Morse code on the odd little box. Then she cursed and stamped her foot. "I'm an imbecile!"

"I have no evidence of that. What have you recalled?"

"It didn't say 'grave.' It said 'monument.'"

"What's the difference?"

"Baudelaire has two markers. His actual grave, where his remains were hijacked and placed by his family, is right here. But there is a cenotaph, an empty tomb that is his memorial."

"And where is that?"

She made a sour face. "The other side of the bloody cemetery. I strolled right past it before running into my friend at the windmill. Must have been there before the others arrived at it, else they would have pounced on me then."

"So our ring-thrower was left here just in case you made a mistake? Disturbingly-thorough planning on their part."

"Isn't it, though? We should take care as we travel there.

They are less incompetent than I had hoped."

They consulted her map, hiding the light inside Ahmed's suit coat so as to not give themselves away. With her knowledge of the cemetery's lanes refreshed, Molly led the way on a roundabout route rather than retracing her steps. That meant approaching the windmill from the opposite direction, where they found that her Hindu had either risen from the dead or been taken, for he was gone, along with all of his gear. Molly managed to find the buried poison claw despite the katara having been taken, as the ground was still disturbed. She marked it with her handkerchief. Sanglier's laboratory men might be able to tell her just what the dreadful poison on it was.

The rest of the way to Baudelaire's cenotaph saw no more attacks. The quiet was disturbed only by the scrape of their feet on the path and the distant sounds of auto horns and traffic rumbling. Molly thought of how odd it was to be back in a necropolis again, fearing for her safety. That had been the standard state of affairs in Mesopotamia, Egypt, the Transjordan, India, and all of the other places she had disturbed the dead in the name of science. It seemed that there had always been some armed band either outraged that she was committing sacrilege against its ancestors or, more often, perfectly willing to reap the benefits of her sacrilege by stealing artifacts from her at gunpoint.

I should probably just give up cemeteries altogether as a bad job and stick to ancient rubbish pits.

Ten meters from the monument they took cover on either side of the lane, watching and listening. Ahead the white stone structure rose tall and slender, surrounded by a low hedge. Its vertical and horizontal planes were the same size, resembling an open notebook. On top of the former, which backed up against an ivy-covered wall, a pedestal had been carved in relief. Atop it a puckish image of the great modernist poet, chin in hands, stared out. Down on the flat portion, as if it were a mortuary slab, lay an effigy of Baudelaire, tightly wrapped in a shroud. It resembled a mummy. Molly frowned when she inspected it. For there were two forms there. And one was moving.

Someone's making love atop his monument. Is that a thoroughly French artistic statement or couldn't they afford a room?

Sure enough, a pair of intertwined figures writhed beside the stone image. It looked to be more kissing and groping than shagging, at least at this juncture. The taller of the two was in the dominant position, leg draped over the other. For a long moment Molly just stared, petting Hector to keep him quiet, wondering what to do. It had to be some sort of ruse, a means to put them off-guard. What were the chances that a random pair of lovers would be there? Paris was full of parks and woods that would serve for better love couches. She caught Ahmed's attention, motioned to him to scout for more assailants. He nodded, moved off to the right flank, while she did the same to the left, letting Hector sniff for trouble.

He found it immediately, increasing his pace as much as his stumpy legs and the leash would permit. The hound towed her unerringly on a zigzag route through the monuments, statues, and small structures until they came to the porch of a mausoleum, where she found the body of the poisoned Indian assassin, laid out reverently by someone who cared for him.

Then that caretaker tried to shoot her.

If his bow had not scraped a headstone as he tracked her, she might never have had a chance. Reflexes vibrating from the evening's dangers, Molly dove away from the porch without pausing to look for the source of the threat. The arrow smacked into the lintel of the grave-house's door, shattering itself on the limestone. Holding Hector down to prevent him from charging the fellow, she poked her head around the marble wall that covered her, hoping to spot the shooter. He was not bothering to hide as he hauled back on the bowstring. Her instinct to rush him before he could fire again got her into a crouch, but the cautious part of her moved her head to the left.

There were two of them.

Bloody hell! Pinned down like a new recruit on his first day.

The black-clad pair -- Hindus, of course -- knew their business, covering one another and not taking wild shots. If she made an assault or tried to move down the lane in either

143

direction, they had her. That left only her rear, maneuvering back through the stones, and finding her way to Ahmed. She had to get to him before he missed her and came looking, or they would drop him before he knew there was a hazard.

Head low, taking care not to give herself away with a clumsy foot placement that might betray her with a snapped twig or kicked pebble, Molly crawled back around the mausoleum, away from the two snipers. Their aim would be immediately spoiled as she disappeared into the maze of the cemetery. Then all she would have to do would be to return to Baudelaire and find Hassanein.

Another arrow crashed into a bronze statue of a child, not ten inches from her face. Hector whined and burrowed beneath her.

Damn! Three of them. This one has my retreat stymied. What now, Aulis?

Her stick and torch were of little use against arrows. Moving was fatal and staying put just as dangerous. Foot-tall Hector was more than game, but he was no police dog when it came to direct combat. Losing her only friend in a vain attack held little appeal. Uprooting the stanchion of a plant hanger, she staked her dog's lead amidst a cluster of sturdy graves that provided perfect protection. After two more arrows came perilously close, making her wonder how her foes could see so well in the murk, she belly-crawled back to the porch of the mausoleum, leaving her lit torch on the ground to draw fire. A shot creased the sole of her boot, but she made it otherwise unscathed. She slithered across the poisoned corpse and pulled it before her as a shield. No more shots came from the Hindus, possibly out of respect for their fallen friend.

That gave Molly inspiration. The fellow with the chakrams had proven to be superstitious. Likewise the one at the windmill. Why not these others? Their recurved bows resembled the Vijaya, the invincible bow that sounded like thunder, used by the demi-god Karna in the *Mahabharata*. Likely not a coincidence. Giving thanks for her husky frame and vigorous physical training, she got to her knees and hauled the dead body into a sitting position, taking care to remain concealed behind it, cane hung on her arm. Still no fire came from the bowmen. Encouraged, she stood with a grunt, making the deceased assassin seem to stand on his own. To sell that idea, she lowered her voice and called out, imitating the dead man's voice in as eerie and moaning Hindi as she could manage, "Brothers! Why have you abandoned me here?"

The confused alarm from the pair across the lane was immediately felt. Molly heard their whispers to one another but could not make out the words, which created tiny jagged purple lines in her mind. At the same time, she kept an ear cocked for signs that the third killer might be advancing on her. Detecting nothing there and hoping that Hector would bark if the man moved, she used her foot to make the dead body's leg kick out in semblance of a lurching step.

"How does this woman's life advance our cause? Look what it has brought me. Agony and death. Do you wish to leave your mothers alone for such a slight thing?" She made her burden take another step, feeling the strain in her arms and back now. She couldn't maintain this for much longer. "Perish on the field of battle against the English if you must. Send the white soldiers to their hell or back to their foggy island. But abandon this dishonorable fight against one woman."

To her annoyance they did not wail in fright and flee, tossing their weapons aside. Instead, they came out from cover and approached her, cautious but not terrified, bows aimed at the impossible figure before them. She knew that the closer they came, the sooner they would realize the trick. Raising a clumsy corpse arm in a warding gesture did no good. The man on her left laughed and waved to his partner to flank her. In another moment she would be between two point-blank fires, with only shield enough for one of them.

And to make the ruination of her evening complete, Hector whoofed and footsteps advanced from behind her.

Molly considered shoving the body at one and leaping at the other with her cane. That might work, but even if she took down the one bowman before he could fire, that left two others free to riddle her. Running back into the monument maze was an option, but the three of them would soon hunt her down.

This is what I get for leaving the Webley at home.

Just as she had given up hope and decided to try the

desperate plan anyway, two black demons materialized out of the shadows behind her enemies.

The Indians must have heard or felt something, though Molly would have sworn that the fiends made no sound. They spun and loosed their arrows. Neither struck anything but damp night air, as the dark shapes anticipated the move. Both dropped low, one sweeping a foot out to trip the man on her left and the other snapping out a vicious kick to the hip that doubled the target over. Molly grinned, having seen that style attack many times. Now she had no more concern about surviving this encounter.

Jason followed up his kick with a left elbow to his foe's jaw that staggered the man. Incredibly, the assassin did not fall. He shook it off, growled, and swung his heavy bow at Molly's savate trainer. The Frenchman's cane caught it, hooked it, stripped it from his hands. Before it hit the ground a roundhouse high kick smashed into the side of his neck. This time he did go down, his face flattening as it met the path.

Five paces away, Hecuba was having more of a challenge. Her opponent proved to be adept at fighting, even when her cane smacked his wrist and made him drop his bow. He flicked out his own kick, in combination with a proper English one-two with his fists. Clearly, he had learned some pugilism at the schools of his oppressors. But it was matched by Hecuba's decade of experience against street thugs. The kick's force was wasted on her lower leg block and the first punch met the same fate against her forearm. His wicked follow-up blow met her cane. Before he knew he was in trouble the petite woman had wrenched his arm down and around with the crook, jerking the wrist up while crushing the elbow joint with her knee. Shrieking, he collapsed, no fight left in him.

So engrossed was Molly by her masters' display that she almost forgot herself and made their rescue futile. Only another frantic bark from Hector reminded her that peril still lurked in her rear. She whipped the dead body around, so heavy in her arms that it felt like turning an ocean liner, just as the bow twanged. Head buried between the broad lifeless shoulders, she felt the impact of the arrow in front and above her. The fletched shaft vibrated, stuck in one eye of the late murderer. Feet stomped hard at her. Now Molly could safely risk her original plan. Her legs bent, sprung, and she shoved the corpse at her assailant, mouthing a rude Hindu curse in the feigned voice of the man.

Whether or not the third bowman was more superstitious than the others or merely surprised by her stratagem, he gasped and bounded back, calling out to Shiva. But he was too slow. The falling form's limp arm snarled in the bowstring and they both fell, the living man beneath the dead. His frantic attempts to wriggle free merely worsened the entanglement. Almost pitying him, Molly stomped on the bow several times until it cracked. For good measure she booted him along one ear, too. That kicked up the familiar curry scent. *Hmm. That restaurant will be short-staffed tomorrow.* She left him to his private terrors and freed poor Hector, beside himself with worry for his mistress. The shaggy hound leaped up into her arms, warm wet tongue drenching her jaw beneath the mask. She nuzzled into his fur, shivering and nauseous, glad they were both alive.

How long they might remain that way was still open to question.

"What now, La Dame Masqueé?" asked a cool throaty voice.

She stiffened, then realized that it was Hecuba, her tiny frame barely visible over the top of a grave. The enormous dark Hellenic eyes twinkled even in the poor cemetery light. Molly had always marveled at her teacher's constant sunny disposition. Perhaps it came from her Greek island ancestors. No Aphrodite, she owned a nondescript oval face and what would politely be called a Hellenic nose. Her wide smile was so bright that it would have made her a target if their enemies had not already been disarmed.

"I'd love some wine and a nap, but we still have pressing business here," Molly answered, setting Hector back down and taking the end of his leash.

"You are unhurt?" Hecuba tugged at the cuffs of her black jumper, a tight turtlenecked affair. She had removed the feminine skirt and blouse she had used as a disguise in the café. A knit cap restrained her curly black hair.

"Yes, thanks to you. How did you know where to find us? I

sent you to the wrong spot."

"That you did, but we ignored you and came straight here. When a Parisian thinks 'Baudelaire,' this is where he goes. The poor poet absolutely did not want to be buried with his less-than-understanding relations."

"Awkward for me if you'd been wrong."

"For us, as well. We would have missed all this entertainment."

Hecuba recognized the distress Molly was in and hugged her tight, one of the few proven calming techniques. Despite her aversion to embracing people, Molly had always relaxed when someone did it to her this way. She felt as if back in a safe womb.

When the post-combat shuddering subsided, Hecuba stroked Molly's hair beneath the flat cap. "Better?"

In any other such situation Molly might have kissed her, but that was a line she dared not cross. "Much. Thank you."

They let Hector lead them back to the lane. "The other actors are subdued?" Molly asked.

"Yes. Apparently you accounted for the other one yourself."

"Yes and no. I restrained him, but the poisoning was all his doing. He seemed to fear failing his employers more than arrest."

"Then we should take that as a warning."

"Agreed. This is a serious enterprise."

"So...do we proceed to Monsieur Baudelaire's attractive monument?"

"Yes, but carefully. Where is Jason?"

"He tied up and gagged the miscreants. They had nothing of interest on them. Now he is stowing them out of sight. We can alert the police later."

"Good. I'd rather not be here trying to explain all of this."

"Can you?"

"Not really. But I'll get to the bottom of it eventually. They wrecked my flat."

Hecuba made a show of horror. "Mon Dieu! They would have done better to murder nuns!"

Molly chuckled along with her. "Silly, I know, but that's how I'm made."

"If I were of the same mind, I would have to kill my husband. For a man so physically dynamic he has great difficulty bending over to pick up a sock."

The rakish object of Hecuba's ire appeared before them, all strong jaw and even stronger legs. Lean and powerful, Jason's tawny hair was long and unruly, and a razor had not touched his chin in several days. His thick eyebrows shot up into the edge of his wine-colored beret. "Are my praises being sung yet again? Should I tie myself to the mast so the sirens cannot tempt me to my doom?"

Hecuba and Molly traded disbelieving glances. Then his wife snorted. "How do you know we aren't Scylla and Charybdis?"

With that jab, and an impatient snuff from Hector, they fell silent and moved south on either side of the lane toward the poet's monument. Just like the first time she had approached it, no more attacks were launched from the gloom, no more assassins appeared to hinder them. The resulting quiet scraped Molly's nerves nearly as harshly as fending off murderers had. Her hound kept his formidable nose to the ground and seemed to find nothing. Molly's own freakish senses of scent and sound were no more effective, as colors failed to flash in her head. Had they all fled? Hecuba and Jason fanned out as flankers. Remaining in a vulnerable clump was a bad idea, and they wanted to clear out any unpleasantness before arriving at the cenotaph.

Molly wondered again about the lovers she had seen writhing on the monument. Most likely they were part of whatever plot was being hatched against her. But what if they were not? If by some incredible cosmic absurdity they were simply a pair of randy Sorbonne students who mistakenly believed themselves to be the first to combine sex with death? *Oh, the supposed cleverness of the French. 'Come, monsieur, let me show you my flower of evil.' That sort of playfulness could get you killed tonight.* If innocents had truly blundered into the evening's mess, she would have to take care to get them out of harm's way.

She arrived at her objective for the second time that night. From across the lane, she could now see the monument, even clearer than before. The lovers had decamped, which at least eased her mind of having to consider their welfare. On either side of her, Jason and Hecuba knelt behind stones to observe as well. *Nothing. Nobody. After all this brouhaha they just picked up and went home?* Still, she stayed put. Then, following two more minutes of inaction on the monument, Molly told Hector to stay and ventured out to inspect it.

Which was when the lower carving of Baudelaire moved.

Despite herself, Molly gasped and froze, cane jerking up into guard. It had only been a twitch of the foot, but that was enough under the circumstances. Cocking her head and longing for her old binocular vision, she stepped to one side to examine the phenomenon. That showed her that, to her great relief, the statue had not shifted after all. Someone lay immediately next to it, stretched out along its length, half his body atop it. In the poor light it had been impossible to tell that man and stone figure were not one. She half-turned and waved her partners back, as they had popped up to assist her. Then she walked up to the monument.

Sleeping off your little death, are you? Did your lady love gambol away once she'd had her fill of you?

She poked the spasming foot with her stick. No reaction. Twice more she jabbed at the sleeping fellow but got no more response. Out of the corner of her eye she glimpsed Hassanein, gliding along the wall on her right. Gesturing him to join her, she stepped up next to the prostrate man and rolled him over.

Dead. Comprehensively so.

In life he had been a dapper young man, slim and handsome, his dark pomaded hair parted in the center. His light double-breasted suit fit him in the manner that only a bespoke item could, and the silk tie boasted of attendance at some upper-crust school where they bred this sort of gentleman in herds. Everything about him bellowed 'posh,' except for the pathetic bit of sagging pink protruding from his open trouser fly. That, and his dark swollen face, eyes bulging, spittle bubbling on his open lips. The familiar smell of the wet mess in his lap announced that he had been dispatched at the moment of his completion.

Just as Molly's mind registered 'garrote,' smooth fabric

slithered across her own throat.

Despite her instant panic she still had a corner of her brain that cursed her for being a fool. She clawed at the satiny instrument of death, naturally, but she also kicked herself for fairly swan-diving into the trap. Whoever had looped the thing over her head crouched above, near the upper statue of Baudelaire. He had hidden behind the monument, standing on the old stone wall, until she had made herself vulnerable. Now the makeshift garrote, apparently a scarf, tightened, hauling her back until her spine smacked against the tall plinth that supported the bust of the poet. A thrust up with her cane merely resulted in it being yanked away. Vision already blurring, blood roaring in her ears, she could just make out Ahmed rushing to her aid. With failing strength, she tried to wave him off.

No! That's just what they want! Get out of here!

Hector yowled, but there was nothing he could do. Jason and Hecuba dashed from cover, clearly believing that three could handle this one assassin.

"Ah, ah, ah!" warned a husky voice above her. "That's just the sort of thing that will kill the esteemed Miss Aulis. "Every step will get her that much closer to Tartarus."

All three would-be rescuers stopped. Hector kept up his growling, but even he stayed put. Molly put a foot atop the reclining Baudelaire's skull, relieving some of the pressure on her throat so that she could catch a breath. She was helped by the apparent interest of the garrotter in not immediately dispatching her. With that bit of leisure, Molly sucked in more air, catching some of it up the pitiful remnant of her nose. Pinkish-yellow streaked across her vision. A particular camellia scent.

Bloody hell. It's that same bitch from the Panthéon.

"You, the handsome Arab," ordered Antiope, "drop that stick and come here. Slowly. Hands out where I can see them." The scarf tightened a bit. "The rest of you, let's not entertain any heroic pipe dreams, eh? She's been through enough in her life as it is."

Molly reached behind her but knew that it was a vain effort. Several Parisian old-timers had regaled her with café tales of the pre-war Apache gangs, who had employed this very technique to rob pedestrians. A second thug would do the actual pocket picking while the man with the scarf hauled back until the victim was off his feet and helpless. It was nearly impossible to defeat if surprise had been achieved. She knew this first-hand from practice sessions at the savate salle. Even her masters had been hard put to escape it. Given enough time and with no accomplice to worry about, Molly might have managed a rear kick or simply sagged into a dead weight. But her attacker was safely atop the statue and the plinth made for a fine lever to immobilize Molly.

Ahmed arrived at the edge of the monument, a sour look twisting his patrician features. He gave Molly an apologetic shrug but did not risk any more than that on her behalf. The dominant woman's voice resumed her commands. "Well done. You follow orders well for one of your class. Let's maintain that fine tradition. Reach into your coat -- slowly, mind you – and pluck out that pretty little bauble you received at the café this evening. Don't bother denying it. Be quick about it. Her neck grows more fragile by the moment."

Despite Molly's frantic pleas with her bulging eyes not to do it, Hassanein reached into the inner pocket and removed the deadly gem. He held the small leather pouch up between thumb and forefinger so that she could see it.

"Take it out, with the utmost care, and prove to me that it is the Gaze of Zeus. No tricks, sudden movements, or any of that nonsense. If you drop it, toss it, or run away, the lady is off to whatever afterlife there may be." The scarf hauled Molly up onto her toes. "And you two in the shadows there! I meant what I said! Stay put! Your intrepid flanking maneuvers are useless. Know when you are beaten."

With a sigh Ahmed tugged open the pouch's neck and lifted out the gem. Even in the pathetic cemetery light it gleamed with inner fire like a small locomotive lamp. The pressure on Molly's throat relaxed a bit. "Good lad. So pretty for such a nasty thing, eh? Now tuck it back up nice and tight and toss it to me." She caught the glint in his eye and barked at him. "No, no! Cleverness is dangerous. You only get one try. If it flies out of my reach, even inadvertently, her neck breaks. If I clumsily drop it, the same. Use all of your fencer's coordination and make damned sure that it lands on my hand like a trained sparrow."

The scarf jerked slightly as she collected both ends in one fist. To Molly's chagrin that did not lessen the fabric's hold on her neck. She craned her neck back to try to spot the woman, but the short brim of her flat cap blocked the view. Yet that gave her an idea. It might not keep the jewel in their possession, but it had a chance of leaving her alive and free to pursue it.

Hefting the pouch to gauge his throw, Ahmed stepped up onto the platform to get as close as he could for the delivery. Once, twice, three times he lifted his arm, practicing like a golfer preparing a shot. With part of her mind Molly stared at her life, literally in his hand. The other part calculated her next, and possibly final, move. Timing would be everything.

The tiny leather packet flew toward Antiope's grasp, perfectly aimed.

With the enemy focused on her waiting palm, everyone else exploded into action. Hecuba dashed forward, Hector taking that as his cue to yelp and follow her. Jason vaulted over the grave he had been using as cover and sprinted across the lane, his stick raised for throwing. Ahmed lunged for the scarf to jerk it from its owner's grip.

None of it worked.

Like a master puppeteer, Antiope slackened the scarf, whipped it away from Hassanein's reach, and pulled it taut again. At the same time, she snatched the jewel from the air and pocketed it. Before the others could reach her or Ahmed recover for another try, she heaved Molly into the air with both hands, a full three feet off the stone surface. In an instant Molly hung, vain fingers clutching at the noose that was killing her. Now she was out of Hassanein's saving reach. Hecuba and Jason skidded to a stop in the middle of the lane. Hector ran all the way onto the monument, growling in futile threat.

"So predictable," Antiope chuckled. "Gallant comrades, all. The old college try and all that." With a puff of effort, she dragged the kicking Molly farther up the wall until their cheeks nearly touched. Kissing her victim at the seam of the mask, she purred, "In other circumstances I might peel this off and have my way with you. Never shagged a real monster before. Unless you count the odd politician. But those were contractual obligations."

Molly bent her knees, tried to walk up the plinth to gain some measure of relief. But her boots skidded off the slick surface. A snake-strike of her taloned fingers at Antiope's eyes was anticipated and avoided. With no more air getting in, and her arteries so constricted that she was seconds from oblivion, she knew that she had to act immediately. There would only be the one chance. Her other hand slid up along the opposite side of her face.

"Let her go," said Hecuba, risking a sly advance as she spoke. "You got what you came for."

"True enough. I came to kill her and here we are."

"But why?"

A shrug came with the reply. "Bruised ego. Removing a powerful queen from the chessboard. The sheer sport of it. What you will. I'll grant that this is less entertaining that I'd hoped. A straight-up fight would've been better. But the boss said no, so instead I have to use this excuse."

Her composed boasting turned to a long yowling screech. One hand flew to her left cheek, where a long line had already begun to leak. No sooner did it touch her face than it, too, suffered damage. She cried out again and the scarf fell from her grasp. Molly collapsed to the platform, choking and gasping, knees up. In one hand she still held the instrument of her salvation.

The flat cap, with the blade of a razor sewn into the brim.

She barely recalled pulling off the hat and slashing the brim edge at her captor's face. The second strike to the hand had been a lucky bonus. Now agony replaced the dull ache that blocked circulation had blessedly given her before. Her throat felt as if an automobile had driven across it. Giving thanks that she had been strangled with a fashion accessory and not a wire, she sucked in wagonloads of air along with drool from the relieved Hector.

All around her feet pounded. Some pursued the fleeing Antiope to the wall, others stopped beside the fallen Molly to render aid. Ahmed fetched the torch from her pocket and half-blinded her with its beam. Far off, tardy police whistles sounded. She would have to somehow make her way out of the cemetery to avoid awkward questions.

"Get me up," she tried to say. The voice she heard was barely audible, that of a frog squashed in a roadway accident.

It must have been enough, though, for strong hands pulled her to her rubbery feet and held her there. The light stabbed her eyes fully this time, as Ahmed examined her. "Less damage than you left that fellow in the Panthéon with," he observed unhelpfully. "Nothing seems actually broken. Normal color's coming back to your, er, face."

"What there is of it, anyway," she wheezed, touching the cheek around her remaining eye.

Jason returned from his chase, holding out Hassanein's fallen stick to him. "They had a car waiting for her, of course. Headed west. She's gone."

"We'll find her," promised Ahmed. "She's too flamboyant to hide for long. Let's get Miss Molly home before the gendarmes do it for us."

13 / Kiki's flat

"You're lucky to still have your eye," observed Kiki de Montparnasse as she applied sticking plaster to the cut on Antiope's lovely cheek. She wore a green and gold silk dressing gown with kimono sleeves, with a matching head scarf. "Two inches up and you'd have an eyepatch."

The patient grunted in agreement, keeping her face still. *And wouldn't that Aulis bitch have liked that. Probably what she wanted, some company in her misery.*

Man Ray, smoking in the corner as he examined photographic proofs of a nude Kiki, asked without looking up, "You say a thug tried to rob you? Where was this? I want to make sure Kiki avoids the area."

Antiope had already established the false story in her mind by the time she had reached Ray's apartment with blood drenching her face and clothes. She had fled the scene, abandoning her allies and casualties to their respective fates. Now she licked her wounds in a two-room walk-up, wearing one of Kiki's much too short robes. Her own garments were ruined. "Outside the cemetery, can you believe it? And I wasn't the only one. It seemed like a gang of some sort was waylaying every pedestrian there."

"You should've just surrendered your handbag and spared yourself the damage," Ray advised her with the usual smug attitude of a male who had never been in danger.

"It was a gift from Coco. Would you blithely give up your

camera without a fight?" she retorted.

Kiki gave the plaster a gentle pat. "There. You'll be just fine in a few days. It's not as deep as it looks. But anything on the face bleeds like a mountain waterfall. And it shouldn't be too visible, either. A very sharp blade. It should heal without a big scar. Makeup will hide it."

"That's good." Antiope raised her chin. "This is what pays the bills, after all."

Ray snickered. "They'd come to see you on that catwalk if your face were blown completely away."

The unintentional reference to her assailant caught Antiope by surprise, but she hid it well. "Somehow I doubt that even novelty-starved Parisians would go that far."

"I don't know," Kiki said, "have you seen how they gawk at road accidents?" She stroked the hand in her new friend's lap. "How's it doing?"

The model made a fist, wincing as the bandage abraded the wound. "Fit enough to wallop the bastard if I ever see him again."

"Use the other hand," Ray told her. "Better still, whack him with Coco's purse. Those metal beads will leave a lovely mark."

"Or a proper kick to the bollocks," Kiki suggested, sliding her fingers into Antiope's.

"A gentle 'accidental' nudge beneath an omnibus," their wounded friend mused.

Antiope really intended to employ her favorite wire garrote next time, after tying her nemesis to a chair, yanking out her nails with pincers, and gouging out the remaining eye. And she intended to take hours doing it.

"So much violence," Man Ray complained. He waved the women over to him. "Come look at the shots from the show."

They dutifully moved behind his chair to peer over his shoulder. The fringed floor lamp between them cast a soft golden glow onto the large photographs in his lap. Kiki absently toyed with his receding black hair while Antiope daydreamed about doing the same to hers, only lower.

"Ick! Do I really make that silly pout when I'm out there modeling?"

"It's adorable," Kiki protested, imitating it to tease her. "So charmingly ducky."

Ray was just as bad. "Quack, quack!"

Antiope pretended to be enraged. "Perhaps I will see how lethal that handbag can be, after all."

Ray flipped the offending image over to reveal another. It was a masterpiece of light and shade, turning her into a chiaroscuro goddess. "Here. Is this better?"

Purring in satisfaction, Antiope said, "Ooh! You know it is. Can I have a print of that one for my portfolio?"

"Just so long as you remind your employers who it was that took it."

"Of course. Don't I always?"

They kept on like that for a good long while, gushing over the flattering ones and the artistic gems, joking about those that were less successful. Ray saved his avant-garde examples for last, the photos that he had manipulated via double-exposures and other tricks to turn into something odd and thought-provoking at the same time. One was of Kiki full-face, dark hair slicked back, with delicate foliage superimposed. Another made Lucita look as if she were flying like an angel, but with a pair of nude legs on her back for wings. Cosette's portrait was blended with the front end of a Bugatti racing auto, her eyes where the enormous headlamps would be.

"I swear, Manny," Kiki giggled, "you smoke too much hashish."

"Is that even possible?" he joked, stubbing out his perfectly ordinary cigarette.

To investigate the concept, they spent the next hour puffing away on Lebanon's finest through a beautiful glass hookah that Kiki had found in a Left Bank shop run by a wizened old Egyptian. Its colors closely matched her gown. Head full of the drug, which was doing wonders for her pains, Antiope accused her friend of buying it solely for that reason.

"Guilty!" Kiki confessed, lying across Ray's legs and laughing like a hyena. It was an open question whether the hashish or her own native silliness was responsible. "I just thought it was pretty. Never occurred to me I could actually use it."

Somehow Ray was managing to balance his lover on his lap,

keep the hookah upright as she thrashed about, and still sketch even more bizarre ideas for pictures than the ones he had already displayed. "I should've been using this all along. The quality of the dreamed images is much better than relying on mere chance."

"Manny's new thing is using dreams to release the imagination," Kiki explained to Antiope, who was slumped, red-eyed, in a corner of the old sofa. "There's a new movement preaching it."

Ray nodded, coughing out some smoke as he passed the hosed stem to Antiope, who held up her hand to say that she had had enough. "Surrealism. Preaching's a strong word, though I imagine poor Apollinaire might've embraced it. He coined the term, though the war got him before he could advance his theories."

Antiope nodded. "I've heard of it at some artsy parties lately. Is that Miró one of them? I got dragged into a show of his. Odd stuff. Flat, almost collage-like paintings. Nothing made any sense. The only objects I could even recognize were a tree, a bull, and an ear."

"It's symbolic language with him, and if you don't grasp his Catalonian allusions it will be even harder to puzzle out." Ray sat up, easing Kiki off. She slithered over to Antiope and proceeded to put herself inside the model's robe at several points. All their eyes were red with the drug. "A lot of us were involved with Dada, angry kids rebelling against the culture that led to the Great War. Tearing down anything conventional. If the old guard thought art and literature were supposed to be pretty, to have order and balance, then Dada would do the opposite. Entering a common urinal in a show, merely signing the artist's name to it. That sort of stuff. They called it Anti-art. Stunt art, I'd say. Like every revolution, destruction was easier than building something to take its place. That's what we're about now. You're familiar with Freud?"

Antiope chuckled. "Isn't he the fellow who's all about sleeping with your mother?" She sighed as Kiki's probing fingers made her loins gush.

"That's the sort of thing that the public seizes upon. The

sensational. But we're interested in his theories of dreams, his ideas about the subconscious mind. Rationality is played out."

Ray became more animated, as an enthusiast smoking hashish tended to get when seized by his imagination. "Look what it's gotten us. Millions dead, cities in ruins, wrecked economies. We try to release the unconscious, to let it shape our work without attempting to mold it into something conventionally pretty or immediately understandable. Art should make you think! It should start furious arguments, even fisticuffs! It's a chisel for sculpting a new society."

Sleepy, her bones turned to rubber, Antiope had little interest in art as politics. She needed to rest a bit and get home. Kiki's rubbing made her gasp with pleasure. *Well...eventually.* "I thought Princep's pistol bullets were the chisel."

"A clumsy cleaver! Art has always been the true utensil for effecting change. Maybe chisel is the wrong term. Surrealism hopes to be the surgeon's scalpel, cutting away the gangrenous tissue left by old regimes."

He went on in that vein for quite a while, but Antiope heard little of it. She drifted off in a lavender haze. Her final conscious thought, as Kiki's face slid between her long legs, was if a Serbian revolver could sunder nations, what might the Gaze of Zeus do?

~

Tugging at his blue bow tie, Harry Matthews gulped as the helmeted bobby strode past him. He unconsciously clutched his briefcase closer to his brown wool waistcoat like a mother afraid of losing her baby. All around him was a great mass of fellow travelers, every one of them, in his churning imagination, a potential government operative eager to arrest him for treason. Beside him a fellow in a trim black beard, bowler hat, and thick spectacles perused the *Times*. This gentleman appeared to have no concerns about policemen or spies. To him Charing Cross Station seemed to be nothing but a delight. Matthews' fidgety terror threatened to undo his enjoyment of the soaring steel and glass skylight and the charming French Renaissance architecture. Sweat beaded on the scientist's lip and his bulging eyes made him resemble a fish lying on ice at the market.

"Oh, do take a breath and calm down," muttered the man behind the newspaper. "The only way anyone is likely to notice you is if you continue to call attention to yourself. Might as well fire off a Very pistol and tattoo 'Here stands a traitor' on your forehead."

"Easy for you to say," grumbled Matthews, pulling his worn flat cap down lower on his forehead. He had on rumbled workingman's clothes to make him less conspicuous to anyone on the lookout for a proper learned man. "You aren't the one they'll hang."

Terremoto pressed down on the edge of his costume beard. The spirit gum was losing its grip there. "You do me a disservice. If it will relieve your mind any, I am more than liable for the same fate were an agent with access to the proper records to pinch me." Remaining in France had been even riskier until the heat brought on by Aulis' interference cooled. That was why he had left the rest of his crew a message saying only, 'Sometimes too hot the eye of Heaven shines,' their cue to go to ground until he told them otherwise.

"So we're equally culpable if caught? I suppose misery does love a little company, particularly if we're dropping through the same trapdoor."

"Such a gloomy outlook. Cheer up. You've invented a method of ending all war. With your device powered by the Gaze of Zeus, it will grant us the means to overawe any despot who might want to bully his neighbors."

"Any save the one you work for."

"One man's tyrant is another man's world savior. My Duce bears a constellation of wounds from the Great War. His friends died in windrows, as did yours. If he could guarantee that this would never happen again, even his most bitter enemies would carve mountains in his likeness."

"Somehow I doubt that my government will take that view if they get hold of me."

"The British Empire does tend to be a tad short-sighted. Can only see as far as the nearest ledger sheet." Terremoto folded his paper and tapped the other man's shoulder with it. "Chin up! We are two perfectly respectable chaps traveling to see friends in Gloucestershire. No breath of suspicion touches us. Come, our train won't wait."

The Italian inspected the heel of one shoe to satisfy himself that it remained secure. Inside its hollow core the alien gem lay hidden. Certain that he was not about to leave it behind him on the platform, he pulled the quivering Matthews up, threw his Burberry trench coat over one arm, and strolled toward the waiting train, umbrella in hand. His irksome wig itched like some biblical scourge, but he mastered the urge to scratch it, not wanting to risk dislodging the wretched thing. He was sure that he must have looked like some poorly-done stage villain, but so far no one had given him a second glance.

Until a policeman stopped them not ten steps from their carriage.

Matthews let out a tiny squeak of alarm that, fortunately, came out like a hiccup. Their way was blocked by a wall of dark blue wool. Safety lay only meters away. Accustomed to intrigue and war, Terremoto blinked through his lenses and gave the bobby a placid smile. "Good morning."

"And a good day to you, too, sir," said the officer, a tall beefy specimen who was a shining example of his type. He crossed his thick arms and gave them both a hard look.

The disguised Italian maintained his false air of relaxation, scanning the obstacle for signs that he had been looking for them. Seeing none, he ventured, "Is there a problem?"

"Well, that depends. I confess I'm worried about your friend. He seems unwell. I hope he don't have something catching."

Almost in audible relief Terremoto answered, "Oh, no, but you are wise to be vigilant. That Spanish influenza was appalling, wasn't it? God forbid we should ever have to go through that again. Barely survived it myself. Doctors despaired of my life for days."

"True enough, sir. My regiment lost a hundred men to it. The ruddy Germans hadn't managed that sort of execution on us. So...he's not sick, then? Because to be honest, he looks it."

"I confess that he does, but his sickness is in the soul, not the body." He threw a comforting arm around Matthews. "Poor cousin Edgar's brother just passed away. Terribly sudden. No warning at all. Tremendous shock. We're headed home to Tewksbury for the funeral."

That earned him a bemused frown. "If you don't mind me saying so, you don't precisely sound like a man from that part of the world."

Terremoto guffawed like every bluff Englishman he had ever heard. "Haw! I daresay I don't, what? My parents moved us all to Pisa when I was barely able to walk. Pater was in the diplomatic service, don't you know. I was raised a proper garlic-eater, in the shadow of that absurd tipping tower of theirs. Rarely been back here for any length of time. Things have certainly changed. Bigger, busier."

"Can't argue with you there, sir. But if you're sure he's not contagious...?"

"Right as rain. Merely distraught, that's all. And who dares blame him? The bond between twin brothers isn't sundered lightly."

"Twins, you say! I know something about that. My little nephews are twins and they practically read each other's minds."

"Remarkable, isn't it? Some brilliant science laddie should study that, find out what's going on there."

"Indeed he should, sir." The bobby touched the brim of his helmet. "You gentlemen have a safe trip. My condolences."

The large fellow moved off to patrol other parts of the station. When he had turned the corner Matthews let out a long-held breath that rivaled the volume of the steam boilers in the trains all around them. His complexion was so pale, with perspiration fairly streaming down his forehead, that Terremoto wondered if the inventor wasn't infectious, after all.

"A damned good thing that one of us lies for a living. Stick to the search for scientific truth, Harry. Spying isn't your game. One wonders how you managed to fight the Boers with so little aptitude for courage."

Matthews produced a half-acre of handkerchief and mopped his face. "I was twenty-two. Everyone is brave and foolish then. It's civilized living and having something to lose that makes a man soft. How do you control such fright? I nearly soiled myself."

"By making a game of it. And by keeping in mind the simple fact that unless you confess your guilt, the average person will always take you at your word." They climbed aboard the train, Terremoto propelling Matthews before him and into a seat in the rear corner, with the least possibility of eavesdroppers. His voice went low and soft. "Now what you have to do from here on out is to stay silent unless directly questioned. If that happens, remember the tall tale I just spun for that genial lout. Your name is Edgar, we're going to Tewksbury for your twin brother's funeral, and I'm your cousin Thomas, home from the Continent."

"As you say. Rather a lot to remember."

"Nonsense. What's the formula for the Lorentz force?"

Though frowning, Matthews immediately replied, "$F = q [E + (v \times B)]$. Why on earth --- ?"

Terremoto winked at him and grinned. "See? Nothing wrong with your memory. If you can recall that, then 'Edgar + dead twin + Tewksbury + Thomas = funeral' should be simple."

"Telling everyone I'm a mute would be even simpler."

"Not true. That's the sort of oddity that attracts attention. We want to be unmemorable."

With a slight jerk and a hiss of steam the train began to move. "I'm all for that."

"Enjoy your anonymity. Soon the whole world will know your name."

"Just so long as it isn't the same way they remember Guy Fawkes."

"Bah! He's a national villain because he failed to blow something up. With our new-found bauble explosions will be as easy as flicking a finger."

"In theory. It remains to be seen how well that terrifying sparkler of yours will match with my device. We may leave a smoking crater in Gloucestershire."

"Nothing ventured, nothing gained, is that not the adage?"

"Nothing ventured, maybe live to a ripe old age."

"Not so." Terremoto leaned in to whisper in his comrade's

ear. "If you fail to venture upon this, you most assuredly shall not live to a ripe old age." He sat back and smiled. "I say this as a friend."

14/ Olympic Opening Ceremony, July 5

A full week later Molly still had trouble swallowing.

She had made the iceman happy with her extra custom, as the neck swelling made her look like a snake that had just ingested a giant egg. An ice-filled towel wrapped around her throat provided some blessed relief. Much aspirin was downed, though she longed for a bit of morphine. Precious little writing got done, as the discomfort proved too distracting. Thankfully, the doctor had pronounced the damage surprisingly minor, despite her misery. Molly had little difficulty tolerating it. Compared to the months of agonizing recovery she had had with her facial wound this was no more than the scratch of a rose thorn in comparison, though the arrival of her monthly scourge at the same time seemed a blow too low. *Ah, well, get all the misery done with at once, I say.* Lying in bed re-reading her autographed proof text of Lawrence's *Seven Pillars of Wisdom* (which she had helped him to rewrite after he had left the first draft in a train station five years earlier), while flexing her toes and bobbing her head, was the extent of her day. Though he had changed her name and sex, she recognized herself as one of his comrades in Arabia.

Hector had dutifully cuddled with her, certain that this would put her on the road to recovery, along with claiming his hound-taxes in a bid to prevent her from poisoning herself with too much rich food. Madame Planant, the building concierge, had made it her mission to ascend from *la loge* on the ground floor to fuss over Molly with tea, cakes, and soup. A tall scrawny stork of a woman, she would burst in unannounced, inquiring after her charge in a cheery songlike voice, burdened with a tray of 'Parisian medicine.' For the first few days Molly had forced a smile and a mumbled *merci*, though she had been able to down only the liquids. Those had been heady days for Hector, recipient of all those dainty morsels that she had to forego. His mistress had invented a story about catching her scarf in a revolving door. If poor Madame Planant had been given any inkling of the sort of activities her tenant actually got into, the poor old Breton might have fainted dead away.

Those sordid adventures, particularly the ones of that day in the Panthéon and Montparnasse Cemetery, two oddly-similar sites of the honored dead where she had fought for her life, might have given the withered concierge nightmares. Certainly, they had done so for Molly. Several times since that day she had been jerked awake, clawing at sweaty sheets, by horrific images of the dead and injured men. Their skulls, worm-eaten and grave-stained, screamed at her as the bodies lurched after her while she desperately tried to run away through knee-high piles of bones, getting nowhere. And the longer each dream lasted, ever more angry animated corpses joined them, wearing Turkish or German uniforms full of the bullet holes she had put there. Every time it all ended with Molly being surrounded as they all laughed and chanted that at least their decaying faces did not look as bad as hers.

Several times the fancy purple car that had pestered Ahmed had cruised down her street, slow as a donkey, so that its unseen passenger might possibly catch a glimpse of her. Molly would make a sour face and stick out her tongue at it, hoping its owner would see. She knew who it was and was not about to grant them the satisfaction of flinging open her door to them.

At least no one tried to kill her.

The surly Italians had vanished from her life as suddenly as they had appeared. Having gained the Gaze of Zeus they had forgotten her and moved on to whatever the next part of their scheme might be. As welcome as that was to her, Molly could not help but be concerned as to their intentions. If half of what Hassanein claimed about the crystal was true, it could power a weapon of frightening destructive potential. Having that in the hands of the Fascists was unsettling, to say the least. But something that dangerous would be hard to keep secret. She would need to pester her contacts in the foreign and intelligence services, as well as the Sûreté, to see if any bizarre happenings sprang up on the international scene, such as blue Hindu gods cavorting about.

Her most recent talk with Sanglier, the morning after the affair in the cemetery, had hardly been a collegial chat about geopolitics. He had stood beside her bed and turned nearly as purple as the flesh of her neck, threatening to jail her on a list of charges as thick as the Paris phone book. For some reason he had been particularly upset about her tricked-out cap with the hidden blade, as if that had been the most heinous offense of the evening. She let him rant, recognizing it as more born of having to complete the paperwork involved than true anger at her. After all, she had been flat on her back with a doctor fussing over her at the time, more a victim than a perpetrator.

Eventually he had stopped to take a breath and let slip that the dead man on Baudelaire's monument had been a British intelligence operative. He also seemed to think that the self-poisoned Hindu was a member of an Indian nationalist group. What they had been doing in the cemetery with Italian agents was anyone's guess. But he had few thanks for her for dropping it all into his lap. At least he had the Gallic grace to inquire after her health and be solicitous for her safety while badgering her. Then he had stomped out, grumbling about the wretched mess she had brought him.

All of that could wait, though. Today was the first Sunday of July and she felt well enough to venture out with the rest of Paris to the grand opening ceremony of the Olympic Games. Ahmed would be marching in with the rest of the tiny Egyptian contingent and she felt that, at the very least, she owed him the favor of her suffering the torment of being trapped in an immense noisy crowd. After all, he had pulled her chestnuts out of the fire more than once that day. So she walked Hector twice as long as usual to inspire a good doggy nap while she was out (as usual, talking to every dog she met while completely ignoring its owner), donned a dropped-waist white frock with embroidered strawberries on it, the loathed silk stockings (*might as well suffer all the way*), and employed cosmetics to make her mask look as realistic as possible. Then she added gray smoked lenses to it, plopped her favorite veiled straw mushroom hat onto her head, plucked a dainty white lady's cane from the stand, shouldered her handbag, and set off for the stadium.

She had anticipated the mobs of people being enough to make her collapse into a corner and weep, but her imagination had fallen far short of the reality. Just getting to the Métro stop was difficult enough, thanks to so many tri-colored bodies on the sidewalks that she felt like she was being carried along by a patriotic ant colony. It seemed that every breathing soul in Paris had come out. After the horror and privation of the Great War it was certainly understandable that the city was more than ready for a party, particularly one meant to showcase the resurrected nation. Well-lubricated citizens laughed, shouted, and sang as they pressed to the trains. Molly's clenched fists dug fingernail marks into her palms, her usual response to being trapped with so many people. Her teeth clicked and her head bobbed as she stared at the ground, stepping across sidewalk seams while desperately willing herself to relax. Every sound created a blinding splash of color behind her eye, swirling and exploding like demonic fireworks

Maybe this was a bad idea. No one will notice if I go back home and lie down for a year or two.

Her respect for Ahmed Hassanein overrode the natural inclination to flee, however. Mastering her fears, she bought her ticket and let the throng bear her onto the car. No seats were available, so she clung to the strap, knuckles white, and tried to ignore the color-bombs created by the smell of sweat, wine, and packed lunches. Underground, the noise of the train over-topped all else and soon a steady gray-gold wave danced at the edges of her vision. That became almost soothing, but just as she almost grew adjusted to the circumstances, the car halted, and she had to endure the stampede and the thoughtless jostling all over again.

The Métro had not yet reached the suburb where the Stade Olympique de Colombes lay. New lines were under construction, but they still had to be completed. Thankfully, extra omnibuses had been laid on by the city authorities to handle the massive flow of humanity from the last Métro stop to the stadium. To Molly's great annoyance, however, they all rushed the buses as if they were the last lifeboat on the *Titanic*. Again, she was elbowed and shoved. Just before she managed to arrive at the steps of an available bus, an unaware matron's parasol handle fetched her a fearsome whack on the side of her tender neck. Red-orange agony throbbed up into her head. A pained yelp escaped her, sounding like a kicked puppy. Everyone around her turned to give her the briefest of concerned glances, then kept on with their job of swarming the transports. Only one of them actually stopped to render assistance.

"My Lord! Are you all right?" a kind voice inquired. "That lady didn't even seem to worry that she'd hurt someone."

The accent was polished American. Molly blinked away the tears in her eye and examined the friendly woman before her. They were nearly of a height even with the other woman's low-heeled shoes and she did not have to look down at her. She saw rich blue eyes, dark hair in an Eton crop, so short that it belonged on a young man, lovely fair skin worthy of a Grecian statue, and thin exquisitely maintained lips. About Molly's age, she wore a dropped-waist forest green frock with gold trim embroidered with little black birds. A long *de rigueur* strand of pearls hung down her front. Her splendid little felt hat with a tiny hint of downward brim seemed to be a feminized man's trilby.

Not beautiful, but handsome and striking. Casts a spell on people. She knows it, too. I'll bet she usually gets what she wants. And my intuition tells me that she wants a woman in her arms as often as not.

"I'm fine, thank you," she muttered, voice hoarse, looking away, as she always did with strangers. No doubt that puzzled the other woman, who clearly possessed all the social graces, but it could not be helped. Molly dropped her chin so the mask remained as unobtrusive as possible, hidden by the veil and her hat brim.

"Are you, too, an American?" she asked, nearly squealing in delight as she switched to English. "Wonderful! Come sit with me. We'll gab like a pair of schoolgirls all the way to the stadium."

Before Molly could think to object to that worse-case-scenario, or could even decide if she wanted to object, her arm was commandeered by the other lady, who towed her on board the nearest omnibus with a patrician wave of her long, manicured hand. "Make way, please! This poor mademoiselle has been injured! She simply must have a seat and some air. Merci beau coups!"

The crowd scattered before her like gazelles avoiding a particularly well-dressed lion. In a trice Molly found herself deposited in a corner seat as far as possible away from the crush, her savior beside her. Pale orange glow-worms called attention to her new friend's perfume, a heady mixture of lavender and citrus. At least it did her the favor of covering the car's other scents, which were rather less floral. When Molly tensed every muscle at having her knee familiarly patted, the glamorous woman next to her cocked her head and gave her a hard look.

"Oh, come now, I won't bite!" She leaned in closer, whispering. "Unless you want me to." One finger lifted the veil to get a better look at the young object she had acquired. When she caught sight of the mask she let out a tiny gasp, instantly stifled.

"Don't say you're sorry," begged Molly, more harshly than she had intended. "Don't make pitying little lady-noises. And for God's sake don't hug me and commiserate over my supposed plight."

The other woman primly set her hands in her own lap. "I am sorry, though. Not that you were injured – it is an injury, yes? – but that I let myself react like a startled child. It's not as if I've never seen that sort of thing before. We all have, sad to say. Everywhere one turns there are empty sleeves and worse. I should know better than to make you uncomfortable and for that I do apologize."

Molly waved it off. "It's fine. At least you didn't shriek and point. 'Mama! Look at that! Halloween isn't for six months yet.'"

Her companion shuddered. "Awful."

Snorting, Molly chuckled, "No, awful is when I take it off and yell 'Boo!' at the little darling."

Sympathy frowned the other's brow. "That bad, is it?"

"They wet their pants."

A brief pall fell over the conversation as her imagination no doubt conjured horrors. "Well, enough of that. This is supposed to be a party. Let's put on a happy face."

"So to speak."

Again, the elegant American blushed at her faux pas. "Lord, I'm hopeless today."

"But not helpless. You handled my situation with aplomb."

"Is that the snooty French word for 'being bossy'?"

"If not, it should be. I was about to have a screaming fit."

"I should say. Your neck is terribly swollen."

"No, it was already like that. A more recent injury. Healing, though. The near fit was from too many people around me. I have limited social tolerance."

The bus lurched and rumbled north and west toward the stadium. From the look of the traffic, it would be a long trip. "Then this mob must really set you off. One wonders what the enraged masses were like in 1789 if they behave like this for a mere sporting event."

"Yes, they're awfully rambunctious. But it's France's first chance to shine since the war. They've had to put up with an awful lot."

"You've been here that whole time?"

Molly nodded, recalling the food shortages and the uncertainty, not to mention the influenza nightmare that she had been lucky to avoid. "Not the war itself, I was in the Transjordan for that. But they evacuated me here in 1918 after I was wounded."

The other's eyes widened. "You were wounded? In action? I thought...I mean I naturally assumed ---"

"Don't worry, you aren't the first. There are precious few women foolish enough to go charging into battle."

"I should do an article about you. That's what I do. I'm a writer for the American magazines." She threw up her hands. "What am I doing? You don't even know my name." Her hand came up. Barnes. Djuna Barnes. Pleasure to meet you."

Now it was Molly's turn to be surprised. "Really? I adore you! Your work, at any rate. If I weren't so shy, I might have come looking for you. That piece about James Joyce in *Vanity Fair*. I ate it up."

They shook hands, Barnes holding on a trifle longer than necessary. "Awfully nice of you to say so. Though with a subject like that, it was hard to fail."

"I appreciate good writing. It's my job, too. Molly Aulis."

Barnes grinned in recognition. "The travel writer! You do those marvelous articles about faraway places like Arabia and Persia. Make us feel that we went there ourselves."

Molly laughed. This was turning into a better day than she had dared to hope for. In order not to ruin it with too many of her oddities, she adopted the persona of a cheery young schoolgirl who enjoyed chatting. It would not last for long, but playacting helped her with Sanglier and others. "If you'd ever seen the ladies' toilet facilities, you'd be glad that I went there in your stead."

"You're an archeologist first, aren't you? I seem to recall that your father was famous for it."

"He was my teacher. Had me out on digs when I could barely walk. That was why I was in the desert when the war came. Ended up fighting with T.E. Lawrence." She touched the mask. "That's how I got this lifetime souvenir."

Of course, that turned the conversation to her exploits during the war. Fifteen minutes later they were still trapped behind innumerable autos and buses, Molly's injured throat ached from talking so much, and Djuna gaped like a goldfish.

"Astonishing! That a woman, an American woman, could do all of that and no one knows the first thing about it. I could churn out stories about you for a year."

"I'd rather you didn't. I can barely tolerate the postman coming to my door, let alone crowds of gawkers."

"I could make you anonymous then. 'The mysterious sharpshooting lioness of the desert.' That sort of thing."

Molly cocked her head. "Well, maybe. I'll think about it. But don't you usually write about the arts these days? Why are you going to the ceremony? Surely your editors at *McCall's* don't have you on assignment for sports?"

"No, they have chisel-jawed men with cigars for that. But the Games have an arts competition. That's my bailiwick. I'm here today to get a feel for the atmosphere." She grimaced as a much-mustachioed gentleman sent a toxic cloud of pipe smoke her way. "And there's more of it than I care for."

"Shall we walk, then? It's a goodly hike but I'm up for it."

"Yes, let's. I'll wager that we'll arrive before this lumbering conveyance."

Moments later they took advantage of yet another traffic pause to get off and stroll toward the stadium. Crowded as the sidewalk was, it still felt better than being trapped on the foul bus. Djuna took Molly's arm again, talking breezily of her own life and work, since her friend had already done the same. As she did so she coolly adjusted to Molly's quirky manner of walking across cracks and seams, as well as her other idiosyncrasies.

Molly learned of Barnes' upbringing in New York, easily as odd as her own. She had been born in a log cabin along the Hudson River, daughter of a free-love polygamist and granddaughter of a literary suffragette. Her formal schooling had been almost nonexistent, though her remarkable grandmother, who had hosted her own literary salon, made sure that she learned to read and write well. With essentially no training or official qualifications, she had breezed into the office of the immensely popular *Brooklyn Daily Eagle* newspaper and declared, "I can draw and write, and you'd be a fool not to hire me!" They had taken her at her word and soon found that she had told the truth. So did all the other New York City papers, and she wrote for them all as the Great War began, specializing in daring 'event journalism.' It thrilled Molly to hear of the wild spectacles Djuna had staged in order to write about them in admittedly-purple prose, such as hanging from a building to be rescued by firemen or entering a gorilla's cage at the zoo.

"People often accuse me of living an intentionally wild life, in order to have fodder for copy," Molly said, "but you seem to have literally done that."

"It was mostly out of necessity, to tell the truth," smiled Djuna, steering them clear of a rowdy knot of sailors. "I didn't have the posh education or experience of the other reporters, so I staged stunts to get into print and to stay in my editor's eye."

"I heard about the forced-feeding one even in Mesopotamia. My colleagues didn't know why I was cheering while reading the paper."

"Yes, well...that was the one that I felt was more legitimate than the others. Though it looked like a put-up job to sell copy, I truly wanted people to know what those poor women went through. Who knows? In a small way it may have even helped us get the vote."

For the *New York World* Djuna had submitted to a medical forced-feeding in 1914, just as the imprisoned suffragettes on hunger strikes had endured. They had wrapped her like a mummy (Molly particularly remembered that photograph) and run a rubber tube up her nose. Terms such as 'torture and outrage,' 'brutal usurpation,' and 'futile defiance' had made the experience akin to a rape, which was accurate enough. The illustrated story had caused a sensation at the time and could still evoke shudders in any woman. Djuna gained enough respect from that to progress to theatre reviews, features, fiction (often accompanied by her own delicate drawings that resembled Aubrey Beardsley's), even a few boxing pieces from a woman's perspective. She also managed to write scripts for the Provincetown Players, as they were part and parcel of her Greenwich Village Bohemian circle.

"That was all splendid training, of course," she declared. "One should dare and risk everything when one is young and ignorant." Her hand squeezed Molly's. "Nothing like what you went through, brave girl."

A warm thrill went along Molly's arm and down into her loins. "It's easy to be brave when you have no other choice."

"I rather doubt that. I know enough about the British upper class and the Arab mind to know that they would have moved heaven and earth to get a woman out of a war zone."

Molly snorted, ducking her head to shade her eye from the glaring sun as they changed direction. "And out of their way. None of them took me seriously or wanted me there except Major Lawrence."

"There's someone I'd dearly love to interview. Like a character in an adventure novel. Could you get me a meeting, do you think?"

"Hard to say. He's a queer duck, especially now that he's out of his beloved desert. I hear that he's even rejoined the army as a private soldier. Ordinary peaceful living is proving more difficult than cruel war. But I can write him and see."

Barnes stroked her beneath the chin with one long finger. "That would be lovely," she cooed.

Her voice created lush brown velvet curlicues in Molly's mind. Used to being in control, holding all at arm's length with her attitude or even by physical force, she felt faint terror at being so moved by this smooth fragrant demi-goddess. Perhaps it was merely tactile starvation, the novelty of anyone honestly wanting to touch her that way, no matter how innocently. But was Djuna being coquettish, likely her default mode, or was there honest interest behind her fripperies?

"*Repulsive Women*," Molly said, barely audible.

"What's that?"

"Your *Book of Repulsive Women*."

"That little old thing?" Djuna shrugged. "Juvenilia, better off forgotten. You've read it? Hardly anyone else has."

"I own it. It's in my bedside table drawer."

Lines crinkled around Djuna's eyes as she smiled. "Well, aren't you full of surprises."

Molly thought of the lines that had made the most impact on her nearly a decade before, when she had stumbled upon the pamphlet of sultry erotic imagery, thinking that Barnes was speaking directly to her, an odd young woman with unpopular urges. Pausing in a shop doorway, she recited them to their author while staring at a sign across the street.

> *We'd strain to touch those lang'rous*
> *Length of thighs,*
> *And hear your short sharp modern*

Babylonic cries.

"Why, aren't you sweet?' Djuna said, voice lower and breathier than it had been only a moment before. Her warm hand slid along Molly's neck, painted thumbnail grazing the mask's edge. Molly sighed and leaned into it, recalling all of the times she had been touched by loving hands, feminine and masculine, before the maiming. A single tear oozed out of her eye, making Paris and her new friend resemble something seen through the bottom of a just-drained wine glass.

Djuna leaned in close and Molly sucked in her scent as she waited for a kiss. But the lovely lips passed by her expectant mouth to nip at the left ear. As that was the artificial one, she felt nothing. A second's surprise could be felt in Djuna's hand as she stiffened, then recovered. Teasing the short hair at the nape of Molly's neck with one finger, she quoted her own poem back to her.

> *We see your arms grow humid*
> *In the heat;*
> *We see your damp chemise lie*
> *Pulsing in the beat*
> *Of the over-hearts left oozing*
> *At your feet.*

Unable to hold off any longer, Molly clutched her close and kissed her with all the ardor that her damaged body and soul could manage.

While Djuna returned the favor with a half-laughing *mmmm*, as if savoring a delectable chocolate, Molly squirmed to the unfamiliar warm tingling beneath her skirt. It had been long years since she had felt that from any agency but her own hand, heat and swelling and dampness. She almost feared leaving a puddle on the sidewalk. Shoving that silly image aside, she tongued and nibbled the other woman's mouth, lost in the warm sensations.

A shout and a great impact knocked her back into the shop door. Minimally apologetic male French voices blurted out something inaudible. The pack of well-sauced young men continued toward the stadium. Molly felt an ache in her lower spine from colliding with the door's brass handle. That was nothing, though, compared to the delightful feeling of Djuna's body crushed against her front from breast to knee. When the other American peeled herself away the sense of loss was an agony.

"Rude louts," Djuna grumbled, sending a fiery glare after the men.

"Lovely butts, though," mused Molly, laughing.

That set Barnes off, as well. For a long moment they giggled like girls in their little niche, which at least let Molly's passions settle down. Now it occurred to her that she had been more than halfway to sapphically copulating in public with a stranger. She imagined getting arrested for that after evading Sanglier's threatened prosecution for much worse offenses and started laughing even harder.

"What's so funny now?" asked Djuna as they resumed their trek to Colombes, surrounded by what seemed like three-quarters of the French nation.

"Oh, nothing I care to explain. Just thinking about the absurdity of what we just did."

"Love is nothing but an absurdity. Giving into the sort of insanity that we shoot mad dogs for. And the act itself is comically undignified." She sighed and took Molly's hand, not caring who might judge them. "That said, we are adhering to life now with our last muscle -- the heart."

"Are you quoting yourself again? The last bit sounded awfully polished."

"Guilty. What's the use of being a writer if one can't spread pat phrases about like rose petals?"

Molly took an awkward extra-long step to avoid landing on a pavement crack. "Most of mine would hardly have the same cachet. I don't write fiction. Hard to wax poetic about Armenian politics or cultural norms in Afghanistan."

"I don't know about that. Have you read this young Hemingway fellow? Another ex-pat, like us. He has quite a knack for making the truth sound like fiction. Very simple sentences, not flowery at all. Manly, I suppose you'd call it, but not dry. I hear that he's working on a novel in that same sort of style. Thrilling if he can pull it off. We may see him here today. He's frightfully sporty. Probably doing a piece on the festivities."

Now the Olympic stadium appeared over the heads of those in front of them. A line of trees made it difficult to see clearly, but as they passed through them, they saw the pale roofs that covered the straight portions of the cinder track. The rest of the crowded oval was open to the sunny summer sky. Molly hoped their seats would be in the shade. Her sensitivity to light was as pronounced as her weakness to noise, even with her shaded glasses and hat. Already she was dreading the experience and clutched Djuna's hand to the point of turning the fingers blue.

"Why, what's the matter, sweet thing?" Barnes asked, peeling her hand free and using it to hug her close.

"I don't do well in crowds. Or in bright light."

"Yes? How on earth did you manage a battlefield in the desert then?"

"Necessity is the mother of toleration. Plus, it didn't get truly bad until after the injury. Readjusted something in my head."

Djuna kissed her. "Poor baby. I'll make sure we get some shade. Shall I stick my fingers in your ears?"

"No need. *I know some other places you can stick them, though.* I brought wax to plug them. Gets a bit dodgy getting it into what's left of the bad one, but I'll manage."

The women were in line waiting to present their tickets. They could hear the noise of those already seated, clapping and chanting to something unseen. As the official start of the ceremony was not for another forty minutes, it must have been a spontaneous reaction rather than part of the festivities. Molly blinked in the sun, finally blocking it with one hand. Whether from that or the anticipation of the misery to come when packed in the throng, her head was beginning to throb. She hoped that Hassanein appreciated what she was enduring for his sake.

As Djuna chattered on about something fashion related, Molly's attention wandered. Her interest in women's clothes only extended to what was necessary to blend in or to do her job. Frequently she had to interview people who did care about that sort of thing and she would be required to look professional to be taken seriously. So she had not only acquired a few attractive dresses but had even cultivated an acquaintance at Madame Formidable's, one of her models, to instruct her in the proper selection and wearing of such articles. Colette was a vacant sybarite, but Molly had to admit that she knew her business. She also had to admit that the girl's splendid physical charms had kept Molly coming back far beyond what had been required. The model had suggested that her remarkable height might make her suitable for that line of work. Either she had been making polite vacant conversation or she had not gotten a good look at the face beneath the veil. Molly rather doubted that Madame Formidable could be so broad-minded as to put such damaged goods on her catwalk.

The thoughts of fashion led her to appraise what other women at the stadium entrance were wearing. It beat dwelling on the pain in her throat and head or the upcoming sensory assault. Peter Pan collars looked to be popular, along with narrow little belts or drawstrings to cinch the low waists of the dresses at the hipbones. Fabrics were light and airy, as the day promised to be warm. After all, it was high summer. Cloche hats were everywhere, of course, many with attached scarves. Some had the front brim turned up, though most did not, to combat the sun. There were many wide-brimmed straw affairs, too. Molly felt positively trendy, which lightened her mood and irked her at the same time.

Then she saw the woman who had tried to kill her.

15 / Olympic Opening Ceremony

It was only a fleeting glance, mostly from the rear, but she was positive that it had been the dusky monster with the deadly scarf. Cosmopolitan as Paris was, there were still few women of that striking tawny complexion and high lovely cheekbones.

Even fewer with a neat razor slice across one of the latter.

The tall woman – Molly's current circle certainly ran to altitudinous ladies – was on the arm of a richly-dressed man in a top hat. His companion wore a blood-red silk dress with an irregularly-cut hem, and a wide-brimmed black hat with a huge white camellia flower on one side. They were being greeted by Olympic officials at a special entrance reserved for dignitaries. Just before they vanished inside Molly spied the cut on her face that Molly's cap brim had left there. Covered in skillful makeup, it was not obvious, but Molly's eye had been immediately drawn to it when she had recognized her assailant. To confirm her identity, there was another on the back of one hand, as well. But an instant later she was gone and there was precious little Molly could do about it. She rather doubted that the hard-eyed men pretending to not look like security guards would permit her to stroll in after her and fetch the bitch a clout to the head with her cane.

By the time Molly ceased fretting over spying her enemy, while feeling concern for the hapless gentleman escorting her, they had reached the front of the line. Their tickets were for a spot facing the sun, as she had feared, but once again Djuna worked her magic -- a combination of glamorous imperiousness and using Molly's status as a tragic war victim -- and got them prime seats beneath the immense awning. Molly's relief at that was palpable, as she now only had to worry about the noise and odor of over forty thousand enthusiastic spectators. Both of those issues were already creating spikes of raw red color in her mind. From her handbag she plucked a small lump of yellow beeswax. Tearing a thimble-sized bit off it, she rolled it in her hands until it was soft, then worked it into her right ear. Immediately the ugly hues somewhat subsided. After glancing about to see if anyone was staring, she reached up under her artificial left ear, using the large hat brim as cover, and found the little nub left after the surgeries. She knew it looked like half of an old, dried apricot. Another piece of the wax entered the channel there. When the mask had been resettled at its proper angle, even more of the unsettling images had faded. With a relieved sigh, she relaxed as much as she was able, settling against Djuna's body.

"All better now?"

"Much. Though I won't know until the real shouting starts."

Djuna produced a pair of small binoculars, the kind favored for horse races. Made of brass and decorated in mother-of-pearl, they perfectly matched the rest of her. Smiling, Molly dug into her bag and found her own version, a collapsible monocular lens that packed flat as a cigarette case. She thumbed the switch and it popped into life. Her companion pronounced it adorable.

"Not much point in having paired lenses," Molly said, scanning the field, "except for keeping up appearances. Anyway, I grew so accustomed to peering into a rifle telescope, this seems more natural."

While Barnes perused her program, Molly surveyed the stadium, examining all of it for sign of the beautiful would-be murderess, and also for any of her accomplices. It could hardly be a coincidence that the dangerous woman was here today. Her instincts, which had long ago learned to mistrust coincidences, told her that something nasty was afoot. As she gazed out, she took note of the impressive scale of the whole affair. It reminded her of an ancient Roman triumph, which was precisely the organizers' intent. Colorful banners and national flags danced atop the rim of the stadium. Enormous posters abounded, including one of a javelin thrower and another of a gaggle of half-naked men giving a stretched-arm salute à la Mussolini. They dwarfed the people standing beneath them. Legions of fit lads marched in procession. For all the lip service paid to the Greeks who had started it all, it seemed that the Caesars were more present in spirit than Pericles.

The Italian Fascists must be drooling over it all.

As the opening ceremony began, Molly split her attention between the events on the field and the patrons in the stands, toes clenching and shoulders twitching. The straw boater manufacturers were certainly getting rich nowadays. Not that the bowler sellers or homburg hawkers were going broke. All outnumbered the ladies' headwear, though the distaff element had come out in more force than she had expected. Now all the heads they decorated turned as one toward the end of the stadium, where an enormous white Olympic flag was being carried out flat, like a wounded man on a stretcher, by young men in blue blazers and white trousers. Its colored rings gleamed in the strong sun, as did the brass instruments of the military marching band that followed it. They entered from a tunnel, above which the new Latin motto of the games had been painted: Citius, Altius, Fortius.

Well, if there was ever any doubt about the Romans inspiring all of this...

The dignitaries in the front row near the cinder track, led by Baron Coubertin, all stood, inspiring the rest of the spectators to do the same. Slim and dapper, with white hair and a matching brushy moustache, the founder of the modern Games doffed his hat as the flag came by. Others mimicked the gesture. All cheered and applauded, including the newly-elected French President Doumergue and England's handsome Prince of Wales to his right. Everyone remained standing, their enthusiasm growing, as phalanxes of athletes paraded behind the flag. Each group marched behind its national flag, with a sign identifying the nation. Molly was pleased to see a smattering of women competitors, though she was less enthused that they were forced to wear skirts. Through it all a film crew just on the infield cranked their camera, immortalizing all present at eighteen frames per second. No doubt that would be in Parisian cinemas the next day and around the world soon after.

She saw that the numbers of athletes for each country looked to be about what one would expect, with some notable exceptions. Naturally, the host's contingent was the largest, prompting such insane noise from the crowd that she winced and covered her already-plugged ears. Black and blue flooded her vision like a moving bruise. Next largest were the Americans, of course, and the British. All victors in the Great War. Germany was notably absent, still banned as a pariah. Italy had brought nearly as many as the English. Molly wondered how many were working for the people who had tried so hard to dispatch her.

Better luck next time. Faster, Higher, Stronger...

Incredibly, the Belgians and the Dutch nearly as numerous as the Italians. Who was left at home there? Ireland, that newly liberated nation, brought a few dozen. *If they play the English in rugby there'll be more blood spilled than at the Somme.* Egypt boasted around thirty. Though she spotted Hassanein, looking dashing in his green blazer and boater, Molly failed to catch his eye with her wave. Poor India had only seven, despite all their teeming millions. Someday that would change, when Gandhi finally mobilized them to nudge the English out. Perhaps it might take more than a nudge. She knew old-timers who could recall the Great Mutiny of 1857. They still shuddered at the memory. As she entertained that gruesomely happy thought while examining the proud Indian athletes, her mouth dropped.

One of them had attacked her in the cemetery.

Naturally, she scoffed to herself. Surely, she was mistaken. But as the competitors all took their places on the field for the Olympic Oath, facing the grandstand, she got a good long second look with her monocular. Sure enough, it was the archer who had nearly got her before she had tangled him with his dead comrade's corpse. She had been nearly nose-to-mask with him while rejoicing in his terror. He looked very young, now that she had the leisure to examine him, and handsome. Probably Kshatriya caste, a warrior, to judge from his bearing and the government's likely selection bias. The man stood so proud you would have thought he was already being awarded a gold medal. Molly snickered to herself that he had not looked so haughty when her boot had been on his face.

Two known assassins at this affair. Doesn't look good.

Now that the Games of the VIIIth Olympiad had officially become more interesting to her, she applied her lens and attention skills with more gusto. Squinting at every face on the field, she spotted one amongst the Italian contingent who might have been a Panthéon troublemaker, though she would not have bet her life on it. None of the other athletes tingled her memory. But that hardly meant that they were all innocent. There had to be a sizeable cadre of others supporting the ones she had already encountered. She could have met a dozen while standing in line with her ticket. One could be creeping up on her that very instant with a stiletto and she would never have known it.

Excusing herself to Djuna, who was cheerily chatting about perfumes with the fetching young lady next to her (*ah, well, so much for our eternal romance*), Molly announced that she was off to find the ladies' facilities. She promised a full report on their convenience and cleanliness. That permitted her to stand, stretch, and assure herself that there was not actually a man with a knife sneaking up on her. With many muttered apologies she squeezed past innumerable knees, gained the aisle, and made her way back toward the entrance. Before she got that far she detoured to the open space in the rear, to recover from having been so confined and to get a wide view of crowd and athletes. It was a splendid sight, despite the noise and brightness. Flags, banners, bands, ranks of strong young women and men she wouldn't mind seeing in her bed. Coubertin was giving a speech about camaraderie and courage that sounded as much about the Great War as about the Great Games. Despite it all seeming just a bit too martial, she hoped that it would live up to its promise and promote peace. The world – France, in particular – could certainly use it.

An orange-painted aeroplane rattled overhead, a

photographer leaning out of the rear seat to capture the moment for future generations. Molly hoped that there would be some. *If we don't recover that damned crystal, it may not come to pass.* Higher up and farther off, a giant cigar of an airship hung in the sky. She smiled at the memory of her single time aboard one of them, a captured German zeppelin. Having learned the rudiments of flying a standard biplane, she would not mind a turn at the controls of that gassy behemoth, just to see what the difference might be. That whimsical thought was erased by the return of the plane for another, lower, pass. It kicked up some debris, to the clear annoyance of the richly clad dignitaries. As it flashed by, she brought her lens up to look again.

"Nieuport 12," said a low warm voice beside her in good French, but with a southern American tone. "The two-seater version. Never wanted to mix it up with a Fokker Tri in one of those, but they made for a right nice flight. Stable, easy to handle. That's what you want in a recon bird."

Molly stiffened when she felt someone come up on her blind side. The accent had relaxed her somewhat, but she still shifted her weight and prepared to use the cane. But a good look at the man beside her allayed the fears. Three inches shorter than her, he stood with the erect bearing of a successful soldier, notwithstanding his well-tailored tan suit, red tie, and stiff celluloid collar. To judge from his sturdy frame and balanced movements, he was trained in a warrior's art. Boxing, most likely. His skin was the color of the darkest mahogany and his black hair was wooly and short. She was reminded by this handsome fellow of the proud features of African masks she had seen, all designed to inspire respect and awe. *I wonder how much respect he'd get speaking to an unescorted white woman back home in Georgia or wherever he's from? No wonder he prefers to live here.*

He held out his hand for her monocular. "May I, ma'am? I'm thinking I know those boys."

When his arm stretched out the movement revealed the inside of his coat. Molly spied the ribbons of several war decorations there, tastefully out of sight but kept close to the heart of their winner. She recognized the *Medaille Militaire,*

France's second-highest award, a yellow bar with green at each end, and the *Croix de Guerre*, green with thin red stripes, bronze star in the center. In the hospital Molly had seen quite a few of those awards for valor given, pinned to the pillows of other grievously disfigured patients. One had been pinned to hers. This American was an authentic French war hero. And a combat volunteer to boot. As a foreigner he would have had to enlist, probably first in the Légion Etrangère. He had actively sought the fight when he could have avoided it easily. Not for the first time it struck her how differently he would have been treated by his own country.

"Of course." She let him take the little lens, noting his swollen and misshapen knuckles. *As I thought. Boxing damage. Looks like he nearly ruined that hand. But judging by his face, he hit the other fellows a lot more often.*

He squinted through it, tracking the sunset-hued plane across the sky. As it vanished beyond the edge of the stadium to come around again, he grinned, nodded, and returned the glass to its owner. "Uh-huh. Thought so. That's Billy Jackson taking the pictures. I'd heard that he'd bought a surplus plane and gone into the newsreel business. Looks like he's rigged his camera to work on the Etévé ring, so he can swivel it nice and smooth like a Lewis gun and not have to hold it up himself. Clever." His handsome head nodded up to her. "Thank you, ma'am. Bonnie little item you have there."

Despite her distaste for engaging strangers in conversation, Molly stiffened her spine and spoke to him. No doubt he had quite a story to tell. "It's easily packed. And in my case binoculars would be a waste of expensive glass." She flicked a finger at the left side of her face.

"I spied the mask but didn't want to mention it. A touchy subject with most folks. Beautiful work, though. Not easy to notice, but us pilots get used to looking for the little things. An accident? Cancer?"

"Boche potato-masher, actually."

His eyes widened, then his features hardened with rage. "No? Those bastards. Pardon my language, ma'am. Attacking women never did bother them much. How'd it happen? Were you nursing at an aid station that got overrun?"

She forgave him for assuming that she had been a non-combatant. After all, that made more sense. Not making eye contact, as usual, she elaborated, assuming in her mind the persona of a bluff male veteran to make conversing easier. "Actually, I was looking down the barrel of my sniper rifle when it went off in front of me. The concussion drove pieces of the scope and bolt into my face."

"Lord God Almighty!"

"Though I don't recall any of it, I'm told that my language was less than godly."

"I'd imagine so. The first time I got hit I turned the air blue with my cussing. The boys almost needed to put on their gas masks."

They both laughed at that, old soldiers improbably joined in mutual suffering. He held out his hand again. "Sorry. I never introduced myself. Eugene Bullard."

Molly shook his hand, returning the same firm pressure he offered. "Molly Aulis. Obviously, you aren't from around these parts, as people say back home."

"No, I most certainly ain't," he confirmed. "Columbus, Georgia. And you're no French lady yourself. You mind if we talk English? Don't get to use it as much as I'd like."

She followed his lead, more than happy to switch to a language a bit less vulnerable to eavesdropping. There were too many spies at the Games for her liking. Not that she planned to discuss anything sensitive with this new acquaintance. "Happy to. Georgia, you say? I don't believe I've ever been. I was born in Chicago. Family's mostly still there."

"That's no Chicago accent, if you'll excuse me saying so."

"Likely not. I've rarely been back there since I was a teenager. Dad was an archeologist and I preferred being with him at exotic dig sites to the charms of Illinois and my mom. I've spoken more Arabic than anything else the past fifteen years."

"Mom's a gorgon?"

"Oh, no, just the opposite. Clingy and dingy." She pretended to search for the plane again, but really used the monocular to inspect the crowd for unpleasantly familiar faces. "An old money type. Didn't want her baby girl to go gallivanting off into trackless deserts, hobnobbing with dangerous bandits and white slavers. That's actually how she put it."

"Can't say as I had that sort of upbringing. We didn't have any money, old or new."

"To be honest, it isn't like having a genie's lamp. Solves some problems but just creates new ones."

Bullard laughed. "I'd have been willing to risk it."

Molly saw no new dangers and tucked the lens back into her bag. "You've risked plenty already, I think." She employed her observational skills on him, taking those tiny details people generally overlooked and creating a portrait. He had already made it easier for her with his talk of planes and Georgia. "Left behind a large family. A good many brothers and sisters. One of your parents is an Indian, Cherokee maybe. Left home after only a little schooling. Lived in Glasgow, probably after working on a ship. Did manual labor to survive, then became a professional boxer. Good at it, too. Had to give it up when you broke your hand badly. Working in France when the war broke out. Decided that your treatment here was so much better at home that you felt like a citizen. And good citizens enlist when their country is attacked. You were a pilot, of course, but not at first. Infantry. Foreign Legion. Wounded, more than once, decided to get out of the trenches and up into the air. You were in a French unit, not an American one. In fact, you weren't permitted to fly with your own force. Now you live in Paris, teach physical culture for a fee and are also a drummer in a nightclub, and are married to a wealthy French woman who will have a baby very soon."

He gawped at her as if about to cry 'Witch!' Then he shook his head and whistled. "You been talking to my friends behind my back?"

Shrugging, she chuckled. "It's a parlor trick. Observation and intuition...and guesswork. Comes in handy when you're an archeologist. How accurate was I?"

"Spooky is what you were. It's all the truth except that Ma's Creek, not Cherokee. How the deuce did you manage it?"

"Well, your familiarity with warplanes, and those ribbons inside your jacket, helped me out quite a bit. There's a hint of the native in your face, so I took a guess on that. By your using 'bonnie' I gathered that you'd been in Scotland as more than a transient. Your bearing and your fists proclaim 'boxer' and the more serious boxing clubs there are in Glasgow. As a non-citizen you would have had to join the Foreign Legion, especially early in the war. Later France wasn't nearly so particular about the rules. Since you're barely thirty years old I gathered that the extreme damage to that hand is why you aren't still fighting professionally. But your muscles have certainly remained stout enough, so you must have remained in shape for a reason. You'd not likely abandon what you know and your attire does not say 'laborer,' In fact, that suit is so expensive and in vogue, more than you could probably afford otherwise, that I'm thinking that your wife – wedding ring, that one's easy – is fashionable enough and has enough family money to have selected it for you. The tie bar, though, bears the bull insignia of the *Escadrille SPA 85*. If you'd been allowed to serve in an American unit you would proudly wear that instead. As for being a musician, every time the band plays, I see your hands pantomiming the drum parts. You aren't aware that you do it. American Negro jazz musicians are in great demand in Paris, so you must work in a club."

"And the baby on the way?"

"Peeking out of the pocket inside your suit coat is a sample birth announcement from a printer. You've been shopping. First child?"

Bullard laughed like a man who's had a clever card trick explained to him. "Sounds so easy when you say it like that. Aye, this is our first. Proud papa's planning to tell the whole world. Might borrow Billy's plane and tow a banner past the Eiffel Tower. Just what Marcelle would expect of me. And you're right, her family's bluebloods back to the Bourbons. Why they let me marry her is still a mystery. But I work for a living. Not about to sit on my duff and swill brandy."

"Do you still fly?"

"Naw. Once the killing stopped, I was more than happy to keep my feet on the ground. I could still do it if pressed. Not the sort of thing a man forgets."

"If I obtained a plane could you take me up? I took lessons but they aren't eager to license a cyclops. I would dearly love to feel that breeze again, smell the fumes, hear the wind playing the wing wires like a harp." *And give myself a sensory fit at the same time.*

"Come to think of it, I might have a hankering for a bit of that myself." He pulled a green and gold card from his pocket. It was for *Le Grand Duc*, a well-known club. "You can reach me there easy enough."

After a few more pleasantries Bullard gave her a slight bow and moved away, saying that he had an appointment with the French boxing coach. Molly was happy to let him go, for though he was charming, the strain of forcing herself to be social and suppress her tics was already wearing on her. She escaped through the standees at the rear of the stadium and sought refuge in a mercifully clean and fragrant stall in the ladies' room. Ten minutes of deep breathing and Tibetan chanting calmed her inner turmoil enough that she could go back in search of Djuna, who probably felt abandoned by her new amour.

It proved to be the briefest of searches. Barnes' tall slim form barred her way as she left the facilities. Her crossed arms and cocked head announced her mood. "There you are," she said with a tight mouth. "I was worried that you might have fallen in and we'd have to send Inspector Javert to hunt the sewers for you."

Molly snickered and tried to joke her way out of trouble. "I've been down there before. Not as entertaining as you might think. The cafe offerings are...unfortunate."

Djuna's lips sank into a pout. "You had me worried, La Dame Masqueé."

That forced Molly against her will to jerk her head up and actually make eye contact. "Where did you hear that?"

"What? My little pet name?" A smoky look crept into Djuna's eyes and she leaned closer. "Do you like it?"

"My savate instructors call me that. No one else ever has."

"Ooh! Romance and violence." Barnes frowned. "Come to think of it, I did hear that term someplace." She considered for a moment. "Ah! I was visiting a film set last week. Albatross Studio. They're shooting over at Montreuil. A bunch of émigré Russians, mostly. That's the name of the film, *La Dame*

Masquée. Breathtaking scenery and costumes. Russian designers certainly know their business. Have you seen Leon Bakst's work for Diaghilev? Scrumptious! This film's a delight along the same lines. The costumier is a feisty woman who dresses like a man and calls herself Claude. For the longest time I thought she *was* a man." Her voice fell to a conspiratorial whisper. "She proved me wrong later that night."

Molly laughed and took Djuna's arm, steering her toward the exit. The ceremony was about to end, and she hoped to avoid the terrible crush that would follow. "A lot of that going around in Paris these days."

"I know! So many Sapphics strutting about that you wonder how the population keeps growing. Not that I mind."

"Only in Paris. Back home they aren't nearly so welcoming about that sort of thing."

Molly fell silent as she recalled a sordid incident from her youth. Her chaste kiss with another lonely girl had resulted in threats and ridicule from their classmates and all manner of horror from the teachers. At home, her father merely shrugged and muttered something about Chicago not being Sumeria. Naturally, her mother had been appalled, though more for having to deal with the fool of a school headmaster and the minor scandal than any concern for her daughter being a sexual reprobate. Barnes seemed to recognize the pause for what it was and hugged her close.

"Those people are prisoners of the same sort of fossilized thinking that started the war," she said as they left the stadium. "You'd expect that with such a shortage of love in the world they'd be keen to have more of it, but..."

"I'm used to it. Been so different from everyone else in so many ways that I wouldn't recognize 'normal' if it parachuted down in front of me with a band playing. This mask isn't the first I've worn."

They turned toward the line of omnibuses waiting to ferry the spectators back to the city. Molly gulped at the thought of being crammed aboard one of the rolling sarcophagi again and said so. With a laugh Djuna picked up her pace and towed her clear of them. "Let's keep walking, then. It's a fine day and I don't want to share you with the rest of Paris just yet."

A smooth Egyptian voice, all honey and spice, came from just behind them. "Might I beg you to at least share her with me?"

As one they whirled -- Djuna in a mix of alarm and curiosity, Molly with pleasure – to face Ahmed Hassanein, still wearing his athlete's blazer and white flannel trousers. Now that she could see it up close Molly thought it looked more like a smoking jacket than a proper man's suit coat, but it fit him well and he still managed to cut quite the handsome figure in it. Djuna seemed to think so, too, as her look of apprehension immediately became one of appreciation.

Hmm. Apparently, she shares kisses with both sides of the street. Another thing we have in common.

"That depends," Barnes said with a smirk. "Who would be asking?"

Before her flirting could get awkward, Molly interceded. "We could use a proper gentleman as an escort. The crowd was a bit rough and rowdy on the way here."

She introduced Djuna to Ahmed, who kissed her hand with all of the considerable charm that he possessed. Fanning herself in a mock swoon, Barnes gushed over the Egyptian as if he were a particularly flavorful dish at a swank restaurant. With practiced ease she flowed into the crook of his arm, leaving Molly to take the other side.

"I can only take you ladies as far as the first Metro stop. I'm due back with the team in an hour."

"That's a considerable distance," Molly said, "don't exhaust yourself on our account."

Djuna muttered, "I wouldn't mind it."

An unbidden thought of the three of them tangled together in a Bedouin tent made Molly shake her head to rid herself of it. The other two interpreted that as a pain brought on by too much sun and society. They made sympathetic noises and fussed over her as they walked away from the stadium. That soothed her mind. Anything to shove the daydream aside. There were too many dangerous agents about for her to afford to be distracted. As that occurred to her, she looked behind her as if the silken garrote might be about to throttle her again.

Ahmed twisted to follow her gaze, immediately on his guard. "Someone following us?"

"I imagine not," she told him in a low voice. "Though a few of our unsavory new friends are back in the stadium."

"Truly?"

"I'm afraid so." She put a hand to her throat. "Including that scarf-loving charmer, dressed to the nines, and hanging on the arm of one of Coubertin's cronies. A couple are even competing."

"Did she see you? Did any of them?"

Molly shrugged. "No bullets flew my way."

"Well, that doesn't mean that ---"

Hassanein froze, jaw set, staring across the street like a spaniel on point. Before either woman could follow his gaze to see what had set him off, the Egyptian had sprinted toward his prey. Dodging motorcars and bicycles, creating havoc and near-mayhem on the road, he ignored the angry horns and made it alive to the opposite side. Confused, Molly pursued, all thought of Djuna forgotten. Again, the horns and curses responded to an impertinent pedestrian. Unused to running in a skirt, she took a long while to catch up to the fleet Ahmed.

He jerked open the driver's door of the long purple auto that kept appearing wherever they went. A black-clad chauffer tumbled out, the newspaper he had been reading floating after him. Ahmed opened his mouth to remonstrate with the man, only to be greeted by steely Oriental eyes and the barrel of a broom-handle Mauser pistol. In pure reaction Hassanein reached for the man, precisely the wrong thing to do. His opponent squeezed the trigger.

16 / Parc de St. Cloud

The bullet struck the ground between them, making both men hop away. Molly's cane had hooked the gun arm and yanked it down. A tumble of angry Mandarin spat from her mouth. Just as much Chinese vitriol came from the driver, who turned with a hand stiff as a blade to engage the new threat. But as soon as he recognized Molly he gasped, stood at attention, and bowed his head. The rear door on the car's far side popped open and its occupant emerged in a flurry of white hair and enormous much befeathered hat.

"Quántóu!" the matron barked in over-educated nasal American English. "What in the names of all of your tiresome ancestors is going on?" Hearing the Chinese name, Hassanein gasped in half-recognition.

Tall, though not standing quite as high as Molly, the angular old lady spoke in English with the imperious attitude of one who expected an entire foreign nation to adjust to her language. Her buxom frame was almost sufficiently restrained by a corseted lavender gown nearly twenty years out of fashion. The immense hat was just as far from la mode, resembling a black velvet beehive awash in the tail feathers of innumerable inconvenienced ostriches, as well as a few piqued peacocks. Pince-nez spectacles clung to the end of her long nose, a black ribbon fixing them to her dress. Squinting through them made her look like a well-to-do myopic weasel.

More Chinese burst from the chauffer's mouth. She held up her umbrella handle to interrupt him. "In proper American, fellow, you know I can't make any sense of that gibberish you spout."

Before Quántóu could reply his employer was met by an irate Ahmed Hassanein, whose customary sangfroid had deserted him thanks to his too-close encounter with nine millimeters of German lead. The Egyptian adventurer charged as if to knock her down, face dark with rage. Trapped on the other side of the huge auto, Molly could do nothing to prevent him.

"See here, whoever you are," he bellowed, fist raised, "I've had just about enough of your constant --- *urk!*"

The brass tip of the matron's umbrella caught him beneath the jaw, turning his words into pained gurgles. Before he knew what was happening, Hassanein found himself face-down across the roof of the car, the umbrella's crook holding his arm up between his shoulder blades in a distressingly effective hammerlock. Quántóu made a move as if to rush to his mistress's aid, but she held up a heavily ringed forefinger and he froze in place.

"I detest violence," she said to her restrained victim, "nearly as much as I loathe rudeness. Now if you would like to engage in civil discourse, rather than impertinence, I would be more than happy to entertain that option."

Ahmed grunted and struggled against the hold. "Let me go!"

"I second that motion," Molly said, making her way around the rear of the car. "You're abusing a friend of mine."

The elder lady raised an eyebrow. "How is this abuse? Quántóu assured me it was a merciful restraint when he taught it to me."

"Wait...you know her?" Hassanein asked of Molly.

Molly sighed and crossed her arms. "Regretfully, yes." She reached out to tug the umbrella's hook toward the ground, releasing his wrist. He stood back up, shaking out his arm, glaring at them both. With a shrug Molly said, "This is the womb from which I sprang...astonishingly."

That earned a long pause from him. He frowned, backed up a step, straightened the knot of his tie. Waves of competing emotions – confusion, ire, mirth -- washed across his dark face. His head cocked, he finally stammered, "Your m-mother?"

"Eulalia Honoria McAllister Aulis," his abuser chimed, patting his cheek as if he were a toddler. Now she sounded as if she were hosting a tea party. "Pleased to make your acquaintance, dear boy. Any friend of Molpadia's and all that. Let's hope our future interactions are of a more cheerful nature. Try not to be so dim in the future." She pointed her umbrella at the driver. "Well, pick up your gun and straighten that collar! And stop glowering in the street. It's undignified. Don't want the locals to think we're a great bunch of colonial Philistines, do we? Everyone in the car before the local constabulary wakes up from its nap and thinks to inquire about the gunplay. Not even the French are that relaxed."

Ahmed slumped into the rear seat of the limousine like a sleepwalker. Mrs. Aulis let her driver assist her in beside him as if she rode with Muslim aristocrats every day. When Molly hesitated to follow suit, she waved her in with impatience. "Hurry up, child, we need to get going."

But her daughter was paying no attention to her. Instead, she had turned to greet the tall chic woman who had finally managed to negotiate the crush of traffic and reach them. "Is everything all right?" Djuna asked, clearly apprehensive about the turn of events. She had lost some of her self-assurance.

Molly sighed, half-laughing. "As much as it could be when my mother's in one of her dramatic moods."

"Your mother?" Barnes sounded dubious as she squinted into the Isotta Fraschini.

"Everyone always sounds the same when I say that, as if I'm expected to have sprung fully-formed from the forehead of Zeus."

"Be honest. That does make more sense."

"Perhaps. But I did come into the world in the usual way, difficult as it is to believe that mom would lower herself to do anything so conventional."

Djuna surveyed the six-acre hood of the car. "Pardon me for saying that I doubt you were as normal as any other baby. Silk diapers? Solid gold rattle?"

"What? This monstrosity? She only acquired it to annoy me. Wants me back in Chicago in the bosom of my doting family."

Eulalia shouted across the still-stunned Hassanein. "Let's go, dull girl! There's a curious gendarme headed our way!"

"And would that be such a burden?" Djuna asked.

Molly opened the front passenger door. "Believe me, nothing cloys like money with strings attached. Can we drop you anyplace?"

"Thanks, but no. I'd be afraid I'd scratch something."

"Please do, it would be worth it to hear some of Quántóu's creatively-profane Mandarin. He doesn't curse nearly so well in English, despite his fluency and education."

Barnes slipped her a card. "I'll be fine walking. But I wish you'd phone me. I'd dearly like to...interview you."

Placing herself directly between her mother and her new friend, Molly kissed Djuna lightly. "I'd like that. So long as you write bold lies about me."

"I would have to. No one would believe the pure truth."

With Eulalia growing more vocal, Molly said goodbye, evaded the driver's attempt to assist her, and dropped into the front seat beside him with as much a display of petulant aggravation as she could manage. Quántóu took his place, started the enormous engine, unset the handbrake, and let the auto glide into the road. All traffic seemed to magically part for the great violet machine, as if it were a shark scattering prey fish before it. The policeman who had been making his way toward them immediately lost interest, the Games giving him plenty of other things to be concerned about.

"There," grumped Molly, flexing her toes and fists in a fierce rhythm, "you caught me. Happy now?"

Eulalia was setting dark glasses onto her face in place of the pince-nez. The sun was dazzling. "I'll be happy when you come home and start being an adult."

"I am home, as I keep telling you. And I'm thirty years old, damn it."

"No need to swear."

"Oh, believe me, there's plenty of need. Shall I share a few of the reasons?"

"Your wretched dreadful mother is smothering you with her demanding love. She doesn't understand you. She thinks your injury has crippled your decision-making capacity. She only wants to control you and run your life as if you're a marionette. She uses her wealth as a weapon. Are there any more?"

Molly crossed her arms despite knowing that it only reinforced her mother's belief in her immaturity. She remained silent, tracing the outlines of the mahogany dashboard's instruments with her eye while clicking her teeth. The rich smell of leather and linseed oil sent little black-and-gold waves across the perimeter of her sight. Tugging off her hat and veil, she set them in her lap and stared out of the window as Paris passed by in an attractive blur. Quántóu had cleverly maneuvered them north and west to escape the press of stadium traffic and was now driving toward St. Cloud, probably to take the bridge of the same name back to downtown Paris. No doubt her mother had rented some enormous centuries-old maison as a temporary residence. *At least I hope it's temporary. Surely she hasn't packed up and moved here? Oh God, kill me now...*

Just to be contrary, she slid shut the communication port in the thick glass partition behind her and locked it. Now Eulalia could stew for a while. "So," she said to the chauffer, "spill it. What's she up to?"

"What do you mean, miss?" asked Quántóu in the rich plummy voice that surprised all who heard it for the first time. He sounded like an Oxford don, which he was certainly qualified to be if that venerable institution ever climbed down from its high horse and entertained the notion. It had taken all of Eulalia's considerable influence and family lucre to get them to accept him as a student. It had been a brutal experience for him. The privileged over-bred students had treated him like a serf. Plenty of abuse and violence had come his way. Instructed to never fight back or that would be used as an excuse to expel him, Quántóu had shown a thicker skin than even the followers of that Gandhi seemed to have. When Molly had asked him about it afterward, he had merely winked and said, "Oh, miss, after growing up a street rat in Shanghai, their pitiful efforts at mistreatment hardly rose to the level of mild ribbing."

Since then, he had become a medical doctor, blending Western medicine with traditional Chinese arts, a skill he rarely used except in the odd minor emergency around the

Aulis home. Now he contented himself with driving Eulalia wherever she needed to go to charmingly intimidate someone, guarding her person and household, and keeping the machinery of her large establishment in Chicago well-oiled. Despite her offer to establish him in a lucrative medical practice, he had dedicated himself to Eulalia for being his mentor and patron. She had need of protection, being a wealthy ransom target.

"Don't 'what do you mean, miss' me, you old reprobate." He raised an eyebrow at that, being only six years older than her. She let it pass. "Why is she here? Why is nagging me by mail and sending me unsolicited checks not good enough anymore?" When he set his eyes on the road and refused to respond, repeatedly glancing at Ahmed in the rear-view mirror, she did the sums in her head and sagged back against the seat. "Ah. Feeling her mortality, is she? Is it all in her head still or has she managed to finally develop an actual malady?"

"Her...heart isn't as good as it should be," he finally murmured.

Molly turned to glance back at the pair in the rear seat. Her mother was laughing and patting poor Ahmed on his manly knee. The fencer hardly looked like a fierce Olympic competitor at that moment. More like a sparrow being teased by a falcon. Eulalia seemed not to notice. *Putting on a show for me. Nothing new there. Been performing that same role forever.*

"Well, that may be her only vulnerable spot. Her spine certainly shows no sign of weakening."

"No, miss. They'll use that to break granite when she passes."

"So she thinks she's on borrowed time, does she? Wants to reconcile with her only daughter before she heads off to Millionaire's Valhalla?"

"We're all on borrowed time."

"Don't! Don't presume to lecture me on that point." Her fingers touched the painted copper cheek of her mask. "I, of all people..."

"As you say. Sorry, miss."

"How bad off is she? Truly?"

"Bad enough to worry her. And you know what that takes." He turned the car east toward the Seine. They were nearing the Parc de St. Cloud, the stunning grounds of an old royal château lost to fire in the Franco-Prussian War. Five kilometers away lay her flat and Hector, both of which she was desperate to get back to. It was past time to make tea and cuddle with the hound in a darkened room. There had been far too much stimulation for one day. Already the headache was growing into a clanging in her fragile skull. But before returning home she needed to have a tête-è-tête with the sixty-year-old coquette currently tormenting Sheikh Ahmed Hassanein.

"Turn in here, please," she directed the driver, who frowned at the request. "Mother-daughter arguments always work out better in pleasant surroundings."

Quántóu steered the enormous auto into the entrance of the old estate and stopped it beneath an oak that looked to have been mature when the foundations of the great house had been built. Glad for the shade, as the sun's brightness nearly overwhelmed her dark lenses, Molly got out before the driver could dash around to open the door. As she donned her hat again she told him to stay put and to keep an eye out for trouble. What form that might take was an open question, so she left it to his discretion. Ahmed popped out of the back like Edmund Dantes fleeing the Château d'If. Molly sympathized. Eulalia had made her feel the same way since birth. Her mother remained in the car for a long moment, possibly considering whether she could withstand a siege. Eventually she chose to sally forth on a spoiling attack.

Oozing out as soon as Quántóu pulled the wide door for her, the grand dame's dangerous smile pained Molly more than the glaring sun. She told Hassanein that they were going to take a stroll about the gardens and that he might want to remain to compose himself. Before she parted from him, she leaned in and warned him to be on his guard. Their enemies had proved irritatingly tenacious and she did not want her mother harmed.

By anyone but me, anyhow.

Her arm slid into Eulalia's and the headed off down the path, severely cut topiary flanking them for the length of a football pitch. The famed garden had been landscaped within an inch of its blue-blooded life in the old geometric style, not the wilder Victorian mode. Cone-shaped yew trees marked the foundation of the old house. Fountains sprayed iridescent plumes high into the air from the mouths of old statues. They climbed the stunning Grand Cascade, a terraced hill covered in so much decorative stonework and still more bubbly water displays that it looked like the main stairway to Olympus. Molly felt concern for Eulalia's heart on all those steps, but her mother showed no weakness.

Few other visitors were about, most either at the stadium or avoiding the traffic and mobs by staying home. Or possibly even going to church. It was a Sunday morning, after all. Grass and flowers and the nearby river's tang provided her with pleasant orange and yellow colors across her sight, while the twittering of little buntings accented those with rich blue speckles. What resulted was almost a stained-glass effect before it all faded into the background of her mind.

"It's pretty here," observed Eulalia at the top of the climb, using her umbrella as a cane while catching her breath. She seemed to be a bit slower and heavier than Molly remembered, though whether that was illness or merely natural aging she could not tell. "The French take good care of their old things."

Molly evaded that obvious opening gambit. "Marie Antoinette owned the house at one point. Gave it to Louis as a present. She was quite hands-on with the grounds."

"That explains the Germanic precision of the arrangement."

The tips of the cane and umbrella struck the ground at the same time as they walked. To Molly that was likely to be the only point of symmetry in the next few minutes. She guided her mother to the crest of a hill called La Lanterne that provided a spectacular panoramic view of the City of Light. Below them the bend in the Seine sparkled, a line of trees trimming its banks on their side. In the east the Parisian skyline was accented by the dominating Eiffel Tower, of course, but the blinding white gleam of the new Sacré-Cœur Basilica challenged it now. Sitting atop the Montmartre butte, Paris' highest point, it had been built as a sort of atonement for the humiliation of the Franco-Prussian War defeat. In exquisite irony it had been completed in 1914, just in time for the Germans to come calling again.

"I've little use for the French," said Eulalia, "but they do make nice things. A pity they pat themselves on the back about it so much."

Again, Molly bit her tongue. She could not count the number of times Eulalia had crowed about the wonders of American this-or-that in general and the muscular marvels of Chicago in particular, as if she had been personally responsible for erecting her city's towers, museums, and stockyards. Her family's enormous piles of money had certainly been involved, but Eulalia herself had never produced anything of value except the occasional bit of needlework. And she wasn't even American. She had been born in Scotland and her parents had moved to Chicago in her infancy.

She's responsible for me, I suppose, if you want to give her credit for such a mess.

As if reading her mind, the older woman patted Molly's hand and gave her a loving look, which alarmed her daughter more than a declaration of war might have. Eulalia pointed at a stone bench beneath an absurdly round tree. The product of some overly-dedicated landscaper, it looked like a green lollipop on a slender stick. But the silly thing did throw shade on the seat, so Molly helped her mother onto it, remaining standing.

"That's better," purred Eulalia, setting the umbrella beside her. The two women made quite a sight with their matching dark spectacles and equally unusual height. "Don't get old, dear. The benefits don't seem to quite match the drawbacks."

"I'll be happy to reach your age," Molly said. "I nearly had the option taken from me."

Eulalia looked up into the veiled and masked face, her own not much more expressive. After a long moment she turned her head to look out over the river again. "Yes, I know. I was there."

Trying not to show her astonishment, Molly said, "Really? I recall waking to an empty room."

"Your brother thought it best that I go home, that three weeks of watching you lying there like one of your beloved mummies was doing neither of us any good. And he said that the sight of your poor face when the bandages came off might give me heart failure." She pressed a hand to her bosom with understated drama that did not fool Molly for a moment. "He was right about that, only it took longer."

"More likely he was afraid that we'd start fighting again and that I'd burst my stitches. Ruining the doctors' fine handiwork would've gotten you shot." It had taken hundreds of sutures just to stabilize her after the first emergency operation. Then many more in the seventeen procedures that followed, just to leave her with the horror show that she had now.

Closing her eyes, Eulalia shuddered. She had never seen what lay beneath the mask and Molly had no interest in showing her. Let the old lady remember her baby girl as she had been. "Give me some credit for a modicum of tact. Be that as it may, I let him put me on the ship. That was a weak error that I regret. I should have been holding your hand when you came to."

Confusion clouded Molly's mind. This was not the knock-out drag-out she had expected and planned for. More like a fearful mother making amends. Perhaps Quántóu's health report had been accurate after all. "That wouldn't have miraculously healed me, you know. Nothing could. Titus was there, even if you weren't, and my nose and eye and ear didn't grow back."

Her mother sighed and shrugged. "Still..."

Molly set her jaw. Her thumb tapped out a rhythm against the cane's handle. If Eulalia would not address the issue, then she would. "Why are you here? And why are you shadowing me and my friends? Quántóu says you're sick. How is this helping that?"

A many-ringed hand waved off her concern. "It's not as bad as all that. They give me pills and the pains go away for a while." Though she tried to be cavalier about it, Molly could tell from the tight voice that it was not the whole truth.

"Is this a 'see the precious daughter before I die' moment?" Molly's throat was hurting again, though she was not sure how much of it was from the injury and how much was from the tension of the encounter. Her fingers rubbed her palms at machine gun speed, matched by the flexing of her knees.

"If it were, would that be a crime?"

"No, just silly. Who stalks their loved ones in a grape-colored automobile instead of sending a telegram?"

"Would you have responded? You ignore my letters."

"Because they come with checks and whining. No sincere inquiries about how my life is going, what I'm doing and planning. Never any ordinary mother-daughter chit-chat. Just guilt and manipulation. And not one mention of serious health problems or 'living on borrowed time.' Good God, how difficult is it to just say what you mean?"

"Just because you have no sense of proper restraint or...decency ---!"

Eulalia caught herself and bit the words back, though not before Molly could grasp their intent. "Ah...so this is my fault...as usual."

"Did I say that?"

"No. Because you never do. Good breeding and all that. Proper ladies fight with scented cards and a raise of the eyebrow. Only barbarians like me curse and spit."

"You're very good at putting words in my mouth."

"If only you were as talented." Molly plopped down beside her, head pounding. She lay the cane aside and interlaced her fingers, tips of thumbnails snapping against one another to make a noise like a cricket chirping. Immediately growing unsettled, she stood again, turned her back on her mother, and pointed at the spot where the grand chateau had once stood, just where the view of Paris was best.

"Great things happened there, you know. Not necessarily pleasant things, but great. Monumental. Napoleon's coup of 18 Brumaire, for instance. He overthrew the government inside that house. Turned a democracy of sorts into a dictatorship."

Molly spun back around. "I'm reversing that. Your velvet tyranny ends today. All of the tears and wheedling and pretending that you care about what might be best for me, rather than merely convenient for you." When Eulalia opened her mouth to speak Molly stopped her with an upraised palm. "No. Please, no. I'm not a doll for you to dress up. Or a puppy you can parade on a leash. Let me live the way I want, no matter how foolish you think it is. Yes, I ended up a big ungainly thing with an occasional yearning for other girls.

Sorry, not my choice. You didn't get a prissy version of yourself to show off at cotillions. That may be annoying, disappointing even, but it's not as if I sat down and hatched an insidious secret plan to make you uncomfortable."

Molly's voice caught and she clenched her fist so hard that she could feel the blood trickle out from beneath her nails. Control restored, she drew a deep breath. "Don't you think I'd like to be what you want? To be normal, whatever the devil that is? Men and marriage and babies and frilly dresses and snooty garden parties. That'd be so much better than being stared at and ridiculed. Called names behind my back. Even with just the one ear I hear them."

She sniffed, cursing herself for the weakness of tears when she wanted to be so tough right then. Spitting onto the sacred soil, she growled and stomped off down the hill with a parting, "Sorry I've been such a disappointment to you."

Using the hill to control her speed, she descended the Grand Cascade, its beauty lost on her. By the time she got to the bottom most of her rage had passed and guilt at leaving a near-invalid at the summit had replaced it. She half-turned to see that hourglass figure silhouetted at the top. Eulalia had stood to follow her but had stopped, daunted by the steep angle. Hand on her hip, Molly looked over at the car. Ahmed and Quántóu were staring back at her. The stern Chinaman's eyes squinted in a sort of accusation. Spitting again, twitching her shoulders furiously, she stabbed the cane into the ground as if trying to kill all her troubles with one thrust. Then she made her way back up to her mother, grumbling every inch of the way.

You've won again, haven't you? All you had to do was wait and I'd start feeling this way again. Well-played...as usual.

When she reached her mother, she reached out to take the lavender-clad arm again, but Eulalia pulled back. The dark glasses had been placed by the pince-nez, so that her red eyes could be on full display. She cocked her head so far that only the long pearl-headed pin held the huge hat in place.

"What?" Molly asked, more harshly than she had planned.

"Disappointed...in you? Is that what you think I am?"

"Clearly."

"Not in the least."

"Funny. Your every word and action shouts otherwise."

Eulalia sighed and shook her head. "So brilliant. And so thick."

"Thanks for that loving tribute."

"Even when you had two good eyes you couldn't see with much clarity."

"If this is supposed to be a rapprochement ---"

"Just stop!"

The old woman's voice had turned deep and sharp, almost masculine. It had the desired effect. Molly's mouth hung open, but no sound came out. After a moment she closed it and crossed her arms, cane hanging from one wrist, foot tapping.

Eulalia's hand caressed her daughter's hair and good ear. "It isn't disappointment. It's fear. I've always been so scared for you...and maybe of you, too, a little."

Again, Molly had to hide her amazement. Eulalia Aulis, intimidated by anyone? That was like the Great Pyramid backing down before a street vendor's cart. But rather than question the statement she just let it hang there. An elaboration would surely follow.

"I've always known that you were different. Too tall, too smart, too brusque, too...everything. At first it upset me, offended me, even. I suppose all mothers want their only daughters to be little copies of them, or of what they imagine themselves to be. And when you not only weren't that, but seemed to be so...unusual...that you'd be at risk for being bullied, or worse..." She threw up her hands. "I didn't know what to do. When shoving you into a mold didn't work and I saw that you weren't just going through a phase, I suppose I just gave up trying anything else. I certainly wasn't raised with any example of how to deal with you. Forces of nature don't come with instructions."

The shoulders-wide black hat cast a cooling shadow on Molly's face as Eulalia stroked the mask with one delicate finger. "They did a wonderful job with this. Looks just like you." She stared at her toes, barely visible beneath the long skirt. "I know a little something about masks."

Molly could not tell where the sincerity left off and the

manipulation began. She often had that difficulty with people, not being talented at reading emotions. Her brain tended to seize up around sentiment. The other little clues that told a story were never any trouble for her. So, while she saw that her mother had breakfasted on pain au chocolat and had visited the Louvre that day, she still was not certain how honest she was being about her feelings. Given that, she decided to take her at her word, for the moment.

With a dramatic gesture Eulalia indicated the whole of her person. "A lifetime of masquerade here, sweetie. Playing the Grande Dame, browbeating the servants, stalking the halls in corseted glamor, overawing all who come within my orbit. More enjoyable than letting anyone see the Nervous Nellie underneath."

"Nervous?" Molly snorted. "You're a better actress than any on the stage then."

"I had to learn to be, didn't I? Do you think our family enterprise runs of its own accord, like the solar system? Don't I wish it did. Then I could relax and play whist instead of juggling all the clubs. Lord knows your father is useless in that regard."

The use of the present tense caught Molly's ear, but she let it pass. Even though he had been gone nine years, Eulalia generally spoke about him as if he had just stepped out for the evening paper. "You could always surrender some of that burden to your sisters. My aunts would hop with glee at the prospect."

"Wouldn't they, though? And we'd all be dressed in rags and eating out of dustbins in a month."

Molly waved for Quántóu to come up and help her mother down the hill. As he ascended to do his duty she asked, "None of this explains why you've been following me and Mr. Hassanein around Paris."

The reply was shockingly nonchalant. "Oh, that. I was hoping that your father would try to contact you. Titus saw him in London last week. It seems he's still very much alive."

17 / Rue Le Goff

Hector nearly bowled Molly over when she opened her door an hour later. The hound spun like a shaggy top, whining in a combination of distress that she had left him and joy at her return. Then he shook his head with such vigor that drool exploded all over the flat. That nearly got him brained by the elder woman, who took umbrage at having her dress befouled.

"What on earth is that thing?" she grumbled, dabbing at her knee with a silk hanky. "Why can't you have a proper dog like everyone else?"

"In France this is a proper dog," Molly assured her. "A venerable breed and much prized. And useful, unlike that whatzit you keep." She hung her bag on the coat rack, setting her hat there with it, and made her usual rounds, touching things in the proper and reassuring order while taking care to step in the calming places.

Eulalia surveyed the tiny space with the judgmental eye of someone who had lived in mansions all her life. "That whatzit is a thousand-dollar bichon frisé."

"Of course it is." Molly sat at the kitchen table so that Hector could hop up into her lap for his apology biscuit. When Eulalia stayed frozen where she was, her daughter sighed. "Oh, sit down, for God's sake. You won't catch some tropical disease. I just had the place sterilized by a team of doctors on the off-chance you'd drop in."

Eulalia cracked a smile despite herself and took the chair opposite her. Quántóu was off in the car taking Ahmed back to the Olympic Village. The athlete had to practice, as his preliminary epee bouts were coming up. To Molly's astonishment, it turned out that the two already knew one another, having been at Balliol College together. They had joyously relived some of their wilder moments as 'those brown foreign student chappies.' Though Quántóu had not wished to leave his employer and benefactor undefended, Eulalia had assured him that her daughter was perfectly capable of being unnecessarily violent in his stead.

"It looks charming, actually," she said. "And with your proclivities I expect that you're only half-joking about the fumigation."

"I was worse about germs when I first got out of the hospital, worried about infection. But everything's all healed up now." She shooed the appeased dog off and stood to make tea. "Well, as healed as it will ever get."

A shadow passed over her mother's patrician features. "Does it still hurt?"

"With weather changes, stress, and exertion. But I hardly notice that anymore. Nothing like when it first happened, of course. More than once I begged the nurses to give me a bucketful of morphine and let me end it all. They would just laugh and claim that the fellow in the next ward had it so much worse than me."

"And did he?"

Molly stopped fiddling with the tea and stared out the window. After a long moment she said, "Arms and legs gone. Jaw shot away. Blind. Had to communicate by banging his head on the pillow in Morse code."

Eulalia gasped. "Dear God."

"I heard that a lot, too. Never saw him pop his head in, though." With a wry smile she looked back over her shoulder. "Dad hasn't either, in case you were wondering."

"Well, I can say the same. At least there we're on equal footing. And he didn't exactly jump up and wave to Titus."

With the kettle hissing on the stove, Molly turned to her, leaning back against the counter, arms crossed, toes flexing. "You might as well spill it, now that we're stuck here."

The ride in the car had been sullen and uncommunicative.

As soon as Molly had heard that her father was alive and that Eulalia had kept the news to herself, no doubt as a trump card for the next argument, she had started shrieking in a meltdown like the one she had had upon seeing her dwelling wrecked. It had taken the combined strength of both men to get her down the hill and into the auto. A gendarme had feared that she was being kidnapped and moved to intervene, until assured by Eulalia that it was a case of pathetic madness and their destination was the sanitarium. That had set Molly off again, which merely confirmed the truth of the statement to the policeman. He had even ventured to assist in bundling the bellowing Molly into the back seat, receiving an elbow to the nose for his trouble. After that any possibility of polite discourse had been erased for the trip's duration. Now, though, Molly was entirely herself again, as the paroxysms were always of short duration.

"All I know is that it was entirely fortuitous, according to your brother. He turned a corner in Whitehall and ran smack into Nathaniel. Literally."

"No possibility of his being mistaken. This is Titus we're talking about. Was he sober?"

"As a judge, he swears. After all, he was going to a meeting with Arthur Henderson."

Molly's head cocked to one side in disbelief. "My wastrel of a brother and the Home Secretary?"

"Yes, well...he's somewhat less of a wastrel these days, though he enjoys keeping up appearances. Says it disarms the enemy, whatever that means."

"As I recall, he has plenty of those."

"Rather more now. He apparently has a position with our Department of State."

Now Molly's head tipped the other way. "Pull the other one."

"As I live and breathe," Eulalia swore, hand to heart. "It's all very hush-hush, but since he's hobnobbing with Henderson it must be in security or intelligence."

"There's a word I never much associated with darling Titus."

"You always sneered at him. He's no fool. Not as brilliant as you, but who is? And he seems to have sown most of his wild oats and matured." Eulalia held up a warning finger. "Do not tell him I said so."

"Wants to preserve his reputation as a hellion, hm? That means he's spying, mother dear."

"You think so? How dashing. Lovely to have a spy in the family."

"I'd think we've more than our fair share already."

"So catty. Have you always been that way?"

"If you'd taken more of an interest in me you might have ---" Molly caught herself, bringing her palms up. "No. I'm trying to be good. Tell me about this chance meeting. I warn you that now that I know what Titus has been up to, I'm beginning to believe that it was no coincidence."

"They collided in Horse Guards Road. Titus says that he automatically started apologizing to the old gentleman, who looked decidedly down at heel, but the fellow just stared at him as if he had two heads. 'Titus!' escaped him, then he dashed off as if the devil were in pursuit. Titus recognized the voice and eyes and gave chase, but lost him in St. James's Park. It would seem that Nathaniel's fleetness of foot hasn't left him after all these years. Your brother couldn't search for him, as his appointment was urgent."

Molly sniffed and wiped her eye. "What the hell's going on? Why wouldn't he contact us? It's pure cruelty to let us think he's been dead all this time. And why Whitehall, of all places? Is he in some sort of trouble?"

"Titus seems to believe so. Says he had the look of a hunted beast."

"In downtown London?"

"They didn't get an empire by playing nice, dear."

"I'm more inclined to think that he went there for refuge. After all, he vanished in Persia in wartime. Plenty of enemies in that neck of the woods for a nosy American. You know his utter lack of any sense of self-preservation when he gets on the scent of a find."

"That's what concerns me. Just what did he find there? Surely not the absurd Shield of Alexander or whatever he was after."

With a shrug Molly said, "I've come across crazier things." *And lost them, too.*

Her mother snorted. "Perfectly happy in retirement. I got to see the man for more than three months running. Then he galivants off the first time someone dangles an archeological lure in front of his nose."

The tea water was boiling, and Molly poured it over the infusers and into the matching cups to steep. "Family trait."

"No doubt. By now we should be majority stockholders in steamship lines."

"I'm fairly certain that I'm a camel magnate."

"Every little girl's dream."

"In Arabia that would be true. A fine camel there is worth more than that swanky purple monstrosity you bought."

"And I expect you have to feed it less oil and petrol."

Molly placed the cups on the table and sat. "Just fodder and water. And the odd bit of skin when it nips you out of sheer pique."

"Quántóu would say that last bit applies to his motorcar, too, especially when he's tinkering beneath the hood."

"The difference is that when your Isotta strands you on the side of the road it doesn't laugh at you."

Hector chose that moment to woof at his mistress. Molly wagged a finger at him. "And don't think that you're any better, you." The hound set his wet chin upon her knee and gave her his patented pathetic look until she rubbed his head and smooched his nose. "You're a fine fellow, you are. I love you, boyo."

Eulalia made a noise in the back of her throat. "I see that your preference for animals over people hasn't changed. You can look them in the eye and express affection."

Her daughter shrugged, still staring into Hector's face. "Can't blame that on the Huns. Born that way, I suppose. I can shoot any number of enemy soldiers but can't abide cruelty to the lowliest mutt."

The older woman placed a hesitant hand on Molly's arm, feeling it reflexively stiffen before finally relaxing again. She left it there for quite a while, but when it did not lead to a warm response, she took it back again, accepting a warm cup of tea instead. After a long silence she said, "Born that way. I wonder."

Molly's teacup was half-lifted to her lips. She stopped, sighed. "You had nothing to do with it. Don't start boo-hooing about your maternal failings, hoping that I'll contradict you. I can't bear another fight today."

Instead of replying Eulalia reached out to Molly's swollen neck, touching it with two fingers. "What happened here?"

"Somebody wanted something that was mine."

Eulalia's eyes widened. "You don't mean ---?"

"No, not my precious virtue, which is as dead and gone as the Pharaohs anyhow. An artifact. Very old, very precious."

"And he choked you for it? Seems a bit much for some old pot shard."

"Believe me, it was worth the effort."

"I thought your voice sounded awful. When was this?"

"A week ago."

"And you didn't think to tell me? I could have ---"

"Could have what? Put me up in a private hospital where you would've given me the best care that money could buy, all the while hovering over me so that I'd never be able to forget who I owed it all to?"

A hurt cloud darkened Eulalia's face. "Is that what you think of me? That anything I'd do for you is to trap you with an obligation?"

"Isn't it? I only have experience to go by."

Knuckles whitening as she gripped the edge of the table, Eulalia made as if to get up and storm out. That was what Molly fully expected her to do. Perhaps that was what she wanted her to do, to abandon the field so that she could declare victory without suffering any wounds. Then she could curl up in her bed with Hector and sleep away the stresses of the day. To her amazement, that did not happen. Instead, Eulalia sagged back into her chair, both hands wrapped around the little china cup. Her voice dropped so low that Molly could barely make out what she was saying.

"You weren't supposed to live, you know. Born over a month early, me with a fever. Doctors despaired of your life, and mine. Advised me to prepare to bury you. Puny withered thing you were. Looked too frail to be able to let out those god-awful caterwaulings. Perhaps you were just angry at being thrust into this breathing world scarce half made up." She sniffed, kept her head down, not looking at her daughter as she sipped the tea. "I told them to stuff it. I finally had a baby girl and no one, not even God, was going to pry to her from my grip. I...We...lost two before you. Stillborn. Both girls. They told me that I likely couldn't have any more, that I was risking my health trying. 'Be happy that you have Titus.' But I'd been reared in a house of men, mother passing while giving birth to me. And I was living in another male establishment, with your father and Titus. I had precious little interaction with the maids. They were all terrified of me."

Molly chuckled. "But I wasn't."

"No. Not of me, anyone else in the house, or anything that drew breath. Born that way, I suppose." When she parroted Molly's earlier phrase, they both looked up and smiled. "The only thing that seemed to scare you was emotions. Feelings closed you up like a clam or sent you running from the room. Anger was the only exception. I was no paragon of empathy myself, but you were on another plane entirely. Some days it was like trying to hold a conversation with a ceramic doll. I got nothing back unless I put my own words in your mouth. Other times you would reply with lists of facts that you found fascinating, or train schedules." Eulalia bit her lower lip and shook her white head. "I thought that I was the worst mother in the world, that something I had done, or not done, had made you that way. A couple of the doctors seemed to believe it, too, until Nathaniel booted them from the house and assured me that it wasn't so. But after a while when you didn't change, I guess that my frustration corrupted my common sense. I hadn't ended up with the ideal daughter I'd imagined, and half gave up on loving the one I had in hand."

Molly hesitantly started to reach for her mother's quivering hand. Before they could touch, however, a knock at the door interrupted the moment. She started and turned her head that way. With a low woof Hector wagged his tail and sniffed at the door, then stood up against it. He looked back over his shoulder as if wondering why his mistress was not rushing to open it.

Checking the antique wall clock, Molly stood up. "Probably

Madame Planant. She's taken to bringing the papers and mail so she can check up on me." That said, she preferred to err on the side of caution and seized a stout stick from the stand before opening the door. With her foot set against it so that the door could not easily be forced open by a sudden push, she cracked it open an inch to greet the visitor. Hector hurled himself at the gap.

"Ooh! Good day, Monsieur Hector!" chirped a high child-like voice, thoroughly French. Long bony fingers with nails painted the color of coral poked into the sliver of space to hand the hound a bit of mutton. The ecstatic dog slurped it down with gusto and forced his nose toward the potential source of more yummies. "Ah, ah, ah! No more for you. Mademoiselle Molpadia would not want a fat doggy."

Molly relaxed and let the door swing open all the way. Framed there was a woman nearly as tall as her but much narrower. Only the completely season-inappropriate black wool coat gave her any bulk at all. Large blue eyes and a long sharp nose made her resemble a gawky bird. Close to Eulalia's age, she did not embrace the fashion of an earlier age but was turned out in the height of chic. Her wrap was of the finest astrakhan, with the collar and cuffs of a silver fox. The head was still on the thing, dangling across one shoulder. That made Molly slightly sick, but she made no mention of it. Madame Planant's crème cloche sported a fetching rust-colored silk band that matched her trim pumps. Sumptuous rhinestone earrings with pearl pendants brushed against the fur collar. Dark pencil-line eyebrows and succulent red lipstick popped against her white-powdered skin. The overall effect was of a well-to-do society matron about to attend the Opera, not a widowed concierge living alone.

Passing the cane behind her to slide it stealthily back into its stand, Molly stepped back to let her visitor into the room. She leaned out to make sure that no one else was taking advantage of the open door to creep up on them. That turned out to be a bootless worry, as Quántóu had already returned and stood guard at the top of the black wrought iron stairs. He gave her the slightest of nods and continued to stare down the steps, motionless as a gargoyle. Satisfied that no terrors would visit them from that direction, she closed the door, gave Hector a rub, and headed back to her tea.

Already her mother, true to her breeding, had bonded with Madame Planant in the half minute that Molly's back had been turned. Secretly Molly was gratified, as introductions and social chit-chat were missing elements in her skill set. She could perform for a thousand patrons in a theatre, assume a disguise to spy on a brutal enemy, even teach a class of curious children in a museum. But simple honest conversation about nothing usually closed up her throat even more than Antiope's scarf had. Generally, when her redoubtable concierge trapped her into conversation, she imagined herself to be a peer of the lady and played the role for however long the torture lasted.

"Did you know that Sophie was a nurse in her youth?" asked Eulalia, as if speaking to a foreign woman from the 'lower orders' was the most natural thing in the world. Her French was better than Molly's, as all girls of her class had learned it in their rarefied finishing schools. Molly wondered how she could recall command of it so easily after many decades of disuse. *Probably drilled like a fiend before getting on the boat, just to show me up.*

"I did, actually." Molly waved Madame Planant into the chair she had been using, preferring to stand and wiggle her toes and rhythmically cluck her tongue while Hector nuzzled her knees. "Thirty years ago, though she volunteered for the Great War, too."

Sophie Planant shook her head. "I did little more than empty bedpans for that. Medicine had changed so much, I felt like a novice student again. But patients still respond to simple kindness, no matter how clumsy the nurse."

"You do yourself a disservice," countered Eulalia. "Those sorts of tender mercies are invaluable. Did not Napoleon declare that in war the moral is to the physical as three is to one?"

Molly's jaw nearly bounced off her flexing toes at hearing her mother quote Bonaparte. But she mastered her amazement. "He certainly did."

"True," agreed Madame Planant, offering a bit of biscuit to a grateful Hector. "Reading letters and newspapers to them, telling them jokes, sharing gossip. They needed that kind of thing."

Though she happened to know that the gracious lady had performed heroic work with horrifically burned men, Molly thought it wise not to bring that up. As with her own hospital ward, the caregivers had come out nearly as scarred as the patients. "I'm sure there's many a soldier who thinks fondly of you for it."

The old nurse clapped her hands as she recalled her errand. "Ah! I forget myself. But the talk of the papers reminds me." She scooped up the bundle of mail from the side of the table where she had set it upon entering. "You've been remiss in collecting your letters and things. Here are the last few days' worth."

Mumbling thanks without looking at her, Molly accepted the armload and moved to the kitchen counter to sort through it all while listening to Sophie and Eulalia discuss Paris as if they remotely traveled in the same circles. There were a few bills, advertisements for various shops, a flyer for an avant-garde fashion show, letters from various contacts in the worlds of archeology and journalism, yet another check from her tireless mother, and the newspapers. She took half a dozen of them, needing to stay abreast of international developments for her writing. Paris, London, New York, Rome, Istanbul, and Peking. There were others that she read frequently without subscribing. And her friends in the digging and war-reporting communities mailed or telegraphed her story tips. The bills she set aside for payment and the unopened check she lay in front of Eulalia without comment. A brief examination of the adverts caused them to be dropped into the dustbin.

Her hand was poised over it with the fashion house flyer, as well, when something in the single photo made her frown and pull it back. Photography in brochures was unusual. Generally they were color drawings. After squinting at it for a moment she shook her head, interest still piqued though she could not say why. It went into the pile with the letters from friends and associates for later leisurely examination. All the papers she took to the divan table. One of her favorite past-times was Turkish coffee and an afternoon with the news. Looking forward to that, she kept the London *Times* and returned to the pair at the kitchen table, where Madame Planant was finishing an anecdote.

"--- And I told him that if he insisted on taking that attitude then I would have to take my lingerie custom elsewhere."

Eulalia guffawed as if that were the cleverest bon mot ever to pass human lips. Molly winced at the garish colors the sound created, swallowed a comment about hypocrisy, and forced a smile, imagining herself to be a Parisian housewife as she perused the paper. "Do tell. Is it juicy?"

"Oh, nothing that would interest you," said Sophie with a chuckle.

The other woman nodded. "My daughter is a formidable and learned woman, but the intricacies of dainty undergarments are quite beyond her."

A fat lot you know. My nether regions are clad in the most wonderful silk knickers as we speak. A trick I learned in the field long ago. Makes a world of difference to have something soft between you and your jodhpurs when kneeling in the sand. "You might be surprised."

Hearing that made both ladies laugh some more. They went on discussing other elements of couture, especially the new hats, as if Eulalia ever wore anything up to date.

Molly scanned the headlines for anything interesting, planning on devouring the paper in detail when her guests were gone. There was much on the just-opened British Empire Exhibition at Wembley in northwest London, an immense affair showcasing over fifty nations. Despite their being garish monuments to oppressive colonialism, Molly loved to visit such pageants. She had been to the one in Marseilles two years before, a much sunnier spectacle, no doubt. The Grand Palais had resembled a giant wedding cake designed by a sybaritic student of Bernini. She made a mental note to drop in on the one in Wembley as soon as she could. There was something to be said for wretched unapologetic excess. Other news was mostly sniping at Ramsey MacDonald's Labour government and kowtowing to the royals. Molly made an impatient noise and journeyed deeper into the paper, toward the news about more rural issues.

And stopped dead as if turned to marble.

She read the piece three times to assure herself that there was no possibility of misinterpretation. Satisfied that the facts were as she had read them, she flung the *Times* onto the divan with a whoop and dashed into her bedroom. Reaching beneath the bed for her favorite old valise, the one covered in leopard claw scars, bullet holes, and travel stamps that had been gathering dust since 1918, she called out to the other women that she had to get to Gloucestershire.

"Whatever for?" asked Eulalia, approaching the divan to look at the headline that had prompted Molly's frenzy. It read 'Three Airplane Engines Mysteriously Stop. Lightning on a Sunny Day. Authorities Baffled.'

18 / *Rural Buckinghamshire, July 6th*

"On the one hand," said Colonel Terremoto from behind his false beard, "the experiments with the Gaze were a spectacular success. On the other, we've outworn our welcome in England."

He muttered to himself as he transcribed his words in Italian into a little leather journal held in his glass hand. The hired Crossley saloon boasted excellent suspension and the pen rarely jerked across the paper. Later he would send the message to his masters in Rome, as they expected complete documentation for the largesse and freedom of action that they granted him. They also demanded results, which had been hard to come by in Paris until Catalessi had somehow managed to wrest the Gaze from that masked demon and her sheikh. She had saved their bacon, as the Black Shirts had been on the verge of pouring their much-dreaded discipline on Terremoto's band. It had been bad enough that the mangled woman journalist had inflicted incredible losses on them. Outright extermination, lingering and creative, would have been positively inconvenient.

Outside the car the pleasant landscape of rural Buckinghamshire rolled by, attractive despite the lack of sun. Though he actively strove to annihilate the nation and all that it stood for, Terremoto had to admit that it was lovely to behold. He preferred his native Umbria and fewer clouds, but the green pastures of England were a delight, nonetheless. Off to the right the Thames flowed toward London, escorting him and his comrades to their rendezvous. One of the latter, Soffocare, drove the big auto disguised as a gentleman's chauffeur, looking uncomfortable out of his priest's togs. To Terremoto's mind the fellow hardly looked more at ease in those, either, but the lad would have to overcome his inner demons on his own. Next to him in the front seat sat a heavily armed Seguire, his sawed-off shotgun hidden beneath an expensive overcoat. His nervousness was palpable as he constantly swiveled his head looking for pursuers or ambushers. Equally as fidgety, Matthews hunched in the seat beside Terremoto, going over scientific calculations in his own journal. Only the commander of the group seemed unruffled.

"I seem to spend half of my time calming the nerves of my minions," he announced to the whole car. "I expect the good doctor here to be nervous. After all, he is a man of science, not war. But the rest of you have proven yourselves on battlefields large and small. Setbacks do occur, my friends. One day you are the wolf, the next day the sheep. After all, even Caesar lost to the Gauls at Gergovia. And how did he respond? By weeping in his tent? Of course not. He recovered and destroyed them at Alesia."

"Don't see us destroyin' no Gauls," Seguire observed, chewing on a toothpick. "Looks to me like we're runnin' away with our tails between our legs."

"Winning pitched battles with the local constabulary is not our objective. We must take the long view. Yes, with the Gaze we could have annihilated those detectives and half of the village, too. But that would have alerted even more police and citizens to our activities. And we had already accomplished our goal. The professor's marvelous death ray now truly lives up to its hyperbolic name. On low power it seized half a dozen engines from nearly a kilometer's distance. With the gem's boost it blasted a hectare of forest like a child's magnifier torches a dry leaf. Splendid, yes? But just as in France, we attracted too much attention with our success." He shrugged. "The price of victory. Now the time will come, and soon, when we shall boldly display our might to the world. But the whole world must be watching, must have its attention fixed on us. Until then we must blend in, be unobtrusive. Obey all laws, tip our hats to ladies, and buy drinks for the men." He smiled, an expression that on him looked like a wolf expressing gratitude for a napping shepherd. "So all of you, please relax. No one knows who we are or what we are about unless you announce it by word or deed. If you behave like guilty men, then you shall be taken that way."

"But we are guilty men," proclaimed Soffocare in a gloomy tone. The priest had the air of one of the damned in Michelangelo's *The Last Judgement*, if such a wretch could step out of that painting and bring his doomed culpability to Buckinghamshire.

"Only if we adopt the old order's worldview. They would have us grovel at their feet, these English and French and Americans. 'We made the world safe for democracy.' Ugh! And what is democracy? Letting the common rabble choose their betters. What a revolting idea. Did Caesar agree to that? Did Bonaparte? Tamerlane? Men of ability and vision have better things to do than pander for votes. We have a world to run! And submitting themselves to the judgement of those whose simple empty lives have proven them unqualified for that task is absurd. No, comrades, laws written by such as they hardly apply to us. So abandon any notion that we have aught to apologize for. Might they thwart us? Imprison us? Slay us, even? Of course. The envious Senate, after all, dispatched the great Julius. But that did not make them right, only victorious...briefly. Remember what followed that ignominious event. Glorious empire for half a millennium."

The car fell silent after his speech, the only sound being the rumble of the engine and the whirr of the tires on the pavement. Terremoto sat back, satisfied at the effect of his words. He had always had a knack for inspiring men. Truth be told, that had earned him promotion to colonel more than any display of tactical brilliance. His easy manner and grace under pressure were valuable commodities. Violent men were plentiful in Italy. Rarer were those who could inspire that violence toward achieving a worthy goal, and who could adapt to inevitable setbacks with aplomb.

He returned to his journal, relating the details of their sojourn in Matthews' native county. Before interesting His

Majesty's government in his proposal for a wonder-weapon for the post-war age, the scientist had naturally needed to test and refine it. His small engineering facility in the countryside near Bristol, not far from his birthplace, had proven to be equal to the task. It had been where he had conducted his first experiments in electrical marvels, such as a radio telephone that could communicate with aeroplanes and a device that could control engines remotely. When his new employers required a place to install the Gaze of Zeus, he had immediately brought them back there. But Terremoto had realized that the place would be known to British agents hoping to lay hands on Matthews. So in a single night he had moved the entire enterprise, really only the contents of one large shed, to an island in the Bristol Channel. They had told the few inhabitants that it was a new type of radio antenna and bought their silence with generous bribes.

Though they had hoped to make the weapon small enough to carry like a machine gun, that proved to be impractical. The Gaze could power it at that size, but only at full devastating force. Controlling it so that it could be employed for more subtle uses such as stopping engines and igniting gunpowder or petrol at a discrete distance mandated complex lenses and mechanisms that made the gun bulky and heavy. Despite Matthews' best efforts he could not get its weight below one hundred pounds. Just the triple-Fresnel lenses alone were a third of that. And the smallest dimension proved to be two meters in length and nearly half a meter in diameter. So they had been forced to mount it on the bed of a covered lorry to transport it. That slower vehicle had already gone ahead, the wonder weapon carefully broken into components and boxed, bound for London where a Dutch ship would take it to France. Terremoto's car would meet them there so he could ensure that all went smoothly. He had few worries. Any inspection would only reveal disassembled electrical parts. No one would identify it for what it was. Its deadly heart, the jewel from a distant star, again slept in the heel compartment of Terremoto's shoe.

The inability to make the ray man-portable had been the only disappointment. All other tests had been gratifying in the extreme. On low power Matthews had exploded a box of gunpowder at a range of half a mile, burst cartridges inside a pistol cylinder at shorter ranges, and set alight the petrol tank of an old automobile. He explained in confusing technical gobbledygook that it excited atoms or some such thing. All that Terremoto cared about was that it worked splendidly. Its ability to silence any engine had been particularly impressive. Soffocare had ridden a motorcycle away from the lorry at high speed, yet Matthews' toy had killed its motor even though it had barely been in sight nearly a kilometer away. This time the explanation had involved doing something to the magnetos.

A car had fared no better in a later test. As a final demonstration of what had been achieved, Terremoto had insisted on aiming the ray at a hapless civil aeroplane some five kilometers away. Just as with the ground vehicles, its engine had gone quiet mere seconds after the weapon had transmitted its invisible beam. Matthews had been upset that they had possibly just killed an innocent, but the pilot proved to be very handy and glided to a safe landing in a field on the mainland. Two others had also been given an opportunity to display their skill in the same manner, though the last episode proved to be a near-run thing when the flyer had been forced to ditch in the Channel. Luckily, a boat had been nearby, and he was picked up swiftly.

Most impressive and spectacular had been the final test: using the Gaze's full charge. Terremoto waited until all else had been proven to unleash the ultimate potential of the ray. After downing the trio of aircraft, he knew that they had drawn attention to themselves and someone official was bound to investigate. So after packing all of the professor's equipment into the lorry, leaving space to set in the device later, he had carefully slid the gem into its niche, aimed at the motorcycle, and pulled the firing lever. Even in broad daylight, with all of them wearing smoked glasses, the hellish beam's glare had half-blinded them. A sharp sustained crackle, like bacon sizzling, had been accompanied by a most un-breakfasty stench of ozone. Metal and leather had liquefied into a glowing mass. In only two seconds nothing remained of the vehicle but a steaming puddle. The car needed scarcely any more time to vanish. It required little imagination to think of what short work the ray would make of enemy tanks, ships, fortifications. And as for what it might do to a poor soldier, well...

Finishing his journal entry, the Colonel scratched his itching crepe beard. He longed for the day when he would no longer have to wear the absurd disguise. But his shining metal skull plate and unusual features drew attention even from ordinary citizens who were not agents of the Crown. Il Duce had taken his glorious war wounds on the back, out of sight, when a trench mortar had exploded. And his head gleamed without benefit of steel. Terremoto had doubtless performed greater exploits for Italy, but God and Fate had conspired to foist upon him an unnerving appearance that precluded any ventures into the political realm. While he could charm a rabid mob with his cool voice in the dark, his disturbing face would undo all of that as soon as the lights came back on. A certain envy of the Aulis woman struck him. Her no doubt appalling face could remain hidden beneath that pleasant mask of hers that made her nearly normal to the casual eye.

He shrugged and put her from his mind. Unlike Catalessi, he held no grudges against his enemies. They held as much reverence for their state and cause as did he for his. Far better to treat them like opponents on the football pitch. Too much emotion blinded the aim. Besides, without strong foes one could achieve no glory. If they were small and mean, so would be his victory. That said, if she had survived his minion's throttling, he would happily meet her again. No sense in leaving a powerful queen on the board.

Matthews had set aside his formulae in favor of the London paper. He leaned toward his employer and pointed to an extensive article on the front page. A photo of the King observing the operation of an immense dynamo took up most of the page. Terrifying bolts of jagged electricity flew through the air. The scientist grew animated, as excited as a hedonist viewing bare flesh.

"Just look at that! Remarkable! We should visit this British Empire Exhibition. It's in Wembley, on our way."

Terremoto laughed as if he had suggested that they march into MI5 headquarters and surrender themselves directly to

Vernon Kell. "Are you dying for a lolly and a brown ale? Perhaps you'd like a trip down to Brighton and take in Palace Pier while we're at it."

"A brown ale, no, but another Brown would hit the spot." Matthews pointed at the photo's caption. "Look. Jennings Brown is there." When that earned him a shrug from the Italian he sighed. "The greatest genius that no one has ever heard of. He worked with Tesla in America. Helped him in Colorado with the spectacular experiments in transmitting electricity without wires."

"I appreciate that he's a hero of yours, but we can't risk blundering in there and being noticed. It's the largest exhibition in the history of the world. Police and spies everywhere, not to mention ordinary citizens who might recognize you. Too risky."

"You misunderstand me. I'm impressed by his achievements, yes, but that's not why I need to see him. He may be able to help us solve some of our problems with the gun."

"And when he's done that, he'll promptly turn us over to the authorities."

"Not necessarily. The man's mind operates on a single track: the problem before him. If I present it in a vague enough manner, he won't realize what sort of device we're working on."

"If it's that vague then he likely won't be able to solve the problem."

"Give me some credit. It's not an impossible task to fool an egghead just enough that he'll do as you ask."

Terremoto bit the inside of his cheek so hard that he could taste blood. His own egghead clearly had no grasp of irony. "Still too dangerous."

"More dangerous than demonstrating the weapon for your masters and having it malfunction?"

That gave the Italian pause. Perhaps Matthews was not as dim as he often appeared. The ray misfired nearly a quarter of the time. And often it hesitated before discharging. His Blackshirt superiors' firing squads had none of those issues.

"All right. You have until Aylesbury to show me how you'd manage it. If I'm convinced, then we'll duck in for a quick consultation." He leaned in close so that the others in the car could not hear, resting the lethal glass finger on the scientist's hand. "Be very sure of this."

19 / *England; July 7th*

Gloucestershire had been a bust.

Molly had left Hector and her beloved flat in the capable hands of Madame Planant, given Eulalia a more-or-less sincere embrace, and taken the boat train to Calais and thence to Dover. She had eschewed the temptations of her London acquaintances and spread bank notes in a profligate manner to get the fastest trains to Bristol. Hardly sleeping despite the lush berth she had bought, she had arrived in a half-comatose state, ready to do glorious battle with the bastards who had throttled her and stolen the Gaze of Zeus.

But they had already fled.

It had been easy to track them with her prior knowledge, augmented by police reports and a helpful constable who had been impressed by her letter of introduction from a certain highly placed personage in His Majesty's government and had escorted her to the proper site. The miscreants had been careful to eradicate most evidence of their activities, probably with the Gaze itself. Standing on that spit of rock in the Bristol Channel and seeing the molten puddle that had once been a motorcycle and sidecar, she was more convinced than ever of the danger posed by the Italians' possession of the artifact.

After giving the constable what information she dared so that the authorities knew what they were up against and could start a proper search, she had dragged herself back to the station to rain more money into the laps of the British railroading establishment. Before departing the enemy camp, she had gleaned enough from her constable and from the local ferry master to guess that her quarry had not left by rail but had taken a heavy lorry and car. Hard-looking men had headed east two nights before. If they were trying to remain unobserved by sticking to the notoriously bad rural roads, she might be able to get ahead of them. Of course, she had no idea where they might be headed and what their intentions were. But clearly, they intended to either employ the Gaze on a target themselves or sell it to those who would. Neither was a pleasant prospect to contemplate.

Either way, I'm betting that they'll ship from London. Easier to hide there, more vessels to choose from. Best to alert someone and have all the other Channel ports watched, though, just in case.

At the station in Bristol, she cabled a friend in the Home Office and suggested in the strongest possible terms that steps be taken to prevent a lorry full of Italian priests from leaving England. She did not mention the Gaze, as they would have either dismissed it as a prank or insisted upon more information, probably in person. Instead, she told them that classified war material of an electrical nature had been stolen and was being smuggled to the Continent. Even if The Home Office did no more than increase vigilance and slap up a few posters that would probably suffice to keep her foes from the smaller ports. They would depend upon the anonymity of London's millions to keep them safe.

Satisfied that she had done all that she could for the moment, Molly slid the bolt of her cozy compartment, hung a skirt on the mirror to disable it, and peeled her mask off with a sigh. She turned off all the lights and stretched out in her berth. Though her poor throat was improved, it still hurt too much after all the traveling and talking to police and newsmen. A towel full of ice from the champagne bucket, worn as a collar, greatly helped as she lay on her back pondering events. It was disturbingly clear that the Italians had succeeded in installing the Gaze into a weapon of some sort. Not only could it destroy substantial metal objects on full power, it could also knock aeroplanes out of the sky and kill other engines, as well. Just the one device promised to deliver disturbing power to

Mussolini. It was unimaginable what might happen if he managed to duplicate the space jewel and mass-produce the things. He could make the Great War look like an elementary school food fight.

The headache that wearing the mask all day normally engendered only increased with anxiety over the loss of the Gaze and its potential use for harm. That she had been the one to clumsily lose it made the pounding in her shattered head even worse. Molly sat up, downed two glasses of champagne to cool her throat and ease the overall pain (though it would likely return in the morning as a hangover) and made a plan to consult some of the experts she knew in London who could advise her on how to proceed. There were any number of eggheads at the British Museum, the Royal Society, the War Office, and in tiny basement rooms in Whitehall who doubtless had experience to share, even in such a bizarre case as this. Perhaps gems like the Gaze had been found before and hushed up. If so, maybe others were already investigating, and she could wash her hands of the whole thing.

Who am I fooling? I could never let this go. It's the story of the century, for one. Assuming the powers that be would ever let me write it. And I'd like to make sure that whoever secures this bauble doesn't plan to abuse it just as terribly as the fools who have it now. Besides, I have a score to settle with La Dame aux Camélias. She needs to know what a ruined throat feels like, preferably by having that scarf jammed down hers.

She had grown agitated dreaming of vengeance, though knowing full-well how hollow the wish was. Nearly two years of searching for it through a rifle scope had not worked out well for her. Diana was still dead, and shooting holes in men who had not had an actual hand in it never amounted to satisfaction. Another glass of champagne calmed her mood. London promised satisfaction of a different sort if she could overcome her trepidations and surrender to it. Virginia and Leonard and all their Bloomsbury friends had left a standing invitation. Any time she was in town and desired a romp in Aphrodite's garden, they would be more than happy to accommodate her. It was the age of radical free love, after all. Three times before she had bolted when the opportunity had presented itself. Killing – at a distance, at least -- she could handle, but tenderness still eluded her. That brief interlude in the stadium with Djuna had been a surprise. Perhaps she might manage it after all, so long as her partners were not there out of pity or macabre curiosity.

Thinking of the bold American woman and her perfumed skin took Molly out of her worries about an imminent apocalypse (after all, she had already survived one, so why agonize over another?) and into a cozy fantasy involving smooth flesh and wriggling forms. She imagined an absurdly enormous bed, impossible really, essentially a room with a down mattress for a floor. Once she had been undercover, so to speak, in such a place in Damascus, though not as a participant. Then she had only been in hiding until her people could extract her and her dangerously acquired intelligence. This one was rather more British in tone, with paler bodies and less incense. Still, it would do. A variety of lips kissed her in an equally diverse number of places. There were even a few hard-muscled masculine participants, faces in shadow. Molly did not mind. "Any part in a storm" was her motto. Though she generally preferred the less-threatening touch of a woman, she was not averse to romping with a bloke every now and then, if she liked him and he did not behave like an ass. *Someone like that silky Hassanein would do, in a different set of circumstances. Coupling with one's battle partner, though...bad form.*

The fantasy resolved itself into a comfortable ménage with long-limbed Djuna, all coltish eagerness and puckish charm, and the mature Virginia, cooler and more measured. As their loving fingers stroked her in the champagne fog, she mimicked the imagined touches with her own hands. They slid down below the hem of her camisole to flirt in her dark curls. Tension uncoiled with every breath. Soon tiny tingles became hot flushes as her own spasming cries created lush and lurid bursts of color and chased away the pain in her head.

For half an eternity Molly lay in the berth, soothed by her own completion and the cradling rock of the car as it rolled along the track. Its distant clickety rumble made her think of being back in the womb, before the war and its dreadful result.

Virginia embraced her in the dream, murmuring endearments and reassurances while continuing to pleasure her in lazy fashion. Soon Molly's back arched again as she gasped and grinned. Twice more she cycled down, then built to another delightful peak. Eventually she sagged into the narrow mattress, damp and panting, desperately wishing for more reality and less imagination.

She jerked awake as morning light filled her little berth with a pinkish glow. Head thick from champagne and pleasure, she groaned and half fell out of bed. By the time she had sponged herself clean, donned a white frock with blue satin belt, and set the mask back on so not to engender cardiac arrest in the other passengers, the train had come to a hissing stop in Paddington Station. With a green felt cloche upon her barely combed hair she handed her single bag to a porter and sallied forth to endure the masses.

Though her hangover was hardly a hellish one, it still served to magnify the expected torture of the morning crush of work-bound London travelers. Try as she might, she could not avoid being jostled by bodies and overwhelmed by noise. The cavernous station's ironwork shell made it all worse, amplifying each echo into howls of lava-red hues. Mercifully, the gauntlet proved brief, as she made it across the platform and into a taxi before the urge to shriek took hold. She let the garrulous driver prattle on about the weather, traffic, and whatever other inanities struck him as they crawled south into Kensington. The amount of necessary tooth clicking, toe flexing, and head bobbing nearly exhausted her.

Her mind was foggier than the air, which was mostly clear for once, and she barely noticed all the splendid sights of Hyde Park and Albertopolis that glided past her window. That may have been for the best, for viewing the detested Albert Memorial in her present mood might have caused the taxi to combust. Its overwrought glory always made her teeth clench. But she liked the symmetry of the Royal Albert Hall, which reminded her of the Panthéon in Rome. Even more she adored the home of the Royal College of Organists near it, with its sgraffito friezes and reliefs that seemed to be of ancient Greek scenes, until one got up closes and saw that they were of modern musicians. As the cab passed its almost Turkish facade Molly even managed a smile.

That turned into a near grin when the driver pulled off Kensington Gore to stop at her beloved Lowther Lodge. The gloriously asymmetrical Queen Anne pile, all lovely mahogany-hued brick, seemed to invite her in like a fussy maiden aunt. Its white wooden balconies and matching window frames, along with the almost comically tall chimneys, gave it the look of a particularly ornate Elizabethan theatre set. Home of the Royal Geographical Society for the past dozen years, the fifty-year-old place was one of the few spots where Molly could almost fully relax.

After paying the driver and taking her bag, she leaned back against the black iron fence and let the tension of the noisy ordeal in the station subside. When it had mostly oozed out of her pores and evaporated into the London air, she strode through the front door, obligingly opened for her by a staff member approximately as old as Egypt, and into the main hall. She gloried in its white-paneled majesty, admired the dark timbered ceiling as she always did, saluted the portraits of the great above the blue-tiled fireplace, and headed for her room. By the time she reached it, just off the east ambulatory, all trace of her headache and the lingering effects of rather too much Veuve Clicquot '93 had vanished. The lock creaked a bit with disuse but admitted her easily enough. With an appreciative sigh she let the suitcase slide from her fingers and bumped the door closed with her backside.

Quiet. Blessed, blessed silence.

So quiet was it that no colors teased the edges of her vision. The subtle odors of the Lodge – dust, Turkish carpets, a curry-like mixture of faint scents brought from every continent by the Society's well-traveled members – brought a tingle of lavender but that immediately faded as she grew used to it again. Molly hummed an old Syrian folk tune as she turned the light switch and re-familiarized herself with the windowless room that hard and dangerous service to the Crown had earned her. It was necessarily cozy, as too much open space made her feel like a prey animal on the veldt. Her bed hugged the far corner, beside the lavatory door. Its embroidered curtains were the color of rust, with the decorative bits in gold and green. They had been the gift of an Arab chieftain whose imminent execution had been interrupted by a shot that she considered her finest. She had accepted them in lieu of his first offer, to join the rest of his wives. Declining the honor had required all the tact that she could muster.

Slipping off her shoes, too tight and girly for a woman who preferred well-worn boots, she wiggled them in the lush pile of the fine Khorasan carpet. A memento of her father, he had bought the 18th century marvel as a fitting gift for her eighteenth birthday, which she had spent on his dig in Kurdistan. Delicately blue on a pale background, its kaleidoscopic motif of reflected peonies and other florals still made her marvel at its illiterate maker's skill.

Thinking of her father reminded her of the staggering news, if true, that he was alive and in this very city. She slumped into the upholstered wing chair and inspected a small pile of mail while considering what to do about that. It struck her that he might very well have contacted someone at the RGS, since so many of the more venerable members were his friends. Would they conceal such a thunderbolt from her, even if he asked them to? And why might he do that?

The mail proved to hold little of interest. Most of it, and anything that looked to be important, was forwarded to her Paris address. She lay it on the small writing table, beside her spare Underwood. For a long while she sat there, feet tucked up, secure in the sheltering wings of the huge chair, pondering her options while in London and prioritizing them.

Try to locate the Gaze, certainly. Much depended on that. Finding her father, or at least gleaning reliable news of him, was now essential. If he were truly alive, she could use his help in this desperate matter, quite apart from her personal joy at finding him. Seeking out a few friends – Virginia Woolf, Dora Carrington, Freya Stark, Gertrude Bell if she were taking a holiday from essentially running Baghdad -- would be nice. It was not as though she had trainloads of friends to choose from. One should seize the opportunity when offered. And taking in that immense Empire Exhibition would be wise, as it was so much in her bailiwick, sensory overload or no.

A timid knock at the door sparked a red swirl in her mind. She admitted a stooped gentleman not much younger than the antique who had greeted her in the main hall. He wore a rumpled suit from the previous century and held a round silver tray heaped with newspapers, snacks, and a glass of Pimm's with lemonade. Molly swept it from his hands, set it on the table, and gave him as warm a hug as she was capable of.

"How have you been, Jenkins?" she asked, aware that he was at least as uncomfortable as she with such familiarity. "Still breaking all of the ladies' hearts?"

"Now and then," he wheezed, "now and then. Whenever I can get the missus out of the house." He winked and permitted himself a ghost of a smile.

Molly sorted through the treasures on the tray, making a geometric arrangement of the papers and a separate one of the biscuits and chocolates. She poured half of the fizzy Pimm's concoction into a second glass and held it out to Jenkins while sipping hers. *Ah, he remembered the mint. Good man.*

"Oh, no, Miss Molly, I daren't," he said, palm out in polite refusal, but they both knew that it was a token resistance for form's sake. He shut the door behind him and cradled the drink in both hands as if it were a precious idol of some beneficent god.

She touched his glass with the rim of hers. "To the glorious Society. Long may she reign." After a mutual swill of the refreshing gin cocktail, she cocked her head at him, imitated garrulous people she had seen, and smiled. "So, how have you all been managing without me, eh?"

That was the old gent's cue to launch into a rambling tale of renowned explorers, expeditions both famous and botched, and great men in states ranging from exalted to inebriated. Molly let him go wherever the scent took him, both because it quickly caught her up on the Society news and because it put Jenkins in the mood to tell tales out of school if she asked a pointed question. And the alcohol certainly helped her cause. By the time that he had gleefully recounted an episode from his youth about Sir Richard Francis Burton being caught demonstrating a page from the *Kama Sutra* with rather too much verisimilitude, though not strictly a current event as she had requested, Molly was fairly giggling.

"He did not do that!" she insisted, desperately hoping to be wrong.

"As I live and breathe, miss," Jenkins swore, hand to heart. But he also winked again, so the jury remained out on the great explorer's saucy exploits.

"Ah...speaking of living and breathing." She set down her empty glass and glared in his general direction with crossed arms.

Immediately he froze, like a witness asked a damning question in the dock. That was all the proof she needed, but she pressed on, just to be sure. "I've been assured, by a fairly unimpeachable source, that my dad has turned up, safe and sound."

Jenkins' face wrenched with the pain of having to make an uncomfortable choice. "Oh, now, you oughtn't to believe everything that you ---"

He trailed off and she waited him out, knowing from experience that his own temperament would break his will. After half a minute of silent agony he moved in close, as if fearful of spies in the walls. "Your source is true. I wouldn't have believed it if I hadn't seen him with these old eyes. He was as close to me as you are now."

That clinched it for Molly. Her brother was capable of error or mendacity, but not this ancient paragon. "Where? When?"

"The President's office, not three days ago."

"You're absolutely certain?"

"Didn't I live and work with him for seven months, digging up half of Transoxiana?"

"Fair enough. What was he doing?"

"Pacing like a caged leopard. Had a hunted and haunted look."

"And Lord Ronaldshay knew him, too?"

"He did. Called him by name in my presence, brief as it was. I was only delivering some dispatches to his lordship."

"How was he dressed? Did he say anything in your hearing?"

"Queer for both. Your father wore old country togs. Looked more like a Lancashire gamekeeper than a famous man of science. A good stone lighter than when last I saw him. Gaunt almost, like a Boer War prisoner. And the one thing I heard him say made even less sense. It was so odd that it stuck in my memory."

Molly was about to burst with expectation. "What was that?"

"The gaze of Zeus can kill a man at a great distance."

20 / Royal Geographical Society

Two minutes later Molly was in the office of the President of the Society, breathing fire.

Jenkins had been unable to tell her any more. She supposed that at his age it was a minor miracle that he had recalled even as much as he had. But he had been firm in his insistence that his memory was accurate on those points, particularly the last. As 'gaze of Zeus' was an unlikely phrase to be coming out of anyone's mouth since around 325 A.D., it was clear that the RGS leadership knew more about terrifying space gems than they had bothered to share with her. But it was neglecting to alert her to her father's survival that truly stuck in her craw. Not that it surprised her. Lawrence Dundas may have been a titled bureaucrat, on the Privy Council even, but he was a bureaucrat, nonetheless. To them giving away information was like having their pocket picked.

Naturally, bursting into his office did her no good, as he was absent. His position was chiefly ceremonial, after all. His deputies ran the show day to day. After kicking a divan, then launching a throw pillow across the room – no sense wasting a good tantrum – she settled into a corner, forehead against the wall, to wait out her anger. Once the mini-seizure had passed and the sparkling lights in her brain had faded, she turned to face the poor secretary, who looked like a condemned prisoner being offered a final cigarette.

"Can I...help you, miss?" the condemned one inquired with a squeak. Clearly word had already gone round about the masked lady's moods.

Fingers flipping in a rapid rhythm, Molly forced a bland smile. "I hope so. You may lose too much furniture otherwise. I gather that his nibs is not here?"

A frown. "His nibs? You mean Lord Ronaldshay?" The poor lady, who looked like a retired primary school teacher, seemed aghast that anyone would refer to the Exalted Presence so.

"Quite. Out lording it somewhere more important, I suppose?"

The flustered secretary consulted her appointment book. "Well, at the moment he is...meeting with the Secretary of State for India and then lunching at his club."

"Ah! Perfect! Which club?" She snapped her fingers and held up both palms. "Never mind. I can guess. The Carlton. That's where all of the upper-crust Tories huddle."

Her victim had no reply to that, other than to offer to call one of Dundas' underlings for her to speak with. Molly announced her intention to speak directly to the oracle and left before the spectacled spinster collapsed in sobs.

She returned to her room, where she lay on the bed with the light off for half an hour until she felt calm enough to venture to teeming Pall Mall and beard the lion in his plush den. While lying there she worked up a few plans of attack, discarding those most likely to result in damage to a peer of the realm, and settled on one most likely to get the result she needed. No matter the result, she would take in the Empire Exhibition as a reward to herself for not murdering a future marquess.

That mandated a change of clothes. Though she had packed little in her hurried departure from Paris, her RGS closet was always full of whatever she was likely to need, be it a swank dinner party or a winter expedition to the Caucasus. Today's outing called for splitting the difference there, so she pulled out a light gabardine suit. The dark green three-piece affair – cream silk blouse with a belted jacket and matching skirt slightly longer than currently fashionable – fairly screamed 'conservative woman of business' when matched with an almost surly black cloche and low-heeled mannish shoes. To complete her look, and make it more likely that she would gain entrance to the club, she plucked a velvet-lined box from a drawer. Inside lay an item that she had yet to use, though it had cost her an unholy amount of money.

A new face.

As a documented war veteran, wounded in battle, Molly had received her first mask and any follow-up maintenance gratis. Naturally, it was made to resemble her original face as closely as possible. But when she had embarked on the life of a journalist, she had thought it wise to be able to look like someone other than Molpadia Aulis, particularly when poking her manufactured nose into sensitive matters. So she had commissioned a second mask, one that would make her look younger, more feminine, less like her original strong-planed face, less threatening to the silly pompous men she so often had to deal with. It had not seen its first field trial, as she wished to use it sparingly so as not to make it widely known. The proper occasion had not arisen. This seemed like the perfect time to test it.

Which was how a tall young woman came to exit a taxicab in Westminster at around noon. She wore tasteful garments and a wool hat pulled down low. Green-tinted tortoise-shell spectacles sat on her delicate nose and a beaded bag hung from a shoulder. In one hand she carried a thin briefcase such as a government employee might require. The other held a stout umbrella, despite the pleasantly sunny day. With determination she marched up to the huge Italianate edifice before her, a great hulk of a building that resembled a bank, but which housed the most powerful club in the land. Only the choicest thoroughbreds of the Conservative Party could claim membership in the Carlton. So influential were they that two years before they had voted to bring down the government of Lloyd-George in a sort of palace coup against their own establishment.

"Lord Ronaldshay, please," she told the trim gentleman who met her in the foyer.

"He is at lunch. Who shall I say is calling?"

"Miss Fisher from Whitehall." She hefted the briefcase. "A Privy Council matter requires his attention."

It was a stretch of the imagination that Dundas would receive such an urgent Privy Council summons, but it would doubtless get him to move with alacrity, if for no other reason that sheer curiosity. Once Molly had him in arm's reach her tactics would shift.

While waiting for her prey to arrive, she lingered in the foyer and took in its almost cloyingly posh décor. Being the playroom of the Tories, the Carlton had more funds to lavish on itself than most clubs. Much of that self-congratulatory old money hung from the patterned rose wallpaper in the form of ornate gilt frames for the portraits of their great robed statesmen. Pitt, Peel, Disraeli, Balfour, and their ilk stared down at her in oiled and varnished majesty. The marble staircase and its sleek mahogany banister towered up to the heavens, where no doubt the membership believed its authority was derived. Having dug up the moldering remains of many such places from ancient cultures, Molly had little room for awe. Someday another archeologist would likely come across a shard of a Royal Doulton commode from this site and shrug.

A door to her left opened, the clink of silver on crockery causing a brief flutter of pewter stars to twinkle in her vision before it closed again. Just shy of 50 and fairly vigorous, the gentleman who passed through it was of middle height and weight, with center-parted graying hair and a silly little brush of a moustache that turned up at the ends. His double-breasted suit was navy blue with the faintest of pinstripes, and the tie was speckled with the tiny red and white shields of Trinity College, Cambridge. He peered up at her through gold wire-rimmed pince-nez, betraying mild confusion. His voice was mild but held a tone that was used to deference. He had just returned from a stint as the Governor of Benghal, after all.

"Hello? I'm told that you have an important delivery for me?"

Molly took a deep breath and made a bit of a curtsey, imagining that she was a perky but ambitious girl fresh out of a top women's university, eager to make an impression on a great peer. She put on the affected accent of a country girl who had learned Public School English after much trial. "Lord Ronaldshay? Sorry, m'lord, but I was expressly instructed to make certain of your identity before going any further."

His eyebrows shot up nearly to his hairline. "I beg your pardon?"

She knew that she spoke to the real man but enjoyed twitting him. "These are sensitive documents. It's as much as my position is worth to ---"

He cut her off with a ruffled sigh. "Never mind." His hand reached into his suit coat and produced an expensive wallet. It opened to display his driving certificate. "Will this suffice?"

Angling the most lifelike side of her face toward him, Molly made a great show of examining it, hoping that he did not ask her to prove her own identity. She had not had the chance to forge anything this time. "Why, yes, m'lord. Thank you very much. My apologies for the inconvenience."

"Now what is this all about?"

A trio of paunchy old gents, looking like overdressed walruses, came into the foyer from the dining room. Molly seized on the opportunity that gave her. "Is there someplace more private that we can go? My instructions were quite clear."

Clearly in a hurry to get back to his lunch, Dundas nodded to a door near the stairs. "We have a lounge for visiting ladies."

Of course, you do. Can't have us polluting your precious establishment, can we?

He led the way and held the door open for her. It lay dark and empty. His finger twisted the light switch as she passed him and opened her briefcase. Though as richly appointed as the rest of the club, the room was only the size of a servant's bedroom. When he turned toward her, she sidled over so that he would have to go through her to leave.

"Thank you for your patience, m'lord. This won't take but a moment."

She handed him a single sheet of heavy paper and let him peruse it. Her hand then went to the umbrella that hung from her arm. If he tried to bolt, she would take bold, drastic, and quite illegal action.

His voice was soft but held danger. "What the devil is going on, Miss Fisher?"

Molly abandoned her false accent now that she had him where she wanted him. "I believe that that should rightly be my line."

He reversed the paper. It was a large photo of her father on a dig in Libya, her favorite. She had taken it from its frame in her room at Lowther Lodge. "This is hardly a Privy Council concern."

"You know this man?" He did not seem to have noticed her changed voice yet.

"Yes. He's an American archeologist. Name of Aulis."

The use of present tense did not escape her. "Is? Then he's alive?"

Now Dundas realized that he had blundered into a trap. "Well...not that I know of. Been missing for years."

"Until he turned up in your office at the Royal Geographical Society not three days ago."

Ronaldshay fell back on bluster, the favored technique of his class. "I don't know what you're talking about."

He made to shove past her. But the brass tip of Molly's umbrella in his sternum put a stop to it. "That won't do, Larry."

The familiarity seemed to upset him more than the physical contact. "Do you have any idea what you are ---?"

"Just stop. I know that he was there. You were seen together."

He muttered "Jenkins" under his breath, then tried more bluster. Standing up straight, though still forced to look up at her, he growled, "Young lady, I could have you arrested with a word."

Molly leaned in close, lifting the veil so that her mask was plainly visible. She whispered, "And I could have you lynched with a scream."

Dundas stepped back, fully aware of his situation now. Like a good politician, he changed tactics. "Miss Aulis. Forgive me, I did not recognize you."

"You weren't meant to. You would've bounded down Pall Mall like a startled antelope." She leaned against the door, swinging the umbrella by its crook, assuming the character of a feared prison interrogator. "Now...tell me about Dad. And the Gaze of Zeus." As he made to profess his ignorance, she stopped him again. "We both know that you met with him. And we both know what the Gaze is. In fact, I had it in my hand just over a week ago."

That completely altered Ronaldshay's manner, turning him into a concerned public servant. "My word! Where is it now? Can you get it back? Have you any idea what it can do?"

"Lost it in Paris to a nasty piece of work. A talented assassin working for Mussolini. At least I think so. Il Duce may have lost control of some of his bully boys. Anyway, I was lucky that the bauble was all I lost." She rubbed her throat. "And yes, I've been told what it can do, by someone who's seen it in action. He was terrified of it. I traced it here. They tested it near Bristol. Weren't any too careful about it, either. But they've bolted. Heading for the Continent again, I expect. I put some of my old intelligence contacts onto them. The Channel ports are being watched. But if they've made it to London they can hide forever."

"I'll alert every pair of eyes on this island. If Matthews has installed it in his gun, then the whole bloody world's in danger."

"Matthews? The fool with the so-called death ray? That's not a hoax?"

Since Molly's cards were on the table, Dundas did likewise. "Would it were. He brought it to us, making all manner of wild claims. It did some of what he promised, in a small way. But when our scientist chaps tried to look at its workings, he balked and vanished. If the fool has offered it to Italy, or worse…"

"I'd say that he has, from what I've learned. Probably too naïve to think it through. Just wants his research funded and accepted."

"That's the perfect word, yes. Naïve. Doesn't recognize that governments and ideologies have different aims."

"Well, my aim is to locate Dad."

"Understandable." Ronaldshay gestured to a divan. They both sat. Molly kept her umbrella ready to hook his ankle if this was just a ruse to clear a path to the door. "Please believe me when I tell you that everyone thought him dead until ten days ago. Generally, when men vanish in a remote war zone, they don't pop up again years later."

"But he did. How did that happen?"

Dundas shrugged. "Unknown. He did not choose to enlighten me during our brief meeting. In fact, it was difficult to get him to say much that made sense. He refused to sit, kept pacing the room like a caged leopard. Insisted that I draw the curtains so that no one could take a shot at him. Alarming, really."

"And was there actually anyone out there to worry about?"

"I did look, of course. Kensington Gore is hardly a hotbed of crime. It's also not heavily traveled. There was an Indian across the way who looked decidedly out of place. Loitering without obvious purpose. Tallest man I've ever seen. Many races pass through here, of course, but he seemed disinclined to enter the building."

"An Indian? I had some trouble with them the very night I lost the Gaze. Had to fight several of them hand-to-hand. Very determined, they were. Apparently in league with the Blackshirts."

The thought of the young woman before him, seemingly vulnerable in her skirt despite her height, fending off multiple attackers made an impression on Ronaldshay. She appeared to rise in his estimation. Ladies in his day had done no such thing. "Indians and Italians? Queer. Can't see them with much common cause. But I should make some inquiries. Naturally, I have many resources on the Indian side. If anything funny's happening there I should get on top of it."

"Agreed. But back to that meeting. Tell me all that you can, particularly anything that might lead me to him."

"I received a hand-scrawled note a few days ago at my residence, asking me -- no, begging me, rather – to secretly meet Nathaniel Aulis at Lowther Lodge in a week's time. I thought it odd, of course."

"That he requested secrecy?"

"That he made the request at all. I'd never met the man. Had to have my secretary dig up information about him and a photograph. I only became President two years ago."

"In that case, one wonders why he chose you."

"I did wonder. But I came to believe, and it was borne out by the event, that he needed a politically connected stranger. He had little trust in old associates. And the RGS had always been a second home to him."

"How did you confirm receipt of the note and agree to the

meeting?"

"By following his instructions to leave a rose with a broken stem on my doorstep."

"This is all sounding like a cheap espionage novel."

"Doesn't it, though? But it appears that he had sound reasons for such behavior."

"How so?"

"When he appeared on the appointed day, he showed me a bullet graze on his neck."

Molly's hand went involuntarily to her own damaged throat. "Who fired the shot, did he say?"

"Unclear. He believed it to be a man in a turban, with a scarf covering his face."

"Here in London?"

"So he said. Regent's Park, at night. Near the zoological gardens"

"That eliminates many groups, assuming it wasn't simply a disguise to throw him off the scent. But London is full of turban-wearers. Sikhs, Muslims, Hindus..."

"Given my experience with the unknown man across from the RGS, I'm inclined to suspect the latter."

"As am I. But leaping to conclusions may undo us. Pray continue. He did meet you at the appointed hour?"

Dundas nodded and gave her the rest of the particulars. Her father had, indeed, arrived on time, though he had no inkling of how he managed it. No one saw him enter the building and no one spotted him in the corridors, either. Ronaldshay simply walked into his office and found him there, pacing. Molly chose not to enlighten the Society President about the hidden passageways built into the Lodge by its original owner. They had come in handy for her more than once.

Nathaniel's identity was confirmed for Dundas by Jenkins, whom he summoned under pretense of providing refreshment. Aulis had certainly been in need of food and drink. While waiting for the old fellow to arrive, the President had urged his visitor to relate the reason for an urgent meeting with a man he had never met. The response had been to draw the curtains and meander to and fro in a secure corner. For long minutes, the archeologist had rambled about international conspiracies, threats to the Empire, occult artifacts, unending pursuit, and near-assassination. Dundas naturally thought him mad, driven out of his wits from exposure. But when Aulis mentioned the Gaze of Zeus and Harry Grindell Matthews, subjects discussed in recent government meetings, the politician began to take his guest seriously. When the jewel's terrifying properties were described to him in such detail that there could be doubt about the man's first-hand knowledge, all thought of explaining it away as madness was abandoned.

"How could Dad have seen it in action? It's only just been found."

Dundas lowered his voice to a whisper. "He said that it isn't the only one."

Holy hell. That's a looming nightmare that beggars description.

"Really? Well, one horror at a time. What did he want with you? Surely not to merely unburden himself of secrets."

"No, that wasn't it. He desired me to assemble a group of scientist, explorers, and military men for an expedition into the Persian mountains."

That was unexpected. Molly blinked. "Did he give a reason?"

"None that made sense. He claimed that he knew where to find an ancient artifact that could negate the beam of the Gaze."

Again, Molly was surprised. She cocked her head and tried to make sense of it. *Could he really have found the mythical Shield of Alexander? And can it really neutralize energy? That would explain why he's been on the run all these years, if someone discovered that he had it, or that he knew where to get it. But it would have to be someone awfully scary to make Dad run and hide. A thuggish government or ruthless gangster.*

Or a demon.

"Nothing more specific?"

"No. He claimed that it was extraordinarily dangerous for me to know even that much."

"Why? Who is he running from?"

"Again, he wouldn't say. But he was afraid of every little sound, even in a locked room with the windows covered. Not much of his muttering made sense. Even said that the old gods and demons had returned, whatever that means."

Molly froze. "You're certain of that phrase?" Dundas' claim of ignorance did not ring true. *He knows more about that end of this business than he's letting on.*

"Oh, yes. Not the sort of thing you expect a man of science to say. Why?"

"Because an Indian assassin said those very words to me right before he killed himself."

"Queer. But on a par for this business." Again Molly detected hidden knowledge, and even a bit of fear.

"Did he tell you why he was on the run, why he disappeared on that dig during the War?"

"Only that it was the best way to protect his family. If his pursuers thought him dead, they wouldn't bother his wife and children."

"Well, that game must be up, if they're shooting at him. Unless the current villains aren't the same as the ones in Persia."

"He did indicate that such might, indeed, be the case."

Molly leaned back into the divan's plush cushions. "So, to summarize: nine years ago, Dad gallivanted off to remotest Persia on a wild goose chase that may have turned up an actual goose. Something valuable, at any rate. So much so that unsavory men tried to take it. Apparently, he stowed the McGuffin, or a piece of it, someplace safe when the miscreants arrived, so that they couldn't lay their grubby mitts on it. Must be near where he found it, if he needs a big expedition to retrieve the thing. And it sounds like it's made of some rare metal or mineral that can protect against the Gaze of Zeus, which would make its value beyond description. To keep Mom and me safe from extortion he faked his death and has been in hiding ever since, wandering the world so that no one has time to ask inconvenient questions about him. But someone's finally recognized him and now he has assassins taking potshots. One has to wonder, though, how they expect to pry the location of the mystery object from a dead man. Leads me to believe there are competing villains here. And what's he been using for money all this time? I'm guessing he's had help.

There's more here than we know."

"A clear and succinct account," observed Dundas.

"The habits of a journalist. Anything else I should know, like his current whereabouts?"

"I can't help you there, though I did probe him with some insistence on that point. All he would say was that he would contact me again to see if I had arranged the expedition. When that had happened, I was to alert him."

"By placing the broken rose on your stoop?"

"Just so."

"Do me a favor, then. Put the rose out today."

"But there is no exped --- ah! I see. Very good. I'll go home directly and see to it."

Molly stood, eager to get out of the stuffy room and on to more productive pursuits. "Tell him that the expedition is approved. Say that Sir Percy Sykes has agreed to lead it. He'll believe that, with Percy's reputation. I'll talk to Sykes and have him confirm the lie. Take steps to have Dad followed when he leaves you. Employ clever men and several of them. Women, too. Be creative. By now he'll be very difficult to track." She handed him her card. "If I'm not at the Lodge you can leave a message here. My service will relay it."

Standing and tucking the card into his suit pocket, Dundas set his jaw. "I know just the people in the Home Office for this sort of work. And where will you go now?"

"I need to clear my head while waiting on events. As I can't very well search the London docks for departing ships carrying electrical horror-weapons, I shall tour your British Empire Exhibition, see what they've done with the archeological bits."

"You'll enjoy it. I did. A splendid show."

With that they shook hands and parted. Molly left Ronaldshay with a higher opinion of him than before. Though she still saw him as a well-placed bureaucrat, he seemed to have more resolve and intelligence than she had given him credit for. That was fortunate, as she had need of that now. It would require a great many dedicated men and women to stop the Gaze from being used for evil ends.

She consulted the Tube schedule to Wembley, but almost immediately decided that it would be the height of poor judgment to subject herself both to that and to the ensuing press of the Exhibition. Instead, she rained still more bank notes upon the Public Carriage Office and hired a taxi again, hoping for a quieter trip. Alas, she drew a driver who was all too keen to demonstrate his mastery of The Knowledge, rambling about every point of interest, no matter how tenuous. Eventually she took the drastic step of clutching her middle and mumbling about 'female trouble' to silence him.

After disembarking from the black Austin near the Exhibition grounds, she sought refuge in a tiny restaurant before braving the crowds. Somehow, she managed to get a dark corner boot and put her wax earplugs in, where for thirty blessed minutes she huddled in relative silence, filling herself with potato soup, muffins, and porter. Fortified against the coming ordeal, she checked her mask in her compact's mirror, refreshing it with makeup to look as realistic as possible. Being pointed at by some artless child was something she preferred to avoid.

To Molly's chagrin the great Exhibition was more crowded than the Olympic Games. All of London and half of the Continent, not to mention many other continents, seemed to have decided that this was the perfect day to swarm the grounds. Already having bought her ticket, and with going back to Lowther Lodge likely just as onerous as what she had already suffered, she opened the umbrella as shade against the unusually bright sun and waded through the masses to take it all in. After all, this was a once-in-a-lifetime event.

True. But so was the Great War and I didn't have to pay good money for the experience.

Against her will she had to admit that the place was fairly awe inspiring. It sprawled over two hundred acres and included large permanent concrete structures as well as dozens of temporary ones that would be removed after the run of the festival. The former would likely be turned into public buildings. There were even man-made lakes. Molly scowled when she spotted the huge new stadium that had been put up, wondering if she was fated to spend time in such packed places this month. As it was, the crush of bodies was already making her teeth clench and garish colors flood her mind.

She squinted in the painful sun, ducking her head as she walked east from the entrance along the main path while consulting her program. On the left stood the Palace of Arts, with the cavernous Palaces of Industry and Engineering, showplaces of the Empire's scientific achievements, taking pride of place beside it. All of them looked to her like creatively designed banks, intended to convey the power and solidity of Britain. Behind it ran something called a Never-Stop Railway, slow driverless carriages that anyone could hop on to travel the northern and eastern perimeters of the lot. Actual road transport at the Exhibition was limited to electric trams called railodoks that carried a dozen visitors. They ran so silently that one of them nearly ran Molly down from her blind side while she stood and gaped at the spectacle.

To her right lay a pair of lakes, covered with sightseeing boats. Across it were the columned Australia and Canada Pavilions, as white as all the other buildings. Everything gleamed as if calculated to annoy her. Straight ahead could only be the India Pavilion. Though she could not make out the name yet, the Taj Mahal-inspired domes and minarets gave it away. Farther right were the Africa Pavilions, some of which resembled mud forts in Timbuktu, though the South Africa one seemed more Western in style. Scattered amidst the pavilions were other edifices, such as the British Government's, festooned with great carved lions, as well as gardens and arbors; Cyprus, Ceylon, and New Zealand; and native villages representing the more far-flung points of His Majesty's holdings. And the children had not been forgotten, for the designers had included an amusement park.

Even cynical Molly could not help but be impressed, though she was well-aware that this was precisely the intent. Bald-faced manipulation could still be appreciated for its artistry and professionalism. But quickly the feeling returned to her that it was all little more than an elaborate zoo, particularly 'Races in Residence,' the areas where so-called less-enlightened people had been uprooted from their home and brought in to re-enact their traditions. Had they been politely asked to do so or simply herded onto ships and hauled over like cattle? Her work had taken her to many places lorded over by the British and it would not have surprised her if genteel kidnapping had been involved. Had not they already betrayed her beloved Arabs, after getting Lawrence to seduce them with his soft promises of a nation? Besides, she had spent so much of her life living with supposedly benighted people that she knew that what passed for modern civilization was hardly superior to some of the marvels that had come before. One could not rummage through the ruins of Persia, Babylon, Sumeria, and Egypt without being struck by their achievements.

Already grumpy after only being on the property five minutes, Molly thought of Egypt and considered visiting that exhibit. But that reminded her of how envious she was that her friend Howard Carter had managed to find Tutankhamen's hoard the year before last. No sense in wallowing in her misery there. Better to take in something that she had only a moderate interest in first. So she turned left toward the Palace of Engineering, large enough to construct zeppelins in. *That should offer some diversions.*

It certainly did, so many that after being there for only a few moments she retreated into a dark corner to adjust to the myriad sights, sounds, and smells. The great open place's iron latticed roof echoed with voices, music, footsteps, and mechanical noises. Half-blinded by the colors that her wounded brain produced in response, she huddled with her fists clenched until it all faded to the edges of her vision. After some Buddhist chanting to settle her senses she managed to venture back out into the throng, fearing this had been a mistake.

She overheard someone say that the building occupied thirteen acres. That was perfectly believable. Five rail lines had been put into it to carry the huge exhibits of modern science and commerce. Besides actual locomotives and their ilk, she saw intimidating artillery, boats, automobiles, even aircraft. Thinking of the charming and intrepid Mr. Bullard, she headed for the aeroplanes. Near them she came across a display of all that was new and wonderful in bicycles. That made her forget her fears of her surroundings for a while, as she assumed the character of a retired road racer and chatted amiably with the fellows in charge of it. They showed her several improvements on her own cycle and she made note of the manufacturers in order to obtain them. After talking her leave of the helpful gentlemen, she turned to her blind side to continue toward the planes and collided with someone.

"Oh, I do beg your pardon," said a woman in a warm plummy voice. "I should have watched where I was ---"

Without even looking at the stranger Molly waved it off, eager to avoid the interaction and proceed on her way. "Quite all right. My fault entirely." She tried to escape but slender fingers touched her shoulder. "Molpadia?"

Few people knew Molly's given name. Even fewer dared use it. And one of those who did spoke with just those refined vowels. The memory of past conversations, combined with the familiar scent, conjured up violet and burgundy swirls in Molly's mind that she immediately recognized. She turned with a genuine smile to look down at a face she admired.

But she did not have to angle her head down very much, for Virginia Woolf was fairly tall. *Do I know any short women?* She was a thin and angular forty-two, so fearful of growing fat that she scarcely ate. Virginia's large protruding eyes blinked back at Molly like a handsome and learned cow's. Long and straight, her nose ended at kissable lips, at least to Molly. Her hair was gathered at the nape of her neck as usual and she wore a wide-brimmed straw hat. The low-hipped frock, embellished with a necklace of chunky black beads, was brown and unremarkable, for the author was no slave to fashion.

"It is you!" she purred, opening her arms for a hug. "I thought I recognized that brusque Yankee manner."

Molly awkwardly returned the embrace, prolonging it longer than she would have for her mother. "Not to mention the gaping hole in my face."

Virginia kissed her cheek. "Oh, hush. Most people I know have a great whacking hole in their face...and don't I wish they'd just shut it."

"Half the United Kingdom is here, and I still managed to run into you. Coincidence?"

Virginia gave her a sheepish smile. "Absolutely not. I have stalked you like a spaniel, my girl. Got your telegram about coming for a visit and went to sleuthing. Impersonated your mother when I called Lowther Lodge. The secretary told me that you'd gone in search of Lord Ronaldshay. Though I arrived too late to enjoy the undoubted fireworks display there, I did just spot you getting into a taxi. Managed to get one of my own, great good luck, and had the fellow follow you like I was a character in one of those spy thrillers people like to read. He seemed positively tickled at the prospect. Claimed no one had ever asked him to do that in seventeen years on the job. Lost you when you came in here, though, and nearly despaired."

"Yet here you are, victorious as Napoleon."

"And less than half as dead. Though if I don't get some tea..."

That was a suggestion to Molly's liking, so they linked arms and repaired to the nearest restaurant for chatter-broth and biscuits. It sat one of the hall's main avenues and gave them a splendid view of all the comings and goings of visitors who were enthralled by terrifying machinery. Virginia was in one of her jollier moods. This pleased Molly, who had more than once had to aid her friend through black fits when her natural melancholia seized her like a terrier on a rat. Things were difficult enough without having to nurse Virginia in a funk. Perhaps that was due to Vita Sackville-West, who was rumored to have recently enchanted her. Thinking of that writer reminded Molly of meeting Djuna. She told her friend the story of the encounter, omitting nothing.

"Well, I'm not at all surprised," Virginia said with a smirk. "You're the spitting image of her current live-in lover, Thelma Wood. Same height, same features, similar manner, matching... predilections. She even wears those tall cavalry boots you fancy."

Well, that's an interesting bit of news.

"Sounds like Djuna prefers apples that haven't fallen far from her tree."

"Or perhaps she simply has elevated tastes." Virginia gave her a look that spoke volumes and made Molly almost blush.

"So, how goes the journalism game?" inquired Woolf, her fingers teasing the back of Molly's hand. "Still enlightening the masses with your tales of exotica?"

Silently enjoying the warm shiver that went up her arm,

Molly smiled. "A beacon of enlightenment, I am. Scribbling away about places I never get to visit now."

"And whose fault is that?" Woolf pinched the younger woman's hand now, making her jump. "You sell yourself short, thinking you're so terribly fragile. I've seen men with war wounds ever so much more debilitating than yours who are racing cars, climbing mountains, crossing deserts. Shaking their fists at fate. You should do the same."

Molly shrugged and stared into her teacup. Only Virginia could get her to open her vulnerable self up. "It isn't so much the physical end of the business. I've taken up flying aeroplanes, hiking, cycling, even hand-to-hand combat training. It's getting up the nerve to go back into the field, after Arabia and Syria. And I don't mean this." She gestured at her mask. "What happened to others weighs more heavily on me."

Hearing that made Virginia lean in close. "Poppycock. Letting your emotions run the show. And I happen to know that you do have them, despite your pretending otherwise. Now you listen. I'm something of an expert on this, as I think you'll agree. Right at this minute I'm writing a novel about a chap affected by the war. Lost an...intimate, as you did. Yes, I know all about poor Diana. You told the tale at great length once when you were in your cups. He has awful dreams, hallucinations, believes himself unable to feel anything. My character leaps from a window. Felt like doing that myself more than once. And why haven't I yet?" She plucked a pen from her purse. "The work, my child. Better than a visit to that Freud or one of his ilk. Opening our veins and bleeding the pain onto the page. This is the way out. True, I tend toward fiction and you do not, but that's irrelevant. Love the language. Tame the wild and whirling words." One long finger stroked Molly's lips. "Bend them to your feminine will." She let the last word linger like a lover's sigh.

Sagging against her, Molly nearly moaned. This was what she had yearned for when she had sent the telegram to Bloomsbury. To hear wisdom from an empathetic mouth. Any touching of sensitive skin was of secondary importance. "I did try. I wrote some of Lawrence's new book. Practically fiction, as I had to disguise my name and femininity, as I did then."

"Perhaps you need to do more of that. Create a bold persona. Shed all the old in one stroke. Considering something in that line myself. Just sketches in my head, at the moment. About a man who wakes up one day, transformed into a woman."

That made Molly snort. "Well, that will certainly knock him for a loop."

"I think not, actually. That will be the joy of it."

Sipping her tea and munching on a biscuit, Molly pondered her situation. "Perhaps I shall take your suggestion. Write some lies for a change."

"Oh, that's the beauty of it, dear. You can find more truth in clever lies than in pedestrian facts." Virginia squeezed Molly's hand. "Not that one could accuse your prose of being pedestrian. On the contrary, it soars like those great birds in the Andes. What are they called?"

"Condors?"

"Yes, them." Woolf trailed her fingers across the mask. "A savage beauty that doesn't call attention to itself but nonetheless is apparent to all."

"I had this savage beauty manufactured in a laboratory. Do you like it?"

Virginia lifted the veil to get a better look. "It is prettier than the other one. Doesn't look much like you, though. Seems to be trying too hard to be something you're not. Good as a disguise but not as a testament to who Molpadia is."

"And who is she?"

Virginia leaned in to brush a kiss on her ear. "She is sorrow, sculpted in iron and gilded with pain."

Molly realized that all of her eccentric tics had gone away ever since meeting her friend.

She slid her hand down to Virginia's thigh, unseen by passersby thanks to the tablecloth. "And you are ---"

She stopped, hot blood rushing through her loins, as several men strolled past them and turned the corner. One was the boyish priest she had met in the Panthéon, the one Farouk had stabbed. Though he now wore an ordinary suit instead of vestments, his bandaged hand gave him away. Even more shocking was the sight of the gentleman in the center of the group. She had seen his face before, in her Paris newspaper.

It was Henry Grindell Matthews, inventor of the death-ray.

21 / British Empire Exhibition

Molly must have made a startled noise as her eye tracked the knot of passing men, for Virginia reacted by seizing her hand. "What is it? Are you all right?"

"Oh, I'm fine. Just spotted someone I need to talk to. For a piece I'm writing." Molly popped up, then turned with a hurried smile and bussed her friend on the cheek. "See you tonight?"

"We'll be there with bells on." Woolf gave her a wink. "And possibly little else."

Molly gathered her briefcase and umbrella, resuming her disguise. As she reluctantly left Virginia at the table she caught up to Matthews' group, remembering to alter her walk from the customary robust stride to something more mincing and secretarial. She hunched her shoulders and drew her arms in. No sense counting entirely on the mask. In her mind she adopted the character of a naïve newcomer to the city, recalling the Warwickshire accent of a nurse who had treated her in the facial ward. While getting the details straight she kept her eye on the pack just ahead of her, curious as to where they might be going and why wanted men would risk being in such a public place at all.

Matthews remained protectively surrounded by the others, as if were the Prime Minister. They looked to be hard men, not the sort to be escorting a more-or-less legitimate scientist through an international exhibition. The tallest one, who seemed to be giving quiet orders, caught her attention. Slim to the point of being gaunt, wearing tight black kid gloves, he wore false hair and beard. They were well-done, but Molly's long and intimate experience with facial appliances could not be fooled. Now she began to wonder if Matthews was being guarded for his own safety or for his companions' convenience. Might he be a prisoner? Were they exploiting his knowledge in order to craft a weapon out of the Gaze? That made sense, given what she had discovered in Gloucestershire. Of course, he might be aiding them for his own selfish motives. After all, his government had been less than accepting of his electrical ray device. Had he sold it to *Ardire* ? Committed outright treason? If so, then it was sheer madness to return to London.

Unless they need help. Maybe it doesn't work as it should and they're looking for advice from another expert. This building is likely full to the rafters with them.

As if in confirmation of that thought, her quarry turned as one man into a side hall full of humming generators and crackling electrodes. Black iron wheels and cranks spun. All manner of man-made lightning leaped between tall metal poles. Molly's hair stirred as unseen forces toyed with it. Similar jagged bolts, only in sickening colors, flashed across her vision as the sounds screeched in her ears. Panic began not churn inside her. She felt as if she had been swallowed by some great metal beast and was trapped in its bowels. The room's other spectators seemed to feel the same way, as enthralled and alarmed as a mouse hypnotized by a cobra. They all made sure to remain on the safe side of the wooden railings that separated them from the rumbling, sparking marvels.

The corner display was less spectacular but was the objective of those she pursued. Matthews, in his element now, shed his imprisoned aspect and strode with confidence toward an odd asymmetrical little fellow with thin orange hair that stood out in wisps like a dandelion puff. He wore round spectacles beneath protective goggles that covered half of his round face and made him resemble a confused baby bird awaiting its mother. A name tag pinned to his white laboratory coat proclaimed him to be Jennings Brown, former associate of the great Nikola Tesla. Few patrons had ventured to his display, which was decidedly low-key in comparison to the spectacular behemoths vibrating the rest of the room. It consisted only of a single long table with magnets, wires, small generators, a few black boxes, and one thing which snared Molly's interest immediately.

Crystals.

None of them resembled the Gaze, which was a relief. They were much rougher, nearly opaque, not cut or polished, almost as if they had just been plucked from the earth. Most were simply set out for viewing as samples, not attached to anything. A few, though, had been placed between metal clamps with wires running to devices that registered a charge on dials. A placard announced the wonders of piezoelectricity. Molly's linguist's brain immediately broke the word down into its constituent origins. Electricity was simple, as it came from the Greek for amber, electron. Piezo took her a moment, but she plucked it from her memory – it meant 'to squeeze' -- just before Matthews and Brown greeted one another.

They were squeezing, too. Their warm handshake spoke of long mutual respect. Molly was not quite close enough to hear much of what they said to one another. The intimidating cluster of men kept her away, and also the cacophony of the machinery in the echoing room drowned them out. Strain as she might, she could not focus enough to push away the furious riot of colors and shapes the disparate noises created in her mind. And the pungent stink of oil and ozone just made it worse. It was all creating a bubbling nausea in her stomach. Soon she would have to flee the room and hide in a dark WC for ten minutes to recover. She decided to seize that small snatch of time to pry into their affairs.

Adopting the attitude of an enthusiastic amateur, she boldly shoved through the stern escorts until she was just behind Matthews. In the dialect that she had been silently rehearsing, she gushed, "Oi! I love scientific things! Just brilliant! Say, ain't you that death-ray chappie from the newspaper? Gonna give them Huns the business if they try to get funny again?" Before he could answer she pushed between the inventors and addressed the astonished Brown. "This your patch? What's it all about then? Is them real diamonds and such?"

Looking like a puzzled ostrich with his fuzzy scalp and pop eyes, Jennings Brown opened and closed his mouth three times, at a loss for how to deal with this loopy force of nature. Finally, he fell back to the inevitable fortress position of the English gentleman when dealing with a lady: polite condescension.

"Your keen inquisitiveness and enthusiasm do you credit, ma'am. And might I say, extra marks to you for recognizing Professor Matthews so readily." Molly saw that none of the others were particularly happy that she had done so, but he did not notice. He was already off on a windy explanation about how certain substances – crystals, ceramics, even bone – could generate an electrical charge when compressed. Pierre Curie had discovered the principle many decades before. Warming to his topic now that he had a new apostle at hand, he demonstrated the principle for her by switching on lamps and ringing bells simply by twisting the clamps on his crystals.

Molly made all of the naïve cooing sounds her sort of woman would be expected to emit. "Smashing! And what good is it?"

"I beg your pardon?"

"What's it all for? Your genius friend here can knock aeroplanes out of the sky. What can your pizza thingamabob do?"

"Piezo," he corrected her with a disconcerted sigh. "Well...sonar for detecting submarines, radio telephony, igniters..."

It required no great leap of the imagination for Molly to see just why Matthews and his crew had decided to pay Brown a visit. No doubt they believed that his charming toy could improve the death device they had installed the Gaze in. And that did not bode well for world peace. Controlling her alarm, Molly tried to rein in the growing sickness from the chaotic surroundings as she manufactured an exit.

"You see, chaps," she giggled, turning to the glowering escorts, "this is why there'll always be an Empire. Who else could dream up such things?" She waved her umbrella at the rest of the immense room. "Why, just look at all these marvels."

But one of the men had moved in close to her blind side and

before she realized it she had caught him in the cheek with the brolly. In reflex he snatched at it with some anger and tried to jerk it from her hand. A muttered oath in Italian accompanied the move. In response, also an automatic one, born of hard training, she spun the tip around his wrist and brought him to his knees with a submission lock.

Instantly she realized her mistake. The dim character she had been playing was unlikely to have such a professional move in her repertoire. Suspicion replaced irritation in the eyes of the group of friends or guards or whatever they were. The fellow with the false beard, in particular, stared at her with narrowed eyes. He began pulling off one of his gloves while whispering to the young man with the bandaged hand. When that one looked hard at Molly and then returned a nodding whisper, the leader gave a brisk gesture and two of the men began to move behind her. Now the glove was entirely off and she saw that he had a bizarre artificial hand, apparently made of green glass.

He acts like he's preparing it for battle. That must not be a simple prosthesis then. Best stay clear of it.

Molly remained in character and tried to play it all off, despite knowing that it would not work now. With a vacuous titter she released her victim from the umbrella's hold. "Oh! Dreadfully sorry! Had a few blokes go all 'octopus' on me, so I got some tips from my cousin. Trench raider in France. Too, too effective, what? I do hope I haven't twinged you too badly." She retreated with tiny shuffles, trying to be unnoticeable while keeping her briefcase up as a pathetic shield. "I had better toodle off before I start breaking bones or bring down the roof, eh?"

Almost immediately she collided with a wall of muscle. Turning to look the obstacle in the eye, she knew that he could see the mask at such close quarters. Yes, it was different than the one he'd seen before, but that would not fool him. How many unnaturally tall, masked women with combat training was he likely to encounter? In confirmation, his biceps flexed, and he angled sideways to pre-empt a knee to the groin. Molly gave him a silly girlish smile, shrugged, and apologized. When he frowned in minor confusion, she hooked his neck with the umbrella crook and jerked it down into the corner of the rising briefcase.

It caught him dead in his beaky Latin nose. As blood gushed like the Trevi Fountain she thumbed the catch on the case and dropped it behind her. It opened, spilling scrap sheets of paper while blocking the advance of those moving upon her. She shoved the bleeding man into his partner and dashed for the exit. A quick glance back revealed the gratifying sight of the boyish one stepping into the briefcase and sliding as if on ice. But she also saw the fellow with the stage beard calmly pursuing her while punching keys on a little communicator box like the one she had taken at the Panthéon. Somehow his cool and unruffled advance terrified her more than the enraged charge of his minions. And through it all Matthews and Brown kept on discussing the marvels of electrical engineering, oblivious to the violent disturbance.

Molly squirmed through the crowd, rudely shoving aside an old gent in morning coat and top hat, and cleared the side hall. Once in the main traffic pattern, she stopped running and tried to lose herself in the throng of exposition visitors. Now there were even more of them than before, perfect for blending in. She bent her knees, calmed her breathing, and tried to look as dull as she could. In hopes of finding Virginia again, where she could walk arm-in-arm with her friend and make it impossible for her enemies to attack, she headed back toward the little snack shop. But Woolf was already gone.

So much for that clever plan. But perhaps...ah! There's a handy policeman. Even better.

The soul of innocence itself, she made for the helmeted bobby, intent on spinning a tale of purse-snatching and mayhem that would earn her the protection of the law. But not five steps before she reached him, fate spat on her. He turned to speak to another outraged citizen.

The very fellow whose nose she had bloodied, pointing straight at her.

Swearing in Arabic, she froze. Then she composed herself, doing her best to look like someone who could never bring herself to commit assault. Her foe, however, must have had a masterful command of persuasion, for the copper glowered at her and hefted his truncheon. As she backpedaled, he aimed the club at her and growled a command. "Come here, miss! This gentleman says you ---"

Not pausing to hear the rest, she whirled right and bolted toward the main exit, clearing a path by simply shrieking that she was about to vomit. It always amazed her how people would hurl themselves the length of a train car to avoid that. To discourage pursuit, she managed to 'accidentally' hook a few boxes, bags, and arms with her umbrella, leaving a trail of obstructions – and profanity -- behind her. Bursting through the giant doors and into the terrible sunlight, she took a deep breath and congratulated herself upon her escape.

Which was when the police whistle screeched.

Her blue-coated nemesis was calling for aid from his brethren, who responded with discouraging alacrity from several quarters of the Exposition. To make matters worse, quite a few men with dreams of glory offered their assistance in apprehending the dangerous felon. Once they were assured that the tall young lady was, indeed, the criminal mastermind in need of foiling, they bounded after Molly. For a moment she thought of simply surrendering, which would likely be as inconvenient for the Italians as for her. But then she considered the likelihood that they would use the moment to ruin her blouse with a covert stiletto, and she ran.

For the next few minutes she led them all on a merry chase that reminded her of lads trying to catch a greased pig to win the prize at an Illinois county fair. Her long practice with Hecuba and Jason served her well, as she deftly squirmed out of a captor's grip several times. The collisions gave her the opportunity to pick a lady's pocketbook and filch her compact. Armed with a rear-view mirror, Molly gave herself a dizzying tour of the Exhibition, dashing through the Australia, India, and South Africa pavilions as she looked for a refuge. Kangaroos, yogis, and Zulus blurred past her as she ducked into displays and doubled back whenever her way was blocked. Somehow that occurred with more predictability than made any sense. Frustration grew as every clever stratagem she employed still brought her up against a policeman, security guard, or burly Italian menace.

Are they all mind readers? How can they possibly...?

At that moment she caught sight of the tall bearded one, still tapping at his little box while advancing upon her through the crowd.

So he's maneuvering his troops with it. Well, doesn't that stink.

As she thought those words, she darted off to her left to avoid him. At the same time, an elderly fellow not an arm's-length away gasped and slapped at his cheek. He shuddered and sank like a granite rowboat. In the little mirror Molly saw the ringleader curse under his breath, that disturbing glass hand still held up so that one cleverly designed finger could fire another spring-propelled dart. Gnashing his teeth, he put the digit away and motioned for one of his minions to cut her off. She saw the man she had taken down with the umbrella move across her path, his dark face full of resentful fury. With a stream of feigned apologies for her clumsiness, she tripped a lady from behind and nudged her into him as she fell. When the victim landed heavily in his arms, Molly changed direction again and made for the only opening left...the bridge across the Never-Stop Railway.

Designed to be a modest replica of Old London Bridge of Shakespeare's time, complete with a line of shops along each side (though, mercifully, without the heads of traitors hanging from it), the structure offered a significant incline before leveling off as it crossed the tracks. People swarmed it, looking to either leave the Exhibition or get onto one of the cars to travel its perimeter. One of them was the young man she had tripped with the briefcase as she had made her escape from Brown's corner display. His face was pale and the hand that held the stiletto trembled, but he stood his ground, the dagger half-hidden against his trouser leg. With enemies closing in from every other direction, Molly had no choice but to power through him. Her concern was less for herself than for the unsuspecting families pressing into him. That blade could do nauseating damage to some poor child's face if she failed to control it.

Her training and the umbrella gave her the tools to manage that, but now the noise, the sun, and the crowds were sending her wounded mind into a tailspin. Her hat had fallen off long ago. Harsh jagged colors obstructed her vision. Clamorous sounds were building up in her brain like a logjam on a river. If she could not escape soon, she would collapse in a shrieking fit and make her enemies' task all too simple. Chanting lightly in Arabic to soothe her nerves, she scooted directly up to him, flicking her handbag at his face. When he predictably over-reacted, she spun to the opposite side of the knife and was past him before he knew it. He tried a desperate swipe with it, but Molly had anticipated that and spanked his wrist bone hard with the umbrella handle. His weapon dropped harmlessly onto the bridge planks and he yelped.

"Find another line of work," she told him, not unkindly. "These people will be the death of you...and your soul."

She threaded her way amongst the bodies milling about on the bridge. The bearded fellow had already caught up, towing a policeman with him. Another bobby was two steps behind and the first Italian she had struck was also closing in. Flashes of red, orange, and now black made her half-blind. Her stomach heaved. All the world was collapsing in on her, making her heart pound and her breath short. If she did not get across the bridge and out of the Exhibition in the next two minutes, she was lost.

Someone, apparently a too-helpful citizen, seized her wrist. Rather than fight him, she simply shrieked that he was trying to molest her. In alarm he reflexively released her and protested his innocence to all who stopped to stare. Molly bolted past him and fled across the bridge. But more police blocked the way to freedom. Two of them stood like marble statues to Justice, just across the other ramp. The pursuers had nearly caught up to her, so retreat was impossible. Only one avenue was left open. She clenched her jaw and took it.

Molly ducked into a hat shop, hoping to hide from the clever bearded leader and his henchmen, then either double back or continue across the bridge when they gave up the search. But she was spotted, and several arms pointed at the door. Her enemies rushed it like hounds on a cornered fox. With only surrender, and likely death, awaiting her if she remained, she feigned nonchalant browsing as she worked her way to the window. As no less than four grim men advanced on her, she opened her umbrella and left it behind her. blocking the window to impede them as she climbed out and dropped onto the railway cars.

The fall was only a couple of meters. Luckily the Never-Stop Railway was also the Never-Go-Quickly Railway, as it moved at a comfortable walking pace. She landed on the end of one car, her skirted legs dangling into the open carriage below. Squeals of surprise and alarm came from inside. Her mask askew, making her even more blind than usual, she slid down with a noticeable lack of dignity until she stood safely inside. That put her face-to-face with one of the African tribesmen who lived at the Exhibition. His dark face frowned, then jerked back as what lay partially revealed beneath the mask shocked him. Molly hastily covered the spot with one hand while replacing her false face with the other, already moving across the car to bound out onto a dirt patch beside a concrete abutment.

Directly into the hands of an enormous policeman.

He was even taller than Molly. She stared directly into a black moustache the size of a hoplite shield. That was appropriate, for the fellow seized her in both hands with a grip that Achilles could not have broken. But he was only trying to help her. His superiors had placed him on the perimeter to respond to accidents on the railway and to prevent anyone sneaking in without a ticket.

"See here, miss," he rumbled in a Northumberland accent, "you'll do yourself an injury like that."

Molly played her only card, aware that those chasing her would soon arrive. "Well, isn't it lucky then that your great strong arms were here to save me then, eh?" She put every ounce of frail femininity she could muster into her voice. "Some oafish lout got all grabby on the car and when I tore myself free of him, I fell completely out."

"Truly?" He frowned, his manly ire up at such an affront to English womanhood. "Come on, then. You'll need to swear out a complaint against him. Otherwise, who knows how many other ladies he'll assail."

Before she could react, Molly found herself being towed

back toward the bridge. Her pleas that she had no wish to confront the man again fell on deaf ears. In a trice the copper hauled her right up to his superior, who stood with most of the other bobbies she had evaded, as well as the dangerous bearded man and two of his cohorts.

"Ah! You got her, Williams. Well-managed!" the sergeant crowed, as if his entire career depended on capturing this horrid felon. He glared down his long nose at Molly. "Quite the merry chase you led us on, young lady. Well, that's all over now. This gentleman is more than willing to testify as to your thievish ways."

The bearded man with the unsettling eyes approached her, tugging at one glove again. "I wonder if my watch is still on her person. Shall we search her?"

His accent was as false as the beard. Though both were expertly done and likely to fool nearly everyone, Molly had much experience with disguises. Her familiarity with clever weapons also told her that she wanted no part of that terrifying glass hand that was reaching out for her arm. Though still held in an unbreakable grip, she thought that she might manage to bat the hand aside and yank the fellow's beard off. That might upset his plan and create much suspicion in the coppers' minds. After that, she was unsure what she could do to escape a likely murder.

"I say, old thing, half a mo'," said a plummy voice from behind the sergeant.

A silk top hat bobbed through the curious crowd, a pearl-handled walking stick encouraging people to move aside. Molly saw creamy spats on mirror-polished shoes, striped gray trousers with a crease she could shave her legs with, a splendid waistcoat, and a black morning coat with a white carnation in the buttonhole. It all shrieked 'upper crust' and 'make way, I'm important.'

Molly's head cocked like a dog hearing an odd sound. It was the old fellow she had pushed through while fleeing Brown's exhibit.

Can't be a coincidence. Did Dundas send him? Or even my duplicitous mother?

"Sorry to interrupt. Frightful nuisance, I'm sure. Can't be

helped, though." The elderly man put himself precisely between Molly and the artificial hand she so feared. His white hair was somewhat longer than was fashionable. Red and round, his plump nose spoke of a fondness for port, while the generous belly announced an equivalent love of dinners. A monocle glinted in one eye.

The sergeant eyed him with the automatic deference such togs engendered. "I beg your pardon, Mr. ---?"

Instead of a verbal reply, a satin card was instantly delivered into the senior bobby's hand. The copper peered at it, then stood up straight. "Good day, m'lord. How can I assist you? We have this feisty miscreant to process."

Again, the well-dressed one handed over a document rather than directly answering. This time Molly could make out the royal seal. "I'm afraid that I have the prior claim. As I said, frightfully inconvenient. But look at all of the paperwork I'm saving you."

Nonplussed, the sergeant hesitated, looking from the card to the other paper and back several times. "This is most...unusual."

"You doubt my authority in this matter? Are the documents not in order?"

"Not at all, m'lord. It's just that I never thought to see..." He chose the path of least resistance and addressed his officer. "Well, release her, Williams! This gentleman will have her in his charge now."

The giant policeman let her go as if burned. He shrugged. His not to reason why...

Grinning, the lord touched the brim of his hat and turned to salute everyone in sight. "His Majesty is much obliged for your assistance in this matter. We've been hunting her a long time."

"You'll need no more help from us, sir?" asked the bearded one, replacing his glove with evident disappointment. "I assure you, the lady is more dangerous than she seems."

The toff let his smile fade as he looked the fellow dead in the eyes. "As are you, I imagine. And I."

For a long moment they took one another's measure. Then the beard was split by a tight smile. Its owner bowed his head a bit and retreated a step. "I leave her in your capable hands.

England is blessed to be under such protection as I have witnessed today."

With that he vanished into the crowd, followed by the group he had arrived with. Matthews joined them a moment later. No one seemed to wonder that the man's concern for his stolen property had evaporated so quickly. Molly had no time to ponder the question, for her savior was nudging her ahead of him toward the main entrance.

"Let's blow out of here before they get wise," he said in her brother's voice.

22 / Savoy Hotel

Her knees unsteady from the chase and the sensory overload, Molly let Augustus Titus Aulis maneuver her out of the park. He got her away from the bustle and noise and into a copse of trees across the street. There, on a bench in the shade and quiet, head between her knees and bobbing, teeth chattering as if it were cold, her muscles began to unclench. As he massaged her neck with surprising tenderness and began to explain himself, she noticed the familiar colors aroused by his voice. They had been obscured by all the other chaos when in the Exhibition or she might have recognized him despite the elaborate disguise and accent.

"Sorry I couldn't bail you out sooner, sis. Turns out His Majesty's Exhibition's a damned sight bigger than I thought. And by the time I tracked you down to that electro-thingamajig corner, you took off like a prize racehorse. This getups's not conducive to sprinting."

Molly took the deepest of breaths and let it all out in a long shuddering sigh, willing the knots in her stomach and back to flow away with it. "This skirt's not, either." She hesitantly reached up to take one of his hands in hers. "Glad you...made the effort. That was a close one."

"I nearly shat myself when you fell off of the bridge."

"Again, that makes two of us."

"Yeah, but you were merely scared of getting sliced in two by a train. I had to worry about explaining it to Mom."

That drew a sardonic chuckle from his sister as her shoulders twitched. "You'd need a cigarette and blindfold for that."

Titus sat beside her, pulling off his putty nose and chin. Then came the wig. In a surprisingly short time he turned back into his usual handsome self, all manly cleft chin and blonde hair. No mask required, to Molly's annoyance. It looked odd with the old lord's costume and false belly still in place.

"How'd you find me, anyway? Is the whole world spying on the Royal Geographical Society?"

"Near as. I followed the Paris policeman who was tailing you."

That made her jerk upright. "What?!"

"Ouch! Missed him, did you? Don't feel bad, he was damned good at his job. I only spotted him because he was smoking a suspiciously fine pipe for a cab driver. Let him pick me up in front of the RGS just as you left it. Never mind how I knew you were there. Long sordid tale of favors repaid and telephones tapped."

Molly gave him a hard look with her throbbing eye. "And since when have you done either?"

He replied in his usual fashion, with the irritatingly charming puckish grin that had caused his mother to spoil him and countless other ladies to surrender in more carnal ways. "Well, I admit, I don't tap the phones myself. We have clever fellows who manage that."

"Who is *we*?"

Titus winked. "Maybe later. And as for repaying favors, surely I just squared my account."

Against her natural inclination, she squeezed his hand again. "Some of it, I think. You're still in arrears for shoving me out of that treehouse when I was nine."

"Aw, shush. You landed nice and soft, didn't you?"

"The manure pile was soft, yes, but not so nice. Much like you...most of the time." Molly leaned back and concentrated on rhythmic breathing to flush the tension out. Eventually she muttered, "Now you're less soft, and somewhat nicer."

"The first comes from living rough all over creation, much like you, though in more covert ways. And the odd assassination attempt does help focus one's powers."

That chilled Molly to the bone, but she let it pass for the moment. "And the niceness?"

"It was always there, though admittedly not on the surface. You just wouldn't stop fighting long enough to notice."

"I'll grant that that could be true. So why have you miraculously appeared today, Galahad? Surely you aren't on the trail of those scoundrels, too?"

"Not at first. I'm with Dad."

That shot her up straight as if jerked by wild horses. "What?! It's true? Where is he?"

He held up a hand. "Whoa! Calm down. You'll do yourself an injury. I should've said, 'I'm trailing Dad.' He keeps giving me the slip."

"How? And what does he have to do with me and these murderous Italians?"

"He knows all about them, somehow. Says that he's been 'stalking the Gaze like a jealous lover,' whatever that means."

"It means this is even more complicated than I thought it was, and that's saying quite a lot.' She grasped his arm, knee tendons flexing twice a second. "Help me up."

"You sure?"

"No, but languishing here does me no good. Have you a car?"

"I do, but you won't like it."

That made Molly sag. "Sweet mother of the Prophet, it's purple, isn't it?"

"Afraid so. It fit the character I was playing."

Precisely on cue, the irritating Isotta appeared at the curb in front of them like a battlecruiser arriving in port. The crisply uniformed Quántóu popped out, opened the rear door, and saluted with a smirk. "Good day, my lord," he said in a perfect British accent. "I trust you had an enjoyable sojourn at the Exhibition."

"I did, thank you," Titus replied in kind, despite having already removed his makeup. "Please see to the lady."

Molly played along, permitting herself to be handed into the car as if she were royalty. Sinking into the leather seat, which supported her like a heavenly cloud, she let the soothing pastel colors of the new surroundings push away the harsh hues caused by the extended pursuit at Wembley. As she began rocking to and fro a bit, scents of patchouli, mahogany, even gun oil swam across her mind, calming her. Titus slid in on the other side, telling Quántóu to head back to the Savoy Hotel. That relaxed her even more. A bit of pampering would be just the thing. A hot bath, soft towels, silky sheets...

Except that the Gaze is still in the wrong hands, no doubt heading to the Continent for dreadful mischief.

That -- and the thought that if the Isotta was in London then, no doubt, so was her mother -- ruined Molly's pleasant reverie. Growling, she shot up straight again. "Damn! Damn! Damn!"

Alarmed, her brother moved closer. "What? Stop bouncing up and down. Are you all right?"

"I got away from those bastards, but the Gaze got away from me. We can't rest yet, Savoy or no."

"The ports are all watched if that's what concerns you. They'd have to be deucedly clever to get a lorry out of England right now."

"But deucedly clever is just what they've been so far. Always a step ahead, always getting their way even when supposedly trapped."

"Their luck may have run out. My people have finally impressed upon His Majesty's government that they've been underestimating the threat."

Molly sighed and sat back again, unwilling to wind herself up again so soon. Every muscle ached and the nausea had barely subsided. Perhaps this once she'd have to trust in others. "And just who might your people be, I wonder?"

"Let's call it an obscure arm of our State Department and leave it at that, for now."

"How long have you been toiling in obscurity for them?'

"Since 1914, straight out of college."

Again, Molly jerked erect, nearly giving herself whiplash. "What?!" She ran a series of calendars backward in her mind in that pictorial way of hers. "Then that would mean --"

"That the drunken wastrel bit was all an act. Sorry to disappoint."

She punched him in the arm, making sure it was hard enough to hurt. It shocked her how solid he was beneath the poufy lord clothes. "How about telling somebody next time!"

"It wouldn't have been a proper disguise if half the world knew about it. And telling mom would have amounted to the same thing."

"What about me? I'm no blabbermouth."

"No, but the mails are. You were already out of the house and off digging by then. Couldn't risk an intercept, especially in some of the dubious locales you worked in."

She shook her head and laughed. "My brother the spy. And a good one, it seems."

That earned a shrug. "Well, good enough to not be dead yet. And I've scored a few hits on the other side." He patted her knee. "Don't pretend that you're a newcomer to this business. They didn't give you that private room at the RGS just for finding a few unique pots, did they?"

Molly winked at him. "Um, maybe not." She leaned forward to speak to Quántóu. "I'll need to stop and pick up some things. What little I brought is at the ---"

"Already in the trunk, miss," came the immediate answer. "Mister Titus arranged that. And some extra things you might have use of."

That made her sigh. "Why am I always two steps behind everyone lately?"

Titus snorted. "Oh, poor little genius sister, lamenting her idiocy. Now you know how the rest of us usually feel around you."

"What's that supposed to mean?"

"You're the Great Intimidator. Not that you mean to, but you make everybody feel like a bunch of schoolchildren."

"Everybody? Have you met Virginia Woolf?"

"All right, then. Most people. That Sherlock Holmes thing, for instance. Unsettling."

She waved that off. "A glorified parlor trick, really."

"Oh? Who else do you know who can do it? The parlors I frequent have to settle for charades and champers."

"Speaking of champagne, you really shouldn't have had that extra glass at Claridge's this morning."

When she realized what she had just done and slapped her thigh with a grimace, Titus grinned. "As I said."

"Even granting you that, it's still small consolation for being so often at sea lately over this Gaze business. If I don't get ahead of events, things are going to go very badly for very many."

"Agreed. At the hotel, we'll put our noodles together and decide how to proceed."

"Fine. So long as it's after my cozy bubble bath and not before."

The co-noodling did, indeed, happen after that truly decadent bath. Her tub at the Savoy rivaled the sarcophagus of an Akkadian prince she had once excavated in Mesopotamia. Molly was certain that she enjoyed her entombment more than he had. With the lights off and the bubbles up to her chin, she had soaked away most of the day's trials with as much sensory deprivation as she could manage. Then she submitted herself to the insistent ministrations of Quántóu's magical hands. She had been away from him for so long that she had forgotten that, before all else, he was a master of Eastern and Western physiology. His acupuncture treatments, at first terrifying, had helped ease her pain immeasurably when she had first left the hospital. He had taught her some pressure techniques that she could apply herself, which she did when one of her fierce headaches came calling. This day he maneuvered her bones, muscles, and sinews to flush much of the aching caused by the chase and the fall onto the train, to say nothing of the knots caused by simply having to endure the Exhibition's crowds.

Cuddled up on a divan in a fluffy hotel robe and slippers, mask back in place, she turned off the lamp beside her and gave Titus everything she knew about the Gaze of Zeus and those who had taken it from her. It took a long time, much aided by a fine old (and appallingly expensive) Armagnac, but eventually he knew as much as she did about the convoluted business.

He, in return, gave her next to nothing.

No explanation of who employed him, what they were up to, how his organization fit into her affairs. He gave her only teasing generalities while sucking up all that she offered. And all the while maintaining that utterly charming, yet oh-so-irksome, smile.

Bloody spies! Won't even tell you your arse is wet if you're sitting in a swamp. I should've known.

So, in revenge, she shamelessly applied her 'parlor trick' to guess at some of it and fling it into his smug pretty face. His clothing, his manner, things he said or omitted, the mud on his shoes, responses to little probing comments of hers, oblique mentions of his activities by her mother and Quántóu, even his suntan, haircut, and fingernails, all painted a picture -- or at least a sketch. The gaps could be filled in with educated guesses. Anything she got wrong would likely tell in his reactions.

In a sleepy, casual murmur she said, "So, when next you're in New York, drop in at Herbert Yardley's little shop and give him my love, will you?"

Titus was good. He almost managed to control his face. But the corner of one eye twitched. "Come again?"

"You heard me. On East 38th, isn't it? Near Fifth Avenue? Is Bill Friedman still there, reading other countries' mail? And does he still think Francis Bacon wrote Shakespeare's plays?"

His half-second's hesitation before replying was all the confirmation she needed. "Well, not everybody is a Stratfordian, you know."

"Only everybody with a brain. But we can debate that some other time. This is the place where you confess all."

He plucked a cigarette from a gold case, then thought better of lighting it when he saw his sister stiffen. "While confession may be good for the soul, it would be less salutary for my head if word got back to the shop."

"Call it confirmation, then, if it makes you feel better. I'm fairly certain of my facts already. You work in the Black Chamber, breaking codes. So does Friedman, and his delightful wife. I met Elizebeth once. Mind as sharp as a talwar. She's probably Yardley's most-prized asset, yes? Can't believe she wasted all of that time at Riverbank hunting for non-existent ciphers in *Much Ado About Nothing* for Colonel Fabyan."

The Black Chamber was the U.S. State Department's code-breaking office, in cooperation with the Army. Its cover was a New York commercial code office in Manhattan, creating ciphers so that international companies could protect their trade secrets. Headed by Herbert Yardley, it actually spent its time breaking the diplomatic codes of friend and foe alike, though it did not mind taking a few peeks at the messages of its corporate clients, particularly those who were cozy with Germany, Russia, and Japan. Molly supposed that Mussolini's letters were also an open book to them, which made Titus that much more interesting just now.

Her brother said nothing, but his shrug-and-smirk combination was as good as a shouted proclamation, so she continued to make it clear how much she already knew about his supposedly secret operation.

"Don't worry, I haven't been rifling your pockets. And it's not magic. I've done some work for Hugh Sinclair, your opposite number in London. That put me onto the scent, once I noticed a few tiny things that aimed me down the proper path. For instance, you're wearing the same make of shoe that the Hugh Sinclair boys favor. They're new, so you just acquired them here, probably after meeting with them. The heels are more than usually thick, easy to hollow-out for hidden messages and such. And your left heel is not quite straight, because when you last stowed something in it you didn't get it set all the way back in its notch."

He stared at her as if she were worthy of burning at the stake and risked a quick glance down at his foot. "How did you...?" The heel was perfectly aligned. Titus groaned and let his head hang back over the chair. "You took a stab in the dark and I walked right into the knife. Touché."

"Well, I won't twist it if you spill some of the beans. Nothing too juicy, just catch me up a bit."

"Sounds to me like you're so caught up that I'm looking at your back." Titus laughed. "Well, so much for my clever covert manner. You're right, of course. I'm one of Yardley's tools. But I don't break codes. That's not only beyond me, but indescribably boring. My job is field corroboration. I take what they glean and then gad about the world seeing if it's true. And I act on it, if required. Ever so much more fun than giving myself a headache staring at numbers until my eyes cross."

That had been Molly's guess, but she was happy to hear it from him. Though quite clever – an Aulis family trait -- Titus had always been more a man of action rather than pure brainwork. She imagined that his 'take action' involved rougher work than she would want to think him capable of.

"Not that I look down my nose at the geniuses in the Chamber," he continued. "Without them I'd just be a big lug fumbling about breaking things at random."

From what Molly had heard, 'geniuses' was no mere turn of phrase. William Friedman apparently could break machine-crafted codes by hand with ease, and his wife Elizebeth worked the same wizardry on codes in other languages, even Chinese. They had honed their craft at George Fabyan's Riverbank estate near Chicago. That textile tycoon had a positive mania that Shakespeare's plays contained hidden messages revealing that the texts had really been written by Sir Francis Bacon. With his vast funds he hired the Friedmans, not then husband and wife, and several others to crack those supposed codes. Almost by accident he created the only civilian cryptology service in America. When Yardley needed talent, he naturally lured the best of Fabyan's people to his employ.

"Do you break a lot of things for flag and country?" she teasingly inquired.

"More than my fair share, though the more of that you do the dicier things get. Attracts inconvenient attention. Much like when a certain someone breaks heads in a major Parisian shrine full of tourists."

"Well, in my defense, they were Fascist assassins."

"Were they? Then I tip my hat, sis."

"As if you didn't know that. Since we're on the subject, what else do you know about the representatives of the ersatz Roman Empire who are so prevalent nowadays?"

"Easy to ridicule, but still dangerous. Mussolini's penchant for funny outfits can blind you to his competence in select areas. Though I doubt that his military is ever likely to be first-rate – I fear the Germans more in that arena, if they ever manage to get off their backs – he does seem to have some crack specialized outfits. Kill squads and science teams, especially. The former draws from old Camorra and Mafiosi, of course. No surprise there. Those fellows have always been handy with stilettos."

"I've come across more of those than I'm comfortable with lately. And some more creative toys. I'll show you one later."

"Always happy to ogle death gadgets with you. As for the science department, the heirs of Galileo are no slouches."

"All I know is that they make lovely, but infuriating, cars."

"True. But they're clever with machinery of all types. After all, they have a tradition. Roman engineering. Da Vinci, Volta, Marconi. It's not just autos and radios. After the less-than-stellar performance of Italian arms in the Great War, Il Duce has set his best minds to the task of ensuring that his troops have every advantage for the next conflict. Chiefly, that involves improvements in the standard systems, but he also has a dedicated crew who explore less conventional avenues."

"Like death rays from outer space?"

"Well, who doesn't like a little drama with his conquering?"

"I admit that there's been plenty of that lately thanks to the Gaze. I had a calmer time of it with Lawrence."

They both knew how untrue that was, but it made a nice oratorical point. After a silence that no doubt indicated that Titus was recalling the time he had spent at her bedside at war's end, he sighed. "Anyway, this Terremoto you keep running into oversees the exotic end of that operation. His head scientist is a fellow named Rospo, who's been drummed out of every legitimate professional organization in Europe. Has a penchant for the seamier side of science: vivisection, destructive testing on living subjects, outright theft of others' ideas. It's hardly a surprise that he'd want to pick Matthews' brain."

"He's given Terremoto quite the frisky set of digits, too. A glass hand that shoots darts. One of them just missed me at Wembley before you rode in on your white charger. I expect it might do other nasty things, too."

"The good colonel had to be put back together like Humpty Dumpty during the war, thanks to an anti-aircraft shell bursting atop him." Titus paused, reminded again of his sister's similar story. "Steel plate in his skull and hand blown off, among other things. We hear that he has to take all manner of exotic drugs to dull the pain and make his muscles work. That's why he looks like a monster in a sideshow. It's all ruined him as a human being, too. Before the war, he was a moral, ethical, empathetic officer, beloved of his men. Now he's a fanged serpent in a human skin. You'd do well to steer clear of him."

"I haven't been steering at him at all. He keeps appearing all on his own."

"Well, make sure you see him coming, then."

"I'll keep an eye out, so to speak. Do you have any intelligence on where they might be headquartered in Paris?"

"They're smart enough to change bases frequently. But didn't you say they had Hindus helping them in that cemetery affair?"

"They did. Let them do most of the dirty work, too."

"Odd. Normally not a lot of interplay between Italy and India. But perhaps the mutual distaste for the British Empire makes for allies of convenience. You might look into Parisian haunts of known Indian separatist groups, especially ones on the outs with that Ghandi fellow and his nonviolent tactics. There must be a band of young hotheads who lack the patience to play the long game against London. War veterans, I expect, who long for glorious action against their colonial masters. If Terremoto is employing them, he might also be hiding amongst them. Not an obvious place for enemies to look for Italians."

"Good idea. I have some contacts there who can help. While on that subject, what do you know about Hindu gods and demons walking amongst us?"

"There's been some wild chatter about that lately, but the shop seems to think it's either a metaphor or a code for something else."

"I wonder. The fellow who poisoned himself in front of me seemed very literal about it."

After a few more minutes catching one another up on details of other operations and of family issues, they retired for the evening. Alone in her two-acre bed, Molly slept little. She longed to be with Djuna, or with Virginia and any other

Bloomsbury playmates who might be interested, but every muscle ached from the fighting, chase, and fall onto the train, to say nothing of the crowds, noise, and social interactions. That would have to wait until the next evening, barring some death ray apocalypse. At least the hotel had obligingly sent a message over to 52 Tavistock Square, Virginia and Leonard's new house, sending her regrets.

With no Hector to keep her company either, she hugged a spare pillow and spent much of the night worrying about Matthews' nasty toy and the possibility that its enhancement by the Gaze would lead to unspeakable horrors. The Great War had been awful enough with its mechanized mayhem. How much more dreadful might things get with an all-destroying beam mounted on a tank or aeroplane? Terrible films ran across the screen of her mind, playing ever-worsening scenarios. In each one, suffering multitudes pointed accusing fingers at her for failing to stop it.

23 / Kensington Gardens, July 8

In the morning, after a lush breakfast that a sultan might have envied, Titus dropped Molly off at Lowther Lodge. Her brother reminded her of their communications plan and kissed her on the cheek, saying that he had business with the Home Secretary about the Royal Navy sealing off any likely egress from London for the Gaze.

She returned to her room, where she checked the mail for anything of interest – a vain hope -- and changed into a decadently-masculine pair of gray woolen Oxford bag trousers and tight matching waistcoat. The spare mask went back into its box and she set her primary one on the desk. Wincing from all the previous day's exertions, she took up an umbrella and went through a few la canne practice routines. That and a cup of chai improved her outlook. After the evening's dreams, though, anything would have been an improvement. Energized from her kicks and strikes, she donned her mask and toured the RGS displays, refamiliarizing herself with the beloved building. Glass cases full of exotic artifacts, as well as old maps and photographs, birthed warm umber hues and recalled the delightful excursions with her father. *Here's hoping there will be more, if I can restrain myself from strangling him when we meet again.*

In hope of bringing the potential strangulation nearer, she searched for Lord Ronaldshay to see if there had been any new contact, but he was out of his office attending to public business in Whitehall. Molly flirted with the idea of sneaking into said office and rifling through his desk for any information that the politician might have withheld. She decided that it was unlikely that anything she had not already intimidated out of him might be available. So she sighed and headed back toward her room, idly looking out of the tall windows toward Hyde Park across the street.

Where she saw a short fellow in Western togs, but with a neat white turban on his head, peering at the building through binoculars.

He made a show of pretending to be a birdwatcher, occasionally looking up at a tree and taking notes in a little journal, but Molly was not fooled. To her trained eye, he directed his lenses entirely too often at the Lodge. Precious few birds of note were there, except for pigeons. It was not the same Indian fellow Dundas had seen spying, who had been freakishly tall. Possibly the same man who had taken the potshot at her dad, though. As soon as that last thought struck her, she growled and raced for her room. Seizing a simple curved stick, she set her specialty bowler on her head and a small false moustache beneath her equally false nose, tossed on an old coat, and exited through a side door to take him unawares.

I wish this whole business would proceed with more leisure. Still stiff from yesterday's bumps and bruises.

She zigzagged across Kensington Road, between a pair of honking lorries, and reached a line of short ornamental trees that bordered the park. Her prey was somewhere to her left, out of sight at the moment because of all the greenery. Adopting a shuffling masculine gait, she put her head down and leaned heavily on the stick. While she was imitating a plodding older gentleman out for his morning constitutional, Molly kept her one eye out for the Indian and for any confederates he might have brought with him. *Hector would be handy right now, as ally and disguise. Ah, well...*

Dropping the pitch of her voice, she sang a profane soldiers' song out of tune as she approached the spot where she had seen the fellow.

"Oh, landlord, you've a daughter fair,
With lily white tits and golden hair,

Inkey pinkey parlez vous..."

It did not serve to disarm her enemy, as he was no longer there, but it certainly shocked the graying matron reading her Bible on a bench. Molly gave the old girl a wink and turned into the trees in search of the turbaned man. She was aided by the subtle and familiar aroma of a particular curry blend. Snaking through the narrow trunks, she let the scent lead her, alert for an ambush.

There was no sign of her quarry, which made her think that he had spotted her and scarpered. Though she had been careful in her approach, perhaps he had a friend on lookout. That made her slow down and think. Retired snipers were always considering the possibility of being on the receiving end of their services. Unlikely as it was that anyone would take potshots in Hyde Park in broad daylight, stranger things had happened in this affair so far. She crouched down and surveyed the terrain while pretending to tie her boot lace. The area before her was open, except for the copse she occupied, all the way to the Serpentine. Few people were in sight and none with a turban, though she examined them closely in case he had removed it. No one suspicious. Mostly nannies with prams.

Where the hell did he go, then?

No sooner had the thought flitted through her mind than she hurled herself behind the thickest tree she could find, trying to get lower than the well-shorn grass. Because the map of London that she kept in her memory had just reminded her of an unpleasant structure to the left. One that a sniper would love to occupy.

That hideous Albert Memorial.

Fifty meters of wretched Victorian excess, the gaudy monstrosity loomed over the south end of the park like a great Gothic lance about to be hurled at heaven. It was over fifty years old and had seen better days, but it still made an impression, for good or for ill. Once adorned in gleaming gold, it had become dingy through the action of omnipresent coal soot and the application of black paint as a preservative to the giant seated statue. Ornate decoration covered every square inch of the immense structure: scrollwork, faux-Grecian friezes, allegorical sculptures, columns, spires. Though it was supposed to imitate a ciborium, the architectural canopy covering a church altar, to Molly's mind it had always looked like a wedding cake for a particularly effete giant.

So far as she knew, there were no steps or ladders to get up into the top of the thing. But her adversaries had shown a disturbing ability to climb like monkeys in the Paris cemetery. That made her cautious, despite the unlikelihood of open gunfire. Still, someone could clamber atop one of the statues and direct an ally toward her. With no other worthy places to concern herself with, she decided to approach it and satisfy herself that it was safe. She resumed her character of the gruff old soldier and maneuvered as inconspicuously as possible, changing direction and pace often, justifying the shifts as interest in flora, fauna, or passers-by. When no hostile fire came her way and no suspicious figures could be immediately seen, she relaxed somewhat and, after climbing a daunting number of stone steps, got to the base of the structure.

Up close, it proved even more irritating to her trained eye. It was the sort of thing self-important people had always built, to intimidate their inferiors and proclaim their own magnificence or that of their family. Molly had certainly excavated her fair share of such things, be they ziggurats or temples or tombs. Would some future archaeologist dig up this eyesore in another millennium? Or a great museum fill its halls with this dreadful statuary? She shuddered at Albert's huge figure, which gazed out at the great round hall named after him across the road.

Some students were sketching details of the structure. *Probably as a punishment from their art history instructors.* A couple of tourists were taking photographs. No one was obviously lurking for mischief, though it was impossible to see every nook of the thing from a single vantage point. Molly noted that the blackened statue of the prince wore clothes more appropriate to Shakespeare's age than to his own. A sensible frock coat would not have set the proper tone for veneration. To Molly's mind, a toga might have been a better choice, since the concert venue he contemplated looked like a marriage of the Colosseum and the Panthéon.

She moved around to the other side of the memorial, cringing at the decoration, to see if the Indian was there. Mindful of the crossbows in the cemetery, she walked with an irregular gait to spoil their aim. Also recalling the deadly fellow on the rope, she looked up into the top of the spire, just in case the same sort of adversary awaited her again.

Which was how she got stabbed.

Strictly speaking, it was her bowler that was pierced, thanks to a timely vision mark of curry and a soft scrape of shoe on stone behind her. Her assailant bounded down from the cover of the northeastern corner's Africa statue group – Cleopatra on a camel – and tried to deliver a quick thrust to her ribs with a wicked recurved dagger. No doubt he hoped to dispatch her with the one secret blow and vanish before anyone in the park noticed. But the lucky forewarning gave Molly time to whirl to her right and bat the blade away with her hat. She had had it specially made just for alarming occasions such as this. It was lined with steel.

The killer's knife hand bounced away, though he retained his weapon. Molly treasured the look of astonishment in his cold eyes. To reinforce that, she hooked his arm with her stick, pivoted back in the other direction, and jerked him into the wall. Much to her chagrin that did little to dissuade him, as he proved tougher than his placid disguise indicated. He caromed off and slashed at her in one motion, as if he crashed into walls every day. When she hopped neatly out of the knife's path and held her stick out on guard, he smiled.

"Khumal, get behind her while I charm this white sorceress," he said in Hindi in a casual tone, tucking his blade beneath his coat so as not to alarm the middle-class mother and children who passed nearby. "You, too, Sanjeev."

His masters would have done better to warn him about his victim's facility for languages. She thought it best to pretend that she had not understood, while **maneuver**ing closer to the wall to make it more difficult for his confederates to get at her. In English she said, "You have the advantage of me, sir. How have I given offense?"

"To me, personally? No offense in the world," he replied. His accent placed his origin somewhere near Uttar Pradesh. "Though that stage moustache is abhorrent."

"Such a pity. I selected it just for you."

"And my masters selected you just for me." He shrugged. "Inquire of them what it is that you are guilty of."

"Asking too many questions of your Roman masters, I expect."

A cluster of uniformed schoolchildren and their teacher approached. A short thick man with dark skin came just behind them, trying to keep himself between the instructor and Molly. She saw that his forehead looked paler than his lower face. *The birdwatcher. He's pulled off his turban to blend in. Well, there's one. I wonder where his friend is.*

The other assassin proved to be bolder. He simply strolled up to Molly while she was congratulating herself on spying the other one. With a clerical collar at his throat, wide-brimmed hat hiding his swarthy face, and Bible in hand, no one else took note of him, either. Molly moved her stick toward him without seeming overtly threatening, while shifting the armored bowler in the first man's direction. She noted that the priest kept well to her blind side, making it difficult to keep him in view with the lethal birdwatcher.

"Good morning, my child," he said with a grin. His accent was pure posh London. "Have you anything to confess?"

Molly smirked and quoted Oscar Wilde. "Only my own genius." Inside she felt much more anxiety than her quip betrayed and backed up against the wall.

The third Hindu popped out from behind the school crowd and approached her directly from the front. Though he held no obvious weapon, his confidence was alarming. "Hurry up and kill her," he said in Hindi, with the same accent as the first man. "We are losing time."

Heart pounding and mouth dry, Molly did not like her chances. Engaging a trio of trained killers was not something her la canne tutors had ever encouraged.

"We can hardly dispatch her in front of twenty witnesses," that fellow pointed out in the same language.

"That depends on what they believe they witnessed," said the priest. He pointed the Bible at Molly, spine up. She saw a round black hole that shouldn't have been there. "Air gun," he muttered in English. "A marvel of Italian engineering. Nearly silent."

Molly saw the plan, as clearly as if he had written it out for her. The priest would shout something religious, like 'Hallelujah!' that would cover the tiny cough of the gun. When she slid down the wall to the pavement, the apparent man of the cloth would rush to her aid, calling out for a policeman. The others would vanish while all eyes were on him, leaving the distraught cleric to anguish over the poor lady. And to no doubt deliver a pointy coup de grace if necessary. As soon as a bobby arrived, the shooter would disappear while the body was being examined. Then the priestly garb would be quickly swapped for something equally innocuous, and no one would be able to spot him again.

She twisted so that her right eye could keep the priest in view and moved the steel-lined hat in front of her, in hopes that it might intercept the bullet or dart or whatever the false book might send her way. The bowler was not designed to stop firearm projectiles, but that small gun would have a low velocity. Was he aware of the hat's protective nature? Would he try to simply shoot through it? Or might he aim elsewhere? And how accurate could the thing be, with so short a barrel? Of course, if she could not block the shot, none of that would matter.

Here's hoping the bird-fancier doesn't realize that I can't see him anymore. He might just give me a friendly stab and make an end of this thing.

In Hindi, the priest gave orders to his companions. "I've only the one shot, so if it miscarries, one of you make a noisy diversion while the other gives her a kiss of his blade."

Molly tensed, holding the hat far out in front of her to cut down his angle, like a charging soccer goalie. The stick she aimed at the man she could no longer see, to slow him down as well. She guessed that the one who had arrived last would be the most likely to collapse in a feigned fit and draw eyes away from the priest, if need be. Simply sprinting away occurred to her, but the three men had all her escape avenues cut off. Two of them would easily collapse on her before she could get up enough speed to break through.

A desperate idea came to her. In Hindi she spat, "I hope your aim is not as ugly as your face."

Hearing himself insulted in his own tongue took the murderer aback. She was not sure if it was the meaning of the words or the fact that she knew what they had all been saying and was aware of their plan. Either way, the man's irritating self-assuredness had been disrupted.

"Kali shall feast on your balls for this," she added with a wink and a cackle.

The prospect did little to reassure the false priest, but he set his teeth and pointed the deadly book at her again. To Molly's eyes, though, it seemed to wobble just a bit. Behind her, the birdwatcher chuckled, but also began to creep up on her. So did the one to her right. Things had reached the point of no return. So, she did the only thing left to her.

She burst into song...in a masculine Cockney voice.

> *We used to have two tiny dogs,*
> *Such pretty little dears;*
> *But daddy sold 'em 'cause they used*
> *To bite each other's ears.*
> *I cried all day, at eight each night*
> *Papa sent me to bed;*
> *When Ma came home and wiped my eyes*
> *I cried again and said...*
> *Daddy wouldn't buy me a bow-wow! bow wow!*
> *Daddy wouldn't buy me a bow-wow! bow wow!*
> *I've got a little cat,*
> *And I'm very fond of that,*
> *But I'd rather have a bow-wow.*
> *Wow, wow, wow, wow!*

Considering the apparent lack of crowds in the park, the effect was startling. Seemingly from the ether came packs of people of all ages, drawn to the old music hall song that Molly had seen Vesta Victoria perform several times before the war. The schoolchildren all came running, of course, despite their teacher's admonitions not to. When they started clapping and calling out, "It's Charlie!" she realized with some chagrin that she had unwittingly disguised herself as the great Chaplin.

While inwardly kicking herself for being a fool, Molly played up to the role, waddling with the great actor's funny walk and twirling her cane. That made the kids giggle and crowd around her, as she had hoped. With a wiggle of her moustache, no more real than Chaplin's own, she let herself be pulled into the safety of the group. And while she kept singing silly songs, she turned her head toward her would-be murderers, tipped her bowler as the actor was known to do, and grinned.

To his credit, the priest could appreciate the performance and how he had been outplayed. He touched the brim of his own hat, tucked the lethal Bible beneath one arm, and motioned for the other two assassins to follow him out of the park. It was a Pyrrhic victory for Molly, who had embarked on the dangerous adventure to capture the birdwatcher and twist information out of him. But she realized that she had barely survived the encounter and that this time she would have to settle for that.

Well, that and the highly interesting sight Father India just showed me as he saluted.

After finally extricating herself from her adoring public, with thirty shillings in tips to boot, she made her way back to the front of the Memorial, alert for any Hindus who might have got it into their minds to double-back and lay a trap. No one dangerous was there, however. At least, no one dangerous to Molly was there. Quántóu lay beneath a tree, his chauffer's cap brim tugged down over his eyes.

"You should be more careful walking alone in the park, miss," he said, without showing any sign of having looked in her direction.

She jingled her coins. "If I had, I wouldn't have acquired all this loot."

"Not to be insulting to the honorable spawn of my employer, but they somewhat over-rewarded your singing."

"Oh, I don't know. I thought I gave the song a certain ---" She growled and kicked the bottom of his foot. "How long were you there, just watching?"

"I followed you from the Lodge."

"And never gave a thought to helping me with those three bullies?'

"On the contrary, I gave it much thought. But you seemed to have the matter well in hand and I didn't wish to presume otherwise."

"Well in hand! They almost shot me!"

"Ah! 'Almost.' See how my confidence in you was rewarded?"

Molly rattled her shillings again, thinking of how easily her mother's deadly bodyguard might have subdued her three menaces. Then they would have had a prisoner or two to pump for information. "I should reward you by stuffing these where the sun doesn't ---"

That made him slide his hat up and give her a puckish half-smile. "That would make it difficult for you to buy me tea and biscuits."

She gave him a snort and pocketed the coins. It was a toss-up which irritated her more: his not having intervened to rescue her or the fact that she hadn't spotted him tailing her through the park. "I hope you choke on them."

Quántóu got to his feet as easily as if he were a flock of birds taking wing. "Then who would drive you home, miss?"

"Home? I live across the street right now."

"Pardon. I misspoke. I meant my current home. Claridge's."

Molly sighed and sagged. "What room is she in?"

24 / Aardbeving

Terremoto was relieved to have removed his disguise. Besides being rid of the itching discomfort of the wig and beard, he had also had his intimidating appearance restored. The silly appliances had left him bereft of his accustomed disquieting manner. Now, every scar and gruesome bit on display, he made full use of that.

"Twice now you have been humiliated by her," he said in the soft tone of a disappointed father. "And by extension, you have burdened me with that shame. A one-eyed wretch has repeatedly thrashed you and escaped to gloat about it. This has placed me in an awkward position."

He stroked his deadly glass hand with its flesh-and-blood mate. All his minions eased away as far as the tiny room would permit, well aware of the fate of poor Eabroni. That was all to the good. It enlivened his chastisement without requiring him to massacre them wholesale. *Can't be liquidating the help every time a plan goes cockeyed. Il Duce takes a dim view of undue recruitment expenses.*

Behind him, Matthews was tinkering with part of his beloved device, a jeweller's loupe in one eye. He had installed the Gaze in a new portable housing he had made months before in hopes of making it work. No doubt that only added to the apprehension of Terremoto's band. The disquieting Italian colonel felt their unease on that score but had to put on a brave paternal front. At least the inventor had the sense to point it out the porthole.

"It would be simple enough to toss a bomb into her flat," he said, anticipating their natural whim. "Or machine gun her while walking that absurd mongrel. Problem solved." He sighed. "If only it were that simple. I remind you that we are a necessarily clandestine operation. Too much attention may undo all our plans. Yes, our goal is to commit a very public act, to announce our supremacy to the world, but that cannot happen if we are all apprehended."

Soffocare raised a bandaged hand. "What about an ordinary road accident? Those are common enough these days."

"I fear it is too late. If Aulis meets with any violence now, no matter how innocent seeming, the authorities of at least three nations will investigate with oppressive thoroughness. They already hunted us across their wretched little island, vainly seeking to bar us from leaving it. An inconvenience, but a plan is in place to make them give up their chase and presume us dead. It would be madness to resurrect ourselves after that and send up a flare." He waggled his false hand. "Therefore, you shall ignore her. Unless she assaults you and you must defend yourself, she is off-limits. I shall send the same order to Catalessi. We will neutralize the masked annoyance's efforts, in any case. She will be out of the picture long enough to be no bother. That will be risky enough."

He rose, metal head plate nearly bumping the ceiling of the cramped little lounge. Their airship, an Italian commercial vessel painted and doctored to look like a Dutch model, with the name *Aardbeving* on its tail, was no awe-inspiring war zeppelin. It was less than half the length of one of the German monsters, though at 140 kilometers per hour her speed was comparable. It could only carry a couple dozen people. Primarily, it was used to ferry pampered business executives. Terremoto allowed himself a small smile at that, though it looked more menacing than mirthful. In a manner of speaking, he was an executive, though his business involved more killing than commerce. And his employee relations record was...complicated.

They flew over the North Sea, halfway between London and Amsterdam. Once there, they would turn south and cross Belgium and on into France. His *Ardire* masters had clandestinely purchased a farmhouse and enough land to set the ship down. He hoped the winds remained calm, for there was no building remotely large enough there to house it. Tie ropes and clever camouflage netting would have to suffice. A few kilometers outside Paris, they would lay low and perfect Matthew's cumbersome ray rifle. Once he proclaimed it ready, they would ascend and make their statement.

"How are you progressing with that thing?" Terremoto asked the scientist.

Matthews looked up from his work, the single lens making him resemble a technological pirate. "The piezo-electric modifications Brown suggested are a marvel. We will be able to control the beam from low power invisible to a maximum blue-white bolt. You could melt the Eiffel Tower with it."

The Italian's eyes widened. "Truly? That is a delight I dared not dream of."

"Oh, yes. Your Duce possesses the most destructive force on the planet. But it will be tricky to focus. I must get the lenses just so or it will merely sputter...or explode."

That did little to reassure his comrades. Seguire, a muscular fellow with little initiative but a bulldog at following orders, glared at the gun as if the latter were imminent. "And just which of us do you expect to be pulling the trigger?"

"It's hardly more dangerous than rushing English machine guns at Passchendaele," Terremoto observed. "You got through that all right."

Seguire rubbed his forearm, then a scar on his neck. "I did. Just. The wounds hurt all the time."

"Well, that wouldn't be a problem with this thing, because there wouldn't be any more left of you than one would find in a fire grate." Terremoto favored him with his disturbing smile. "Worry not. We shall give it a thorough testing, with a long line tied to the trigger, before we deploy it. And in any case, you will not be firing it. I shall."

"Small comfort. We'll all still be aboard when you do...in a giant bag of hydrogen."

"A giant bag of undying glory, I believe you meant to say." The colonel addressed Matthews. "Is this as small and light as you can make it?"

"For now, yes," the inventor said. "Until some bright lad dreams up new and smaller circuits and tubes."

"A pity. I was so hoping to have one for my holster. All the other terrorists would swoon in envy." He frowned. "What about making copies of the jewel?"

"Theoretically possible, as it was manufactured and not created by nature. But I believe it is so beyond our earthly understanding that we shall not live to see it."

"An awful lot of 'not living' talk here," pouted Seguire.

"If we are going to call ourselves 'To Dare,' that is a risk that is implied," said Terremoto. "But let us dare to be good optimistic little Fascisti and talk about our enemies not living instead. So much more fun that way."

He moved to the door of the cabin. Turning back, he added, "After all, isn't that why we all joined this happy band?"

~

It stupefied Molly to find a hotel more opulent than the Savoy, but Claridge's had managed it. The doorman, dressed as well as any sultan, opened the door of the Isotta with a salute and an assisting hand. To her amazement, Quántóu left his precious car for the valet to park. He accompanied Titus and her through the double-arched, six-columned entrance and into the Grand Hall, where he vanished. There the gleam of brass and tile overwhelmed Molly, reflecting the light of the spectacular chandelier above.

"It's swankier than Buckingham Palace," she said to her brother, squinting in pain and clicking her teeth.

"Well, the Cartes do have more money," he smirked. "They own the Savoy, too."

Though having grown up accustomed to comfort, thanks to the railroad money her mother had inherited, Molly was unused to such richness. Eulalia, and particularly her father, wanted nothing to do with living like royals. They insisted their children grow up to be useful, not entitled. But that did not stop her mother from indulging herself on the few occasions when she travelled.

To the right of them rose a magnificent staircase, gently curved and only slightly less grand than the one at the Paris Opera. The carpeting looked to be plush enough that you would need ropes and pullies to get up out of it. Clinging to the oak banister would be of little help, as it was so polished that one wondered how to keep hold of the thing.

"Up we go," said Titus, waving her toward it. "Mom's on 3."

He strode to it like an overconfident mountaineer, but Molly did not move. Two steps up he stopped, turned, frowned. "Why aren't you ---? Oh."

The floor was black and white checked tile.

Molly remained frozen, shoulders twitching, mind awhirl with the anxiety of having to step only on the white ones while other patrons and staff stared at her.

Titus asked, "Can't you just tip your head up until you can't see the floor?"

"If only," she muttered. Her fingers flapped so hard they were a blur and her teeth clicked at the same rate. *Get it together, Aulis. Whether you stand here and fidget, or do your patented checkerboard dance, they'll still gawk.* Her fists clenched until her arms shook. She stepped on tiptoe into the center of the first white tile. Concentrating as if she were walking a high wire, she slowly moved her other foot to the next. Imagining a mob of people laughing at her, she sped up and fairly dove into Titus' arms. A panicked look behind showed that no one was in the lobby.

"I think all of the stress lately is making it worse," she told him.

Titus hugged her so hard her ribs complained, knowing that it served to calm her more than a light embrace. She had a blanket weighted with sand for just that purpose at home. "I'm only two steps away from joining you."

"Well, let's go visit mom then. That always makes my worries magically vanish."

The trip up the stairs was markedly easier, as they were carpeted in a soothing purple (*why am I not surprised?*) with little cream flowers. They passed no one and the shrieking inside Molly's head faded. When they reached the door to her mother's rooms, she leaned against the wall, eyes closed, and bumped her head lightly against it until the colors settled at the edges of her vision.

"Ready?" asked Titus. "She has aspirin, if things go that way."

Quántóu answered their knock and ushered them in. Although she made no mention of it, Molly noticed he held the Mauser hidden behind him in case the wrong visitor arrived. She also noted that her mother had taken a hellishly expensive corner suite that boasted a pair of bedrooms, a marble fireplace, and a baby grand piano. Molly's room at Lowther Lodge would have fit in the bathroom. Eulalia lounged out on a Rococo Louis Quinze sofa that might have been looted from Versailles.

"You look like you're expecting someone to peel you a grape," laughed Titus.

She favored him with a genuine smile. "Don't be silly, dear. I leave the peels on when I'm roughing it in the field." Her eyes shifted to Molly. "I heard about your walk in the park. Why can't you ever attract the right sort of boy?"

Molly raised an eyebrow at that. Eulalia mimicked it. After a long moment Molly burst out laughing and the other two joined her. In a stagey, snooty voice she said, "Oh, mother, you're such a card!"

"A joker, I expect," Eulalia said, "since all my efforts to be treated as a queen have come to nought."

Gesturing at the absurd room, Molly asked, "Really?"

"I meant by my little darlings."

Titus moved to one of the heavily curtained windows and peered at the street. "If it's any consolation, she treats you precisely as she treats royalty."

"Any of our tiresome friends in sight?" his sister asked.

"Just our Gallic pal in the cab, puffing away on that pipe."

Molly joined him and squinted at the car across the street. "Describe it."

"Straight stem briar, silver band, gold accents."

She kicked the wall and scuffed it, no doubt doing £800 of damage. "Damn him!" Titus gave her the expected questioning look. "Sanglier, Sûreté detective. I thought we had a better understanding than this. And why is he doing his own legwork and not delegating it? He must have found out something that scared that silly moustache right off his lip."

Quántóu asked, "Shall I remove him?"

"That might prove harder than you think. Leave him there. I need to find out what he knows, but not right now."

Molly turned back to her mother. "Speaking of finding out things..."

Sitting up in her lavender dressing gown, Eulalia shrugged. "I told you, I go where you go until we find your father."

"You don't trust me to alert you if he shows up?"

"No, it's that I don't trust him to stay long if he does."

"He's been on the run for years and no one's caught him yet. I rather doubt that your great screaming advertisement of a car will provide the sort of stealth you require."

"Likely not. But if we can get him in it, he'll be safer than anywhere else. I had it armor plated. The glass, too."

"You're joking."

Titus chuckled. "She's not. And the tires will be next, thanks to your friend Hassanein demonstrating their weakness."

"Why on earth do you need a tank?"

"Because I'm a target, dear," Eulalia explained, as if to a toddler. "Always have been. I have enormous pots of money that people would like a bit of. Why do you think I carry a heavily armed doctor with me?" As if on cue, her heavily armed doctor set down a tray of jasmine tea. "Sit down, you two," she commanded, "before you fall down. You both look like wrung-out washcloths."

Molly fell into an armchair, 'fell' being the operative word. It was like being in a plummeting elevator, until the too-thick cushion finally stopped compressing. "If I feel a pea at the bottom of this, am I a real princess?"

"You're my princess regardless, so have some tea and biscuits. What have you been eating? Grass?"

"Terror and cluelessness, mostly. The only reason I have any bacon is because the great fraud over there saved it at the Exhibition."

"So I heard. We have a viscount in the family now. I shall have to redesign our coat of arms."

"We have one?" Eulalia had been born in Scotland and

moved to America as a toddler.

"Oh, yes. One of my more disreputable ancestors bought it from Charles II. I don't know what it's supposed to represent, but it looks like a moulting turkey clutching a chamber pot."

"That explains why I've never seen it."

"Quite. It never did match the drapes."

Molly arranged her biscuits in a perfectly straight line. "Neither did I."

Quántóu answered a knock at the door. He brought a note on a tray to Eulalia. She squinted at it, then jerked up straight. "This is from Lord Ronaldshay."

With a smile, Molly asked, "How is old Larry doing?"

"Old Larry found a broken rose in front of his door."

Now everyone became as focused as a viper eyeing a mouse. "Indeed?" said Titus. "And...?"

"He says there was a note this time, directing him to meet Nathaniel at the zoo rather than Lowther Lodge."

"Odd," Molly mused with a frown. "Did he give a reason?"

"Says the RGS is too carefully watched."

"Understandable, based on my subcontinental contretemps today."

"2 p.m., at the black-tailed gazelle exhibit."

"Just like dad. They're native to Persia."

"Wait until 2:30. If he doesn't appear, then leave carefully, watching for an attack."

Titus glanced at the wall clock. "We have forty-five minutes."

25 / Claridge's Hotel

Ahmed Hassanein stood across from the Claridge's entrance, holding his black-ribboned Panama hat. His epee bouts had gone about as well as he had expected, given that he was an aristocratic dilettante and advancing to the medal rounds was not in the cards. It had been the same in Antwerp four years earlier. Perhaps if the Games adopted the scimitar his people would be on even ground. As it was, he had been no match for the French and Belgians. They understood the use of the point.

At least he now had time to himself. He had a soft spot for England, having attended Oxford. That was where he had learned to fence, and more important, box. Too many of his fellow students sneered at his brown skin and Arab accent. Success in combat, along with patrician stoicism, had earned some respect. Now, over a dozen years later, he could walk these London streets without fear of abuse.

Miss Aulis could not say the same, of course, so he had rushed from Paris after her telegram invited him. Their Italian friends had gone to ground, and an extra pair of eyes and a cool head would be welcome, she had said. When he had arrived at Lowther Lodge, though, the secretary told him that she was visiting her mother at Claridge's.

So now he stared at the grand building, expensive white linen suit and silver-headed sword stick proclaiming him a gentleman who might have business there. Beside him was an off-duty cab, a black Renault. The pipe-smoking driver looked at him through the mirror with more interest than Hassanein thought proper. Perhaps Egyptians were a novelty in his world. Shrugging that off, Hassanein crossed the street, adroitly avoiding traffic as a fencer should. As he neared the doors, an ambulance raced up and stopped with a screech of brakes. It was, of all things, a motorcycle with a torpedo-shaped sidecar. Its goggled driver sat still, waiting.

As Hassanein reached the lobby, two white-coated orderlies carried someone out, face covered. A young doctor followed, black bag in hand. Staff and patrons clustered about, watching with concern. They gently slid their burden into the rear of the metal cigar, closed the hatch, and nodded to the driver, who immediately raced off with his patient. The doctor and orderlies walked off in the same direction. Hassanein wondered why. Was their hospital so near that it was that convenient? Even more mysterious, the cab that had shown so much interest in him pulled out in a U-turn and roared after the motorcycle.

With a shrug, he forgot the scene and climbed to the third-floor suite of Mrs. Aulis. After three sets of polite knocks, the door remained closed. Had they all gone out to tea? It was about that time. He turned away, intending to lounge in the lobby until they returned. A thump inside made him pause. Going back, he put his ear to the door. Now there were more of the same noises, but in a regular pattern. They grew louder, closer together, more urgent.

Hassanein rushed back down and collared the first staff member he saw, telling them that he feared an emergency upstairs. The fellow was dubious until an Egyptian diplomatic passport was produced. Then he led Ahmed up in a rush and unlocked the door.

No one was in the suite. A tea service lay out, pot upended, and cups broken. One of the carpet runners was bunched up. Most alarming was the smell that stung the nose.

Chloroform.

"Call the police! Now!" Hassanein barked in his best military officer's voice. The employee vanished as if fired from a gun.

The frantic bumping sounds came from the bathroom. Sliding his blade out, he cautiously threw open the door and hopped back. A bound and gagged man in black livery fell out, thrashing. Hassanein recognized Quántóu. In a moment he had the bonds cut and had plucked the handkerchief from the outraged mouth. A torrent of Chinese invective seared the suite.

Quántóu struggled to his feet, kicking furniture. Now he swore in posh English. His face was red with minor chemical burns. He dashed about, searching everywhere, even silly places like inside the piano.

"Did they take her?!" He pointed at his rescuer. "Did they take her?!"

"Take who? Miss Aulis?"

"No, not her. My lady. Her mother."

"I don't know. I only just --- the ambulance! Someone was taken off in an ambulance as I got here. Face covered."

"That had to be her."

"Did you see who did it?"

"No, to my eternal shame. The front desk, so I thought, called and said there was a delivery from Mr. Aulis coming up. Like a naive baby monkey, I opened the door without caution. Took a spray of chloroform dead in my face. Blinded me for a bit. Then they held a cloth of the stuff over my face. I held my breath and fought. One of them has broken ribs now. But in the end..." Quántóu collapsed onto the sofa, shaking his head. "I had only the one job to do."

Moving to the phone, Hassanein tried to reassure him. "I am familiar with kidnappings and ransom. The lady is wealthy, yes?"

"Oh, yes. Croesus-level."

"Then they will certainly call with demands for money. And we shall ---"

He snatched up a note sitting beside the phone. "Perhaps not. 'Abandon your pursuit for seven days and she shall not be harmed...*Ardire*.'"

Quántóu jumped up to read it for himself. "It's those Italian scum again! And their curry-loving brethren, no doubt."

"Agreed. But how do you propose finding her in a city of millions? Take out an advertisement in the *Times*?"

"If it comes to that, yes." The chauffer opened a drawer and took out his Mauser pistol and three magazines. One magazine he loaded into the gun, pocketing the other pair. He also pulled out a leather case about half a meter long, hanging it on his shoulder by a strap. After stuffing the gun inside his jacket, he returned to the phone and called the London Zoo to hopefully get a warning to Molly and Titus that they were either decoyed or targeted.

"Best write a note in case they come back, and we aren't here."

Quántóu did so. Then he made for the door. A puzzled Hassanein followed into the hall.

"And where are we rushing off to?"

"Lobby. Perhaps staff or guests noticed something of use. Doormen are famously observant. And I need to take some sort of action to salve my humiliation."

The only aid given turned out to be chiefly what Hassanein had already noted, except that the orderlies looked to be Indian, and they mentioned they were taking their patient to King Edward VII's Hospital.

"That's in Grosvenor Crescent, very near. But it's no doubt a lie. Still, it's all we have."

He marched off down the Mayfair sidewalk in the direction Hassanein had seen the ambulance and the orderlies go. They had not gone a hundred steps when a taxicab pulled up alongside. Its driver whistled, then called out in an East End accent.

"You chaps need a lift?"

Quántóu waved him off without even looking at him. "No, thank you."

"I believe you do." The driver's voice turned very Parisian. "I know where they are. I followed them."

Hassanein stepped to the open window. "Monsieur Sanglier, I presume?"

"Just so. I suppose Mademoiselle Molly has sung my praises?"

"If you call complaining singing, then yes."

"Ah! When the civilians are grouchy, I have been doing my job. Get in. Bring the terrifying fellow hiding the pistol in his coat, too."

A moment later they were hurtling down the street with small regard for traffic laws, other cars, or innocent pedestrians. At the first intersection the detective made a pair of right turns and headed in the opposite direction from where they had been traveling.

"The talk of the hospital was a bluff, of course," he explained. "They took this same route to their hideout."

"Which is?" asked Quántóu.

"An Indian restaurant in Ealing. Large community of Hindus there."

"You saw the lady taken in?"

"I did, through the rear kitchen entrance. Stayed long enough to see the orderlies who took her arrive in a car."

"You saw only Indians?"

"Yes. Why?"

"The Italian *Ardire* group left us a note, warning us away from them for a week."

"St. Adrian preserve me from Fascist secret societies. They've caused much trouble in Paris." He frowned. "A week? And no money demanded?"

"They clearly have an important event planned and it will be completed in that time," said Hassanein. "They want Molly and the rest of us out of their way."

"Then they are smoking much hashish, particularly about La Dame Masqueé."

"Agreed."

Quántóu asked, "So how do you propose we rescue my lady? Brute force will not work. None of us is a citizen here. Blazing away in a restaurant full of civilians will only get us arrested."

"Says the gent packing thirty rounds," laughed Sanglier.

"A last resort only. You can imagine how an armed someone with my face would be greeted by the police."

Hassanein said, "Stealth it is, then, or at least blades that do not attract attention. He considered. "Ah! I have it. We will have to make a few stops on the way."

As they continued toward their objective, he briefed them on his plan. They smiled as they listened.

~

Gurdwara Bhagwa sighed. Across the storeroom, redolent with the smell of spices, Eulalia kicked and scratched, searing the air with the sort of creative invective only well-educated aristocrats could muster. "A full week of this?"

Ladro, the thick-bodied *Ardire* ambulance driver laughed. "You wish to wage war against the British Empire and are worried about one old lady?"

"I bow to no one in courage against English bayonets, but I should be receiving hazard pay for this."

"Just cut her throat," suggested handsome Seddutore, still dressed as a doctor. "Problem solved. Peace will reign."

"It would reign until Terremoto hears of it. You've seen his idea of discipline. Besides, she must stay alive in case things go awry and we need to bargain."

"Which is all too likely the way things have been going."

Eulalia ceased her swearing and grew calm, which was somehow more menacing. "So...how much am I worth these days?"

Bhagwa turned a grumpy face to her. "What?"

"$25,000? $30,000? I would be insulted if it were less."

"You have a high opinion of yourself."

"I have experience in these matters. Someone is constantly trying to snatch me or my friends. Money drives some people mad."

"She was in the Royal Suite," Ladro pointed out. "Must be loaded."

"Are you?" Bhagwa asked. "Loaded?"

"Somewhat."

"How somewhat?"

She shrugged. "55."

Bhagwa's eyes widened "You are worth $55,000?"

Eulalia giggled like a schoolgirl. "You're funny." She looked around the room. "$55 million. Give or take."

Every jaw bounced off the concrete floor. Seddutore snickered. "You joke."

"I do no such thing. It's what you get when you sell a railroad or two to J.P. Morgan."

Ladro turned to Bhagwa. "Is the Colonel aware of this gold mine?"

"I presume he has excellent intelligence, as always," answered their host. "But I shall definitely press him on it when he next calls. Until then, do not so much as breathe in her direction."

A waiter cracked open the door and waved his employer over. "Boss, there's a man here. Frenchie. Says he's a food critic from the *Times*."

"What the devil would he want with us?"

"Told me they're doing pieces on cuisines of all the corners of the Empire, to tie in with the big Exhibition."

Bhagwa straightened his tie and slicked back his hair. "Sounds unlikely, but let me talk to this fellow."

~

Sanglier's new clothes were a bit tight under the arms and itched, but he had to admit that they sold his goods well. From the homburg on his head, watch chain at his middle, and the spats on his shoes, he oozed quality. And knowing the restaurant world as he did, he was confident his French accent would do most of the work for him. The waiter he had first spoken to had reacted as if he came bearing the Holy Grail.

An important looking turbaned Indian in a white coat and tie, confident in his manner, approached the table, the waiter who had fetched him lingering behind. "How may I be of service, sir? My man tells me you are here to write about us?"

"Bonjour, monsieur," Sanglier beamed, as if he would rather be in that restaurant than in a Turkish seraglio. "Le Garcon is most correct. I am indeed on a mission to describe for my readers the splendors of your nation's cuisine. Though the jewel in the crown of your great empire, too many of your fellow citizens are sadly ignorant of its culinary delights." He sniffed the air. "And if the aroma from your kitchen is any indication, I shall regard this as more a reward than a job."

The manager did not seem completely convinced yet. "There

are many Indian restaurants with greater reputations than ours, I am forced to admit. How did you come to select us?"

"Pure chance, will you believe it? My editors do not wish to fawn over an establishment that has been much praised already. So they gave me a list of all others in London and bade me close my eyes and point. And voila! Here I am."

At that the other man seemed to relax a bit. "A strange manner of selection for so important a task."

"You are right, of course. But in my time, I have seen odder things. This is an unpredictable business, food writing. Why, once in Hounslow I was served an American armadillo! You are familiar with these creatures, yes?"

"Only from pictures in books."

"I was astounded. It tasted like excellent quality pork. You would never guess from looking at the little monsters." Sanglier removed his wallet from inside his coat. "I will have you know that I am not one of those food critics who is only doing it to cadge free meals. I shall pay my way." He laid an enormous amount of pound notes on the table.

Any remaining doubts about the veracity of the critic were blown away by the sight. Snatching up the money, the manager waved the waiter over. "Give this gentleman whatever he desires. And then give him what he does not yet know he desires." He smiled at the critic. "We shall begin with a sampling from all our regions and styles. Will that suit you?"

Sanglier patted his stomach. "Perfectly!" He produced a notepad and pen. "I tremble in anticipation."

~

In the spice storeroom, Eulalia had changed tactics. Now she was trying on her 'perfect grandma' to see how it fit. Assisting her was the absence of all the Indians, pulled out by Bhagwa to work in the kitchen to impress the *Times* writer. Only Ladro and Seddutore were left. Of the two, the latter was the easier target, looking younger and less hardened by life than his dour, unshaved comrade, who slumped by the door smoking and reading a magazine.

"Does your nonna know what you do?" she asked him, not unkindly.

He looked at her quickly, then dropped his head and his voice. "No. But I do it for her. The money goes for her doctors."

"I am doubly sorry to hear that. What is her ailment?"

"Her eyes...very bad."

"And can the doctors help her?"

"They say there is a man who can, a new operation, but the cost is...high."

"What a pity. If things were different, I would pay for it."

The baby-faced youngster looked at her again, this time as if she had two heads. "Why would you do that?"

"Because I am an old woman who has seen a great many things. I live in Chicago, in America. You know of it?"

He nodded. "Many Italians there."

"True, many. They come to America because there is little for them in Italy. But there is not always any more for them there, either. So sometimes they feel they are forced to do...bad things to survive."

Seddutore would not look at her directly, only sideways, head down.

"I try to help men like that when I can. You have seen a kicked dog go vicious, only to be tamed by kindness?" He nodded. "That is why. No one is born to do bad things. But desperation leads to anger, which leads to unfortunate decisions sometimes."

"Stop talking!" Ladro barked, finally noticing the exchange. "Get away from her."

Eulalia rolled her eyes and smiled. "And there are some men who need no excuse."

He pulled a stiletto from his leather jacket. "Do not try my patience. I am not naive about what you are doing."

"Oh, put that thing away before you hurt yourself. It isn't scaring me. My heart doctor says I could fall over dead with no warning, so why should I worry about your little letter opener?"

"I am forbidden from killing you, but no one said I couldn't carve my name on your forehead."

"Why? So you can remember it? It is such a challenge to

your mind?"

Glowering, Ladro stood and took a step toward her. But a knock at the rear service door stopped him. His face still dark, he put a hand on it and shouted, "What do you want? Who's banging?"

The voice hollering back at him responded in Italian, "Terremoto will bang on your head until it breaks if you don't open up!"

"Sounds like Seguire," said Seddutore.

"Hurry up, you ugly donkey! This box is heavy!"

"Definitely Seguire."

Ladro tucked his knife away and cracked the door open. It swung outward with a yank from outside. A square meter parcel entered. All that was visible of its bearer were dark hands. Behind him was another, a turbaned fellow in spectacles.

"Well, help me with this damned thing!" the first man commanded. "Rospo's new gadget weighs a ton."

With obvious annoyance, Ladro bear-hugged the package and backed into the room. He failed to notice that Seguire had let go of it.

"Frightfully good of you," said a cheery Ahmed Hassanein in his own voice. "Allah shall reward you in heaven."

And thirty seconds of violent chaos ensued.

Ladro proved to be stronger than he looked. He hurled the bale back at Hassanein, who nimbly avoided it and let it tumble out the door. Both Italians drew knives. Shaking the turban off, Quántóu tossed his partner the sword stick he had been carrying for him. With his hands now free, he shrugged the leather case off his shoulder and pulled a bundle of smooth sticks out. A wrist snap broke them apart to reveal that it was a Chinese three-section staff, connected by short chains.

Epee blade out, Hassanein advanced on Ladro. The *Ardire* man proved to be made of stern stuff. Lighter on his feet than his strength indicated, he dodged the Egyptian's first two probing thrusts and batted away a third with his bare hand. That earned him a respectful nod and more complex attacks with feints and disengagements, backing him up toward the kitchen door. Just as it appeared that he would be forced to yield or bleed, three armed Indian cooks burst through it.

Someone must have seen the rescuers at the rear door and grown suspicious. One cook, holding a cleaver, assisted Ladro. The other two advanced with long kitchen knives on what they thought would be an easily downed Chinaman. They immediately realized their error when Quántóu's odd weapon swirled about his lean body like a snake around a tree trunk. As it came around again it struck at the first cook in the shoulder, making the arm hang, numbed. Believing he had an advantage, the other one cut at Quántóu at the same moment. But another section of the staff blocked it. An instant later, a blurred kick sent the fellow crashing into the wall behind him.

Hassanein had no difficulty disabling his cook, as the man had no idea who he was dealing with and rushed at him blindly. For his trouble he received a disabling thrust in his forearm and a cheek cut. Growling in frustration, Ladro shoved him at the Egyptian as a shield and followed hard to send a knife stab at him. However, he had not reckoned with the cane body, which rapped him soundly across the nose, making it gush scarlet. Another blow to the top of his head took him down.

Quántóu's first opponent had recovered and gamely moved in with his knife, albeit more cautiously. Eulalia's bodyguard spun the staff's front section like an airplane propellor. It kept the cook at a distance, but it also focused his attention there. The staff's rear portion slapped him at the base of the neck. As the knife slipped from nerveless fingers, Quántóu folded the staff into a triangle and throat-punched him with the center part. His knees buckled and he collapsed into a choking heap.

"Out of time!" shouted Hassanein, sheathing his blade. "More are coming."

Nodding, Quántóu folded the staff tight and looked to the kitchen door. It bulged in with the efforts of Indian reinforcements. But Ladro's limp body blocked it. The doctor rushed to Eulalia's aid. When he arrived, he saw with a tight smile that she needed none. Poor young Seddutore grimaced in her clutches, bent over in the same arm lock she had used on Hassanein.

"Now you remember what I told you," she said to him in a sweet grandmotherly tone. "It's never too late to take the proper path. You tell all to your priest and then telegraph me in Chicago. I'll wire you enough money to help your nonna."

26 / English Channel, HMS Thracian

Titus was yelling at Molly, but she had her hands over her ears to mitigate even louder sounds.

Engine roar and spray from the Channel had come near to overwhelming her. With the various smells of oil, salt, gunpowder, and more, the colors in her mind had become a demonic firework. HMS *Thracian*, the long and lean Royal Navy destroyer taking them southeast of Portsmouth, cut through the waves at thirty-five knots in pursuit of its prey.

She shook her head as her brother's mouth kept moving. He seized a wrist and pulled it away from her right ear. "I have proper earplugs for you, silly goose!" His other hand opened to offer them, bits of India rubber joined by a thin cord.

Within a tight grateful smile, she took them, ruing the absence of her wax plugs, left back at Lowther Lodge. She worked these in carefully, taking care that they provided the maximum protection. As the second one was seated, Titus tapped her on the shoulder and offered her something else. It looked like standard winter earmuffs, but they were thicker and lined with cork.

"Experimental," he explained. "Some skeet shooter invented them when he felt his hearing start to go."

Molly settled them onto her ears. Her whole body shrank as the tension melted away. The noise and colors subsided to whispers. "Remind me to get you a Rolls-Royce for Christmas!" she shouted, like a half-deaf person.

"You alive and well will be present enough."

They stood in the high bow, ahead of the 4-inch gun turret. Borrowed petty officer coats and caps kept them warm and somewhat dry, as the ship's speed kicked up great fountains that rained upon the deck. Water kept seeping under Molly's mask. Perhaps half a mile ahead, what looked like an underfed whale swam away from them. Titus loaned her his binoculars. Through them she could see that the small submarine leaked oil due to a hit from the gun.

"She's hurt," she told her brother. "Must be why she hasn't dived."

"Good thing she isn't one of their big ship-killers," Titus said. "Mussolini's subs are no joke. Wouldn't want to have to dodge a torpedo. For that matter, I wouldn't want to be standing here exposed if one of their deck guns let loose. Those are as heavy as the one behind us."

After staring at antelopes at the zoo for so long that their eyes crossed, they had at last realized that Nathaniel Aulis not only would not appear, but that they had been fools to believe in it happening. All the way back to the exit, however, Molly had peered at every face until her head ached, just in case. For his part, Titus kept an eye out in every other direction, wary of an ambush. Molly had told him of Terremoto's murder darts.

He employed his influence as ersatz aristocracy to use the zoo office telephone and call Eulalia's suite. After twenty rings he gave up. A second call, to the front desk, informed him, to his horror, that Eulalia had been taken to the hospital with an unknown ailment. When he gave the news to Molly, she instantly dismissed it.

"What are the odds that the moment we were decoyed here, she got sick?" she asked, more worried than she let on. "I'll bet my remaining eye they've snatched her. Did they say anything about Quántóu?"

"They did. He and a wealthy-looking Arab gentleman left on foot for the hospital. But they didn't act as if they were distraught at a medical emergency. It was more like ---"

"Fury, knowing Quántóu. They would have had to have duped or overpowered him to get to her. Lucky chance that Ahmed was on hand, though." Molly's own demeanor was much the same as Quántóu's. "Get your people onto it. They'll know how to handle this sort of thing. We'll go back to Claridge's and wait."

Titus made some more calls and they set out. No sooner had they entered the hotel, though, than the concierge handed them a message from the Home Office. Men answering the description of Terremoto, Dr. Rospo, Matthews, and several *Ardire* agents had been spotted leaving from a London dock in a speedboat. A photograph had even been taken, though not a clear one. Terremoto's metal-plated skull could be identified. If Molly and Titus wanted to be in on the pursuit, they needed to rush to get on the ship. Judging that they could be informed of progress on finding her mother by radio as well as phone, they had jumped into a cab and raced to the dock.

By the time *Thracian* had caught up with them, the *Ardire* group had transferred to a submarine, of all things. Officers on the bridge identified it as an older Italian one. The destroyer's third shot exploded just beside it, but the sub kept moving.

Despite the oil slick betraying damage, it now submerged. Another 4-inch shell splashed precisely where it had been, its skull-shaking boom right behind Molly nearly giving her a seizure. Using that spot as a guide, the ship's commander circled his craft, rolling half a dozen barrel-shaped depth charges off the stern on the assumption that the sub's captain would have changed course underwater. Explosions scarred the sea in sequence, creating great white blossoms. The crew waited to see if their attack would force the sub to the surface.

After about one minute, another explosion rocked the deck beneath Molly's feet, even larger than the depth charges. Soon debris appeared on the surface, followed by gory bits of mangled bodies. A small boat went out to retrieve them. While it did so, the ensign assigned to the civilian visitors remarked on how unusual it was for a submarine to explode in that way.

"The TNT shock wave breaks rivets, compresses the hull, causes internal leaks that leave it no choice but to surface. They don't bloody blow up, pardon my language, miss."

Molly chuckled. "Think nothing of it. I'm just bloody glad you got her. Words can't begin to express how dangerous those passengers and their cargo were."

Titus agreed. "And now that it's at the bottom of the

Channel where it can do no mischief, we can both get some sleep."

"Here's hoping. Though I wonder what else was on board that made it explode."

"You mean beside a dozen torpedoes?"

She snorted. "Quit being logical when I'm trying to be suspicious."

After an hour, the foredeck was covered with bits of soaked debris skimmed from the surface. The corpses were so mauled that any identification was impossible. Molly commented that her face looked worse than them, which drained the blood from the faces of the crew within earshot. Scraps of torn clothing, packaged rations, papers...none of it was in any out of the ordinary. The life vest held a certain irony. Picking through it all idly, Molly saw a flap of skin. But the gruesome item did not look quite right to her. She nudged it with a toe, squinted, and saw that it was not skin but rubber, about the size and shape of a large, cupped hand, with a triangle of silver paint on one edge. After a moment of contemplating it, she shrugged and followed Titus to the wardroom for coffee.

Back on terra firma, they evaded the shouting members of the fourth estate and made their way to Claridge's. Their relieved mood slid into a darker realm in the taxi. No word had come of Eulalia. Despite all the sturm und drang of being her offspring, Molly shivered at the thought of losing her. A sort of rapprochement had begun. It would be beyond dreadful if something tragic occurred just as they were retracting their claws. Which is why she quite uncharacteristically cried when the suite door opened, and she saw Eulalia calmly finishing her tea biscuits as if nothing had happened.

After the tears came finger-snapping, toe-clenching, walking back and forth in front of the window like a mechanical duck in a shooting gallery, and a minor meltdown ending in mother hugging daughter on the sofa. Then Eulalia related the entire episode to her, making it sound like some silly cotillion from her youth. Molly absorbed it all in silence, fearing she would go off again. When the tale had been told, she rose and faced the three rescuers. As old soldiers do, she acknowledged their heroism with a tiny nod, receiving the same in return.

Her own story, related with her brother's aid, had the virtue of more explosions. After toasting their success and the watery demise of the fearsome Gaze of Zeus, they all questioned another at length about the particulars of the two events. It was important to know how everything fit together. No doubt there would be many loose ends to tie up, and subsidiary schemes to quash.

Hassanein asked her to describe the submarine's detonation again, emphasizing the size of it. She judged it to be perhaps fifty percent larger than the depth charges. He nodded, frowned, but said nothing more.

Molly approached Sanglier, who wore the look of a cornered animal, and punched him in his sizeable shoulder. "You, monsieur, are an enormous shit."

He shrugged. "What can I say, my bosses told me to track down those Italian bastards and I was fairly certain that following you was the quickest way. They seemed to love assailing you. Besides, Paris is hot in the summer and I wanted to avoid Olympic security duty. No job for an old trench raider, that."

That earned him another punch. "A bit of notice would have been courteous. If I'd known I had an ally at hand ---"

"You might have behaved differently and tipped them off."

"Thank you for that vote of confidence in my skill." She sighed. Awkwardly, not looking him in the eye, she mumbled, "And for mom. Without you..."

"I think you overestimate my contribution. I mostly gorged myself on curry. And I'm not so sure she wouldn't have freed herself, in time."

"I can't argue with you there. Another hour and she might have owned the restaurant."

Eulalia chimed the rim of her glass with a spoon to get everyone's attention. "Thank you all for a thrilling afternoon's entertainment. I haven't had that much excitement since Andrew Carnegie proposed an assignation atop the Flatiron Building. Long story, another time, perhaps. But shall we collectively decide on a course of action?"

After much discussion, and a room service dinner fit for a

rajah, they arrived at a plan. Eulalia would remain in London with Titus and Quántóu, in contact with Lord Ronaldshay, and aim for a true meeting with her evasive husband. Molly and Hassanein would return to Paris to restore Hector to his rightful place as lord almighty of the Rue Le Goff. They and Sanglier would work at mopping up stray *Ardire*, particularly Molly's would-be strangler. If Nathaniel appeared, they would naturally alert Eulalia.

Molly returned to her RGS room and succumbed to a long nap full of dreams of decayed corpses rising from the sea, murderous beams of light bursting from their mouths and melting warships. Her father descended from the heavens on a fiery wheel and punched the beams with his fists, annihilating the monsters. She woke with a little smile at that.

27 / Northern France: Oise, July 11th

"Gentlemen, a toast to us, the glorious patriotic dead," said Terremoto, raising a glass of Asti while tapping the bold headline of the newspaper before him. 'Royal Navy Sinks Fascist Submarine,' it read, with the subhead of 'Murderous plot foiled, many lives saved.' "And to the actual dead, as well, I suppose. They played their roles perfectly and perished so that we may complete our great work. They shall be enshrined on the Blackshirt Roll of Honor."

His *Ardire* compatriots all grinned and cried out, "Alla vostre salute!," draining their glasses as one. After so many cockups, it was a delight to have an operation succeed so well. The late actors hired to portray each of them had more than justified their cost. So convincing had they been that not a soul, including that meddling Aulis and her allies, suspected the ruse. More to the point, Mussolini had accepted their lie that the sub's detonation, and the loss of a trained crew, had been a tragic and unforeseen accident.

They celebrated in their makeshift hanger, a clearing in an apple orchard covered by Italian army camouflage nets. In the highly unlikely event that a plane flew over, the airship would not be noticed. Their tests of Matthews' weapon only occurred when they were absolutely certain of not being seen by air or ground.

"When will we do the job and go home?" asked Seguire. "Every day we sit here increases the chance of being found out. I prefer the sham death to a Blackshirt funeral and a pension to my mama."

"Found out by whom?" his commander asked. "No one is searching. And even if a farmer were to come by, what would he see? Trees, to his eye. And in any event, you would shoot him in that eye, and no one would be any wiser." He refilled his glass. "But, to answer your question and put your mind at rest, if this afternoon's test goes well, you will get to see the Olympic crowd burn the day after tomorrow."

"Why wait that long?"

"Because the marathon will finish there on the 13th and the elite of Europe, as well as every journalist and photographer, will be attending. Il Duce desires the maximum attention paid to his demonstration. I also need time to motor into the city and pick up Catelessi. She is positively aflame to see it with us."

Terremoto stood and headed toward the house. The late morning sun was bright and cheery. A pigeon flew low overhead, reminding him of how tasty they were. "At two we shall melt the tractor. If all issues have been addressed by our honored genius here, you may begin loading everything into the ship."

~

Molly strolled through the Luxembourg Gardens, Hector tugging her along and sticking his shaggy snout into everything. Her smoked lenses and wide hat brim tamped down the glaring July sun some, but her usual bright light headache still nagged her. She watched for the first shaded spot she could find that was away from the mobs of families swarming the place. Even the distant shrill shrieks of children filled her head with jagged yellow flashes that sliced through the warm purple haze caused by the flower scent.

Beside her, Ahmed Hassanein seemed to have none of these issues. Naturally, the sun was unlikely to torment an Egyptian much, though he did wear a splendid Panama hat as a concession to it. The kids' laughter made him smile rather than wince. His only concern seemed to be keeping his expensive walking stick away from Hector, who thought it was a fine new chew toy.

"Your hound is a persistent little fellow," he observed.

Taking the hint, Molly reined the dog in. "It's bred into them, so they will stick to whatever scent they're on until they track down their prey. Though his particular prey tends to be whatever yummy I happen to be trying to eat without paying him his taxes."

As if to prove her point, Hector woofed and charged toward a little boy holding a sugared croissant. It took quick reflexes on his mistress' part to avoid an embarrassing disaster. He gave her a surly look and towed her toward the pond in front of the palace. Small model sailboats filled it, pushed out by the proud young boys who had built them. A few of the naughtier ones lobbed rocks, calling out ranges as if they were naval gunnery officers.

The pale palace itself was particularly well-balanced and attractive for a Baroque royal building, though Molly knew from touring it that parts of the interior could not make the same claim. Most notably, the Salle des Conférences dripped with so much excess gold decoration that Versailles pouted in envy. Marie de Medici had built it for herself, but now the French Senate met there.

"So very different from my country," said Ahmed. "Less sand."

Molly nodded and twitched a shoulder. "And more bare legs on the ladies." Her own were on display, beneath her pastel blue split skirt.

"My father would faint dead away. Speaking of fathers..."

"No sign of him yet. I keep looking. So does Titus and mom. They're paying for extra eyes in London and here."

She had lingered in London for a day after the submarine affair, hoping that he would feel free to show himself. When that had not happened, she felt obliged to go home and assuage Hector's wrath. On the way, she had mustered her courage and dropped in on Virginia for an intimate evening of verse and many long overdue *petit morts* until she had glowed in her core. This was her fourth day back. The day before she had received a telephone call from Sanglier, assuring her that his people were on the lookout for Nathaniel, as well as any stray

Italian or Indian troublemakers. So far all was quiet.

"When do you leave?" she asked, moving from shade tree to shade tree, shoulders twitching.

"In a week or so. I have some sights to see and calls to make on some Egyptian government functionaries. Business... pleasure..."

"We should have dinner at Café Scirocco again. It should be less stressful this time."

"I would be honored."

They passed a mother fussing over her toddler daughter. Molly recalled being the fussee at that age, but with less grace. Now that things were tending toward the better, she hoped that she could acquire some grace before she met Eulalia again. After her mother had been rescued, the thought of what might have been had sent Molly into shivering chills so bad she feared she had come down with malaria. And having normalcy snatched away just as her father had reappeared would drive her mad.

Well, madder than I already am.

She was grabbing a morning doggy walk before meeting with Sanglier. The detective had phoned to tell her that some promising information about Nathaniel's whereabouts had come in and he wanted her opinion as to its likely veracity. By good fortune, Hassanein had visited on his way to the Olympic stadium to view the team saber competition and some other events, particularly the end of the marathon, which would happen around 7:30 p.m. because of the dangerous mid-July heat. He had invited Molly as a courtesy, knowing how small the chance was of her agreeing. Of course, she had demurred, citing the crowds and sun. The fact that Djuna would be dropping by, and that she would be spending the afternoon in a rather different sort of marathon, she kept to herself.

She let Hector tug her toward a cluster of children. He was always drawn to them as to a lodestone. In his experience, kids meant adoration and treats. They were gathered around a white-faced clown who was handing out free balloons. Wearing a sort of blue-and-gold Tudor doublet, he had a bald head and slim lines above his eyes and around his mouth.

Something about him stung Molly's mind. Frowning, she

moved behind him, staring to see what might be important. All she noted was that the rear of his head, near the neck, was curled up. The spirit gum was not holding well in the sun's heat and the edge of his bald cap was loose.

Molly grew dizzy as her mind raced back to the odd bit of rubber on the deck of the *Thracian* that had puzzled her. Now she recognized it for what it was. Part of a disguise to make someone resemble Colonel Terremoto, steel plate and all. She turned with eager glee to tell Hassanein what she had realized.

At that moment, her ears exploded as one of the balloons burst, clouding her vision with orange lightning bolts. The Egyptian heard it, and their noses nearly touched as they both faced one another with wide eyes and exclaimed at the same time.

"The sub was a fake!"

"That explosion was too small," Hassanein said. "If the Gaze had been aboard, the enhanced burst would have sunk your ship."

Nodding her understanding, Molly told him about the bald cap. They jumped about with so much excitement that the children turned their attention from the clown to this new entertainment. And Hector squeezed between them, climbing up first one set of legs, then the other. Ahmed did not even notice the damage to his fine trousers.

"Who do we tell?" he asked, as Molly and Hector headed home at a brisk pace.

"Who do we tell who will believe us, you mean," she said over his shoulder as he jogged to catch up. "Sanglier first, since I have to meet with him anyhow. And Titus. He'll know how to make the high muckety-mucks take us seriously. But without more evidence than our manifest cleverness..."

"I may be able to get a fellow I know in our Embassy to believe me. He has pull with the British."

They volleyed possibilities all the way back to Molly's flat, accented by the odd adjustment in stride to avoid sidewalk joints. While Hector plunged his face into his water bowl, the better to drench the bipeds later, his mistress hung her hat on a peg and went through her mail. She had a habit, one of many, of separating it into neat piles – largest on the bottom, smallest on the top -- of personal, business, and advertisements. After leafing through the first two, she gave the other items a cursory glance each and tossed them into the bin.

Hector accepted a biscuit and some loving baby-talk in lieu of half-drowning her with his beard. Molly turned to suggest something to Hassanein when she froze as if she had just sighted Medusa.

"What's wrong?" he asked.

Instead of replying, she held up a finger and returned to dig through the trash. After rearranging the top layer so that all the labels faced up, she plucked out a flyer that she had noted many days before. But now she peered at it with absorbing interest. It promoted a fashion show at that cartoonish Madame Artemisia Formidable's salon. The picture was of a line of models wearing the latest mode. Front and center, a full head taller than the others, was the sternly beautiful Antiope.

Catelessi. And the show was in an hour.

"The gods are with us!" Molly cried. She shoved the flyer at Hassanein. After frowning for a moment, his face also lit up.

"If we can capture her and make her talk ---"

"Then the Sûreté and army will have to believe us." Molly was so charged up she did not even notice she was stepping on all the wrong-colored tiles. "I need to fancy myself up and still be as unrecognizable as possible. You should go to your Embassy and get them out of their cozy chairs."

He nodded and was gone. After calling Djuna to reschedule their planned debauch, Molly made herself up like all the important Parisian ladies did, taking particular care to blend the edge of the mask. The getup required ridiculous shoes that would be worthless in a fight, so she hoped for surprise. But just in case, she emptied her largest knapsack and put the shoes and her best dress and cloche in it. Then she donned green linen knickerbockers, a white dress shirt sans collar and cuffs, and a gray wool vest. Her darkest lenses went onto her mask. There was a restaurant next door that she could change in, if no one got alarmed at a man going into the ladies' powder room.

With sensible shoes on and Hector placated with more treats, she carried her prized bicycle downstairs. It was the most expensive thing she had ever owned, and she treated it like a lover which, given where her tender parts rested on the saddle, was appropriate. Molly had bought it with the only check of her mother's she had ever made herself cash. Hand-made by JB Louvet, dark green with gold accents, it boasted five different gears and a state-of-the-art Cyclo derailleur system that not even Tour de France riders had. She felt like a flying Valkyrie on it. After setting her razored flat cap on her head and tightening the straps of the bike's toe clips, off she went toward the 8th arrondissement and the Rue du Faubourg Saint-Honoré.

Given the heat and the need to not be a sweaty mess when she appeared at the fashion show, Molly rode as easily as time permitted. For twenty minutes, she gave herself a reminder why Paris was worth living in. Just behind her building, straddling the Boulevard Saint-Michel, sat the Sorbonne campus, dominated by its magnificent domed chapel. As she cruised past it, she marveled that when her country gained its independence, the university was already 500 years old. Being a lover and digger of aged things, the fact made her happy. As if to reinforce that appreciation, the Musée de Cluny slid by on her left. A vast collection of medieval artifacts, it was half a millennium old and built atop a Roman bath.

When she reached the Quai des Grands Augustins, on the Seine, Molly nearly turned right reflexively to visit the Shakespeare & Company bookstore her friend Sylvia had recently opened. But instead, she merely shrugged and crossed the Pont Saint-Michel onto the Ile de la Cité. That took her right by Sanglier's office. Despite the unlikelihood of him being on hand to spot her, she ducked her head and sped up. This left her no opportunity to admire the glorious stained glass of Saint-Chappelle, nor the enormous beauty of the Conciergeie. Notre Dame's façade made up for it, though.

On the other side of the Pont du Change, she turned onto the wide Rue du Rivoli and had a long straight pedal past the Louvre. When she reached the Tuileries Gardens, a left turn took her directly and quickly into the Rue Saint-Honoré and Artemisia's salon. A pretty street with many trendy shops, it was fast becoming a magnet for designers of high-end clothing and jewelry. Molly parked and locked her own fancy art piece and went into a café to change into her dress.

She just managed to present herself at the door of the salon, looking as feminine as she ever could. Settling into the last seat, usefully near the exit, she placed her bag full of cycling clothes beneath the chair. When the lights were dimmed, her sigh of relief seemed as loud as the string quartet. The summer sun had nearly done her in.

For the next fifteen minutes Molly happily relaxed, and wondered at a parade of clothes she would prefer to never be caught dead in. Over-beaded monstrosities that looked like they weighed twenty pounds. Long flowing things that would have snagged in her bike spokes. Elaborate ornamented headpieces that a maharaja might drool over. So many pearl necklaces that the oceans must have been denuded of oysters. There was a silk pajama outfit she liked, the only one with trousers, though what Hector's nails would do to it did not bear thinking about. Only the yummy models made up for it all.

Catalessi came last, the pièce de résistance of Artemisia's collection. Here she called herself Antiope, which thrilled Molly because, fittingly, Antiope had been an Amazon queen who betrayed her people.

And Molpadia killed her.

Catalessi wore a black silk gown with a long train. The chiffon top was three-quarters transparent, allowing the world an excellent view of her bare charms beneath. Gold trim in Egyptian motifs decorated the skirt, mummies being all the rage thanks to the Tutankhamun discovery. Bare feet clad only in bits of chain peeked out. Her arms were also uncovered, adorned with heavy gold bands. Sleek and shiny as a black lacquer skullcap, Catalessi's hair had been feathered across her brow in claw-like shapes. That coldly beautiful face bore several pounds of kohl about the dead eyes. White makeup covered any mark Molly's razor slash might have left.

It was both alluring and ridiculous...and Molly wanted to strip it off and devour her right on the runway.

Instead, she shrank back into the shadows in case Catelessi's eyes were sharp enough to spot her. The rest of the audience did the opposite, leaning forward in rapt admiration.

Molly had to admit that the murderous model had a certain something that entranced all who gazed upon her.

Just like the snake on her headdress.

Catalessi reached the end of the runway, turned as if on greased bearings, and slid back the way she had come. When she vanished behind the curtain the whole room seemed to exhale at once. Applause drowned out the musicians, and made Molly's hands and toes rapidly clench, as the turbaned Artemisia popped out for her bow, followed by all the models. There was much fussing over her by her girls and the public. Soon the show poodles melted away to return to their dressing room.

Molly rose, collected her bag, and made for the door. She needed to find the building's rear exit and plan a strategy for subduing her prey. But no sooner had she got into the sun and rounded the corner than she spotted a significant problem.

An undisguised Terremoto, wearing a fedora to call less attention to his unforgettable head, stood at the rear of a black Citroën, fiddling with a wireless communicators. He could only be waiting for one person. The driver remained at the wheel, engine running.

Yanking her head back out of sight, Molly dashed for the restaurant to change clothes again. It took a bit longer than it should have because she tried to do it too quickly and kept fumbling with buttons. She ran out of the restroom, tossing her knapsack and too many coins to a waiter and asking him to guard it until she returned. Again, the process of unlocking her bike was made worse by haste. But after only a mild amount of cursing in Arabic, she was mounted and spinning for the alley.

The car was gone.

She let out a wail like a doomed hero at the end of a Greek tragedy. As that did nothing to solve her problem, she sped through the alley and looked both ways. The gods were with her, for she just spied it as it vanished around a corner. Standing on her pedals, she pumped her legs as if she were doing a hundred-yard-dash. By the time she reached the corner she had gained a bit on the Citroën, since it had slowed for a mother with a baby stroller. *How chivalrous for a bunch of murderous thugs.* But it soon pulled away again, as traffic was light on the Rue-Saint-Honoré.

Molly gritted her teeth, tucked her head down low, and pounded the pedals in the bike's highest gear. Keeping her good eye on her mirror for cars overtaking her, she got into a sustainable rhythm and managed to stay in sight of Terremoto. She had the benefit of being able to maneuver between cars through spaces the Citroën never could. The pace made her feel the best she had in weeks. With the wind rushing past her face and everything beside her a blur, she imagined herself as Mercury, plummeting from Olympus on some business of Zeus.

'Get my damned Gaze back from those obnoxious mortals.'

At the intersection of the Avenue de l'Opera and the Rue du Richelieu, Terremoto turned right and then immediately left onto the Rue de Rivoli, which ran wide and straight for nearly three kilometers to the Place de la Bastille. At that spot he could take any of ten streets that could take him out of Paris in any direction he chose. If Molly lost him before then, the game would be up.

She grunted and stomped on the pedals as hard as she could, gaining a bit on the Citroën a hundred meters ahead. The Louvre slid past, on her right this time. In the distance she could see the St. Jacques Tower, an overdecorated remnant of a church demolished in the Revolution. Molly made a bargain with herself that if did not catch her prey by that spot, she would have to abandon her pursuit. Already she was gasping. Sweat ran under the mask to sting her eye.

Just as she realized that she would likely not make it even to the tower before exhausting her lungs and legs, fortune smiled. An omnibus passed her, moving at the same pace as Terremoto. With her last reserves she caught it and snagged a handrail with slippery fingers. Now she could rest while not losing any more ground. For five minutes that lasted, until her front wheel hit a dip in the pavement. She lost her precarious grip. The wheel shimmied and she jerked it straight, overcorrecting and forcing her to the gutter. With a tooth-crunching jolt she struck the curb and fell over. Only the quick reflexes of a Sorbonne student saved her from a dangerous impact.

But Catelessi and her master were gone. Molly had failed.

Nearly an hour later, after doubling back at a sleepy snail's pace to the restaurant to retrieve her knapsack, remaining for a while to refuel herself with espresso and pastries, she arrived at her building. No spies were evident. With a sigh she hoisted the bike onto a shoulder and began the painful ascent to her flat.

At the door she saw something out of place on the handle. Shiny. Sticky. Red. Leaning the bike against the opposite wall, Molly pulled the tire pump from it. That metal rod would make a serviceable baton. The latch was unlocked, another danger sign. She eased the door open just enough to attract the attention of an ambusher, pump raised high. Nothing happened. A peek inside revealed no one, just spots of crimson on the floor. No onrushing mass of fur and drool greeted her. Odd...and worrisome. Following the trail on tiptoe, she arrived at the bathroom. Her sink was a gory mess, but no one was there. More wet spots led to her bedroom. Bare feet were the first thing she saw, then Hector's fuzzy muzzle. Deciding that if her dog was so calm the danger must be low, she stepped into the room.

"Hi, there, little fa'ara," her dad said in a weak voice. "Planning to pump me up? I could use it."

28 /Rue Le Goff

What made it strike home was hearing him call her *mouse* in Arabic, something he had started when she had joined him on her first dig. She stood as if staked to the floor, sweat itching under her mask. All her joints flexed nonstop, toes wiggled, jaw clenched and unclenched in a fast rhythm. He had not seen her since the ruination of her face. Did he know about that?

"Your arm will get tired if you insist on posing like you're Leonidas fending off the Persian hordes," he pointed out, voice betraying pain. He had Molly's bright brown eyes and Titus' nose and chin, set in a head too large for his frame. Thin gray hair straggled across the top of it. Battered wire-rimmed spectacles sat uneasily on his face. His skin resembled boiled brown leather, baked by innumerable eastern suns.

"Appropriate, though," Molly said, barely audible. She lowered the pump and tossed it into her laundry hamper. "He failed to keep the invaders out, too."

"But his people were victorious in the end. Let's hope you emulate him there, as well."

Molly shook off her amazement and found a towel. She offered it to him, as blood from his head was soaking her good pillowcase. "Do you need a doctor?"

He pressed it to the side of his forehead where the wound was, making no comment about her flat, emotionless tone, despite the drama of the situation, nor lack of a welcoming embrace. "No, it's just a graze from a chakram ring. But heads always gush like fountains, no matter how shallow." His eyes went to the single tiny window. "Besides, can't risk it. They'll be watching the hospitals and clinics."

Molly sat on the edge of the bed next to him, petting Hector with one hand and inspecting her father's damage with the other. "Something more than a graze, I think."

His fingers touched her mask. "Here, too."

She lay her hand atop his, squeezing it as if she were juicing an orange. "If you weren't already damaged, I'd crack your noggin for what you put us through. Mom, especially. You're legally dead, did you know that?"

"There, that's the sentimental reunion I was expecting from you. Molly never disappoints."

"Would that were true." She poked at him all over. "I've dug up mummies with more substance. What have you been eating all this time?"

He assumed a dramatic air, as if reciting. "'Fear and despair,' he said with poetic melancholy. "And a soupcon of anger for seasoning.'"

"A lot of that going around lately." She stood. "I'll find some real food and sticking plaster. You regale me with your tale of woe."

After soundly locking the door and jamming a chair beneath the knob, Molly pulled chicken from the oak icebox in the kitchen. She made sandwiches for them both, chicken for him and portabella mushroom for her, ably supervised by the keenly interested Hector. All the ingredients she arranged in a perfect line. Nathaniel moved to the table. Holding the towel -- now full of ice -- to his head, he gave her a succinct account of his missing years.

"When the Great War began, I was as foolish as everyone else in believing it would be brief. But when the trenches went in from the Channel to Switzerland, and poison gas began filling them, I wept for civilization. Would it ever end? Eternal stalemate? I moped around in a funk, as you might recall.

"But then a strange bit of ancient writing occurred to me. By Callisthenes. You remember him? Grandnephew of Aristotle, Alexander's military historian? It was so fantastic that no one has ever taken it seriously, except perhaps as metaphor. He claimed that at the Macedonian siege of Tyre, in 332 B.C., *'gleaming silver shields' fired a beam of light at the city wall, collapsing it. Alexander's' army rushed through the opening and captured the city."*

Molly froze, knife in hand. "A beam of light..."

"Sound uncomfortably familiar? And lest you're tempted to write it off as Hellenistic hyperbole, the Tyrian historians saw and recorded the same thing."

"And nobody ever considered that corroboration?"

"Corroboration of the impossible? That's not how you get tenure, dear."

She resumed her sandwich-making. "Point taken."

"Here's another one for you. In the Bible, two centuries earlier, Ezekiel predicted the sacking of Tyre, in uncomfortable detail."

"Ezekiel...the guy who saw wheels in the sky? Were those involved?"

"No, but the prophet Amos wrote, 'I will send a fire upon the wall of Tyre.'"

"This is a lot of convergence."

"Not to mention the flying chariots in the *Vedas* of India."

Molly turned. "Is that why half the bloody subcontinent keeps appearing in this?"

"That and wanting Matthews' murder ray, to use on the British garrisons there."

She set two plates on the table, nudging Hector aside before he could fling himself upon them. "I'm guessing Ghandi wasn't consulted about that." After a long sigh, she asked him where he had been for the past nine years.

He replied with an equally long pause, then said, "The first part of it was in a Persian prison camp, interned until the war ended. Some days they would threaten to shoot me as a spy, but it didn't seem that their hearts were in it. As soon as they let me go, February of '19, I wrote a letter to your mom. Apparently, it didn't arrive. None of the others did, either. Later I discovered why. Three days after release, I was snatched off the street in Tabriz. Bag over my head, hands and feet bound, tossed into some sort of wagon. I wasn't mistreated, but I wasn't allowed a long leash, either."

"Who did this?"

"They looked and sounded like Kurds, but they were working for someone else. Refused to tell me where they were taking me. Seemed terrified of their employer."

"Takes a lot to scare Kurds."

"It seems demons do."

"Demons? Literal ones?"

"So I gathered. After a good three months of travel south and east, which would have been less, but they believed they were being pursued by someone and were always hiding in some cave or gorge, we reached the end: Koohaye Merikhi."

Pausing mid-chew – she was eating the sandwich in her usual odd way, making a perfectly even line across the bread - - Molly made a surprised sound and said, "The Martian Mountains. Another coincidence?"

"Possibly. The locals call it that because the formations are so otherworldly looking, like gray fabric bunched up into weird narrow channels. But as thing turned out..."

"Also, within spitting distance of India."

"Correct. That will become a salient point. They untied me and took me into a Bedouin chieftain's tent, where a very odd individual greeted me. He was over two meters tall, muscles of a circus strongman, gleaming black hair past his shoulders, face of Adonis. Dressed like a north Indian prince. But it was his skin that I noted first."

"How so? You find every shade under the sun in those parts."

"True. And at first it looked like your typical north Indian. When I got close, though, it looked painted on."

"Who would wear body makeup in that miserable climate? And why?"

"My very thoughts. Anyway, he spoke Ariya, at first."

"Old Persian? That hasn't been used in over two thousand years."

"Correct. In a very refined and educated Persian accent, not at all in keeping with the natives. Then he saw his error and switched to perfectly-accented British English. Apologized for my treatment, saying it was necessary for my safety and the success of his dig."

"They kidnapped you to help with an archeology project?

Why not just ask politely?"

"Because I might have declined and then they would have been compelled to cut my throat. Again, with apologies."

"Why so secretive?"

"'Good madam, stay awhile. I will be faithful.'"

"Don't you quote Polonius to me, you foot-dragging old reprobate. Get to the point."

"He called himself Akshar, 'eternal' in Sanskrit, which you will have already noted is a name for Vishnu."

"I hadn't, but it doesn't surprise me."

The old gods have returned for vengeance. Demons will feast on their hearts.

"Akshar claimed to be a wealthy merchant with a passion for the antiquities of his people. He believed that a thing of immense significance was beneath Koohaye Merikhi. When I asked what it was, he would only give me vague hints. 'A silver chariot,' was one, but huge. I'd know it when I found it, he said."

"And did you?"

"Oh, yes, that was the easy part. I found it in three days. The hard part was convincing them that I hadn't."

"Why would you---? Ah, the throat cutting. You were expendable and couldn't be allowed to talk."

"So I suspected. Thus I dragged the thing out for nearly two years, until their patience was exhausted and the whetstones came out. Which is why I tucked the bit I'd found under my shirt and stole their truck one night."

"Seems clumsy of them to permit that."

"Well, I'd spent every moment playing the part of the world's clumsiest and most absent-minded professor. They soon ceased to worry about me. But I would have fought like Heracles to get away if stealth had failed. Because I happened to see Akshar applying his makeup."

"Why would that spur you to action?"

"Because the man's skin was bright blue...like the clearest sky."

~

Colonel Terremoto lit a perfumed cigarette with his igniter-finger and wedged the holder into the glass hand. Between that sandalwood odor and Catelessi's camellia, the car's atmosphere reeked of a particular upscale brothel he had favored when last in **Marrakesh**. He let out the tiniest of laughs. That poor girl was probably still in shock from his special desires. She had earned the generous tip he had left. Beside him, in a black and perfectly tailored man's suit, Catelessi twisted her silk scarf in elegant hands.

"You'll ruin it if you keep that up," Terremoto observed. "And the poor worms worked so hard at it."

"I'm just staying ready in case she interferes again. This time I'll wring that worm's neck properly."

"Lost labor. She has no inkling of our grand escapade today."

"You've thought that before."

"Touché. But this time we have been especially circumspect."

"Nevertheless..."

"Feel free to plan your vengeance, if it makes you happy." He pulled a transmitter from his leather coat. "I shall busy myself with more rewarding pursuits. Now that we have you, I can tell the others to ready the ship and the gun."

"Be sure to encrypt it. She has one of those things."

"Fear not. I shall require the confirmation code. I'm hardly a novice at this spying thing, you know."

Catelessi ceased her scarf twisting and shook out her hands. "I almost wish she would try to stop us again." She patted a pocket. "I have a new toy that will drop her to her knees."

~

Molly's mouth mimicked Hector's and hung wide open. "Pull the other one."

Nathaniel held up a palm. "As I live and breathe."

"A blue guy with a Vishnu name? Hunting what I presume is a flying silver chariot?"

"It's shaped like a wheel, but yes. That was all the strange I could take. So off I went, but not before they realized that I had something from their dig."

"And they just cheerfully waved goodbye and went about their business?"

"Alas, no. When they awoke and saw I was gone, they dispatched a plane...and some other things. Dropped hand grenades at me."

"What? They weren't worried about their precious artifact?"

"It would take a great deal more than that to even scratch the thing. They clearly knew it."

"Yet here you sit, intact."

"Thanks to decades of living in that part of the world. And clever driving to make them miss. Aerial bombing is more difficult than it looks. Once I got to Bandar Beheshtī, I sold the car and went native, darkening my skin and posing as a mute beggar. Once I saw my pursuers pass right by me without a glance, I knew I could head out on a camel. Traveled only at night. Made it to Bagdad."

"But it was another three years before you got here."

"Yes. Bad luck. It turned out that Akshar hadn't been lying about his wealth and influence. I thought I was clear and abandoned my disguise. But at the hotel I checked into was one of his paid informers. In two days, I was on the run again."

"To where?"

"Everywhere. Their organization is so vast and so tireless that I was shut out of every city and town in the east. Constantly moving in the most remote of areas, where they were unlikely to be and where I could see a plane or car coming. Doing odd jobs or translating to feed myself. Occasionally I would pay someone to get a letter out to Lalie or you or Titus. No good. I eventually grasped that they were in the post and telegraph offices nearest those I was likely to contact. That made me abandon trying in case they were watching you. No sense endangering anyone else. Once in a blue moon I came across a European or American newspaper. That's how I found about your... injury. That article in the Chicago paper, since you were such a novelty, being a woman patient at the new faces shop."

"I recall that. Made me out to be some grand war hero. Absurd."

Nathaniel grasped his daughter's hand. She stiffened, then relaxed. His other hand traced the edge of her mask. "Honey, if you aren't one, then the word has no meaning."

After a long uncomfortable pause, she said, "How did you finally evade them?"

He pulled the ice bag away and showed her the blood stain. "Clearly, I didn't."

"You know what I mean."

"I spent the better part of a year planning and rehearsing. Without going into all the details, I forged identity papers, disguised myself as one of them, walked right into their plane, gave orders as if I were their boss, and let them take me here. Fortune favors the bold."

"But even then, you didn't let any of us know."

"I still wasn't sure how closely you were being watched. That's why I went to the RGS first, to get the lay of the land."

"And to try to get them to sponsor an expedition back to the rest of the artifact."

"Of course. And armed to the teeth. You've seen what just one of those gems can do. Imagine if Mussolini or Stalin got hold of the others."

Molly felt an icy finger along her spine. Her teeth began to click. "The others?"

"Akshar dropped hints that the 'jewels of the gods' were what he really wanted. Said they could grant favor or death. There are assorted colors that work in varying ways. The Gaze is only one of them. I believe a flying machine broke apart high above the earth, scattering bits from Africa to Asia. Most of it is under the Martian Mountains. Your sheik found one of the random chunks in Libya."

"What do the others do exactly? Did he say?"

"*Magical things* was all I got. But I gathered that one can cure wounds, and another enables short-distance travel in the blink of an eye."

"Those grant favor. What about the death part?"

"Unsure. One may boil your enemy's brain in his skull, and another controls the demons, but that might have been just wishful thinking from the Kurds."

"The demons are real, too?"

"Oh, yes. Here, I'll show you one."

That's it. My head wound has finally wrecked my mind. Next I'll be claiming I'm Napoleon.

Nathaniel shuffled back to the bedroom, returning a moment later with a package wrapped in brown mailing paper. He set it on the kitchen table. Hector jumped up to give it a thorough houndy inspection, then hopped away when he determined that it was inedible.

"This was here when I arrived," Nathaniel said. "Sent from a Paris post office. Here's the note that was inside."

Molly peered at the card he handed her. *'Madamwazeil Molly, here is the stone head I took from the cave in Libya. The Gaze was one of its eyes. Looking at it haunts me, so I send it to you. Many apologies, Farouk.'*

"Interesting. Why does he say it haunts...holy hell!"

Nathaniel had unwrapped the package to reveal every disturbing detail of the bust.

"If I had to guess, I'd say it's a Rakshasa."

"A man-eating Hindu demi-god," Molly breathed, shoulders twitching as she examined it. "Very nasty."

"I know. They sent one after me. I saw it as clearly as I see you now. Seven feet tall, four arms, striped orange and black like a tiger, naked."

Molly put her hand on her father's damaged head. "Hmm. No fever. Yet still delirious."

"If only I were." Nathaniel showed her three long white scars on the back of his left hand. "That's how close she got."

"A female Rakshasa? And nude? The mind boggles." *Well, there's one woman even I would say no to.*

"Mine did. If I hadn't leaped into the sun, I'd be in its foul belly. Sunlight burns them. That's why Akshar generally keeps them close to him, as bodyguards, instead of using them as bloodhounds. And I doubt he would relish the attention they would bring to him. He has to stay close to control them. An unbound rakshasa doesn't bear thinking about."

"But surely they aren't actually demons from the Hindu Panthéon. What are they?"

"My guess is that they originated from where Akshar and the Gaze did." Nathaniel pointed at the ceiling.

Molly hugged herself, suddenly feeling a chill. "The Gaze, and any like it, has to be controlled. It---"

Hector woofed and began dancing around the tiny kitchen. Frowning, Molly stood and asked him what was wrong. In answer, the hound stood up on the counter and nosed her purse. It was buzzing.

"Again?" she muttered. Thrusting her hand in, she pulled out the captured wireless transmitter. Nathaniel asked her what it was and if it was about to explode.

"I hope not. One of the other side's clever inventions." She squinted at the tiny screen, where the green Italian words *Urgent priority message: confirm identity* blinked. Six spaces followed.

"It wants some sort of code, but I haven't the faintest---" With a snap of her fingers she dug back into the bag. After groping around for a moment, she dumped everything onto the counter, pulling out a wrinkled scrap of paper with a triumphant "Ha!" It was the mysterious number she had taken from the wall-walking Indian. She typed in the CR4224 from it. Immediately new letters scrolled across the screen. Molly read it aloud. *All is ready. Activate gun and Aardbeving, wait for our arrival. This will be an unforgettable Games.*

"Bloody hell," she said, "they're going to attack the Olympics."

"Just like the Fascists to want a gaudy demonstration of their new power," her father noted.

"But where? There are venues scattered all over Paris. And how?"

"*Aardbeving.* Sounds Dutch. 'Aard' is earth, like the German 'erd.' So...'earthquake.' That's Terremoto having his little joke. Naming it after himself. And for what it's about to do, I expect."

"But what is it? A boat, coming up the Thames? A plane?"

"Not a boat. Too easy to seal off their escape. Terremoto isn't one for a suicide mission. A plane would let him come in fast and hard. Aiming would be an issue, though."

As Molly paced across the white tiles only, teeth clicking and fingers flapping, her black candlestick telephone rang. The sudden noise and yellow sunburst in her vision made her jump. After taking a moment to compose herself, she picked up the little receiver and answered.

"You just spasmed, didn't you?" Titus said. "Sorry about that. But we have important news. I sent a telegram but it probably hasn't been delivered yet."

"No, it hasn't. And I likely wouldn't open a door to a stranger right now anyway."

"So I figured. Well, here it is. One of our photo-recon pigeons brought back a ---"

"Stop right there. Pigeons?"

"That's right. They wear little harnesses with tiny cameras that take pictures on a timer. Very hit and miss, of course. But sometimes we get lucky. We've been sending them around the Paris area, hoping to spot the *Ardire* hideout."

"And...?"

"And the photo shows a blurry airship tail, poking out of what looks like a military camo net."

"That's it!" Molly told him about the wireless message. "Any chance that *Aardbeving* is proudly displayed on that thing?"

"Too blurry to be sure, but the first letter looks like it could be a capital A."

"Burn a hecatomb to the gods. They've just granted us impossible luck twice in the space of five minutes. They're going to blast the Olympics today, probably the stadium, from a stable floating platform."

"Jesus!" Titus said, hardly in the spirit of his sister's metaphor. "The marathon finishes there this evening. The place will be packed to the rafters."

"I'll alert Sanglier, but it'll be a hard sell without more proof. The French aren't going to send a pursuit sortie over their big national party on a whim. As soon as I say 'death ray' the conversation will be over. You'll need to use your intelligence connections to convince them that this is a real threat. While you're doing that, dad and I will---"

"Wait! Dad's there?"

That set off a flood of recriminations, and Nathaniel and Titus had a reunion over the phone. Mollified, Titus went off to work his magic on the international defense community and, no doubt, call his mother with the news. While the male side of her family had been gabbing, Molly had gone to get Mme. Bernays, the former nurse, who was happy to stitch up Nathaniel's scalp. A large glass of brandy helped him endure it, but Molly noted that his tolerance of misery had increased dramatically.

The call to Sanglier went as she had expected. He understood the reality of the danger and promised to communicate it to his superiors but held out little hope of immediate success. Time might not be on their side. Perhaps she might phone in a false bomb threat to get the stadium emptied?

"The panicked crush might kill as many as Terremoto's attack," she said while stuffing her purse with the items that had fallen out. "I'm at a loss as to...hold on." She squinted at the green and gold business card in her hand. "I may have an idea. But you're going to hate it."

~

Thanks to a Parisian traffic jam, Terremoto's car had arrived at the farm later than planned, but there had still been time to get airborne and make it to the Olympic stadium, though it would be close. All three engines were at full throttle. The ship vibrated but still felt solid. Matthews had remained on the ground with Soffocare as a guard. If things went badly, Mussolini would have need of him. If not, all would rendezvous back at their starting point once the stadium was in ashes.

Seguire sat on a bench, cleaning and inspecting his machine gun. The odd thing looked like a civilian shotgun, even cocked like one, but it had a curved magazine full of bullets atop the barrel. It fired 900 rounds per minute and its owner caressed it like a lover.

Terremoto observed, "If you keep stroking it like that, you'll have to ask its father for permission to wed."

"Laugh if you must," Seguire countered, "but if your balky knick-knack goes belly-up, Maria here will be all that stands between you and a French guillotine."

"No, no, by all means, continue. Fortune favors the

prepared." The colonel smiled a bit inside, as that made him think of the two parachutes he had secreted under his seat. "Is that thing fully ready?" he asked Seduttore, who was fiddling with the Gaze gun. He had assisted Matthews in preparing it.

"Oh, yes, absolutely," he assured his commander. "I'm just naturally fussy with babies."

"Well, finish changing its nappy and leave it alone. In fifteen minutes it will either giggle or shit on us. Nothing to be done about it now."

Catalessi made her usual sour face. "I know which one my money's on."

"My dear, you need to resign yourself to the fact that you cannot strangle a whole stadium full of people."

"No, only the one," she muttered, fingering the scarf at her throat.

~

"I didn't do anything this crazy in the whole war!" shouted Eugene Bullard, his goggled eyes scanning the eastern sky.

Molly, equally bug-eyed, hollered back from the rear seat of the Nieuport as she adjusted her leather flight helmet, toes and jaw clenching rapidly, red and black colors clouding her vision. "I'd like to tell you that this is as insane as it's going to get but lying is a sin."

"If half of what you told me is true, I can believe it."

They were flying over the eastern outskirts of Paris, hoping to intercept the *Ardire* airship before it could accomplish its horrific mission. Billy Jackson had been surprisingly amenable in loaning his garish orange plane for an unstated purpose, but Bullard's name carried weight among pilots. If he had had any inkling of the dangerous lunacy Molly planned, he would have slammed his door in their faces.

"There she is!" Bullard said, pointing dead ahead. "Twelve o'clock and a little high."

"I'll be damned. Titus' pigeon's earned extra seed tonight. We need to get to her, but don't attract their attention. Fly...nonchalantly."

Bullard banked right and climbed slightly, as if heading toward Belgium. The airship gave no indication of any suspicions. Molly had half-expected a bolt of Gaze-light to vaporize them. In a few moments Bullard had corkscrewed in the other direction and got behind and above the aft end, in the ship's blind spot. No one in the gondola could see them. He matched the gas bag's speed and seemed to hover over it, around a hundred meters higher. That distance was crucial, for Molly needed momentum for her device to work. She held it in both hands, inwardly hoping that she was not condemning thousands of helpless people to a fiery doom, and let it go.

A foot-long steel dart, feathered at the back end and full of explosive.

They had been devised by the British during the Great War for taking down German zeppelin bombers over London. Shooting zeppelins had proven surprisingly ineffective. Hydrogen needed oxygen to ignite and punching tiny holes had not been enough. Eventually, the RAF discovered that a mixture of explosive machine gun rounds with incendiaries did the trick. The former tore open the skin and exposed the gas cells to the air, and the latter set the hydrogen alight. But in the meantime, the darts had been developed.

As it plummeted toward the Italian ship, Molly gave thanks that Sanglier was such a thorough weapons collector that he had one in his office. Though not armed, of course, it had taken little time to amend that with supplies from the Sûreté arms locker. He had not revealed to Molly what tale he had told his superiors to make that happen.

The dart struck immediately in front of the tail and punched through precisely as designed. It exploded inside. Molly waited for the hydrogen fireball.

Nothing happened.

The darts had not always worked in the war. Sometimes they were unlucky and went off in just the wrong spot to obtain the magic mix of air and gas. Occasionally they bounced off the hydrogen cell. In any case, this one had failed. And there was no back-up plan, other than suicidally ramming it.

And to make matters worth, angry hornets suicidally rammed the right wing.

Bullard's fighter pilot instincts had not faded since his active duty. He banked hard left and dove beneath the airship. Soon they were at a safe distance, keeping between the Italians and their target.

"How the hell did they know we were there?" Molly asked, blinking away the insistent green sparkles in her eyes.

"He was in the right engine nacelle. Seems they have maintenance bays, so a mechanic can address problems in-flight."

"That's just peachy. Is the wing okay?"

"Seems to be. Didn't hit anything too vital."

"Our only chance now is to keep blocking him from the stadium and pray that Titus convinces the *Armée de l'air* of the danger."

"You'd think that a machine gun letting loose over Paris would get their attention."

"Let's hope so. In the meantime, can we delay them with some aerial harassment? Without getting shot down?"

"I'm game to give it a try. Duck and weave, just like boxing."

Molly thought that it was a cavalier attitude for a man about to be a father, but then, she had just reunited with hers, so they were both mad alike. All other considerations were smothered by the world spinning around her heaving stomach, as the Nieuport performed **maneuver**s she would not have thought it capable of. The plane corkscrewed toward the airship, changing direction and altitude like a shuttlecock battered about by gods. Though she heard the chattering of the machine gun, nothing struck the plane. They plunged beneath the ship and came out behind it. Bullard levelled off and came around for another pass. That was when Molly saw that their adversary was turning away from them. What was puzzling was that it kept going until it made a complete circle....and then another.

"What are they doing?" she asked with a frown.

Bullard laughed. "All they can do, miss. Looks like your shot didn't fail, after all. Control cable to their elevator must've been cut by the explosion. Steering's gone."

Molly let out a breath she had not known she had been holding. Perhaps they *had* saved the day. To reinforce the feeling, three dark specks approached from the north. Titus' powers of persuasion had won out. The cavalry had arrived.

"Let's be gone before they make the wrong assumption and shoot us down," she suggested. Titus was supposed to alert the French that any orange Nieuport they might see would be friendly, but she had experienced enough military foul-ups to prepare for the worst.

Just as they banked away, two dark shapes plummeted from the gondola. While Molly watched white parachutes billow open, the airship glowed orange on the inside. A moment later, flames consumed it, and the craft began to float toward earth like a wayward leaf from a bonfire.

"Terremoto's cutting his losses. And his witnesses. I'm betting he's under one of those chutes. And I'll put double the money on who the other is." She fancied she could smell the camellia perfume. "Follow them down so we can mark where they land."

Descending in lazy circles to keep their quarry in sight, Molly felt the French SPAD S. 20's zoom past them overhead, intent on getting to the airship. She was glad they weren't pursuing her, because the S.20 was one of the fastest planes in the world. Before the thought left her head, though, one of them spotted the Nieuport and veered about in a frightening nimble turn.

"Down, down, down!" Molly yelled. "This guy must have been in the bathroom when they had their flight briefing."

Bullard ceased circling and pointed the plane's nose straight down, diving at the spot where the parachutes were now landing. Molly noted that it was at the south-eastern tip of the Montparnasse Cemetery. *Ending where we began? Is this business going to be that neat?* The SPAD caught them with disturbing ease. Closing her eyes, Molly waited for the pair of Vickers guns to do what that Boche grenade could not.

Blood drained from her head as Bullard hauled back on the stick and brought their craft out of its dive. Both planes roared across the cemetery, just above the trees. Molly opened her eyes to look back at her doom, but the SPAD was not there. Swivelling her head around, she saw that it had pulled alongside them. The leather-coated pilot nodded in recognition, saluted, and pulled up to return to his comrades.

"Just wanted to make sure of us!" Molly called out to Bullard. "Now I have to tell you to do something you're not going to like." There had been a lot of that lately.

Two minutes later, to the accompaniment of honking horns, screeching brakes, and Gallic curses, the Nieuport landed on a broad avenue that was mostly empty of traffic, thanks to the big day at the Olympics. To their right was the wall of the cemetery. On the left was the entrance to a place Molly knew well.

The Paris Catacombs. And the locked gate had been burned through as by a massive blowtorch. It glowed a bright orange.

Thanking Bullard and advising him to leave before gendarmes arrived, Molly unbuckled and tumbled from the plane. Already, the curious and concerned were closing in. She raced across the street, intent on following Terremoto and Catelessi. Whether they were merely hiding or planned to travel all the way to the exit in the Rue Dareau, she could not let the Gaze escape her. So focused was she on reaching the still-smoking gate that her mother's car nearly flattened her.

"Mind where you're walking, dear," Eulalia advised from the back seat. "These European streets are treacherous."

Molly threw up her hands. "Why are you here? *How* are you here?"

"Got a telephone call from the RGS saying that your wayward dad might be in Paris, looking for you." Her head tilted toward Nathaniel, sitting beside her with a bandaged head. "As for how, well, when you're shamefully rich they're happy to lay on a special fast ferry for you."

"I can't talk. The villains of this piece are in there." Molly made for the gate, then turned back. "Keep dad in the car."

"Fear not. I shall leash him like an adored doggie."

Quántóu opened his door, Mauser in hand. Molly stopped him. "No! Watch after them. But do it from the catacomb exit in case they go all the way through."

"What if they try for one of the other exits, the ones not open to the public?" he asked.

"Then they'll be down there until they starve. Only one route is lit. Besides, this is all we can do."

Molly moved to one side of the gate, fearing an ambush.

Then she decided that it was an unlikely prospect, as those she pursued could have no expectation that she would be there. Nevertheless, she stayed low as she dashed inside, taking cover behind the ticket-taker's station while her eye adjusted to the darkness. Since she had needed to aim the dart, she had put a clear lens in the glasses. No attack came. Gradually she could make out details. A shelf held candles that the patrons used as they toured the tunnels. An oil lamp lit the small area where she crouched. Before her was a stone circular staircase that went over sixty feet beneath the streets. She had been down there often enough to know how daunting it would be to find your own way, much less track someone with the possibility of a fight. A weapon would be immensely valuable, but nothing serviceable was at hand. Not for the first time in this business, she lamented leaving her service pistol at home. Sighing, she picked up the lamp and went to the stairs. Halfway there she stumbled over a heap of objects and nearly fell. Moving the lamp showed that it was the Lost and Found area, full of items left by visitors. Her foot had hooked a stout wooden cane.

How did I get this lucky? Let's hope it continues.

Holding the lamp low and to the blind side to keep the glare from her good eye, Molly descended the long, cramped circular stairs. She led with the cane in case she was wrong about an *Ardire* ambush. At the bottom she advanced through the first section of tunnel, bare and free of bones, then paused to listen, seeing and hearing nothing. Six million skeletons had little left to say. The doorway before her did. It proclaimed 'Stop! This is the Empire of the Dead.'

Now she crept through the macabre part of her solo tour, proving the phrase's accuracy. Leg bones lined the walls, stacked tightly end-on, with skulls as gruesome accents. They were arranged in artistic shapes: lines, curves, crosses, even hearts. That might have relieved her anxiety a bit, if she had not been aware that behind the neat displays were chambers stacked to the ceiling with all the other bones. Occasionally signs were part of the mix, with sayings in Latin or French like 'Believe that every day may be your last.' Paris had created the world's largest memento mori. As disturbing as it was, Molly recalled that the chandelier made of bones below a Bohemian chapel had given her more shivers.

She had nearly taken off her insulated leather flight jacket before going down, as it had made her sweat up top in the sun. Now she was glad she hadn't, as she recalled that the temperature was always uncomfortably cool down here. The leather helmet she also left on. Every few meters an oil lamp glowed, as an aid to candle-bearing tourists. The caretakers had left them burning, expecting to return after the Olympic ceremony, no doubt. They revealed sculptures carved into the walls: buildings, a prison, even a complete seaport. All as a complement to the endless walls of bones. Also cut into the limestone were street signs, matching the real Parisian streets above.

At an intersection Molly had to decide which way to go. The rough stone floor left no tracks. Terremoto had not been kind enough, like Ariadne in the minotaur's Labyrinth, to leave a trail of thread to aid her. Sniffing, however, set off a mild burst of the same colors as that Antiope's scent had created in the cemetery. It was strongest to the right, so her path was clear. She stepped in that direction and froze.

Someone was behind her.

Her good ear had not picked up any noise – the bones and stone absorbed nearly all -- but the tiniest hint of color flashed at the edge of her vision. As she had been exhaling at the time, it had to be a sound. Crouching low and turning her head in all directions, she determined that it came from back the way she had come.

Did they run a clever game and leave one of them back to get me from the rear? But how would they know they were being followed? Just assuming someone would? They can't expect it to be me.

Or is it a demon, like dad said? They hunt in the dark. Eerie moving shadows from the candlelight emphasized that possibility, sending ice water down the back of her shirt.

In any event, she had to take it seriously. *Rush on and take my chances, or double-back and see who – or what -- it is?*

Though the danger of the Gaze to the world called on her to advance, sound tactics said to not risk being jumped before she could catch Terremoto. But running headlong down a corridor with no cover was foolhardy. So, she remained where she was, constantly revolving her head to look in both directions trouble might come from.

The wait was brief. Soon scraping sounds and low breathing convinced her that she was truly being followed. Hefting the stick, Molly let the stranger pass her before catching his ankle with the crook and sending him sprawling face-first. She leaped upon him and bent both his knees over her arm, a pin she knew could hold the strongest of men.

"A fine way to treat your pater familias," Nathaniel complained.

Molly let out an annoyed growl. "I should've been 'familias' enough with your ways to expect this."

He rolled over as she got off him. "Says the darling daughter who has never obeyed me in the slightest." With that he took her offered hand and stood.

"You're in no condition to be playing checkers, let alone stomping around in this. Look, your head's bleeding again. Did you hit it when you fell?"

"No, all that did was scuff my knees. It's old ooze from an hour ago. I'm fine. A handful of aspirin is taking care of the pain."

"And the lunacy?"

"Remains at its normally expected Aulis level. Stop mother-henning. How do things stand?"

"Terremoto and his scarf-loving wolf are ahead. No idea how far. Looks like they're planning to get to the exit and vanish into Paris."

"Quántóu's there with his gun. They won't be happy."

"Terremoto has a death ray. Mom won't be happy if her pretty purple paint gets scorched."

"Then let's catch them before then. It'd be cruel to condemn them to Lalie's wrath."

Nathaniel bounded off up the bony corridor. But Molly dragged him back by his shirt until she was in front. "Nope! Pater familias or not, get back."

She moved forward, lamp in one hand and stick in the other. As soon as she rounded a bend in the tunnel, there was a faint electrical hum, then a beam as bright and white as lightning lanced out. But Nathaniel had already jumped in front of her. And took the Gaze of Zeus directly into his chest.

29 / Paris Catacombs

Molly wailed and jerked him back under cover. Tears already filled her light-dazzled eye as she laid him down. His shirt had a black burn half an inch across, just to the left of the sternum. Smoke twirled up from it. She dropped her head onto his shoulder and wept.

"You're getting girl snot on me. Ooh, ick, cooties," her dad said.

She jerked straight up as if electrically shocked. Mouth hanging open, she stared at him as if he had suddenly grown eight heads, which was as likely as surviving Matthews' death ray. "What the --- ?"

Her hands felt around the wound . But there was no wound. Just solid...metal?

"Sorry for not mentioning it before now," Nathaniel said. "Had to keep it as secret as possible."

She tore open his shirt, listening for Terremoto's approach at the same time. "Keep what a secret?"

Strapped to his chest with old army web belts was an irregularly shaped slab of something solid. It looked like dull silver, with faint streaks of violet. Tapping on it produced no sound at all, not the slightest vibration, as if it were a bank vault. But Nathaniel had been moving with it like it weighed nothing.

"I found it, fa'ara. The Shield of Alexander. A piece of the aerial whatzit that he saw two millennia ago. The craft that carried the Gaze of Zeus here."

Molly still detected no one advancing on them. She risked a peek around the corner and saw nothing. "This is what you've been hiding all these years?"

"For most of them, yes. It's all I could take with me when I escaped from Akshar. The rest is still buried where it crashed, and I felt that he was the last person who should know about it."

"So where did it come from? Who flew it? How did it crash?"

"Can't help you with any of that. This bit, for sure, is as close to indestructible as any substance I've ever seen. Must've been an internal explosion. An accident, or maybe enemy action. Had to be high up to scatter pieces from Libya to Persia."

"So, not from anyplace nearby then?"

"I'm figuring you'd need a big telescope to spot it." Nathaniel stood up with her aid. "Maybe they were just exploring. Maybe they were pursued after a battle. Who knows? But the skin of their ship is made to neutralize energy, like from a Gaze-type weapon. A defensive invention."

"But not heavy, it seems."

"No, anything but. This roughly twelve-inch square piece is a quarter-inch thick and weighs four ounces."

"That beam did nothing to you? No impact? No heat?"

"Nope. Like getting hit with a powder puff."

Molly punched his shoulder, hard, making him wince. "Did you feel that? Good. It's what you deserve for scaring the bejeesus out of me."

"Fair enough," he chuckled with a shrug. "But we'd better get after our friends before they get outside and have the misfortune of encountering your mom."

After another check of the corridor drew no fire, Molly moved down it, hugging the wall and staying low. More skeletal arrangements slid by, each odder than the last. Nathaniel followed closely. Every few steps Molly stopped to listen, but no sounds came to ear or eye.

When she came to the Crypt of Passion, she froze, listening again, as it was a good place for an attacker to lurk. A three-sided nook of bones with a tall white cross in the rear, its dominating feature was an enormous barrel-shaped display surrounding a pillar supporting the roof. About two meters tall, it had the usual bone ends accented by horizontal layers of skulls. Molly looked all around it, found nothing, and moved on, waving for her dad to follow.

She saw the camellia scent. Then an alarmed grunt.

Whipping about, stick ready, lamp low, she winced as Nathaniel crashed onto his back with a thud. Antiope had caught his leg with a loop of her long scarf from her perch atop the Passion Barrel. The assassin had hidden inside the gap between the bones and the ceiling. That had masked her smell. Before Molly could react, the other woman hopped down and wrapped Nathaniel's throat, hauling him upright and hiding behind his narrow body.

"It's like my birthday and Christmas all in one go," she purred. "Sent back as a precaution against enthusiastic gendarmes and look what falls right into my lap." Like Molly, she wore action-ready male attire, with a stylish blue beret on her sleek head.

Molly eased right, closer to the barrel, in case she needed it for cover. No telling what her foe had besides the scarf. *A throwing knife would be just what she'd pack.* "Not quite Christmas for me, I'm afraid. More like Walpurgisnacht."

"More of a compliment than you intended. I am, indeed, about to bewitch you and slay you."

In Farsi, Molly told her father something his captor could not grasp. To Antiope she said in French, "Then I shall have to light the traditional bonfire to keep you at bay."

And flung the lamp at Antiope's face.

It missed, as planned, because the woman ducked it. But she had not expected Nathaniel's to go limp, his dead weight pulling her forward. Off balance, she tumbled across him. As she had to break her fall with her hands, the scarf slackened, and Nathaniel squirmed out of it and got clear. The lamp had smashed against the bone wall just behind and flames consumed the skulls like an advertisement for Dante's *Inferno*. Now the quality of the lighting in the Crypt changed into a flickering gold that threw eerie shadows everywhere. It made distances and depth perception even more difficult to judge than usual for Molly.

She had hurled herself after the lamp and landed atop Antiope. But the *Ardire* agent had recovered quickly and deflected her away. They rolled to their feet at the same time. Nathaniel had vanished. Molly backed into the crypt, knowing her adversary would follow. Antiope did just that, fumbling in a coat pocket while twirling the scarf in the other hand.

"The exit is blocked," Molly informed her while keeping her feet ready to react in any direction. "Men with guns will stop you."

That earned a laugh. "I have a man with a gun, too. Can yours shoot through walls and melt cars?"

"All of Paris is alerted now. You're trapped." Despite her vocal confidence, every one of Molly's physical tics was going full-tilt, making her body vibrate.

"You think we haven't planned for something like this? We have more allies and escape routes than you can imagine."

As she said that, the dark woman's hand flew out of her coat pocket and aimed a metal object at Molly, who retreated and tried to get behind the barrel despite knowing it was too late. But instead of the crack of a pistol, the weapon let out a shrill foghorn sound. It was a small canister of compressed air with a flared bell in front. The thing was nearly loud enough to wake the dead, who noticeably remined asleep, and obviously intended to overwhelm Molly's delicate hearing. Antiope leaped at her to take advantage of it.

Only Molly was not cowering in a whimpering heap. She stood firm as an oak and slapped the horn out of her opponent's hand with the cane. It clattered across the stone floor until the crypt's cross stopped it. Antiope's confused look was priceless, but she recovered immediately. Her scarf, stretched between both hands, looped around Molly's cane hand and twisted. The stick fell from numbed fingers. As it landed, she maneuvered to the side and yanked the arm up into a wrist lock, forcing Molly to bend over, arm high behind her. Having trained with that move countless times as attacker and victim, though, Molly saw it coming. Her boot swept Antiope's leg before the hold could set and they both tumbled down, Molly on top.

Alas, she could not remain there. Antiope rolled, releasing

the scarf, then catching Molly's bruised neck yet again. When her spin was done, she knelt atop Molly, strangling her with a triumphant grin. Molly's feet were against the barrel, but she had no leverage to kick off it.

This time the choking was more insistent than in the cemetery. Antiope was in haste and in earnest. Both Molly's arms were pinned by her knees. The deadly fashion model leaned down, clearly aiming to kiss her dying victim with luscious lips.

"Good night, sweet princess. Flights of angels and all that."

Molly's vision was narrowing and darkening. She felt a pounding in her ears and tremendous pressure in what remained of her face.

Her face.

With her last bit of strength, Molly rocked hard to one side just enough to briefly free a wrist. Then she played her last card before dying.

She flicked her mask off, letting Antiope see the full horror show.

Tough as she was, Antiope flinched back a tiny bit, slackening the garrote. That gave Molly just enough room to bend her knees against the barrel of bones and shove with all her weight into a back roll, tumbling the other woman over her. As she did, Molly caught Antiope's slender throat with her own garrote, twisted it, and jerked it like a fisherman trying to land a whale. Antiope's momentum stopped instantly, and she lay still, neck broken like a straw.

Molly sat up, panting, throat damaged anew, sweat pouring from underneath her flight cap. She unbuckled it and pulled it off. With a look back at the horn Antiope had tried to disable her with, she smirked and removed the noise suppressing earmuffs Titus had given her, followed by the wax ear plugs she normally used when flying. For a moment only she permitted herself a bit of calm, resting her forehead on her knees, rocking like a hobbyhorse, teeth clicking, fingers rubbing her palms. All the emotions of killing the Turkish assassin in the bath came rushing back, only five-fold. Only with the greatest effort did she manage to suppress the nausea.

After about two minutes she pocketed the hearing

protection and cap, retrieved her cane and Antiope's scarf, reset the mask, and continued down the eerie corridor in search of Terremoto. Her dad, too, must have already done so, for he was not in sight.

Progress was slow, for she had to guard against another sudden Gaze blast. At every moment she expected to come across Nathaniel's body, his wages for recklessness, but that did not happen. In fact, she never found him at all. The only thing unusual was a bone pile that has collapsed, revealing the random heap of remains behind. What she did find, though, were the long steps leading to the surface exit. Colonel Terremoto stood at the bottom of them, in full black Fascist unform, aiming the dreadful ray gun at her. She froze. There was nowhere to hide from it.

"Ah! So that's how it is," he said with the merest hint of sadness on seeing the scarf in Molly's hand. "I thought she might best you again, but...c'est la guerre. I hope she has a fine time in Fascist heaven."

Molly's mind was a whirl, assessing options for attack or defense. All were pointless. If she ran, she'd be shot in the back. The corridor was too straight here for him to miss. If she rushed him the result would be the same. He was too far away. Throw the cane and zigzag at him, maybe? She doubted that her real face would frighten him, judging by what he saw in his own mirror.

"Is that the heaven with the dungeon?" she said, trying to distract him while frantically thinking. "I can't keep them straight."

"Full marks for grace under pressure, Miss Aulis. I could have used a few like you. But, alas, I must toodle off. Dr. Rospo is waiting to show me his particular secret egress out of Paris. There are so many, apparently. It seems as if people are always trying to leave. Hardly bodes well for the tourist trade." He hoisted the gun up a bit to aim at her. "Arrivederci."

Molly tensed her hips to hurl herself to the side in hopes he would miss, but the blazing shot never came. As Terremoto spoke the word, the bone wall opposite her exploded at him with skulls, femurs, and other bodily detritus. Though it all fell short, it drew his attention and the gun's muzzle. That gave

Molly a chance to sprint at him.

But before she could gain much momentum, a skull struck the Italian in the face. He stumbled back, tripping on the next step up and sitting clumsily down. More skulls followed, hurled with desperate precision by Nathaniel, who emerged from the gap covered in the dust of the dead. Terremoto fended them off with the gun, stood, began backing up toward the exit. Unluckily for him, he stepped on one of the wayward skulls, lost his footing, and fell again. This time the impact made the gun fire. The blinding Gaze of Zeus light shot upward toward Mount Olympus. Stones began falling from above as the ray burned in. One knocked the gun from his hands. Others fell in a continuous mass, blocking him from view with the gun on Molly's side. She leapt to it, snatched it up.

From the other side of the stone-fall Terremoto's voice could be heard. "C'est la guerre, indeed. My congratulations. But a battle won does not a campaign make. Ciao!"

~

The rest was anticlimactic. Molly blasted a path through the stones and got up to the exit. There she found smoke obscuring everything. Quántóu sat beside her mother's car, holding his head. Three or four other people lay on the ground but were beginning to stir. Of Terremoto there was no sign.

"What happened? Where did he go?" she asked as her father came up behind her.

"He threw his bloody fingers at us!" Quántóu shouted.

"What?"

The driver struggled to his feet. "You heard me. Pulled one off, tossed it, and this hell-smoke gushed out. Other one knocked us all over. Some sort of stun grenade, I think."

"But everybody's okay? Where's mom?"

"I made her lie down in the back of the car to be safe."

Molly handed the gun to Nathaniel and opened the door. She stared at her mother for a second and just shook her head. Eulalia was asleep, cuddled in a ball, a little smile on her lips and snoring lightly, still mistress of her world.

"Don't know why this would surprise me." She took the gun back, turned away from everyone and found the compartment that held the Gaze of Zeus. She plucked it out and pocketed it before anyone could notice. Then she tossed the gun back down the stairs to the Empire of the Dead.

30 / Paris, July 16ᵗʰ

"And you have no idea where it is?" Sanglier asked for what seemed the thousandth time. Three days had passed, and it was all he talked about. The pressure from his government must have been enough to crush elephants.

They were in her parents' suite at the Paris Ritz. Its opulence looked about to smother Nathaniel after nearly a decade living rough. Eulalia had, naturally, gone overboard on every aspect of her husband's return. The best doctors in the city. Exquisite barbering. More new clothes than he could wear in a year. Room service orders a Vanderbilt would have envied. She had even rented one of the ballrooms and brought in an entire orchestra to play behind Cole Porter. Her poor husband looked like a puppy squeezed to death by an over-loving child.

"For heaven's sake, monsieur," Eulalia chided, "how many times must she say it? If she had found the wretched thing, don't you think she would have surrendered it someone who could keep it out of harm's reach? After all, she risked life and limb repeatedly to try to find it."

"If it were anyone else, gracious lady, I would concede your point. But Mlle. Aulis thinks and behaves in a different manner from the rest of us...several different manners, if I may be blunt."

"Are you ever anything but?" Molly snickered. "Search me if you must. Search my flat. Search Ahmed there, and Farouk, and Titus, and God himself, if it will reassure you."

"All that assures me of is that you have hidden it well, as I would expect of you."

Sanglier was most accurate on that point. She and Titus had hidden it in a small locked safe...which they had then hurled into the middle of the English Channel.

Hassanein asked Sanglier, "What progress have you made rounding up Terremoto and his minions? I'm especially concerned about the Indians."

"And you are right to be. We rounded up dozens. Most are just peripherally involved, but the hard cases have proven incredibly resistant to interrogation. They claim that their returned gods are more terrifying than us and clam up."

"So is this more religious than political?" Titus wanted to know while rubbing Hector's ears.

"Probably an irritating mix of both. But their Hinduism is of a brand I've not seen before. They speak as if Krishna will literally walk in the door and spring them from jail."

Molly and Nathaniel exchanged knowing looks. They had suggested that the Sûreté search for an unusually tall Indian businessman named Akshar but had kept his idiosyncrasies to themselves.

"And the Italians?"

"Terremoto and Rospo have vanished as if the earth swallowed them up, which may be true, given the geology of Paris. But all the ports, train stations, roads, and airfields are being watched. Our street informers are being paid double for good information about anything Italian. The core group went down with the airship."

"How did you explain the airship crash to Mussolini?"

"Told him it was a medical relief flight that had a tragic accident and that his men were heroes. Hard for him to deny that and use it for any Fascist propaganda."

"What about Matthews, he of the flexible allegiances?"

"Our information says that he may have crept into Belgium, possibly into the Italian embassy."

"My people can likely confirm that one way or the other. Diplomats aren't as tight-lipped as one would think."

Molly struggled up out of the absurdly plush sofa before she had to send up a rescue flare. "So we stopped the one scary thing, but the perpetrators either escaped or won't talk. Where does that leave us? Dad can't hide forever, though he's certainly proved he very well might. And more of those monstrous gems are out there. Rospo has an old map of where."

Titus said, "It leaves us with the choice of waiting around like sheep for the wolf or taking the fight to the enemy and making him fear us for a change."

"I like that," said Nathaniel, Molly, Farouk, Ahmed, and Quántóu simultaneously.

Eulalia shouted, "Well, I don't!" All heads turned at the pain in her voice. "I just got him back. He's not going galivanting off again chasing dangerous people. For Pete's sake, he was almost vaporized by some Jules Verne thingie. His head still has stitches. And Molpadia and I are finally not at one another's throats...as much. I don't want her fighting Fascists with machine guns again. Titus, I suppose, I can do nothing about, as it is his job, not that he shares any of that with his worried mother. You all need to find someone else to save the world."

"Who would that be, dear?" Nathaniel asked, taking her hand. "The more who know about the Gaze and its fellows, the more will be hunting them for their power. Power to destroy, power to change borders, power to enslave. We must keep this as secret as possible until the threat is removed. Can you imagine what the Boche would have done with the Gaze? The war would have ended in a week, with Paris and London and New York in flames. We'd all be speaking German now. You saw what Mussolini nearly did, just as a demonstration. Imagine if Stalin had it. If the stories are true, he makes Mussolini look like a country parson. And no doubt some lunatic in Germany would love to use it for revenge for losing the war. That would be the worst case."

His wife did not reply. She just set her head on his shoulder and wept. Nathaniel whispered to her for a long time. No one else could make out what he said.

Titus asked Molly, "What are we thinking? An expedition to the Martian Mountains, disguised as something else?"

"I'll leave the cloak-and-dagger stuff to you."

"Says the one who impersonated a government official and a nosy tourist. Who had a false face made."

Molly's shoulders twitched. "All my faces are false."

"Yes, well, tell that to your psychiatrist."

"There isn't enough time or money in the world to fix me."

"From where I sit, you don't need fixing, to judge by the results you get."

"Don't waste your charm on me. Save it for one of your floozies."

"You'd be surprised how few of those there are. Sorry to disappoint."

"I am disappointed." She winked. "You could have shared them."

He laughed out loud at that. Nathaniel stroked his wife's hair and announced, "Everyone, my immense powers of persuasion have convinced her to give us our blessing."

Titus whispered, "Meaning he crawled."

"Like a worm," Molly snickered.

"I hate it, but I am assured it is the only way. And a rapid solution will bring you home to my loving bosom all the sooner. To that end, the family funds and assets are completely at your disposal."

Molly sighed. Her mother had found a way to make her stubborn daughter cash her checks, after all.

If I can manage to get back out into the field again. Leaving my cozy den for an hour or two is one thing. Traipsing all over my old stomping grounds for weeks or months, stalked by Diana's ghost, will be another. Maybe I should talk to Djuna about it...during rest periods.

She gazed at a blank spot on a wall, teeth clicking, fingers waggling, toes clenching. No one took any notice of it.

About the Author

Terry Kroenung has leapt out of perfectly functioning U.S. Army aircraft, taught Crips & Bloods on a wagon train, and been paid actual money to portray both William Shakespeare and Chuck E. Cheese. Oh, a side note: doctors cut his misbehaving heart out and threw it away. But at least he got a book out of it (*HeartSnark*).

Brimstone and Lily, the first novel in his Legacy Stone series, started as 'swords-and-sorcery Huck Finn' and went sideways from there. The books include shape-shifting swords, Civil War battles, magic cannonballs, combat pelicans, Captain Nemo's sub, kindly Arab terrorists, swimming trees, cyclopean ogres, 10,000 ancient Greek zombies, lady ninjas, and poop monsters. *Brimstone and Lily* won the Bronze Medal in Science-Fiction/ Fantasy at the 2010 Independent Publishers Book Awards and was a Colorado Gold Rush Literary Award finalist. *Jasper's Foul Tongue* and *Jasper's Magick Corset* followed. *Jasper's Sloppy Smooch* will concluded the series.

An Advanced Actor/Combatant with the Society of American Fight Directors, he has choreographed or performed hundreds of swordfights, from *Hamlet* to *Peter Pan.* That's why his books have such an absurd number of fight scenes. He teaches Bartitsu (Sherlock Holmes' martial art, an actual Victorian discipline), because if you can't kill someone with an umbrella or a lady's hatpin, are you even civilized?

Paragon of the Eccentric, his Steampunk prequel to *War of the Worlds,* won the 2013 Colorado Gold writing contest and the Incite Denver contest for best first sentence ("When a Whitechapel whore waves her tentacles at you, attention must be paid").

He is retired from 30 years of teaching literature in Colorado, supported by his wife Janet and a completely whack-a-doodle basset hound named Moonbeam.

Glossary
(terms arranged in order of appearance in the text)

Prologue
Effendi: courtesy title for an educated, upper-class man
paraffin: kerosene
Webley: army pistol, Mark VI version, .455 caliber
Ahmed Hassanein Bey:
keffiyeh: square cotton scarf folded into a head/face covering
Senussi: political/religious Sufi order in Sudan and Libya
Enfield rifle: Pattern 1914, .303 caliber
Blackshirts: paramilitary wing of Mussolini's Fascist Party
sheik: literally, 'elder'
Jahannam: Islamic hell
hand torch: flashlight
Rosita Forbes: English explorer and travel writer
djinn: magical shape-shifting beings, usually invisible
General Maxwell: Sir John Maxwell, commander of British troops in Egypt until 1916, when he was sent to crush the Irish Easter Rebellion
kismet: fate
Attic Greek: dialect of ancient Greece
Hephaestus: Greek god of metalworking
fasces: ancient Roman bundle of wooden rods surrounding an axe, a symbol of authority; origin of fascism
Negev Desert: rocky treeless desert in southern Israel
MBE: Member of the Most Excellent Order of the British Empire, the lowest rank of British chivalry
Squadristi: another name for the Blackshirts
dulce et decorum est pro patria mori: "Sweet and fitting it is to die for one's country," used ironically in a Wilfrid Owen poem of the Great war, quoting the Roman poet Horace
carbon-arc stage lamp: intensely-bright light invented 200 years ago; the first practical electric light

Ch. 1
Rue Le Goff: very short street, only 95 meters, between the Sorbonne and the Luxembourg Gardens

Major Lawrence: Lawrence of Arabia, leader of the Arab Revolt against the Ottoman Empire
Herald: *Paris Herald-Tribune*, the chief English language newspaper in Paris
Sufi: Islamic mysticism
Transjordan: now called the East Bank; mostly in the nation of Jordan now
Caucasian: referring to the area between the Black and Caspian Seas
Dawes: Charles Dawes, author of the plan that instituted the Versailles Treaty; given a very unfortunate Nobel Peace Prize for this
Bukharin: Nikolai Bukharin, senior Soviet official and allied with Stalin against Trotsky; it didn't save him in the end
Trotsky: first Soviet defense minister, in on the ground floor of the Russian Revolution
Duse: Eleanora Duse, possibly the greatest stage actress of her time
British Empire Exposition: a huge world's fair of all things British, 1925-25
Boche: nickname for Germans in the Great War, loosely meaning "cabbage for brains"
la canne chausson: French stick fighting discipline
savate: French martial art emphasizing kicks, but also includes punches and stick fighting
jiu-jitsu: Japanese unarmed martial art emphasizing throws, grappling, and submission holds
Field Museum: Field Museum of Natural History, one of the largest in the world
Hiram Bingham: American explorer, re-discovered Machu Picchu
Marcel Proust: French author, famed for a scene where a teacup triggers an extended memory
St. Vitus' dance: disorder causing jerky limb movements
Luxembourg Gardens: site of an ornate palace built for Marie de' Medici in the early 1600's
Champs-Élysées: "Elysian Fields;" famous avenue running to the Arc de Triomphe
Amiens: city in northern France, site of final offensive that

defeated Germany in the Great War

Baroque: ornate artist style of the early 1600's to 1750's

Clémence Isaure: medieval sponsor of the Floral Games

Academy of the Floral Games: a famed poetry competition

Dorian Gray: character in Oscar Wilde's novel of the same name; his sins and aging showed on his portrait, not in his face

Anna Coleman Ladd: American sculptor awarded the French Legion of Honor for making restorative masks for wounded soldiers

Ch. 2

Jebel Uweinat: mountain range in southern Libya/Egypt

Jebel Arkenu: legendary mountain discovered by Hassanein

Panthéon: shrine of tombs honoring French heroes

Tubes Pneumatique: air-powered message system, like drive-in banks use now

India House: London hotbed of student resistance to British rule in India before the Great War

Madame Cama: famed Indian independence leader, living in exile in France after the end of India House; designed an early version of India's flag

coup de pied bas: kick to lower leg

direct bras avan: jab punch

fouetté: circular kick with toe making contact

Collier's: famous magazine known for progressive investigative journalism

Colonus: death/burial site of Oedipus

Goldberg Variations: famed series of 32 keyboard works by Bach

Underwood: popular brand of typewriter

Yemeni: from Yemen, on the south coast of Arabia

Lewis gun: popular light machine gun of the Great War

fedora: man's hat with soft brim and indented crown

stiletto: long slender dagger with little edge but a wicked point

damascened: a blade pattern resembling flowing water

hoplites: ancient Greek infantry fighting in phalanx

Fiume: chief port city of Croatia
Gabriele D'Annunzio: ultranationalist Italian poet and rival of Mussolini
Dalmatia: eastern shore of Croatia
Sûreté: detective branch of Paris police
Poincaré: Minister of Foreign Affairs until June 1924

Ch. 3
Place de la Sorbonne: plaza in front of the chapel of St. Ursule in the area of the University of Paris
brasserie: semi-casual restaurant serving the same menu all day
Chapelle St. Ursule: rebuilt in 1642 by Cardinal Richelieu
Cardinal Richelieu: de facto rule of France during Louis XIII's reign 1624-1642
St. Teresa: referring to the Bernini sculpture where an angel is piercing Teresa of Avila with a golden spear
Catalessi: trance
Soffocare: suffocate
Rospo: toad
Eabroni: blacksmith
Gare du Nord: Paris train station
Sobranie: cigarette brand
Seguire: to follow

Ch. 4
allez: go ahead; begin
riposte: an attack immediately after parrying the opponent's attack
flèche: a running attack
saber: fencing weapon where the edge is used as well as the point; everything above the waist is a target
foil: light fencing weapon with a torso target
epée: heavy fencing weapon with the whole body as a target
Vélodrome d'Hiver: indoor cycling track, also used for Olympic events other than cycling
Voltaire: François-Marie Arouet, 1694-1778; French philosopher famed for wit and fighting against Christianity
Isotta Fraschini Tipo 8A Landaulet: very upscale car,

essentially a limousine; passengers are covered, driver is not

Sheffield: the great steel-making city of Britain's Industrial Revolution; known for cutlery

Montmartre: hill in northern Paris home of many famous artists

Prussia: warlike German state that united Germany

Commune: very brief revolutionary government established in Paris after the defeat by the Germans; very liberal and progressive; the French army massacred 15,000 of them

Île de la Cité: island in the Seine, site of Notre Dame

Sorbonne: University of Paris and its district

mansard roof: roof with 2 slopes on each side, the lower more vertical; very popular when Paris was resigned in the 19th century

Renault: largest French car company, established in 1899

5th arrondissement: Left Bank Parisian district containing the Sorbonne, Panthéon, and Latin Quarter

Croix de Guerre: Cross of War; high decoration for combat heroism

Distinguished Service Order: British decoration for combat heroism, similar to Croix de Guerre

gendarme: policeman

Victor Hugo: author of *The Hunchback of Notre Dame* and *Les Misérables*

Edfu Temple of Horus: an immense late-Egyptian temple

Blue Mosque: completed in 1723, it is very similar to the famous Hagia Sophia next door

oculus: 'eye;' a circular opening at the top of a dome

National Convention: French revolutionary legislature responsible for the Reign of Terror; France's first democratic body

Marat: Jean-Paul Marat, radical French revolution writer/politician, deeply involved in the Reign of Terror

Robespierre: Maximilien Robespierre, revolutionary leader who promoted its most liberal ideas, but who also authored the Terror

Ch. 5
Diderot: Denis Diderot, 1713-1784, founder of the

Enlightenment *Encyclopédie*
Rousseau: Jean-Jacques Rousseau, 1712-1778; author and philosopher whose ideas fueled the Age of Enlightenment
Mirabeau: Honoré Gabriel Riqueti, Count of Mirabeau, 1749-1791; early revolutionary leader; the Panthéon was built for him
Saint Genevieve: patron saint of Paris
Homburg: man's hat with single long crease in the crown and a flat round brim with a tight curl on the edge

Ch. 6
Mufti: civilian clothes
Coubertin: Charles Pierre de Frédy, Baron de Coubertin, 1863-1937; founder of the modern Olympics in 1896
Amritsar Massacre: shooting of unarmed Sikh protesters in India in 1919, 1,000 dead
Jallianwala Bagh Garden: site of the above massacre
Brigadier Dyer: commander of the troops at the massacre
Gurkhas: crack Nepalese troops serving the British Army
Neuve Chapelle: 1915 Great War battle with 20,000 casualties
Harry Grindell Matthews: British inventor with a habit of exorbitant claims and refusing to let anyone examine his inventions to see if they worked; **not** a traitor for Mussolini, though
lingua franca: common language
Pamplona: city in Spain known for its Running of the Bulls, popularized by Hemingway in *The Sun Also Rises*
Seduttore: seducer
Boers: 'farmer;' descendants of the original Dutch settlers in South Africa
Kitchener: Herbert, Viscount Kitchener of Khartoum, 11850-1916; credited with winning the Boer War through putting civilians in concentration camps; lost when his ship hit a German mine
Viscount: rank in the British peerage above a baron and below an earl

Ch. 7
Arab Revolt: 191-18; rebellion of varying Arab groups against the Ottoman Empire, with British support; Britain reneged on its promise to recognize an independent Arab state after the war
Ottomans: Turks
Kerak Castle: ancient Crusader castle in Jordan

Ch.8
Sainte-Chapelle: royal chapel and medieval royal residence; most magnificent stained glass anywhere
Le Havre: port on the English Channel
demitasse spoon: the size of a baby spoon, used for stirring froth
Milo of Croton: ancient Olympic wrestling champion, famed for his strength
Vulcan: Roman god equivalent to Greek Hephaestus
Hotel Brienne: home of French Minister of War
Armenian massacres of 1915: genocide of the Armenian people by the Ottomans during the Great war; around 1 million dead
French Guiana penal colony: 'Devil's Island;' 75% death rate

Ch. 9
Montparnasse: Left Bank district known as an artists' haven
haute couture: high fashion
John Hemingway: 1923-2000; first son of Ernest Hemingway
Antiope: Amazon queen in Greek mythology
Oran: 2nd-largest city in Algeria
Marseilles: Mediterranean port and France's 2nd-largrest city; long known as a 'tough' town
garrote: any hand-held line or cord used for strangulation
Horatius at the bridge: he famously held off the entire Etruscan army until his troops could destroy the bridge and save Rome
Man Ray: born Emmanuel Radnitzky, innovative photographer and one of the most influential artist of the 20th

century

Cubism: objects are broken apart and reassembled in abstract form

paso doble: ballroom dance representing a matador and bull

Fitzgerald: F. Scott Fitzgerald, 1896-1940; author of *The Great Gatsby* and *Tender is the Night*

Coco Chanel: 1883-1971; famed fashion designer, influential for 'uncorseting' women after the Great War

Misia Sert: 1872-1950; famous art salon host and bosom friend of Chanel

Cole Porter: 1891-1964; renowned composer of songs and Broadway musicals

Constantin Brancusi: 1876-1957; pioneering Romanian sculptor and proponent of Modernism

James Joyce: 1882-1941; Irish author of the much-banned *Ulysses*

Alice B. Toklas: 1877-1967; famed salon host and Gertrude Stein's lover for 40 years

Le Bain Turc: *The Turkish Bath,* 1859, a painting of nude harem women

Adrienne Monnier: 1892-1955; owned the House of the Friends of Books and supported Sylvia Beach's English-language bookstore across the street, Shakespeare and Company

trilby: man's hat with very short brim, high in rear and tipped down in front

Atrăgător: attractive, pretty

Sylvia Beach: 1887-1962; owner of Shakespeare and Company bookstore (still in business); publisher of *Ulysses*

Lanvin: oldest French fashion house, in business since 1889

Charles Baudelaire: 1821-1867; famed Decadent poet, author of *Le Fleurs de Mal (Flowers of Evil)* and proponent of Edgar Allan Poe

Ch. 10

Praxiteles: ancient Greek sculptor, the first to sculpt a life-size female nude

Hermes: Greek messenger god

Dionysus: Greek god of wine and religious ecstasy

sadeeka: honest, sincere
Provence: southeastern French province famed for its beauty and artists
serge: soft, fine twill fabric
Felixstowe flying boat: twin-engined seaplane, the basis for most subsequent seaplane design
Percy Fawcett: 1867-1925; British explorer who vanished in Brazil; his reports from the Amazon were the basis for Conan Doyle's *The Lost World*
Matto Grosso: large Brazilian region containing the Amazon basin
Sir Henry Morton Stanley: 1841-1904; Welsh explorer who found Dr. David Livingstone in 1871 after an historic and brutal trek through Africa
David Livingstone: 1813-1873; beloved Scottish missionary in Africa
Sir Richard Francis Burton: 1821-1890; English explorer, soldier, and scholar; spoke 29 languages
kufi: cap that looks like a very low fez
mosh fahem: I don't understand
Ibn Arabi: 1165-1240; poet and scholar in Islamic Spain
garçon: waiter
meze: a platter of appetizer dishes
mujaddara: lentils, rice, and onions
baba ghanoush: eggplant and tahini (ground sesame)
kanafeh: spun pastry with sugar syrup and cheese
Roy Chapman Andrews: American archeologist who found the first dinosaur eggs
Gobi Desert: vast, cold western Chinese desert where the fossilized eggs were found
purselane: lemony greens
sumac: tart red spice
dolma: vegetables stuffed with cheese
labneh: cream cheese made from yoghurt
salaam alaykum: peace be upon you
poltergeist: mischievous ghost that throws stuff
Cimetière du Montparnasse: 2nd-largest cemetery in Paris; 35,000 graves

Ch. 11
Virgil: Roman author of the *Aeneid;* Dante's guide in *The Inferno*

katara: wide blade held in an H-shaped grip and pushed at the target

Spanish torero: bullfighter

verónica: holding the cape in 2 hands and slowly drawing the bull forward with it

bagh nakh: held in 2 finger-rings with several tiger-like claws on the palm

Mutiny: the Sepoy Mutiny of 1857, when Indian troops rebelled against the British East India Company; 800,000 dead

mahatma: great soul

Vishnu: one of the great trinity of gods in Hinduism; creator and protector of the universe

jiva: soul

samsara: cycle of death and reincarnation

avidya: ignorance of the true reality

karma: an individual's intent and actions influence the individual's future

Don Giovanni: *'Don Juan;'* 1787 Mozart opera where a living statue drags a libertine down to hell

Ch. 12
Le Fleurs de mal: controversial poetry collection by Baudelaire, full of sex and death; banned in France for nearly 100 years

cotillion: elaborate 18th century group dance, forerunner of the square dance

Rajasthan: large northern region of India, bordering Pakistan

necropolis: 'city of the dead;' any cemetery with elaborate monuments

Karna: a main character in the *Mahabharata* known for his expertise with a bow

Mahabharata: one of the two great epics of Hinduism

Shiva: the Destroyer; one of the 3 principal deities of Hinduism, along with Vishnu and Brahma

Scylla: fearsome monster in the *Odyssey*, opposite Charybdis
Charybdis: fatal whirlpool in the *Odyssey*
Tartarus: Greek mythological hell
Apache gangs: violent Parisian street thugs compared to American 'savages'
plinth: the flat support for a column

Ch. 13

hookah: a pipe with a large glass bowl full of water which filters the smoke
Joan Miró: 1893-1983; Spanish Surrealist painter and sculptor with an Expressionistic edge whose works now sell for millions; believed that establishment-approved art was just political propaganda to control the masses
Gavrilo Princep: young Serbian nationalist who assassinated the heir to the Austro-Hungarian throne and started the Great War
Charing Cross Station: large important central railway terminal in Westminster, London
French Renaissance architecture: the style you see in Loire Valley castles
Very pistol: flare gun
Gloucestershire: western English county containing the Cotswolds
Burberry: British fashion house famous for trench coats
Tewksbury: site of the 1471 War of the Roses battle that destroyed the power of the Lancaster faction and put Edward IV on the throne
Lorentz force: the electromagnetic force in physics
Guy Fawkes: English traitor who tried to blow up the king and Parliament in 1605

Ch. 14

***Seven Pillars of Wisdom*:** T.E. Lawrence's book about his time with the Arabs in the Great War
Brumaire: fog
concierge: person who assists residents of an apartment building
la loge: the apartment on the ground floor occupied by the

concierge

Métro: Paris subway

Stade Olympique de Colombes: main stadium for the 1924 Olympics, built in 1907; later turned into a soccer/rugby venue; will be used again for the 2024 Olympics

Eton crop: extremely short women's hairstyle, created for cloche hats

de rigueur: required

Djuna Barnes: 1892-1982; Modernist writer and journalist, known for *Nightwood*, a major cult work in lesbian fiction

McCall's: major American magazine for 130 years, known for stories by prominent authors and the sewing patterns included in each issue

Brooklyn Daily Eagle: important New York newspaper for over a century, with the largest circulation of any afternoon paper in the country; Walt Whitman was briefly its editor

New York World: Joseph Pulitzer's paper; created yellow journalism and probably started the Spanish-American War

Aubrey Beardsley: English illustrator, helped create Art Nouveau

Provincetown Players: short-lived theatre group that established Eugene O'Neill as a major force in literature

Greenwich Village: Manhattan neighborhood known for its artistic community

Book of Repulsive Women: 1915 book of poems known for its frank portrayals of eroticism and perversity and Barnes' own illustrations

Ch. 15

Baron Coubertin: founder of the modern Olympics in 1896

President Doumergue: very popular French resident, took office on June 13

Prince of Wales: heir to the British throne; in this case the future Edward VIII, the one who abdicated in 1936

Kshatriya caste: the social group asso9ciated with the warrior aristocracy

Nieuport 12: French biplane of the Great War mostly used for reconnaissance or training; 2 seats, with a machine gun on a swivel in the rear seat

Fokker Tri: the Dr.1, a 3-winged fighter plane used by the 'Red Baron'

Medaille Militaire: highest military award in France

Légion Etrangére: the famous Foreign Legion

Etévé ring: a swiveling metal mount that allowed a machine gun to move in a 360-arc

Eugene Bullard: 1895-1961; 'The Black Swallow;' one of the first black American military pilots and one of a literal handful to fly in the Great War; so famous for his nightclub work that Hemingway based a character on him

Escadrille SPA 85: a French fighter squadron on the Western Front

Bourbons: the last ruling family of France, beginning in 1589 with Henri IV

Inspector Javert: antagonist of Hugo's *Les Misérables,* known for implacably pursuing the protagonist Jean Valjean

Montreuil: eastern suburb of Paris

Leon Bakst: 1866-1924; Belorussian set/costume designer, famous for designing *Firebird* and *Afternoon of a Faun*

Serge Diaghilev: 1872-1929; Russian ballet impresario and founder of the famous Ballets Russes

Sumeria: earliest civilization in what is now Iraq, 4000-2000 BCE

Bedouin: nomadic Arab tribes; the Arabic word for them is a'rab

broom-handle Mauser pistol: the C.96, invented in 1896; 7.63 mm, has a box-shaped magazine in front of the trigger, and a rounded wooden grip that gives it its name; Han Solo uses a fancied-up version in *Star Wars*

Ch. 16

Mandarin: language of 70% of China

Franco-Prussian War: 1870-71; lasting 6 months, it was a disaster for France and led to German ooccupation of Paris

Edmund Dantes: protagonist of Dumas' *The Count of Monte Cristo;* he famously escaped the Chateau d'If prison

Château d'If: island prison a mile off the beach of Marseilles

Sacré-Cœur Basilica: that enormous pointed-dome white church you see on a hill in every photo of Paris; completed in

1914 as a

Montmartre: tall hill in Paris long known for its artists
Coup of 18 Brumaire: Napoleon's bloodless takeover in 1799 (18 Brumaire was November 9)

Ch. 17

bichon frisé: little fluffy white toy dog that looks like an actual toy
Balliol College: one of the constituent colleges that make up Oxford University; founded in 1263; alma mater of kings, prime ministers, and the fictional sleuth Lord Peter Wimsey
Whitehall: seat of the British government
Arthur Henderson: Home Secretary until November 1924; won the 1934 Nobel Peace Prize for trying to forestall WW II
Horse Guards Road: site of British Army Headquarters at the time
St. James's Park: next to Buckingham Palace
Huns: slang term for Germans in the Great War
astrakhan: prized wool from the undercoat of a central Asian sheep
Wembley: suburb in northwest London
sybaritic: hedonistic; pleasure-seeking
Gian Lorenzo Bernini: 1598-1680; creator of the Baroque style of sculpture
Ramsey MacDonald: 1866-1937; Prime Minister and founder of the Labour Party
Labour Party: center-left British political party; founded the National Health Serviced after WW II

Ch. 18

Buckinghamshire: English county bordering London on the northwest; now the center of the film industry
Crossley saloon: a large 4-door sedan (sedan and saloon mean the same thing)
Umbria: region in the dead center of the Italian peninsula; St. Francis of Assisi was a native
Gergovia: fortified town in Gaul, in what is now central France
Alesia: walled Gaullic town northeast of Gergovia

The Last Judgement: huge Michelangelo fresco covering the wall behind the altar in the Sistine Chapel in the Vatican

Tamerlane: Timur Gurkani, 1336-1405; brilliant and brutal warlord who conquered most of central Asia

Bristol: large port city in southwest England, on the mouth of the Avon River; slave-trading center in the 1700's

Fresnel lens: powerful lens originally invented for lighthouses; has a series of layered steps instead of a large curved convex surface

lorry: a truck

pitch: a playing field

dynamo: a powerful electric generator

MI5: domestic investigative service, equivalent to the FBI

Vernon Kell: 1873-1942; leader of MI5 for 30 years

lolly: lollipop

Brighton: seaside resort on the English Channel south of London

Palace Pier: famous long pier with an amusement park at the end

Nicola Tesla: 1856-1943; Croatian electrical genius; inventor of the alternating current motor

Aylesbury: English market town

Ch. 19

boat train: train to a port to get on a ship to another port and another train

Calais: French port nearest to England

Dover: English port closest to France

Royal Society: The Royal Society of London for Improving Natural Knowledge, founded 1660; world's oldest scientific society

La Dame aux Camélias: 1848 Dumas novel; the basis for Verdi's La Traviata

Leonard Woolf: Virginia's husband; political theorist and publisher; published Eliot's The Wasteland

Bloomsbury: fashionable London area, home to the British Museum and similar institutions

Paddington Station: central London railway station, original western end of the London Underground

Kensington: central London district, cultural hub, and London's smallest borough

Hyde Park: largest park in central London, founded in 1536

Albertopolis: Kensington district full of arts and scientific institutions

Albert Memorial: overdesigned monument to Prince Albert, husband of Queen Victoria

Royal Albert Hall: world-famous performance space opened in 1871

Royal College of Organists: school for organ players and choral conductors

sgraffito: technique of applying contrasting layers of plaster to a wall

frieze: decorated area atop a columned wall

Kensington Gore: short u-shaped street adjoining Hyde Park

Lowther Lodge: large red-brick house from 1875, headquarters of the Royal Geographical Society since 1912

Queen Anne: British Queen Anne Revival architecture, late 19th-early 20th centuries; corner towers, curved jutting oriel windows, lots of exterior white woodwork accenting the brick

ambulatory: a long covered hall for walking

Veuve Clicquot: major French champagne house; invented many now-common techniques and made champagne popular with the elite

Khorasan: culturally important region of central Asia

Kurdistan: eastern Turkey to northern Iran, home of the Kurds, the largest ethnic group without its own country

Dora Carrington: 1893-1932; androgynous bisexual English artist

Freya Stark: 1883-1993; English explorer and travel writer, one of the first non-Arabs women to travel through the Arabian Desert world

Gertrude Bell: 1868-1926; influential traveler and government administrator; worked with T.E. Lawrence in the Arab Bureau (Intelligence) in Cairo before he went to Arabia

Pimm's: a fruity, gin-based liqueur

Sir Richard Francis Burton: 1821-1890; legendary explorer, soldier, and author; translated the *Kama Sutra* into

English; knew 29 languages

Kama Sutra: Indian manual on living well, best known for the sex stuff

Transoxiana: central Asian region centered on Samarkand

Samarkand: very old Silk Road city in Uzbekistan

Lord Ronaldshay: 1876-1961; British politician known for his expertise on India; later Marquess of Zetland

Marquess: high-ranking title in the British peerage above a count and below a prince

Lancashire: northern English county bordering Yorkshire and Manchester

Ch. 20

Lawrence Dundas: Lord Ronaldshay's given name

Secretary of State for India: former British Cabinet position and politician in charge of governing India

Carlton Club: founded in 1832 in a London district full of snooty men's clubs

Pall Mall: London street connecting St. James to Trafalgar Square; upscale; Casanova used to live there

David Lloyd-George: 1863-1945; Prime Minister during the Great War; the last Liberal Party PM

William Pitt: 1759-1806; Prime Minister during the French Revolution and Napoleonic Wars

Robert Peel: 1788-1850; in 1829 founded the Metropolitan Police force

Benjamin Disraeli: 1804-1881; only Jewish Prime Minister; big fan of British Imperialism

Arthur Balfour: 1848-1930; Prime Minister early in the 20th century; issued the Balfour Declaration, supporting a Jewish homeland in Palestine

Royal Doulton: famed ceramics company founded in 1815

Trinity College: founded in 1546; wealthiest college in either Cambridge or Oxford; has produced 34 Nobel Prize winners; Isaac Newton's alma mater

Cambridge: one of the two most prestigious universities, along with Oxford

Public School Standard: proper accent taught to elite students; better known as Received Pronunciation

Regent's Park: large park housing London's zoo

Sir Percy Sykes: 1867-1945; soldier and diplomat; member of the RGS and Royal Society for Asian Affairs; spent many years in central Asia

Tube: the London subway

Public Carriage Office: licenses London cabs

The Knowledge: the details of routes and other facts every cabbie is tested on; the test is fiendishly difficult and can take nearly 3 years

Austin: venerable car company founded in 1905

Ceylon: now Sri Lanka; the big island at the tip of India

Vita Sackville-West: 1892-1962; successful poet and novelist, lover of Virginia Woolf; the protagonist of Orlando is said to be inspired by her

Ch. 21

Warwickshire: county in central England; home of Shakespeare

WC: water closet, toilet

Pierre Curie: 1859-1906; husband of Marie, shared the Nobel Prize with her; perished in a street accident, but the radiation was already killing him

Trevi Fountain: Roman fountain completed in 1762; featured in countless movies; the one you throw coins into backwards

Old London Bridge: 1209-1831; imposing edifice with over 100 buildings on it

Northumberland accent: Northumberland is a far northern English county

Ch. 22

Savoy Hotel: luxury Westminster hotel built in 1889 with profits from Gilbert & Sullivan operas

Claridge's Hotel: upscale Mayfair hotel built in the mid-19th century, later bought by the Savoy's owner

Akkadia: the Mesopotamian empire that succeeded Sumer

Francis Bacon: 1561-1626; 17th-century statesman and scientist who absolutely 100% did not write Shakespeare's plays

Much Ado About Nothing: Shakespeare comedy featuring a feuding couple who are maneuvered into marriage by their scheming friends

Hugh Sinclair: 1873-1939; influential spy chief who set up MI6, later James Bond's employer

Camorra: criminal society pre-dating the Mafia

Alessandro Volta: 1745-1827; inventor of the battery

Ch. 23

Kensington Gardens: directly across the street from the Royal Albert Hall; I fell asleep on the grass there once

Oxford bag trousers: just what they sound like; adopted by jitterbug dancers who needed their legs free

"Inkey pinkey parlez vous": ribald Great War soldier song actually called "Mademoiselle from Armentieres"

Scarpered: ran away

Serpentine: a long 40-acre lake

prams: baby strollers

ziggurats: ancient Mesopotamian temple structures much like Aztec temples

Uttar Pradesh: most populous state in India, site of the Taj Mahal

Vesta Victoria: 1873-1951; enormously popular music hall singer of comic songs; at one time worth $1 billion in modern money

Ch. 24

Aardbeving: "earthquake"

Passchendaele: horrific Belgian Great War battle with hundreds of thousands of casualties

Cartes: Richard D'Oyly Carte, 1844-1901; got crazy rich producing Gilbert & Sullivan's original operettas

Paris Opera: the staircase in every Phantom of the Opera movie

Rococo: the ornate 18th-century style that followed Baroque

Louis Quinze: Louis XV, 1710-1774; the style features innumerable shell-like curves

Charles II: king of England 1660-1685

Ch. 25

Panama hat: straw hat with a cloth band, a large central crease on top, and the brim turned up in the back
Antwerp: Belgian port, home of 1920 Olympics
Croesus: 6th century BC king of Lydia (western Turkey), famed for his spectacular wealth
Grosvenor Crescent: snooty Belgravia street leading from Hyde Park; average house price is $20 million
Mayfair: district in Westminster east of Hyde Park; one of the richest places on earth
East End: London area east of the old London wall and north of the Thames River; very poor area still, though improving
Ealing: west London district, home of the world's oldest continuously-working movie studio
St. Adrian: patron saint of soldiers
J.P. Morgan: 1837-1913; insanely-wealthy American financier and tycoon
seraglio: harem
Hounslow: west London suburb
nonna: grandmother
three-section staff: Chinese flail weapon made up of wooden rods connected with chain or rope; good for curving around an opponent's defense

Ch. 26

Portsmouth: Royal Navy base on England's southern coast; Nelson's flagship *HMS Victory* is berthed there
India rubber: natural, non-synthetic rubber
petty officer: naval non-commissioned officer
sturm und drang: "storm and stress"
Flatiron Building: triangular 20-story skyscraper on 5th Avenue in Manhattan

Ch. 27

asti: sparkling white wine, the Italian 'champagne'
alla vostre salute: to your health
Salle des Conférences: a truly eye-wateringly overdecorated room in the Luxembourg Palace
Marie de Medici: 1575-1642; queen of France, married to

Henri IV and mother of Louis XIII

JB Louvet: important French bicycle manufacturer and big Tour de France team sponsor in the 1920's and later; their bikes were among then best money could buy; their logo was a female wolf (*louve*)

8th arrondissement: right bank district plopped right atop the Champs-Élysées; home of the French President, the Arc de Triomphe, and the luxury business district

Rue du Faubourg Saint-Honoré: site of most major fashion houses and the U.S. embassy

Boulevard Saint-Michel: the Sorbonne is here

Quai des Grands Augustins: runs along the river; known for its bookshops since the 18th century

Shakespeare & Company: 1919-1941; famous English language bookstore; gathering spot of Fitzgerald, Hemingway, Joyce, etc. another with its name and equal renown has been in business for 70 years

Sylvia Beach: American owner of Shakespeare & Company; published Joyce's *Ulysses* and Hemingway's first book; her store probably hosted more great writers than any other in history

Ile de Cité: the island in the Seine where Notre Dame sits

Saint-Chappelle: chapel of the kings of France, inside the royal palace which is now the Paris courthouse; has the most magnificent stained glass on earth

Conciergeie: old palace and prison that housed Marie Antoinette

Pont du Change: the bridge Inspector Javert leaps from in Hugo' *Les Misérables*

Rue du Rivoli: street running alongside many famous buildings and high-status shops

Tuileries Gardens: public space where the old Tuileries Palace was, a former royal residence burned by the Paris Commune in 1871

Rue Saint-Honoré: upscale street where King Henri IV was assassinated in 1610

Citroën: car company founded in 1919 by a successful weapons manufacturer; known for its many innovations which are now standard on all cars

Avenue de l'Opera: high-class street running directly up to the front steps of the opera house

Rue du Richelieu: long street leading from the Comédie-Française (the national theatre, the world's oldest); the croissant was invented on it

Place de la Bastille: public square where the Bastille prison used to be; a popular site for political rallies

fa'ara: mouse

Ch. 28

Leonidas: leader of the 300 Spartans at the Battle of Thermopylae

Tyre: port and capital of ancient Phoenicia (now Lebanon); it was in the hands of the Persians when Alexander took it with the largest siege engines ever built

Hellenistic: historic and artistic period between Alexander's death in 323 BC and the Battle of Actium in 31 BC that brought about the Roman Empire

Vedas: a large collection of Sanskrit writings of crucial importance to Hinduism

Tabriz: Iranian resort city famed for rugs and handicrafts

Koohaye Merikhi: the Martian Mountains in southeastern Iran; bizarre swirling rock formations carved by erosion, with almost nothing green in sight; they look like gray meringue

Adonis: Aphrodite's gorgeous mortal boyfriend

Ariya: where 'Iranian' comes from; another name for Old Persian

Akshar: 'undestroyable' in Sanskrit;

Polonius: king's counselor in *Hamlet* who liked to give long-winded and unrequested advice

Sanskrit: ancient sacred language of Hinduism

Marrakesh: major city in Morocco, with an ancient marketplace and historic district

Bandar Beheshtī: now Chabahar, Iran; important port on the Gulf of Oman

Madamwazeil: mademoiselle

rakshasa: malevolent creatures with magical powers

hecatomb: a sacrifice of 12-100 cattle to the Greek gods

SPAD S. 20: biplane fighter so fast it was used for air racing

pater familias: male head of the Roman family

Ch. 29
Walpurgisnacht: celebrated on the night of April 30; bonfires are lit to ward off witches
Farsi: Persian (Iranian) language

Ch. 30
Ritz Hotel: literally 'ritzy' luxury hotel, opened in 1906; everyone who's anyone has been there

www.ingramcontent.com/pod-product-compliance
Lightning Source LLC
Chambersburg PA
CBHW031314280626
47169CB00019B/1503